THE
WINGS
OF A
FALCON

Also by Cynthia Voigt:

Homecoming
Dicey's Song
Tell Me If the Lovers Are Losers
The Callender Papers
A Solitary Blue
Building Blocks
Jackaroo
Come a Stranger
Izzy, Willy-Nilly
The Runner
Stories About Rosie
Sons From Afar
Tree by Leaf
Seventeen Against the Dealer
On Fortune's Wheel
The Vandenmark Mummy
David and Jonathan
Orfe

THE WINGS OF A FALCON

CYNTHIA VOIGT

**SCHOLASTIC
HARDCOVER**

Scholastic Inc.
New York

Library of Congress Cataloging-in-Publication Data

Voigt, Cynthia.
     The wings of a falcon / Cynthia Voigt.
        p.   cm.
     Summary: Fourteen-year-old Oriel and his friend Griff flee the slavery
of Damall's Island and seek a new life on the mainland, where they face
raiding Wolfers, rival armies, and other dangers.

ISBN 0-590-46712-3

[1. Adventure and adventurers — Fiction.]   I. Title.
PZ7.V874Wi   1993
   [Fic] — dc20   92-41946
                                                               CIP
                                                                AC

12 11 10 9 8 7 6 5 4 3 2 1   3 4 5 6 7 8/9

                    Printed in the U.S.A.   37

            First Scholastic printing, September 1993

For Ray Haas —
this, in admiration & appreciation

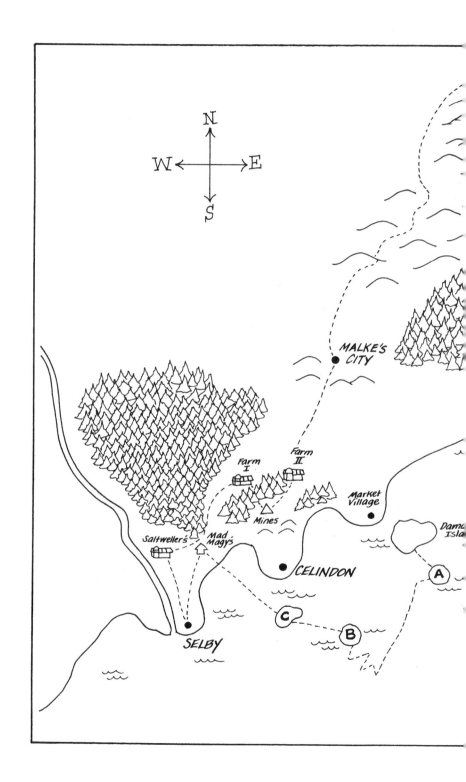

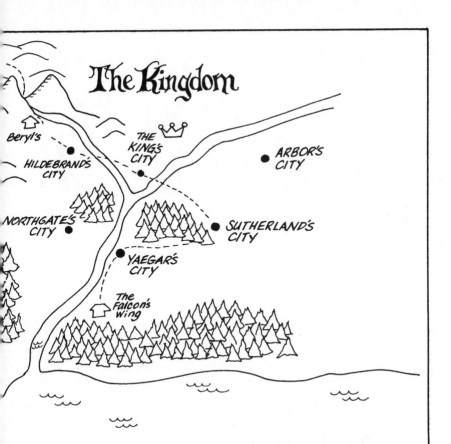

The Kingdom

Beryl's

HILDEBRAND'S CITY

THE KING'S CITY

ARBOR'S CITY

NORTHGATE'S CITY

SUTHERLAND'S CITY

YAEGAR'S CITY

The Falcon's wing

LEGEND

●	– City
🌲	– Forests
△	– Mine
✘	– Damall's House
A	– First Island of Escape
B	– Night Stopover
C	– Night Stopover
🏠	– Farm
⇧	– House
∽	– Mountains
⋯	– Route
∿	– Water

PART I

THE SEVENTH DAMALL

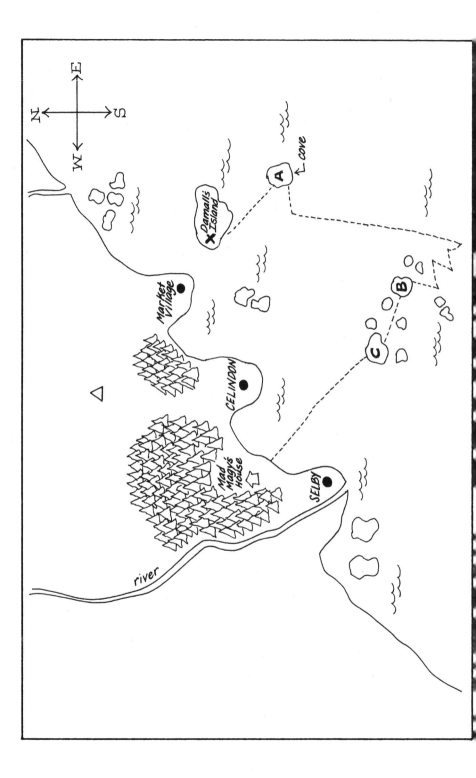

CHAPTER
1

He knew from the first that this man would know how to hurt him. He had to keep the fear secret, and he couldn't cry no matter how much he wanted to. When he was hungry he couldn't ask for food, when he was cold he couldn't try to push himself closer to the fire, when he was tired he had to stay awake, when he was lonely he had to be alone. He knew from the first that he would have to be strong.

Damall's Island rested on stone. Boulders edged the island, and rose up out of the ground in unexpected places all across it. The harbor beach was made up of stones as sharp as shells, as if a giant had brought his hammer down on the boulders, and shattered them. Some of the boulders walked out into the sea, but the waves could no more move them or beat them down than the wind and rain could. He learned to be as strong as stone.

He brought nothing with him to the island but the clothes he wore. The Damall took away his clothes and dressed him in the tied trousers and brown shirts all the boys wore. There was a pile of boots in all sizes — the soles made out of the same soft leather as their sides — for when he could not go barefooted. He didn't know if he had brought a name with him to the island. If he had a name, the Damall took that away, too.

The Damall was master. A tall thin man, with hair as pale as the bellies of fish and eyes that glittered like the sun on water, he was the sixth Damall to be master on the island. The boys, who did not know if they were slaves or sons, obeyed the Damall. They worked the year around, to serve the Damall.

In spring, the schools of fish were netted, then spread out on the flat rocks to dry in the sun. There was the garden to turn over, and take stones from, and then plant with onions and turnips, parsnips, cabbage. In spring, the places where the wind had torn the roof tiles off, or the snow and sleet had worn them through, had to be mended. The sows, which had wintered in a shed, slunk out into the trees to give birth. They had to be found and brought back before they could eat their young. The stench of the long shuttered winter had to be washed out of the whole house.

Spring took the boys out from under the Damall's glittering eye. When winter sleet beat down on the roof, the Damall would as soon call for the whipping box as find any other way to hurry time along. But in spring the boys scattered all over the farmstead, and it was harder for the Damall to get them.

Griff told him that the island boys had to know how to swim before they could be trusted on a fishing boat. On the first warm day in spring, a boy who couldn't swim went out in a boat with older boys. The older boys dropped him overboard and sailed away.

The Damall watched to be sure it was done properly. The Damall sailed a boat by himself and watched from nearby.

Sometimes the boy just couldn't learn to swim and he would sink. Most of the time the boy struggled, and learned, and swam back to the island. But sometimes a boy would be too young, or be someone who couldn't float, and he would sink. The drowned boys were usually never seen again on the Damall's island. Maybe, like fragments of boats that washed up onto the Damall's shores, the drowned boys washed up on one of the other islands. There were many islands here, of all sizes, scattered close to the mainland, like swimmers trying to climb back onto solid ground.

He was afraid of the water, afraid of its cold dark deepness.

Griff told him that the boys who sank were afraid. They flailed their hands around and tried to breathe water, because they were afraid.

He said he wasn't afraid.

It wasn't true.

Griff woke him up one night, in the room where the littlest boys slept rolled up in blankets on the stone floor. Griff led him to a place where the shore sloped slowly down underwater. Griff showed him how to lie on the water, as if it were a floor, and then how to kick and paddle his way along the surface. Griff didn't want him to sink, and die.

Swimming was easy, after all, even at night when the sky was as black as the sea. Swimming was like a game he could play, once Griff taught him how. Not many days later he was taken out in a boat, but he wouldn't let the bigger boys push him into the water. He wouldn't let them think he was frightened. Nikol wanted him to be frightened. Nikol looked over to where the Damall sat smiling in his own boat, his hair as white as the frothy tops of waves. Before he would let Nikol push him out of the boat, he stood up on its side, and balanced there, and jumped into the water, and set out swimming for the island.

He heard Nikol cry out in disappointment. He heard the Damall laughing.

That night he was the one the Damall called up, to sit at his table close to the warm fire and to eat whatever the Damall had left on his plate, which was more and better food than any of the boys got. "Nikol wanted you to drown," the Damall said.

"Aye," he said. It was true.

"Shall we whip him for that?"

He hated the whippings. He hated watching a whipping almost as much as he hated being whipped. The whip had a thick wooden handle and little leather tails with knots tied into them and, in some of the knots, little sharp pebbles.

"Shall we call for the whipping box?" the Damall asked. The Damall leaned close to him, leaning across the wooden table, and looked into his eyes.

To say yes meant to watch — as they must — and know that Nikol would hate him even more and look for even more ways to hurt him. To say no meant crossing the Damall's will and making the Damall wonder if he was a weakling. He sat silent as a stone while the Damall waited impatiently, until he thought to say, "Don't care."

"Ach, you bore me. Get away. Get out."

He obeyed. He hadn't eaten, and he was hungry, but he didn't ask to stay at the table. The Damall whipped Nikol anyway. The Damall wanted to hear Nikol's bitter protests, and loud wailings under the whip, and Nikol's whimperings when he pulled his clothes back on. The Damall liked to see Nikol being angry and not being able to do anything about it. The Damall liked to see Nikol being afraid and being ashamed.

He was walking back from the privies that night when a stone hit him on the mouth. Blood dripped onto his tongue. Nikol thought he could hide in the dark and throw a stone without being known, but Nikol was stupid with anger and slow with the weakness that came after a whipping. Nikol was older and bigger, but Nikol ate a mouthful of dirt before the fight was done.

Griff washed off the cut with wine stolen from the Damall's barrel. When that stinging eased, Griff sprinkled a little of the precious salt from the Damall's cellar onto the open wound, so it would heal clean. If the Damall had caught Griff taking wine and salt, Griff would have begged forgiveness. Griff would have been afraid and sorry and promised never to do it again. When Griff was afraid he would promise. Later, he might take the wine and salt again, and be afraid again, and promise again, and break the promise again, over and over again. Griff had the bending strength of a sapling.

In summer, Griff bent tirelessly over the gardens, pulling up weeds, and tirelessly over the smoke-house fires, where hams and fish were hung along poles, and tirelessly over the oars when the wind died and the sail flapped uselessly. Griff never complained and seldom smiled.

He was like Griff, and didn't complain, but he smiled often, and laughed, too, for no reason. He could run faster and swim farther than any other boy, after eight winters' growth had been added to the three or four he'd brought to the island. He was handiest with the boats, and handiest with the nets, and it had been years since he had lost a fight. He was the one all the boys wanted to sail with, or work beside — all the boys except Nikol. He was the one the Damall liked best to take across the sea to the market town, the two of them sailing away at dawn, in a boat heavy laden with smoked and fresh fish, as well as barrels of the black gostas that were caught crawling around the boulders, with claws so strong they could take a boy's finger off if he wasn't quick. The Damall would sell first, and then buy flour with the money, or buy cloth for shirts and trousers if that was needed, or buy barrels of wine. Always they would buy as large a cone of salt as they had coins for, to add to the Damall's saltcellar.

Once the Damall had given him a pinch of salt on top of his turnip stew. He was the only boy ever to have salt on anything.

Once the Damall took Nikol to the market town, and they bought a dagger, but the dagger wasn't for Nikol, it was for him. The Damall gave the dagger to him, and promised to show him how to use it. But the next morning the dagger was gone from under his mattress. Nikol thought he would tell the Damall, but he didn't.

On the Damall's island, each boy of sixteen falls was taken to the city, and sold. The journey to the city lasted two nights away from the island. He made many of these journeys with the Damall and such a boy, from the time of his own sixth fall on the island. In the boat, the boy had his hands and feet tied, because no boy wanted to be sold as a slave, or to the mines, or to an army. The boy would ask for help to escape, or ask for pity, or ask for mercy. He never answered. He sat deaf as stone at the tiller. After the boy had been sold, he could wander around the city on his own and spend the three copper coins the Damall would give him out of the sale price of the boy. Once he spent all of his pennies on sweet cakes, which he carried back to the island wrapped up in his shirt. He gave them out among the boys, leaving none out. He felt, when he gave out pieces of sweet cake into the open hands, and the boys all looked eagerly at him — he felt clever and strong, the best of all of them.

The Damall whipped him that night, nineteen strokes. He knelt naked in the whipping box, the sharp stones·digging into his knees and into the palms of his hands. The Damall whipped him until he was sorry he'd given away the sweet cakes. The boys crowded around being glad it wasn't them in the whipping box. Griff brought seawater up from the dark when all the rest of the house was silent, to wash his back clean, and he slept on his belly for two weeks, but he never let the Damall see how much his back hurt. He laughed, ran, worked, and ate, just like always, just as if every time he moved any part of his body he didn't feel pain as sharp as a burning branch across his back and his legs. Stones had no feeling so they knew nothing about pain, and he was a stone.

In the long purple evenings, the Damall would tell them about the treasure the Great Damall, who was the first Damall, had won from the world. The treasure was hidden on the island. "Gold coins and jewelry, silver coins and jewelry, even gemstones," the Damall said. His voice glittered. "Diamonds, more like those stars up there than you'd think, and pearls set into necklaces and bracelets, but the best of it is the beryls. Nine beryls there were," the Damall said. "Nine green beryls paid in ransom to the Great Damall by a Prince from the Kingdom. Years ago, when the Old Countess was a child, there was war. This was war between the Old Countess's father and a soldier Captain, and the Captain hired a giant from the armies of the Kingdom — where all the soldiers are huge as trees, and long to die, and can't be killed by steel or wood but only with a naked fist into the forehead, here." He pounded his own forehead, between the eyes. "The Great Damall had captured the giant and his Prince brought ransom, to free him. This was a Prince among Princes, a Prince who might have been a King, and he sat down at the table with the Great Damall, and they ate out of the same pot, and he bought back his giant with four beryls, each one the size of my thumb." He held up his thumb. "What's that face for?"

He wasn't afraid, because it was only a mistake the sixth Damall had made. "You said nine before."

"Four beryls, nine beryls, what's the difference. As long as one beryl remains on the island, we're safe enough. Maybe I like to change the number.

It took one beryl to buy the island from the Countess, it would take the value of one beryl to buy the island's safety, so however many exactly there are between doesn't matter, does it? Maybe I'm just making up a story, maybe there was no Countess who ruled the cities, and there were no beryls. Maybe there isn't any Kingdom, either, with giant soldiers and Princes who value their soldiers at this high rate; maybe it's all a made-up story. Nikol, do you believe in this Kingdom?"

"Naw," Nikol said. He swaggered his shoulders. "Nobody ever went there, did they? Only someone stupid would think — "

"Then how do you explain the beryls?" the Damall asked, in a soft and dangerous voice. "If I'm stupid," in a sharp and dangerous voice. "Who'll bring out the whipping box?"

"Don't, please," Nikol said. "I'm sorry, I didn't mean — "

"Who's going to help Nikol take off his shirt and trousers, since he seems to be having trouble doing that?"

"Please?" Nikol cried, and he had tears going down his face. "You were telling us, about the beryls. You were telling about the treasure. Tell more," Nikol asked.

The Damall shook his head. Four boys carried in the whipping box and set it into place. Two boys were pulling Nikol's shirt over his head and he struggled to pull it back down.

"Tell about the pirates," Nikol cried. "The pirates and the treasure and the fifth Damall."

The Damall shook his head. He reached down for the whip and shook out its arms.

"But you were telling us!" Nikol screamed. "Please don't — I didn't — I'm sorry, I'm sorry."

11

He clutched the top of his trousers. "I hate you!" he screeched.

"Oh," the Damall said. "Oh dear me. Did you boys hear that? Nikol, I wasn't going to whip you, but now I have to."

Nikol knew when he was defeated and he hunched down, weeping and begging the Damall to stop, begging, after each of the five strokes. "One for each beryl," the Damall said. "Isn't that right, boys?"

The boys agreed.

In fall, the pigs were slaughtered, held squealing overhead while Nikol slit their throats with a knife, until his arm ran with blood and his face and hair were covered with it. His teeth shone out white in his blood-dark face. After they bled themselves empty, Nikol slit open the pigs' bellies and everybody helped pull out the guts, then they all worked to peel the skins off. Griff was in charge of smoking the butchered meat, and also of boiling the heads and trotters and bones. Wood had to be gathered into piles so that the smokehouse fires would burn night and day. Buckets of entrails had to be carried down to the sea, and poured into the water.

Apples and nuts ripened on the trees in fall. He was the bravest climber, who went highest. The Damall's island had a small apple orchard and a large woods, as well as two meadows in cultivation and two more for grazing. Before the Great Damall bought it from the Countess, for the price of one beryl, there had been fisher families living on the hill, high enough to be safe from spring tides and winter storms. The Great Damall sent them away, and tore down their cottages, and built his own house there. The Great Damall's house was of stone and had many rooms — a great hall with a fireplace so large a boy could stand upright in it, with his arms spread out, and touch the fireplace stones only with the soles of his feet; the master's bedroom with its own fireplace and a carved bed hung with heavy curtains; a kitchen; three rooms for the boys, one for the littlest, one for the middling, and one for the oldest. All around the yard the Great Damall built a stone wall, with two wooden barred gates in it, to keep the animals in, or to keep the boys in, or to keep the house and those living in it safe. For pirates roamed the islands, hiding during the day and attacking at night with fire and sword. The towns and cities of the coast were too well fortified and defended, so the pirates preyed on the islands. The Great Damall built a house that could be sealed up as safe as a castle against pirates. It had cellars for storing food and a deep well in the center of the walled yard.

Only once had pirates attacked the island. They had come by day when the gates were open, when they weren't expected. They had heard of the treasure. They held the fifth Damall's hand in fire, until it burned off. But he didn't tell them where the treasure was. He died three days later in a fever, but he hadn't told. The treasure was safe and the island was safe. As long as one of the green stones remained on the island, as the story was told, no harm would come to the grassy, forested island that rose up above its circling base of boulders. The Damall's island was too small, and townless, for the pirates to come back to — or so the boys hoped.

In winter, the boys were kept inside, under the glittering eye of the Damall. They were taught to read, the older teaching the younger. The quickest boys also learned to write, which would make them more valuable as slaves in the market. The Damall told them the numbers, and what he knew of how they worked, but only Griff needed to remember that because it was Griff who kept the books of records — household income and expenses; where boys had been found and, if purchased, how much had been paid for them and, when sold, how much had been gotten; the yields of field and fowl and pigs, the catch of fish and gostas and skals; the records of deaths, by drowning, by fever, by coughing, by infected wounds, by wasting away. There were some boys who came to the island only to die, pale and listless, and they were poor weeping things whom nobody grieved over. Their bodies were wrapped in an old blanket, with three stones at the head and three at the feet; they were taken out to sea and set down upon the water. There were other boys who came to the island and it seemed nothing could kill them. Nikol had fevers and infections, and once he was swept out to sea in one of the boats. Nikol always got better, however, and he'd been blown back to the island by a friendly wind. Nothing could kill Nikol.

Nothing could kill him, either. He had never been sick, except once. Once, when he was little and Griff had just been given the job of cooking for the boys and the Damall, too, Griff gathered some wild onions in spring, to put into the soup. Griff chopped up the onions and cooked them in with the turnips and fish bones, and that night the whole house fell ill — the boys went outside to vomit, many had the shits, all had sore and swollen throats. Even the Damall was struck down, lying on his carved bed and calling for pots to be brought to him by whoever was on his feet at the time. The illness lasted all the night long, and it was two days before anyone felt well enough to wonder about it; one of the littlest boys died but everyone else recovered. The Damall asked Griff what went into the soup, and then he went out to the woody edges of the meadow on a damp morning to dig up one of the plants. He took it to the market town and one of the old women told him its name, naked lady, and its poison. First the Damall whipped Griff, then he left Griff crouched naked by the door for day after day, without food, tied with a rope around his neck.

He could do nothing for Griff. He couldn't even drop a crust of bread as he passed the door, because Nikol watched. He couldn't even sneak out in the darkness of night to bring water, because Nikol slept across his doorsill. If he had been caught trying to help Griff —

He had to be strong as stone, and pretend it didn't matter to him. Nikol watched him, to catch his weakness. The Damall watched him, too. He was as strong as stone, and no one saw the anger that burned inside him.

It ended, the punishment, and the memory of both punishment and cause faded. Griff was kept in the kitchen, and made no more mistakes like that. The years rolled by, spring to summer to fall to winter, and over again, and the older boys were sold and new boys came to the island. One day, the Damall promised, he would name his heir, he would choose the boy who would stay on the island and be the seventh Damall. The heir would be master of the island. The heir would be told the secret hiding place of the treasure, which he must never reveal until he told it to the boy he had chosen for his own heir. The Damall's eyes glittered in firelit winter darkness as he told the boys this.

He didn't know why the Damall kept looking at him, whenever the story turned to the heir. Until he finally did understand. He would be the boy named. He would be the heir. He would be — and his chest swelled with it — the master. He would be the seventh Damall.

CHAPTER
2

"Why else do you think I never had a name?" He spoke in a whisper.

Griff shook his head, denying it. Griff's hair was pale brown, the color of dry leaves in fall. Griff was tall and bony faced. His eyes glistened like pebbles darkened in the sea. He and Griff sat by the fire, for light, working on their letters and numbers. Nobody could hear what they said when they whispered. The other boys were ranged back against a stone wall, allowed no nearer, on the Damall's orders. The Damall had taken his tankard of wine into the warmth of his own room. They had heard

17

the carved wooden bed creak when the Damall stretched out on it.

He might be nameless, but he was fourteen winters now, and now when he heard one of the little boys whimpering about the cold he thought of tossing the whiner outside, for a night of real cold, and now he could judge to the minute when he should start crying out under the whip so the Damall would be satisfied. He was fourteen winters now, and better at everything than anybody. "There's no other reason, except if I'm to be the heir."

"It troubles me," Griff said. Griff was carefully copying a sentence from the pages the Great Damall had written down, to use in teaching his boys to read and write. *The King rules, for his father was the King.* Griff finished copying that sentence, then said, "There's no mention of you in the record books, no price paid, no place of purchase. No date, no age at arrival. Nothing."

"Because I'm going to be named heir," he repeated.

Griff wrote the next sentence, slowly. *The Queen rules, for she has wed the King.* "Do you remember anything?" Griff asked.

He shook his head, but tried because Griff asked it of him to search out something from the darkness of memory. "I was afraid," he said, and in his mind there rose darkness, streaked with red and orange flames, heavy grey smoke, a storm of chaos, screams, a blinding fear. It was no clearer than the memory of a dream. Like a forgotten dream, it rose into his memory and then sank away again. He swallowed, as if he might weep. "I was afraid," he said again.

"There are no women on the island," Griff said.

"What does that matter?" he demanded. "And besides, the Damall brings women back, sometimes, for anyone who wants the pleasure." Those women were as sharp as stones, and besides, Griff was right. "What does it matter?"

"Women have a man's sons," Griff said. "He hates you."

"I don't mind." That was true. "He can't hurt me."

"That's what I mean," Griff said, his eyes troubled.

It wasn't more than two days after that cold fall evening that the weather blew in mild from the south, as if summer had traveled halfway home across the sea and then changed her mind. Such a season wasn't unknown on the Damall's island. Lady Days, they called it. This Lady Days, the Damall gave orders. Griff and Nikol would stay at the longhouse to care for their master, but the others must go to the other end of the island. They could take with them nothing but their clothing. They must feed and shelter themselves, which would be no great hardship, the Damall told them, not in this fine Lady Days weather. He did not wish to see any of them back before the weather broke.

They stood around, staring at the Damall, staring at one another, dumb with surprise, stupid with confusion.

Angry now, the Damall pointed at him, jabbing the finger into his chest. "You're in charge. Now, go. Are you all deaf? Does every one of you want to be taken to market and sold?"

It was a long morning's walk. He led the boys, through the woods, over the stony hills. At the island's end, looking down a short cliff to the sea where it fed among the rocks, he found a patch of woods. The leafy trees held branches bare as arms up to the sun. The firs never shed their needles, so those were the trees under which to shelter. He sent the boys to gather armloads of dried leaves, for warmth at night. All of the ten boys, even those who were older, obeyed him. He spoke, and they obeyed.

They had brought no fire nor tinder with them, so he set two of the older boys to rubbing dry sticks together to make sparks that would ignite a handful of leaves, on which they might blow — gently, just a whistle of breath — until the little pile of twigs beneath caught fire, and so by slow steps they would have a fire large enough to cook over, and to give them warmth.

Some of the remaining boys he sent back into the woods to find branches to feed the fire, and the rest he led down the cliff and out onto the rocks, to gather the blue-black skals that clung under beds of seaweed and clustered at the bases of boulders.

They slept that night huddled under piles of leaves for warmth.

He kept their fears at bay by insisting that each boy find his own food. He showed them how to catch a gosta behind its hard-shelled head, where its snapping claws couldn't reach a boy's fingers. He showed them how to burn a stick's end in the fire, and scrape it to a point with stones and shells, so that a boy could spear the fish, if he waited patiently and a fish appeared.

He kept their fears at bay by concealing his own fear — What if they were never allowed to return to the longhouse, for example, then how would any of them survive the winter months? If one of the smaller boys were to slip into the icy water, and drown unnoticed, then how would he be repaid by the Damall for his carelessness?

He kept their fears at bay by telling the old stories over again. He told about the Great Damall, and what he didn't know or remember he made up. He told them about the market town, and the Old City — although not about the slave market and the collars worn by slaves in the cities of the mainland. He told them tales of the faraway Kingdom, hidden away among mountains, a land that didn't have four seasons every year like other countries but was always in harvest season, the orchards always in fruit and the goats always giving milk and sweet cakes always in the oven. In the Kingdom, he told them, the King had no whipping box, for he executed evildoers and all the others served him gladly. In the Kingdom, the children were the last to go hungry.

He kept their fears at bay into the long nights, until they moved from the fire to the sheltered leaf piles and into sleep. He locked his own fears away in a stone prison as he looked up at the cold and empty sky, black above him, and the cold and empty sea black before him.

Sometimes he could see trouble building. When the boys understood that there was no drinking water on the northern end of the island, no spring nor stream, they wanted to drink from the sea. He forbade it. They obeyed him for a day, and then grew sullen. He told them what he knew: "The Great Damall's book says seawater is poison. *As well pour oil on flames to drown them as try to slake your thirst with seawater.* That's what the Great Damall knew."

Why, they wanted to know. He said he thought it might be because so many creatures lived in the sea, and so many things grew in it, like earth. They wouldn't be nourished by eating earth, would they?

Or it might be because of the salt, so strong in seawater that you could taste it.

But salt was good, wasn't it? they asked. Didn't the Damall sprinkle salt on his food to make the taste better?

He said he didn't understand and he didn't know. He said he expected obedience and if any boy disobeyed him, that boy would be left alone, to live or to die.

They were silent.

He said there was liquid in blue-black skals, there was juice in gostas. He said he wouldn't let them die for lack of water.

They obeyed him. And didn't complain.

When almost a fortnight had passed, the wind shifted to the north, accompanied by a cold rain that pelted down from the low grey sky, driving through the fir branches. Their fire was drowned. Their beds were soaked. He led them back to the Damall's house. Later in that winter, the Damall took him aside to say, "You will be my heir. Tell no one. Be patient."

He wasn't surprised, except at the swelling of his own heart, as if it were not made of stone. Every tree and meadow on the island was his, every room in the house, each boat, each fowl, each pig . . . everything. He kept the secret even from Griff. He had given his word.

On one of the last long nights of winter, he was seized out of sleep by a hand like a vise on his shoulder. The Damall's face hung down over him, as pale as his hair in the lightless night. "Come," the Damall said.

He followed without a word, without a question, out into the black night, without a cloak. The Damall crossed the yard to the three-sided shed where the fowl slept on shelves and rafters. The two of them stepped warily into the dark stinking air, and the creatures stirred in their straw beds. The Damall gave him a candle to hold, then struck a tinder and put the lighted twist to its wick. The Damall's finger was across his lips in warning, and his eyes glittered.

The Damall pointed with a finger to the stones that floored the shed, then tapped with the toe of his boot at the rear corner, stretching his leg out to reach under the shelves. The birds didn't wake and cry out. With his toe, the Damall counted off five stones towards the center rear of the shed, then — backing up — eight stones towards the front. The Damall crouched down there, and dug with his fingers around the round-topped eighth stone. It lifted out easily, as did the six stones that encircled it.

An uneven cloth-wrapped shape was revealed beneath the stones. He obeyed the Damall's gestured command to bend down and hold the candle closer.

The Damall lifted the shape up, out of the ground, and removed the cloth wrapping to reveal three lidded boxes, lying one on top of the other. One after another, the Damall lifted off the lids and let him look in.

The largest box had a layer of silver coins over its bottom, the middle-sized box held a handful of gold coins, and the smallest had only a leather bag, gathered together at the top. He reached his hand down to take the bag, but the Damall's strong fingers wrapped themselves around his wrist.

The Damall himself opened the bag, and shook it, until a green stone lay on the palm of his hand. As soon as the stone lay there, the Damall closed his hand around it.

The treasure. He was being shown the treasure, and in its hiding place. He was being shown this because he was the heir.

While he held the candle, the Damall closed the boxes, wrapped them in the cloth, replaced them in their earthy cave, and set the stones back in place. The Damall stood then, and took the candle from him. A puff of the Damall's breath plunged the two of them into darkness again.

Out in the empty yard, the Damall spoke, low voiced. "Southernmost corner. West five. North eight."

He nodded his head. He wouldn't forget.

That summer, he decided to build a boat. The island had anywhere from four to six boats tied to the trees that edged its small harbor, small enough so that a boy could handle one on his own, large enough so two or three boys could go out for a day's fishing and carry back the catch. Boats were sometimes lost, to bad weather or a bad mooring knot or bad seamanship. If a boat floated away from the island, or sank when thin planking gave way, often pieces of it would float back onto the beaches; but that was all the good the island got from it.

He saw no reason, studying the little boats, why the island couldn't build its own boats, rather than spending precious coins on the mainland for a boat. The boys already sewed their own sails and mended leaking hulls. It seemed to him that he could build a boat as well as any mainland man, and it seemed to him that the Damall approved of the idea. For helpers, he had the boys who had been in his care during the Lady Days. They had learned how to obey him.

The finished boat floated buoyantly. He fixed its sail between mast and movable boom and set off alone. The boat sailed as if it were a bird on wings.

It was only a week later that the boat was lost, in a squally night. His was the only mooring line the squall pulled loose. In the morning, all the other boats floated on a quiet sea, the long ropes leading from their bows to the shore still in place. The rope that tied his boat was gone, too, but he had no one but himself to blame, since he always knotted it himself. The loss was sharp. But since he knew that he could build another, starting the next spring, he consoled himself. The Damall whipped him lightly for carelessness, and then seemed to forget all about it.

As soon as the last of the shoats had been slaughtered and smoked that fall, he accompanied the Damall to the Old City. He hadn't expected the journey. One morning, the Damall took him aside to speak into his ear, "Fetch me three silver coins. We take Tomas to market today, and I don't know what he will be worth so I must be sure to have enough coins to get another boy or two. Do it during the midday meal, while everyone eats. You won't be missed."

He thought to argue and say that Griff would note his absence, but decided not to. He remembered where the treasure boxes were buried, and removed three silver coins without even counting how many were left, without even lifting the lids of the other boxes, without trying to hold the beryl in his own hand. He tucked the three silver coins into a cloth he had wrapped tight around his waist, and hid the boxes away again.

When he returned to the main hall the Damall

merely nodded to him. "Tomas," the Damall said then, and Tomas stepped forward. "Nikol, bind Tomas. Today you go to market, Tomas."

"But it's only my fifteenth fall," Tomas said.

"Not true," the Damall said.

"But Griff is older," Tomas said.

"Not true," the Damall said.

"But — " Tomas said.

"All of you, help Nikol, hold Tomas until he is bound," the Damall said, then rose and left the hall. By the time he returned, Tomas was bound and ready, and they set sail immediately.

He had the tiller, following the Damall's directions even though he thought he could probably guide them to the Old City without help. Not a word was spoken, as the wind pulled the boat through the water. Tomas watched him, as if hoping to catch a glimpse of hope, or a glimpse of some reason that hope shouldn't die. The Damall watched him as if to catch a glimpse of weakness. He sailed with a stone face that neither of them could read.

That was the way of the island — the older boys left, and new boys arrived. There was no reason nor use to question the way of the island, established by the Great Damall and carried on by his successors. The way things were was the way things had been. He would be the seventh Damall — he named it to himself — to hold rule over the island.

The wind blew brisk and favorable. They were in time to exchange Tomas for five silver coins, and the Damall was pleased with the day's work. The Damall was in good spirits as they left the enclosed slave market and headed for the market square. "What shall we get for you?" the Damall asked. "Dinner in a tavern? A tankard of wine? A woman?"

The market spread out before them. At its center

a tall stone column pointed like a finger at the sky, and at its back broad buildings stood in a line.

He could make no response to the Damall's questions, and then he thought he could. "A dagger."

The eyes glittered. "You may think I've forgotten what happened to the last dagger you were given, but I haven't. I won't give you another dagger so that you can lose it, as you did the other."

The words wanted to tumble out — that he hadn't lost it, it had been stolen, he suspected stolen by Nikol. But he held his tongue, warned by the glittering eyes. There was something dangerous here, something he didn't understand. He would say no more.

"A dinner, wine, and a woman it is, then," the Damall said. "In the morning we'll stop by the slavery again, and you can choose."

He did not ask what it was he was to choose.

The next morning, after buying a full cone of salt at market, and two of the delicate loaves of sweetened bread the bakers put out in the mornings to tempt the hungry, they returned to the fenced slave market. He was to make the selection alone, the Damall told him. He was to spend no more than one silver coin and five coppers. They needed the rest of the silver truemen to feed them across the winter, the Damall said, and hadn't he noticed that the treasure boxes were not as full as they might have been?

He didn't answer.

"You didn't count when I had you fetch the coins?" the Damall asked, and then he laughed. "I know you didn't steal any. I was there behind you, to know if you were a thief."

Why should he steal what would become his own? He didn't ask. Instead, he turned to a huddled group of boys, ranging as he guessed from two winters in age up to twelve. The biggest boy was too old, too tall, he thought, just as the littlest was too little. He noted that only one of the boys stood bravely, without tears or bent head. This boy had curly black hair and a body as round as a tree stump. He went to the master to ask the price. He asked the price of the oldest, first, then the price of the youngest, and he looked doubtful at each answer. It didn't matter what the answer was, he wrinkled his forehead, as if the price worried him. "How old?" he asked, pointing. "How much?"

The black-haired boy was not the first he asked about, nor the last. When he had heard all of the prices, he stepped back from the master and opened the hand he had held closed. He examined the coins on his palm, as if he were counting them. Then he closed his fingers around the coins again, and wrinkled his forehead again, and bade the master farewell. "I am sorry to have troubled you," he said. He turned, and moved three paces towards another group of huddled boys and their master. Then he turned swiftly around to ask, "I don't think you would take five coppers for him?" pointing at the dark-haired boy.

The master barely hesitated before agreeing, and taking the coins, and pushing the boy forward.

He kept his eyes stony, so the master wouldn't see his pleasure.

As he led the boy away he asked, "Do you have a name?"

"Carlo. I wanted you to choose me."

He didn't answer.

He thought the Damall must be pleased when he

returned the silver coin whole, but the man said only, "There'll be a reason he came so cheap."

No reason became evident when they returned to the island. Carlo made no complaint, learned his chores quickly, and performed them without error. Other boys, especially the smaller ones, would spend a sennight weeping and whining; and the Damall would whip their complaints out of them. Carlo never complained. He became a favorite among the littler boys, who vied to work beside him, and eat beside him, and sleep at his side.

After a few days of this, the Damall called for the whipping box and called Carlo. When Carlo knelt naked and afraid, the Damall said, "I'm a little tired. Would anyone care to do this for me?"

"Me," Nikol said. "I will. I can." A few of the other boys asked for the favor.

He stood silent as stone. He thought, when he was the seventh Damall, there might be no whippings ever again.

"Here, you." He was the one to whom the Damall held out the whip.

He thought, he might decline to take it. But even as that thought was in his mind his hand reached out for the wooden handle. He knew it would be dangerous to refuse. If he couldn't wield the whip, to win order on the island, then it might be thought that he wasn't worthy to be Damall.

He had no desire to whip Carlo, who besides had given no reason to be whipped. "How many?" he asked, each word like a stone rolled from his mouth.

"You decide," the Damall answered.

Nikol watched, the firelight making his face red. He raised the whip and brought it down once, twice, not hard, not gentle, and then a final third time.

Carlo cringed at the strokes, but made no sound.

"That's enough," he said, holding the whip now in two hands. He had shown that he could do it. He asked no more of himself.

Carlo stood up, left the whipping box, and put his clothes on.

"Now it's Nikol's turn," the Damall said.

"Me?" Nikol asked. "Turn for what?"

"I saw your face," the Damall said. "I know your mind. Do you think to defy my will?"

"No," Nikol said. His face was pale now. "How many strokes?"

"Let *him* decide," the Damall said, and smiled.

"You don't dare," Nikol said to him.

He would dare.

"I'll get you back," Nikol said.

"Strip," the Damall said to Nikol. "Kneel."

Naked, kneeling, Nikol shivered, on his skinny arms and legs.

He thought he would do one stroke, and get it over with, because Nikol's fear made him feel ill in his stomach, and the whipping made him feel ill. Even though he knew he had to, if the Damall told him to. If he was to be the seventh Damall, he must. He raised his arm and brought the whip down, not gentle, not hard.

Nikol whimpered.

He felt like laughing at Nikol, whimpering now when just before Nikol had been telling him he wouldn't dare. He felt like bringing the whip down again, and harder, to see if he could make Nikol cry and beg for it to stop. Thinking of the whip, and Nikol weeping and begging, his stomach tightened, and his loins. He brought the whip down hard.

Over the sound of his own heart beating he heard the Damall's voice. "Remember the boat that was lost? When there was a squall and only one boat was lost? Nikol untied it. I saw him."

"You did not!" Nikol cried out. "He's lying! I didn't!" Blood rose up out of one of the welts on Nikol's back.

He held the whip that had made those marks, and drawn that blood, and he was ashamed. He held the whip that could make more marks on the flesh of Nikol's back. While Nikol begged.

"I didn't mean to do it!" Nikol cried out, and the Damall laughed. "It was an accident! It served you right, anyway, and I don't care!"

"A confession," the Damall announced. "You all heard it. And with fishing our livelihood, too, but this boy — " he pointed a finger down at Nikol, "didn't care about our livelihood. He didn't care if we went hungry," the Damall said. "What does he deserve?" the Damall asked.

"A whipping. A bad one," the boys answered in ragged chorus.

Nikol wept and blubbered and would have fallen onto his belly in despair except for the sharp stones of the whipping box.

"A bad whipping," the boys urged. Griff watched him out of dark eyes.

He was ashamed, and sick at his stomach, and he passed the whip back to the Damall without a word. The Damall stared at him just for a minute. Then, "He's right, you're not worth the trouble," the Damall said to Nikol. "Get up. Get out of there. You're disgusting."

He knew the Damall would make him take the whip again, and he knew he could take it, and wield it. He had to be able to, because he was the heir. But he would choose the number.

When the Lady Days came that fall, he hoped to be sent out again with the group of boys. It might be uncomfortable without shelter or food supplies, but those discomforts were a rest from the discomforts of the Damall's house. But he was ordered to stay behind, with the Damall and Griff, while all the others went off under Nikol's charge. When the boys returned a fortnight later, Carlo was no longer with them.

The little boy had disappeared, Nikol said. Carlo had just gone in the night, one night. Isn't that so? he asked, and pale faces nodded in agreement. They had searched for him, all the next day — wasn't that the case? There was no disagreement. They finally had to conclude, Nikol reported, that Carlo must have drowned, somehow. Perhaps he wandered in the night, the way some little boys did, and had fallen over the cliff and his body washed out with the tide. Perhaps he had walked into the sea to escape. He had been low in spirits, didn't they agree? The boys agreed.

The boys who had spent Lady Days under Nikol were exhausted, and hungry, and timid. Two of them needed bandaging and all needed hot food, and water. Nikol didn't look worn at all. Nikol looked as if the days had nourished him well. Nikol looked pleased with himself, as if he knew no one would dare to stand in the way of the words he spoke, as if he knew no one would hesitate to obey him.

The Damall said nothing, not to praise or to blame, not to Nikol, not to him.

He waited, uneasy. When he thought of Carlo,

the uneasiness flamed. Across the winter, it was sometimes Nikol who was handed the whip. He was given the whip rarely. When he at last heard the whispered rumor, he was not surprised.

Nikol, the little boys said, had been chosen to be heir. They had heard it from Raul, to whom Nikol had told it in secret. The Damall had said: It was Nikol who would be the seventh Damall.

He didn't say a word to the tale-carrying boys. He didn't say a word to Griff. He stood, and thought, and his heart turned to a fist inside his chest. His heart was a stone fist.

CHAPTER
3

After the long winter came days of foul weather, cold day-long rains that froze at night into sheeted ice that covered everything, like snow, then melted the next day under the cold rains. The boys stayed inside, except when they needed to feed the animals and visit the privies, day after day. The Damall moved restlessly around the house, a blanket wrapped around him. It was earlier each day that he called for his tankards of wine, and called for the whipping box.

Day after day, the weather went on, unchanging. One afternoon all the boys complained of stomach pains, and thirst, and the shits. Some even stayed miserably outside, to be close to the privies. The Damall stayed in his bed, with buckets to be emptied by whatever boy was well enough to carry out, and dump, and put back. By the next morning all felt eased, as if some poison had worked its way out of their bodies. In the morning, all the boys gathered pale and weak in the main hall, where the Damall waited pale and weak for them. Outside, sleet clattered down. Inside, the Damall's eyes glittered. The whipping box was set out and the whip hung in its place on the side of the stone fireplace.

There was danger. Not immediate danger, but mounting danger. Nikol went up to whisper in the Damall's ear and after a few words the Damall brushed him away. The Damall didn't eat that day's soup, and neither did Nikol.

He thought he could see the shape of the danger, forming out of darkness.

By the second morning, all the boys felt well again, and hungry. The Damall had also recovered. The Damall sat beside the fire, the whipping box on the floor before him, a thin smile playing across his lips. The whip rested in his hands. "Nikol," the Damall called.

Nikol approached, waited before the Damall's chair.

He looked at the two faces, and recognized his own fear. He did not yet know what he had to fear, but he would find it out. He didn't doubt that.

He also didn't doubt the courage of his heart to respond to the danger, whatever it was. He wouldn't let himself doubt his courage. He didn't dare to let himself doubt his courage.

"Nikol accuses Griff," the Damall announced. "Griff. Step forward."

Griff went forward.

"Face them," the Damall said.

Griff turned around and faced the seated boys. Griff's hands clasped and unclasped together. Griff's tongue wet his lips, and wet his lips again.

He looked at Griff's familiar face. He didn't know what the Damall, and Nikol, were playing at. Nikol looked right at him then, and smiled.

He didn't like Nikol's smile.

The Damall also looked at him. The Damall didn't smile. "Come forward," the Damall said.

He stood up. He moved forward, over the limbs of seated boys. There were three boys then, standing before the Damall in his highbacked chair. He faced the Damall, and Nikol, and Griff. Griff held his hands clasped together, and his jaw clamped tight, to keep himself quiet. Griff must think that if he were still and quiet, the danger would flow over him, like water. He wondered if Griff hoped to ride out the danger, as seaweed rides out the tide, by standing still, floating silent. He wondered how he, himself, rode out danger — and knew the answer before he had finished asking the question, when he felt his spirit spread out its wings, to rise up and away over, to look down on and see clearly, to soar free. Griff's way was not his way.

Griff's way would not deflect this danger. He knew that. How he knew, he couldn't have said, but the knowledge set his heart beating fast.

The Damall raised a hand and pointed a finger at him. "You be judge."

He didn't question the choice. The Damall must not see any doubt or weakness.

Nikol accused Griff. "He put something in the soup to make us sick."

"I didn't!" Griff cried.

"You did!" Nikol cried.

"Why would I?"

"To make us sick," Nikol said. "Like you did that other time. You hate me, and you hate the Damall, and you want us to die."

Griff hesitated against this charge. "But I was sick, too, it wasn't just everybody else, it was me, too. If I'd done it, would I have eaten any soup?"

"How do I know you were sick?" Nikol asked. He pushed his face towards Griff, jabbing his chin and nose upwards because Griff was the taller. "Anyone can pretend his stomach hurts. Anyone can pretend he's been outside with the shits, or the vomits. Who made the soup?"

"I did," Griff said, "but — "

"Who knows what the naked ladies look like?"

"I do. But that's because after the time before I found all the places where they grow. Because I didn't want that kind of mistake ever to get made again," Griff explained to the Damall. "I found the spring leaves and the fall flowers. I found the corms. I know what they look like."

"See?" Nikol cried out, triumphant.

"But only so I wouldn't make that mistake ever again," Griff cried out.

"That other time, we were sick the same way," Nikol said.

"If somebody did it on purpose, it wasn't me," Griff said.

Nikol spoke slowly then, his voice hissing. "Are you saying it was me?"

Griff's eyes were wide, like the eyes of a rabbit in a snare. "No," he denied. "I don't accuse anyone. I don't know anything. Except I didn't. I wouldn't do that. I made the soup, it would be stupid for me

37

to do that because I'm the first person anyone would accuse. . . ." Griff's voice trailed off and his shoulders slumped.

He thought what Griff said was true: It wouldn't be the cook who poisoned the soup. He thought that Griff wouldn't want to make *him* ill. He believed Griff was guiltless.

"Here's the whip."

The Damall passed him the whip.

He couldn't say — as the Damall wanted to hear him say — "But I haven't judged." If he said that, the Damall would pass the whip to Nikol.

He couldn't say — as the Damall hoped he would — that he believed Griff. If he said that, he would lose his place as heir. He knew that as surely as he knew — whatever Nikol might have actually been promised or maybe just lied about — that *he* was the rightful choice for seventh Damall. Not Nikol.

He took the whip into his hands and folded its tails back along the length of the handle, being careful not to cut his hands on the stone chips. "For the guilty party, how many?" he asked the Damall.

"Twenty," the Damall said. "No, twenty-five."

The boys murmured, pleased. Griff seemed to shrink into himself.

He kept his face a stone mask.

"After which," the Damall said, "he goes to market. Directly to market. It'll be spring, when the soldiers come shopping, and the mines need to replace their winter dead."

He nodded his stone head and did not let his eyes turn their emotionless glance from the Damall's face. He could see Nikol, out of the corner of his eye, smiling. He saw Griff's body quivering, as if with chills.

"For the guilty party," the Damall said, and showed his teeth.

He understood: This was a test, or a contest.

"I am to judge?" he asked. "As you said," he reminded the Damall.

"So I did." The Damall seemed pleased.

He didn't know how to judge, but he knew what his failure to judge would lead to. So he began to make his careful way into the trap. "What Nikol says is true," he said. "It *is* Griff who prepared the soup, and who knows about the naked ladies. It is Griff who always prepares our food, so it is Griff who could most easily add the sickmakers," he said. "Nikol is correct also when he says that the guilty person could pretend to be ill. But," he asked, "how are we to know which one of us it is who was pretending? Nikol might accuse anyone," he said. "He might accuse me."

"I didn't accuse," Nikol sputtered, "I just told the truth. Are you telling the Damall that I'm lying?"

"How could I know if you're lying?" he asked, and felt his own cleverness. He had asked a question no one could answer. He knew, now, how to win the test, and hold his inheritance. "How can any of us know, without proof?"

Nikol pulled at his lower lip and looked at the Damall. At last he answered. "Raul saw. Raul saw and he told me. Stand up, Raul. Stand up and tell them what you told me. How you saw Griff cutting up little white-brown things. How he'd gotten them from under his bed, in a bag. How you looked under his mattress and found them there. How he didn't see you because he thought he was alone, and you were in the shadow by the cupboard beside the fireplace, and his back was to you, and he chopped them up small, with the biggest knife, and dropped them into the soup, handfuls of them. You saw him. You saw it all. Tell what you saw. Tell what you told me last night, when everyone else slept."

Raul stood up. "That's right," he said, and his voice squeaked.

"No, you tell," Nikol said.

"What Nikol said. That's what I said. It's true. I promise," he cried, his voice rising as Nikol reached a hand out for him.

The Damall interrupted. "Twenty-five strokes, judge."

He didn't like his choices. Each choice must be paid for in coin he didn't have to spare. If he denied his own belief in Griff, then he would have purchased his right to rule the island by the betrayal of the one person in the world he trusted. If he acted as he believed, then he would lose his inheritance. His heart sank like stone.

Griff, pale, and sad, was lifting his shirt over his head. Griff looked right at him to say, "I'm sorry."

He knew what Griff meant to say. Griff understood the choicelessness and was sorry to make things harder for him.

"You hear? Did you all hear? Griff admits it," Nikol said. "But he's just saying it now so he'll get fewer strokes. Are you going to let Griff get away with that?" Nikol asked the Damall.

He felt anger raise his heart, until it seemed that he was soaring on wings of anger above the hall. From up there, he could see the Damall's purposes, and see Nikol's purposes, and see a way to save himself.

He handed the whip back to the Damall, who held it out to Nikol.

He made his accusation. "Griff isn't the one who should be whipped. I accuse Nikol."

Nikol's eyes narrowed, briefly. The whip was between them, ready. "You, I'll whip you first, until you beg me — "

"You'll whip no one." The Damall had risen in his chair. "Not until I tell you. Besides, he accuses you. Have you no answer to make to the accusation?"

"I deny it," Nikol said. "He has no proof."

He had proof ready, and as soon as he started telling it, the Damall's glittering eyes told him he had chosen well. "I think Griff saw you," he said. "I think Griff had gone out to the privy and left the soup unguarded. I think you had the corms. I think Griff saw you dropping something into the soup and I think he asked you what you were doing and I think you told him he made a mistake, you weren't doing anything. I think Griff believed you. I think you are the boy who only pretended — "

By then, Nikol had hurled himself forward.

He was ready, feet apart, hands in fists. He felt nothing, when Nikol slammed into him, he felt no pain of fingers groping for his eyes and cheeks, there was no more than a temporary blackness in front of his eyes. He threw Nikol off, threw Nikol onto the ground, threw himself down on top of Nikol.

Hands grabbed him, to haul him up. Nikol scrambled to his feet.

"Let's do this properly," the Damall said.

The Damall held him back by the arms, until he agreed. Then the Damall said, "Take the whipping box out of the way. These two will fight without interference, until . . . one of them begs for mercy. Yes. Then we can be sure who the guilty person is, and we will deal with him. Understood?"

The boys murmured agreement.

"No boy is to try to help in the fight. No one. If

any boy does that, he'll be punished as many strokes as the guilty person. Is that understood?"

They understood. Four boys carried the whipping box out of the way. They made a circle around the space in front of the fireplace. The Damall sat in his chair. The main hall was dark behind the ring of boys, even though it was morning. Firelight played in the air and fell over the faces, as if it were evening, not morning.

He didn't think. He couldn't think. He held himself ready.

Nikol, too, across the empty space, awaited the Damall's word. The packed dirt floor made a kind of penned area, like a corral for animals or the slave market in Celindon. The fire burned behind its hearthstone. Nikol's eyes burned. He hadn't understood how much Nikol hated him.

He shifted, waiting. Firelight made shadows on Nikol's face.

At the word, they began.

This time they were cautious, with circlings and fingers clenched. There was a roaring in his ears, like fire. He could hear his heart beating, he could see Nikol's eyes and the red blood oozing down from Nikol's nose. His feet scuffed along the floor in their soft-soled boots as he circled, wary, ready.

Then there was a time of feinting and false starts. He jabbed a fist out, to draw Nikol's guard. Nikol rushed forward and he just stopped himself in time from ducking backwards, off balance. They feinted and drew back, circling. He began to sweat, salty sweat running into his mouth. He was aware only of Nikol's burning eyes and the dark moving shape beneath the eyes that was Nikol's body.

With a cry that was half a groan, Nikol broke the circle and threw himself fists first into the fight.

There was a confusion of blows and jabs and pains. He moved his hands and legs, moved back and forward, to protect himself against fists, and clawing fingers, teeth, and hands that pulled his hair back, against jabbing knees and kicking feet, and he had to maintain his balance. He was shoving and hitting, clawing, biting at Nikol's ear — it tasted vile — and biting at the hand that Nikol had over his face, with Nikol's fingers up his nose. He jabbed his knee at Nikol's parts. He shoved Nikol's chest with his shoulder and Nikol's face with his elbow and knuckles. Nikol's nose spurted blood, and he had Nikol's blood all over his face. Unless it was his own blood.

He wiped his eyes, because he couldn't see for the blood, and sweat. The sweat stung.

He jabbed backwards, because Nikol hung on his back.

Nikol fell off and he stumbled for sudden lightness.

There was a sound, the boys making some kind of noise. The sound had been going on for a while, he thought.

The Damall's eyes glittered. The Damall might have been about to smile.

He got up onto his feet, but his knees felt wrong, and he was struck from behind the legs and his knees buckled. He fell over backwards like a tree and heard his head strike on the hearthstone. Stunned for two blinks of his eyes, as he tried to clear his vision, two more blinks — he shook his head.

Nikol knelt on his chest, a knee in his neck, choking him. Nikol had a dagger. The dagger Nikol had was his, the one he had been given years earlier, the one that had disappeared. Did Nikol carry a dagger in his boot every day?

Nikol lifted the dagger up, to bring it down into his throat, or chest.

To cut his throat, like a pig's. To —

He held Nikol's hand up, his arm stiff. He bucked and arched, like a fish on the hook, to knock Nikol off. He brought his knees up. Nikol rocked, but didn't fall. Nikol's hands and legs held him down. The dagger descended and only his own left hand slowed its progress.

He wondered which would prove stronger: the hand that wrapped around the dagger's hilt and drove it down, or the hand that wrapped around the other hand's wrist, to push it back away.

From behind Nikol's head, behind Nikol's bared teeth, the Damall's blanket swirled. The Damall reached down to take the hands that held the dagger. The Damall pulled the dagger free. Nikol groaned, cursed, wiped tears away.

He gathered all of his strength, and bucked Nikol off. He surged up onto his feet, staggering a little until the floor steadied under him.

Nikol lay on the ground, on his side.

He took a minute to pull his lower lip free of his teeth. The blood that followed, he swallowed.

Nikol lay on his belly, on the ground. His back heaved.

"I think I'll keep this dagger for the boy who wins this fight. I think," the Damall said, "that the boy who wins this fight is the boy who should be my heir. Don't you agree?" the Damall asked the circle of boys, who responded excitedly. "Isn't that a good idea? Whichever of you two is the winner — the one who makes the other boy cry out for mercy, he has to say that word, no other word will stop it — that boy gets the dagger. That boy will be the seventh Damall. Yes, I do like that." The Damall backed into his seat, and gathered the blanket about himself.

He was already standing.

Nikol struggled up onto his knees, because tears were running out of his eyes. Tears of frustration and anger.

He knew he shouldn't let Nikol get up. He knew he didn't know how much strength of his own he had left, in his legs that shook and his hands that hung on the ends of his wrists, somewhere. He couldn't think. It was harder to fight if you were standing, swaying. He dove onto Nikol.

They rolled, punched, grabbed. Nikol rolled over on top and pounded with his fists.

He felt wrong — in his mouth and cheeks, his ears rang and there were hands around his throat trying to keep air out.

He rose up, and the arms fell back. He rose free and grabbed Nikol's hair. He was sitting on Nikol's chest and Nikol's head rose in his hands and banged back onto the ground, it rose and banged. He couldn't tell if the blood was coming out of Nikol's ear or going into it.

"Stop," Nikol cried. "Stop, please."

Nikol's mouth was bleeding, and Nikol's whole nose followed the blood sideways over his cheek. The hands that lifted Nikol's head and slammed it down kept at their work.

"All right!" Nikol cried out. "Mercy!"

The hands kept on, and he could feel his heart thudding in his chest. He had been breathing fire.

"Mercy!" Nikol screamed. "Mercy! Mercy! I beg — "

He heard the voice. Nikol's head fell down onto the ground. Nikol lay screaming, like a pig at the slaughtering. He lifted his hand — and his shoulder hurt, too — and backhanded Nikol across his bloody cheek. The screaming stopped.

The boys were crying out something behind them. The Damall put the dagger into his hand. "Nikol wanted to let Griff have twenty-five strokes," the Damall said. "Twenty-five strokes will — I've seen a boy die after nineteen. Nikol wanted Griff to die."

"I didn't," Nikol cried. "I didn't, I didn't."

"He was lying about Raul, too, just to get Griff. That was a lie, wasn't it, Raul?" the Damall asked. "Didn't Nikol make you lie?"

"I didn't," Nikol wept. "I didn't do it, I'm sorry."

He sat on Nikol's chest, the dagger in his hand, but he couldn't understand what to do next.

"You said," the Damall reminded him, "that for the guilty party there would be twenty-five strokes."

"But I'll die!" Nikol cried. Nikol's swollen eyes didn't know who to look to, for help.

He held the dagger in his hand, and the fire burned in front of him. He had won the right to be seventh Damall. He had won what had been already given to him. It wasn't a whipping Nikol needed.

He swallowed, and tasted blood.

"You tried to kill me with the dagger," he said to Nikol.

"I didn't, I wouldn't have, I'm sorry."

"This wasn't a fight with daggers," he said. He knew what he was going to do now. He had his fingers wrapped around the dagger, and he brought it down to Nikol's throat, like a pig's.

Nikol's eyes showed white. He couldn't back his head away from the dagger.

"I don't trust you," he said to Nikol.

The boys behind him murmured.

"I'm not afraid of you. But you'll do things behind

my back," he said to Nikol. "So you have to choose. I could cut behind your knee so you'll never walk straight and I'll always be able to hear you coming. That's one choice." Nikol's head rocked from side to side in fear. "Or I can hold your hand in the fire. Like the pirates did to the fifth Damall. Until the whole hand is burned off, so you can't hurt anyone again."

"No." Nikol moaned now. "No, no. Not fair. Please. No."

"Choose," he said.

Nikol shook his head. Nikol opened his mouth but no words came out.

The Damall crouched down and put his face close to Nikol's. "You have to choose. If you don't pick one, I'll let him do both."

"I can't say. I don't. All right! the leg! I choose — no, don't, please don't, I'll take the — no, please don't, I'll do whatever you say. Forever, until I die, I will. I'll tell you everything I know. I know the Damall's secrets, where he hides things away, what he's afraid of, I know where there's meat — "

The Damall's hand came down over Nikol's mouth, and squeezed until Nikol screamed again.

He felt sorry for Nikol, who didn't even have the courage to pick his own pain and punishment. Nikol was nothing now, not even as much of a creature as the pale lusks that backed down into the mud when your fingers chased them.

He looked around, over his shoulder. All the boys were looking down at Nikol, and some of them were laughing at Nikol, and none of them felt sorry for Nikol.

He stood up, without a word. The Damall tried to stop him, but he eluded the man's grasp. He left Nikol on the floor and walked across the main hall,

47

away from the fire. He walked out of the door, out into the yard. He held the dagger.

Rain sleeted down onto his bare head. It cooled his body and his face. His head was already cool. The boys followed him and the Damall followed the boys and he was not surprised when they followed.

He crossed the yard and went through the narrow gate, down the path to the harbor. The rocks underfoot were slippery, but he didn't lose his balance. He held the dagger up, aloft, as if it were a light to follow. At the water's edge, he waded out to climb up onto a huge boulder, and waited for all to gather on the shore behind him. Without a word, he pulled his arm back and hurled the dagger up, out, over, and then it cut sharply into the grey water. It sank and was gone.

He turned around to let them see it in his battered face: He needed no dagger to rule.

CHAPTER
4

He had only blinks of an eye to escape losing everything: He felt the wateriness of his knees and waist at the same time that he heard a buzzing in his ear and — just for an eyeblink — saw the boys gathered on the shore, the Damall tallest of them, although there was one boy there who might be trusted — to see them all, there, and boats, too, although not all the boats — as if they were behind a cloud, now, or behind —

He took a breath and fell backwards. It might look as if he were diving into the winter sea, in a show of strength.

He fell like a stone into the water. It was so cold that he opened his mouth to gasp a protest. Icy water poured in through his teeth, filling his mouth and choking his throat. His heart, he thought, stopped.

The sea bottom caught and held him and he rested there, until numbness seeped into his skin — face and arms and legs, belly. When he gathered his feet beneath him and stood up in the chest-high water, the boats bobbing around him, the pains of the many parts of his body had been dulled by the cold. He could smile, although it pained his cheeks to move, and his lower lip. He could smile in victory and mastery. He could walk out of the water and stride back up the path, with the others behind him as if they were a procession. It was not until he was ten paces from the doorway into the main hall, where Nikol stood waiting, watching, bleeding from a nose that seemed to have moved under his right eye, that the seventh Damall felt in danger again of collapsing onto the ground, into the soft bed of senselessness that reached up for him.

He made himself walk on. Made his knees bend. Nikol moved back before him, and that was luck. Through the doorway to the fire.

There, Griff took him by the arm. "I'll use wine," Griff announced, "lest the cuts fester."

All eyes were on Griff, who dared to say such a thing. He was glad all attended to Griff, because what little strength he had left was draining out of him.

"And salt," Griff announced, maneuvering the two of them to the doorway into the kitchen.

The boys all looked to the Damall, to hear how he would respond to this. The Damall hesitated.

Meanwhile, Griff carried and pushed him into the kitchen. Meanwhile, Griff lowered him onto a stool beside the fireplace, carefully, so that his back rested against the warm stones.

He closed his eyes. The numbness had entirely worn off, and his body and face ached and throbbed, worse in the fire's warmth. When he breathed in, there was pain waiting, and when he breathed out. His legs trembled.

"Drink," Griff said.

A bowl was put into his hands. "Blood?" he asked, but even he had difficulty understanding the word as it came out through his swollen mouth.

"Wine," Griff said.

Between them they lifted the wooden bowl and got wine into his mouth. The wine was sharp, and bitter; it lay warm on his belly. He drank a second bowl unassisted, and the warmth of wine worked like the cold of the sea, to numb.

Griff washed him off with water, washed his face with wine, which stung, and then rinsed it again with cool water.

He leaned back against the warmth of the stones and dozed. When he opened his eyes, he could see only Griff, bending over the cauldron of soup. "Griff?"

Griff moved to the wine vat, ladled a bowlful, and brought it to him. "It's time for the meal," Griff said.

That made it late in the day. He swallowed wine and felt his head clear. "The Damall — " he said, staring into the wine.

"You're the next Damall," Griff reminded him.

"The seventh Damall." He lifted the bowl to his mouth and emptied it. He had the right, now. "I had better go into the hall and sit at table. And dine." He stood, swaying, and then righted himself, waiting until the ringing in his head ceased. He moved slowly to the doorway, and was not sure where he was going.

Wine fuddled the brains. They had all seen it often enough with the Damall. That thought went through him like flame through straw, and he straightened up, to walk strongly into the main hall.

When he entered, the faces of the boys turned to him and conversation halted. He didn't know what they saw. He saw a half circle of boys, sitting cross-legged or leaning back on their elbows, drawn back from the warmth of the fire because the Damall's chair sat up close to it. He saw the Damall in his chair, a tankard of wine in his hand, a little smile on his face as he listened to Nikol. Nikol stood behind the half circle of boys. His nose still slewed off to one side and one of his eyes had swollen to a slit. Nikol stood stiffly, as if all movement would be pain.

The Damall stood to greet him, with a raised tankard. "This boy is the next Damall, the seventh Damall. I name him my heir." The Damall was saying the sentences just the way the Great Damall had written. "I name him next to rule over the Damall's island and the Damall's boys. I name him master of the treasure. Gold and silver and the beryls — all of these are his, because he is the seventh Damall," announced the sixth Damall.

The seventh Damall didn't speak; as the ceremony required, in the Great Damall's book, he remained silent. The faces of the boys were turned up to him, now, and the first shadows of fear joined the shadows the fire left on their cheeks and in their eyes.

Nikol broke the silence. "What about me?"

The sixth Damall lowered his tankard and sat

down again, before he answered. "What about you?"

"You promised," Nikol said.

The Damall smiled. "But you couldn't win it. Could you. You didn't win it. Did you," he said. "This inheritance isn't just going to be given to you. Do you understand that now? The title has to be won. And you have lost it, Nikol."

Nikol stood absolutely still, as if concentrating on remembering something. Then he turned on his heels and left the hall, moving stiffly. Nikol went out — perhaps, the seventh Damall thought, to the privies, or perhaps to kick the pigs.

"The title has first to be won," the sixth Damall said. "Then it has to be held. We hope you can hold it. Don't we, boys?"

"Yes," the boys said, and "You were always best," and "You'll be good at it." Even Raul joined in the line of boys who spoke into his ear. Nikol didn't return that night.

At morning, however, Nikol stood beside the cold fireplace. The seventh Damall had risen early, in the pain of mending sprains and bruises, cuts and swellings, joints pulled away bone from bone. The seventh Damall had entered the main hall before sunrise to start the fire. He saw Nikol waiting there.

Nikol looked pale, and wet, washed clean as if he had spent the night out in the rain. But the night had been rainless. Nikol's hair was slicked down wet on his head, and his shirt dripped onto the floor. His eyes were cold and he didn't speak.

The seventh Damall pretended not to notice, but he saw as much as he could. He saw Nikol's face, so puffed that it seemed boneless. He saw a pale stillness in Nikol, and in his eyes.

53

He thought he had destroyed Nikol yesterday, by shaming him in cowardice. Now, he saw, Nikol had moved beyond the heat of anger or fear. The seventh Damall thought, placing logs on the grey ashes of yesterday's fire, that he was going to have to win his right to inherit every day, every day win it again, in order to hold it.

He told the sixth Damall that he wished to walk the borders of the island that day. He didn't ask it, he announced it, as befitted the heir. He spent that whole long day clambering over the rocks that tumbled down at the sea's edge, and walking across, back and forth across, the fields and woods of the land he stood heir to. At the end of that day, he had decided what he would do — because he understood that he had no choice.

A fortnight later, the Damall lay dying.

There had been a taste of spring. Under the warmth of sun, the woodland meadows had sprouted up pale grass and little white starflowers. Green petals had reached up towards the blue sky. After three days of such promises, they were broken. The wind shifted to the northeast and settled into a blowy rainy cold.

First the Damall sat day after day by the fire, for warmth he said, drinking tankards of wine to medicine the shits and ease his cramping guts. Then he lay before the fire in the great bed that he'd ordered the boys to take apart, and reassemble there in the main hall. He complained of pains in his stomach, of burning in his throat. He complained of weakness in his limbs. He drank tankards of wine and kept all the boys under his eye. He wanted to see what they got up to, he said. He ate only long after the boys had dined. The sixth Damall shivered in his bed by the fire, complaining that he couldn't get warm. He pulled clumps of hair out of his head.

By the tenth day, every breath the Damall drew could be heard by the assembled boys, and the air he drew in rasped against the sides of his throat like pebbles rolled by waves up and down the rocky shore.

Throughout the sickness, the seventh Damall kept near, to spoon soup into his master's mouth, or lift a tankard of wine to his lips. He helped the sixth Damall out to the privies, then back into the hall again, until the man was too weak to move from his bed. As the Damall's body grew weak, his mind also weakened.

Even delirious, however, he knew Nikol. "I want you under my eye," the Damall mumbled, whenever he remembered Nikol. "I never trust you. Stay back. Death's-head beetle, you. You watch — I know you, what you, you want. You should," he grabbed the seventh Damall's hair and pulled hard, "have killed him. I told you."

Nikol spoke not a word. His pale face and cold eyes showed no expression as he hunched in the corner of the hall.

The Damall turned in his bed, and he sweated. He sat up to throw his bedclothes onto the floor. He lay back to cry out, and to weep with cold. He saw people closing in around his bed when none were there, when all the boys dozed fitfully wrapped in their cloaks on the floor. He spoke to those people as if he were answering what they spoke to him. "I didn't mean," the Damall said. "I didn't mean it, I was only a boy, I'm sorry, don't."

By the fourteenth night, the Damall had no voice and no thirst, either. He lay on the bed, with no motion except the narrow rise and fall of his chest, and no sound except the whistling of his breath in his throat.

All the boys were awake, hoping to see death's moment. Smoke from the fire clung to the stained roof beams like mist. Moisture filmed the stone walls and rose up cold from the floor. The Damall coughed, choking. The seventh Damall rose up from his place at the side of the bed, and leaned over to wipe away the bloody froth.

Nothing would happen, the seventh Damall knew, until the sixth Damall died. It might even be that nothing would happen until the sixth Damall had been first washed clean, then wrapped around in the bedclothes he had died in, with three round stones at his head and three round stones at his feet, and at last rowed out to be laid upon the sea. But he didn't count on that much time. He counted only on the time before the sixth Damall died.

Rain washed against the shuttered windows. It drummed on the roof. He listened to air sucked in between cracked lips. Then he stood up, and looked about him.

Griff sat with his back against the stone wall. At only that standing movement, Griff was wary, awake, ready.

But it was Nikol the seventh Damall signaled, with a gesture of his hand. Nikol rose from his corner and darted to the doorway, to await the seventh Damall outside.

The seventh Damall led Nikol into the shelter of the fowl shed. He brought out a candle and struck a tinderbox. The single flame burned bright in the surrounding darkness. Shadows moved behind Nikol and over his face. Nikol held his cloak close around him. He kept his hands hidden under the cloak.

"Listen."

The seventh Damall pitched his voice low. There was none to hear, but a low voice promised deep secrets. If Nikol thought of murder, he would wait to hear the words such a voice promised.

"This is where the treasure is hidden."

Nikol, who had not spoken for ten days, opened his mouth. "You name me eighth?"

"He won't live the night. The Great Damall's rule says there must be two to know the hiding place."

"But never more than two," Nikol said, low-voiced.

The seventh Damall said nothing.

"Will you kill him yourself?"

"Why should I do what this illness does for me?" the seventh Damall asked. "Listen to me, now. At the southernmost corner, you count west five stones, then north eight. No, not now, Nikol, don't! If you disturb the fowl all will be wakened, and guess our business. Say it back to me."

"Southernmost corner," Nikol repeated, staring into the candle's flame. "North five. West eight."

"Wrong." The seventh Damall shivered and the candle flickered. "You said it backwards. Concentrate, Nikol. Listen."

Nikol clenched his teeth in irritation.

"You have to know it exactly."

"Show me."

"To show you is to show all, if I show you now. And you know what would happen then."

Nikol knew. Or, as the seventh Damall guessed the situation — Nikol didn't know exactly, but he knew it would have to do with blood and death, possibly his blood and his death, and he knew the story of the fifth Damall, he knew the effects of greed. "I'm listening," Nikol said.

"Southernmost corner. West five stones. North eight," the seventh Damall said, patience in his voice like honey in a comb. It suited him that Nikol should be irritated, and impatient. It suited him that Nikol should feel events moving more rapidly than his understanding of them.

"Say it," the seventh Damall ordered.

Nikol repeated the words correctly, staring into the flame. Facing Nikol, whose hands were hidden under his cloak, whose face was hidden under moving shadows, the seventh Damall felt fear coil and loosen at his belly. But he didn't let Nikol see that, not even in his eyes.

"Dig up the eighth stone, and also those that encircle it."

Nikol couldn't help but ask. "The beryls are there?"

"That is the treasure's hiding place."

"And the rest of the Great Damall's wealth? The gold pieces and silver?"

"There are three boxes, one beneath the other," the seventh Damall told him.

"How many?" Nikol whispered. "How much?"

"I've been away too long," the seventh Damall said. "He'll notice. Don't forget."

"Southernmost. West five. North eight. All stones that encircle. I can remember that."

"You won't speak until he is dead and underwater," the seventh Damall asked.

"I might," Nikol said. "Or I might not."

The seventh Damall knew the dangers he ran. But if he knew his man, Nikol would first feed himself on satisfaction at being named heir, and at the foolishness of the seventh Damall in trusting him, and especially at the promise of the power and wealth of the Damall being his. It would be a time before Nikol understood that if you are eighth Damall after a younger seventh, you have been played a trick. But for a little time, Nikol would be no danger.

The other boys were no danger. They cared only that at the end of things they stand behind and under the care of the Damall — whoever that might be. The seventh Damall trusted none of them, trusted no one, none but Griff.

When he slipped back into the firelit hall, with Nikol at his heels, nobody had moved. When he sank down onto his haunches, his back against the bed, Griff's eyes closed. The whole household sprawled around the hall, wrapped in their cloaks. The dim, smoky air was filled with the sounds of their restlessness, and the sounds of the Damall, sucking at the air.

The seventh Damall turned his head until he saw Nikol's corner. A flash of white where an eye closed confirmed his guess.

At the slightest disturbance Griff would waken. The seventh Damall wasn't unprotected, should he need protection. The two couldn't prevail against the numbers against them, but they would not — either of them — stand alone.

The dying man moved. The seventh Damall leaned forward, to catch whatever sounds might issue from between the dry lips. He thought it was wine asked for and lifted the shallow bowl from the hearth to spoon some red liquid into the mouth, one spoonful, two, the wine chalky now with sediment. He wiped the dribble away with his fingers. The throat moved, to swallow; the head moved away from the spoon; the eyes, which had not opened for two days, remained closed.

The cold night dragged on. Slowly, logs burned down to coals. Chilly air rose up from the stone floor. The room slept uneasily.

The seventh Damall thought he, too, must have slept, because when he opened his eyes he saw that Nikol had moved from his corner and lay stretched flat — sleeping, it might seem — with his head by Raul's head, his mouth at Raul's ear.

The seventh Damall stiffened, alert.

Griff, as if in response to a cry for help, was awake.

The seventh Damall noted then what had probably awakened him: a stillness of the sixth. The Damall was dead, and it was time to act.

He leaned forward over the lifeless face, as if the sightless eyes could see him, bent closer as if listening to a request, and drew his own breath in, harshly. He rose to put logs onto the fire, and kick at them until the bark caught, spitting and hissing. The fire leaped up into noisy life, as if it were chattering back to the rain that drummed on the roof.

He was Damall now, should he claim it. With a glance, he signaled Griff to move outside.

As Griff left the room, the seventh Damall bent over the body on the bed, to spoon wine between the lips. He drew in another long breath. He spooned more wine, and wiped it off the body's chin, then set the bowl back down by the fire. Before he turned away from the fire, he gasped, as if in exhausted breathing. Then he rose and crossed over sleeping boys to get to the door, and slip outside.

Griff waited for him in the rainy darkness. They didn't speak. The seventh Damall hurried across the yard. Griff followed. They climbed over the barred gate rather than taking the time to open it. Huddled in their cloaks, they ran along the path to the harbor. Rain sluiced down onto their shoulders, burned icy onto their cheeks. The steep path was slick, slippery. Once, Griff fell, landing with a crack of bone that the seventh Damall could hear even above the sounds of rain and waves. At least, he thought, waiting for Griff to scramble to his feet, it wasn't a wind storm. There was a strong wind but it blew from the fortunate west; the wind would fill their sail from behind.

He could have answered questions, had Griff asked them: They were taking a boat and sailing away from Damall's Island. He had hidden food in a stopping place where, if they made a safe escape, they might rest a while in safety.

Griff untied a boat while the seventh Damall pulled it in to shore. They waded out and tumbled over its sides, tumbling in. Griff pulled the sail open. The seventh Damall poled the boat out into deeper water, then passed the oar to Griff and sat at the stern, taking the tiller into his hand. Griff settled the oars inside the boat.

The seventh Damall let the boat tell him, through its round keel and flapping sail, about tide and wind, about the pull of currents among the rocks of the harbor. Then he hauled the sail in close and watched it belly out, like a woman with a child growing. He held the sail's rope in his left hand, the tiller in his right.

The boat, with its two silent passengers, moved out into the black night, moving among the sharp-toothed rocks as freely as if it were a sea hawk crossing the empty skies of a sunlit noon.

CHAPTER
5

The rainy air was shifting to silvery grey as they arrived. The seventh Damall had sailed the route many times, preparing for flight, and so hadn't felt the lack of visible landmarks. They could have beached the boat in darkness, but it was easier in light.

Griff did no more than turn his face in surprise when the seventh Damall lifted the stubby mast out of its blocks and laid it, with its sail pulled close and wrapped secure, flat within the length of the boat. It wasn't the time for asking questions. Rain dripped down their faces and saturated their cloaks.

Climbing out into the seawater, they lifted the boat and carried it clumsily up onto the stony beach, then up onto a low flat rock where it was hidden behind boulders. They set it on its side, and the mast clattered down. The tilted boat made a lean-to shelter.

Before they crawled under it, the seventh Damall led Griff back across the beach to pick up the shattered shell of another small boat, which he had found after days of patient searching. This they lifted more easily, to carry down to the sea. They stood in the rain and watched the waves carry the wreck away, out to sea.

From the narrow cove where they stood, no other island was visible, but there were many islands, scattered alongside the mainland. It was likely that someone on these islands, somehow, would come across the wrecked boat, and tell a tale about it in the market town. It was likely that, should the tale be told, Nikol would hear it, and be satisfied.

The wrecked boat floated into the rainy distance. They turned back to their own boat and crawled under its shelter.

It had been long days and long nights and little time for sleep. The seventh Damall gathered his knees up to his chest. Now he could sleep. All was now done, accomplished. Griff was already asleep, hunched up under the bow, his mouth hanging slack, his whole body collapsed into exhaustion. The seventh Damall waited impatiently but although his body ached with tiredness, his mind pulled restlessly, like a fish fighting on the end of a line.

He stretched his legs out and that didn't ease the aching.

He curled over onto his side like a little boy, and sleep didn't come to him.

The seventh Damall had made the plan and executed it — what was there now to keep him awake?

He rolled over. Small jags of rock cut into his back, through the thick cloak, and he lifted himself to sit again, shivering. He wrapped his arms around his legs, drawing them in close again so that he might warm himself.

If he warmed himself, he was his own fire. Was there danger in the fire-way of consuming itself? The sixth Damall had lain by the fire until death took him. And now there was an eighth Damall.

The seventh Damall existed only in the past, now, like the Great Damall and those five who had succeeded him. There was no longer any seventh Damall. He could no longer be the seventh Damall.

He fell into sleep then, as a body weighted with stones and wrapped in winding sheets falls into deep water.

He awoke to the sound of rain and the sight of Griff, also awake. In sleep, new concerns had come to him. "We can't build a fire," he said, and Griff nodded, understanding. "There's food here — bread, carrots, onions — but it may all be soaked, ruined." Griff nodded, accepting.

He had wrapped the food in cloth and tucked it behind sheltering rocks, but the bread turned to dark mush in their fingers as they scooped it out of its thick crust, like porridge. The carrots were unharmed, the onions slightly mildewed. They ate to blunt the teeth of hunger. When that was accomplished they ceased eating. Water they could lick up out of the hollows in the rocks. Water was plentiful, under the steady rain. Bellies no longer pinched, they slept again and woke to the last light of day, and an end of rain.

It was a pleasure to crawl out from under shelter, and stand in the evening breeze — fresh and cleansing as a snowfall. In this solitary cove on the barren island, where the rock cliffs rose at their backs and descended at their sides to the sea like enclosing arms, they were, he judged, safe. All they could see was the empty water, stretching eastward, stretching southward.

He stood, looking eastward and southward. Griff came to stand beside him. "You kept your word," Griff said, "for which I thank you. I never believed you'd be able to do it."

Surprised, he asked, "What word?"

"You promised me I'd never be sold in the slave market, even when I grew old enough."

"I don't remember."

"The third winter," Griff said.

"But I was a child, a little boy, just — How could you even think — ? You shouldn't believe a little child."

"Why not?" Griff asked.

He laughed, and the sound sailed out over the darkening water. "Because a child can't — "

"But you kept your promise."

"I have. I did, didn't I?"

He bent down, to pick up a small rock and throw it high out over the water, then bent to pick up another. Griff did the same and they stood there, pelting rocks into the approaching darkness. "We're free of the island," he said, hurling a fist-sized rock so high it almost could have been mistaken for a bird.

"Free of the Damall," Griff said.

"No, because that's me, that's who — "

"No, I mean free of the fear, fear of the Damall, and fear of the other boys. You're not a Damall to be feared, you'd never be."

"First my name was lost to me," he said.

"You never were such," Griff said.

"Now the title, too, a title is almost a name."

"What will you do?" Griff asked.

He considered. "Take a name," he decided.

Griff didn't ask *What name?*

He wished Griff would ask, in case he held an answer on his tongue to answer that summons. He waited, but Griff didn't ask that question. Instead, "I'm hungry," Griff said.

"Tomorrow. In the morning, we'll eat again." He didn't mind hunger. Griff didn't protest.

Even though the rain had ceased, they slept that night under shelter. They awoke to a low, receding tide, and pale sunlight, and a breeze that blew lightly from the south. They divided the carrots equally between them and passed the one onion back and forth.

"I thought of taking one of the kitchen knives," he said.

"Nikol would have seen you. He was watching everything, those last days," Griff said. "Watching. Waiting."

"The Damall shouldn't have given me the dagger that second time," he said. "But I wonder why he didn't teach us how to fight."

"Maybe he thought he didn't need to, because those who knew by nature how to fight would take what they wanted. Would you have taught your boys?"

"I think so," he said. "If pirates were to attack me, I wouldn't know how to defend myself or what was mine."

"It was the fifth Damall the pirates killed, and that was long ago," Griff said. "Pirates haven't been seen since."

"Because he wouldn't show them the treasure."

"Is there a real treasure, then?" Griff asked.

But he was thinking, for the first time really thinking, of that event — which he had always known of but never thought about. "But he'd have told them, Griff. The fifth Damall. He would have. Any man would. When they hold your hand in fire to make you tell, and if the hand burns away and so they hold your arm — he died in the fever of burns and the pain had burned away his mind — that's what they said, isn't it? So he must have told them."

"Under such compulsion, I'd speak," Griff said. "But I don't think you would."

"It's only gold. Silver. One beryl. It's only wealth. It isn't life."

"Would you give the island's treasure to pirates?"

"I would, and I should," he answered. "But afterwards, unless there was urgent need not to, I would chase after them, track them down, come upon them when they suspected nothing and — take back what was my own. I think the fifth Damall must have told them where the treasure lay hidden. Under torture. Under the pain."

"Then the pirates would have taken it. Was there any treasure on the island?"

"There was. Gold, silver, one beryl."

"So," Griff said, "the pirates didn't take it. The fifth Damall didn't tell. Neither would you."

"Unless," he answered Griff, "the treasure wasn't

where the fifth Damall thought it was. Unless he told them where it was and when they went to find it, it wasn't there."

They sat on a long flat rock, watching the sea. They were on guard, although neither had spoken of it. If Nikol were following them, this was a day he would use.

"Who else knew where the treasure was hidden?" Griff asked. He answered himself, "No one. Except the heir, if he'd been named. And he — " Griff didn't want to finish the sentence. Griff had never wondered; he had only feared. "What about the others," Griff said then. "Not Nikol but — what about the other boys?"

"What do you mean?" he asked.

"I mean, because they're still there on the island, under the new Damall." Griff looked out over the water, his eyes dark. "With Nikol," Griff said.

He tried to separate his thoughts. "I couldn't do anything. Because of the way they were. What they expected," he said. "I could have been Damall, I don't mean that. But — I have to make my own way, choose for myself and make my own way."

"What about me, then?" Griff asked.

"You taught me to swim," he said, which seemed to him enough. Then, "It seems so far away, doesn't it? and long ago? Even though this is only the second morning, and we aren't even safely away."

They sat on the sun-warmed rock, with sea birds wheeling above. He wondered if Griff was also remembering fear, and helplessness, and —

He rose to his feet. "I wasn't powerless."

But he had chosen to be. In the circle around the whipping box, each boy was alone. But each boy shared the shame, his heart shriveling up like a leaf

on the fire, like his shriveled-up man-part, everything that might have been strong about any of them
shriveled up and useless, like the discarded skin of
a snake.

"You couldn't have done anything. What could
you have done?" Griff asked.

"I could have attacked him, and I thought of it.
With a log. Or the whip."

"He'd have set the others on you."

"You'd have stood by me."

"But I am only one." Griff thought, and then
spoke the truth, because Griff would always speak
truly, if he could. "Some of the others, too, they
might have."

"And I never tried. Because I was afraid. I never
have to be afraid again." He realized it.

Griff turned to smile at him. "Maybe you don't.
Who can tell? But the sixth Damall never will
be."

It took him a time to understand Griff's meaning,
while waves washed up at the base of the rock, a
time of staring down at the back of Griff's head,
where the brown hair hung down over the shoulders
of the dark cloak.

It took him a time to understand, again, what it
was not to have any name.

It took another time, more waves rolling up, to
understand that he had no idea what it would be
like to live without fear at his elbow, warning him,
keeping him safe, keeping him frightened. Fear was
stones in his mouth, their grey dry gritty taste, and
stones a weight in his stomach, and stones pressing
down on his heart so he couldn't breathe. In a world
where everything changed, the sky and the sea and
even sometimes the land, and especially the mood

of the sixth Damall, and even the faces of the boys changed as the older boys were tied at hands and ankles and taken to be sold —

In that world, only fear was the same one day as it had been the day before, and would be the next day. It was fear of seeing sails on the water, sails that drew closer and became recognizable as the Damall's boats, that governed him now, even though he had made an escape from the island.

He couldn't watch patiently, as Griff did. If they were to be pursued, and captured, and taken back —

He couldn't sit and wait. He walked off the rock and down along the water's edge. Stones cut at the soles of his boots. He looked up at the stone cliffs. He looked across to where Griff sat watching the water. He looked out over the empty sea.

Without their boat, this island would be a sentence of death. The high cliffs were too smooth to climb. The water was too shallow and stony for fish; there was no sand or mud for burrowing skals to live in; no blue-black skals clung to the rocks here, because the sea ran too strongly for seaweed to attach itself. No food, no water, no escape — this island could be a killing place.

He crossed the beach to the cliffs. When he looked up from their base, they seemed to sway over his head, they seemed about to fall over onto him. Almost dizzy, he reached out to the stone.

There were letters cut into the stone. His fingers felt them, and now he knew what to look for he could see them clearly, lines cut deep into solid rock and worn by weather. The letters formed words. The words were names, he thought, two of them close together while the other three were separated, each one alone.

The two together were cut more deeply into the stone. They might have been carved with a knife, he decided, whereas the others were hacked roughly. A rough solitary name was under his hand. SANDO, he read, and then another solitary name, MILLAR, and then — its initial C as ragged as a scream — CORBEL. These names were at different heights and the letters differently shaped; these three must have come to the island at different times.

The two names together, cut more narrowly, worn more smoothly, one above the other, were two who had been together, he thought. ORIEl, he read, and BERYl.

He wondered — his fingertips tracing the O, the sun warm on his back — which names had been first carved, and how long ago, and if those made at a later time had been inspired by the sight of the earlier. Then he thought, he must be more weary than he guessed, not to recognize the gift.

BERYl and ORIEl, weathered yet clear. He knew beryl, and he ran back to where Griff sat, looking seawards.

"I found names carved in the cliff face," he said. "As if people were maybe shipwrecked here. From a long time ago, but there's no way of knowing how long, but — look — " He reached up under his shirt and his fingers worked their way down into the strip of cloth he had wound around and around his waist, concealed by both trousers and shirt. "There were two names together, Oriel and Beryl and — see?" He brought out what he had carried hidden among the windings of cloth, and unwrapped it.

The green stone lay in the palm of his hand.

Shafts of light seemed to lead the eye into its green heart.

"You can hold it if you want to."

Griff reached out his hand and took the beryl. The stone was as long as his thumb, and twice as thick.

"This is the last beryl."

"They said," Griff said, "that as long as there remained one of the Great Damall's beryls, the island would be safe from harm."

That wasn't the response he expected, or wanted. "They also said," he reminded Griff, "that the Great Damall would rise from the sea, his sword in his hand and Death himself at his shoulder, if danger threatened the island. What of that? They also said there were nine stones given to the Great Damall, each one as large as a man's fist. But I know better. I read what the Great Damall wrote: There was a Prince from a distant Kingdom, in the northern lands, who bought the giant from the Great Damall. The Great Damall had saved the giant from drowning in the sea, and the price the Prince paid was three beryls. The Great Damall wrote down what the Prince told him. This giant had been stolen from the Kingdom by pirates; the Prince disguised himself as a beggar and followed after. When the Prince saw how well the Great Damall treated the giant, he revealed himself, and offered the three beryls. Two bought the island. This is the last of them."

He didn't believe all the Great Damall wrote, but that last he did believe. The giant, the Prince, the distant Kingdom, the Great Damall wearing honor like a cloak — those he might doubt; but the beryl he could touch.

"I take Oriel for my name," he said. "Shall I?"

"For what reason?"

"Isn't it reason enough to see the name carved here? and beryl with it? Isn't it reason enough that I must have a name?" He gave himself the name, silently speaking it, Oriel. "Can you name me?"

"Yes," Griff said. At the waiting silence, he looked up. "Oriel," Griff said. "I can name you that. Oriel."

At each saying, the name fitted him more closely. "Name me again," he said.

"Oriel," Griff said. "Did you bring the Great Damall's treasure with you then, Oriel?"

"I did. Not all, though. I left some gold pieces, and silver. For the well-being of those who stay behind."

"Now what will happen there?"

"I named an heir."

"Nikol?"

"If I hadn't named him . . ."

Griff remained silent for a long time. His fingers turned the beryl over, and back, and over again. "There's something — " he held it up before his eyes — "Look, Oriel, isn't there something carved?" He returned the stone.

"A bird?" Oriel tilted the stone so the sun shone onto it. "This looks like a beak, head, and the wings outstretched — Tomorrow we leave this place, Griff, and when we have paper we'll see what there is to see. But who would carve into such a stone?"

Griff didn't know.

"And why?" Even Oriel, who had read the Great Damall's book over and over, couldn't guess.

The day passed slowly, until afternoon faded into evening. Darkness crossed the sea, slowly, approaching. Oriel was hungry and restless. Beside him, Griff was probably just as hungry although neither spoke of it.

The stars came out, faint as distant sails, then clearer. Griff went back to the shelter of the boat to sleep. Oriel remained at the shore, with the sound of little waves for company. In a while the moon would rise up into the black sky. On such a clear night, the moon's light would be so bright it would cast shadows.

They might, Oriel's restless mind thought, set sail on such a night.

But nobody sailed at night. Night sailing was dark and dangerous. Besides, were Nikol to search for them, he'd never look at this stony, eastward-facing cove, at the back of this uninhabitable island. He wouldn't care enough to search. Except —

For the treasure. Nikol wouldn't have read the Great Damall's book, because reading was too hard for him. Nikol would think there were many beryls stolen. Nikol would search long and hard for beryls, and for imagined riches of more gold and silver than the treasure boxes had ever held.

Oriel was on his feet. He turned, staring into the darkness that was cliffs, then back over the water. They should sail this night, and sail by night.

It was already too late, the wind had sunk, if they didn't make a harbor by morning and if Nikol were searching —

But it would be foolhardy to sail out blind, and at night on unfamiliar waters he was as good as blind, and worse if the wind rose up.

Here, everything was known. Everything was stone. Here lay safety, here safety was sure. Here, night shielded them.

Nobody ever sailed by night. Everybody knew better.

Oriel turned back to the shelter of the boat. Sleep came swiftly, as if she had only been awaiting his summons to lie down beside him and wrap him in her soft arms.

CHAPTER
6

They were later than the sun in rising, and clumsy at righting the boat. It was, Oriel thought, the weakness of hunger and thirst. He hadn't brought enough food when he stocked this cove for their sheltering. But he had taken all the food he dared risk removing from the storeroom. If failing to take the greater risk meant that they failed —

But they hadn't failed. They were here, safe, on the third morning. They might not live, but they wouldn't have failed. A surging effort, beyond his own strength, enabled him to lift the stern, while Griff shifted the bow onto his shoulders and back.

They were breathing heavily and could only carry the boat twelve paces before they had to set it down.

When they had regained strength, they crouched down and once again lifted, settled the boat's weight, and bore it twelve slow paces before setting it down again.

In that fashion they made their way down to the water. Once the keel was buoyed up by water, there was only the mast to lift and set into place. Oriel locked the mast into place with its wooden pin.

Oriel and Griff climbed into the boat and each took an oar to paddle them out into deep water. Then Griff lowered the boom from where it had been lashed against the mast, and thereby unfolded the sail. The wind came from the northeast. The sail swelled with wind. The sun shone down, dancing along the uneven surface of the water, reflecting light into their faces. The sky was empty and blue. The cove fell away behind them, and the rocky island fell away.

Griff didn't ask where they were heading, not even when Oriel brought the bow around to point as close to direct west as the wind permitted. This slowed their pace, and the wind — dying into noonday calm — slowed them further. At the pace of a leaf floating on still water, they approached two islands that seemed only a hand's breadth apart, but which they knew from familiarity lay hundreds of paces separate. From those, the Damall's island lay close. Beyond those islands, to the north, stretched the green horizon of the mainland.

"Sails," Griff said, pointing to the east. "Do you see three?" Both knew how unclear vision over distance is, at sea. "Two?"

Oriel bent his head to look under the boom. He

saw at least two, and maybe three, or four. He saw tiny dots that were red sails, the same color as the sail over his head. "Coming closer?"

"I can't tell," Griff said. "Oriel — ?"

Oriel didn't know if this was Nikol, searching. He didn't know if their single boat was visible over the distance. He didn't know if they should fold up their sail, since it was the most visible thing about them. He didn't know what —

Danger made his choice. He pulled the tiller in close, to swing the bow of the boat around until the wind came at the sail from behind. This was the favorable set. This was the set of the sail for speed, and he held it — heading south and west, heading away from what might be boats pursuing. Griff watched behind them while Oriel watched the sail, to keep it filled. They might be pursued, but on this heading they couldn't be caught, not with such a lead on their pursuers. The tiller and rope pulled against his hands, and the boat pulled eagerly through the water.

He didn't dare turn his head, so he watched Griff's face. He wasn't surprised to hear, after a long while, Griff's report. "They're out of sight. I haven't seen them for a long time. I think we're clear of them."

"A little longer," he decided.

It was afternoon when he turned the boat again. They had gone so far out to sea that only a dim greyness at the horizon that might have been a line of clouds marked what he hoped was land. He turned the boat and sailed a zigzag course back to the north, then west again, across the empty water. He thought, he would like to see just one island. If he could see an island coming towards them out of the distance — green-headed within its encircling boulders — then he would know that sooner or later they could find one of the few beaches that appeared on the islands, and make a landfall.

The afternoon passed slowly, as they first saw at a distance and then sailed among unfamiliar islands, bringing the boat in close wherever it looked as if they might make a landing. At last they saw a narrow pebbled beach.

"I hope there's water," Griff said. "A creek, or a spring."

"Yes," Oriel agreed, and he hadn't realized until then how dry his mouth was, how great his thirst. When he had turned the bow of the boat and sailed for speed in whatever direction the wind chose, he might have lost both of their lives, when he let danger make his choices.

It was twilight by the time they had dragged the boat up the slope of shore and tied it to a boulder, in case the tide rose high. From beyond the beach the island's rim of great stones — smoothed by weather until they seemed huge flanks of even huger animals — trees were visible against the darkening sky. "If we sleep until light, we can try then to find water," Oriel said.

"I feared," Griff said, "that we might never make landfall again. For a while I truly feared it. You did well, Oriel. You — I don't know how you do it, we're away from the island, and safe and — You did it."

Oriel heard the wonder in Griff's voice and he knew why Griff felt that way, but he couldn't agree. He counted up the errors he had made, and understood how great a part good luck had played in their escape. Without all of the luck, Oriel knew where they would be. Because his first error was not killing Nikol, when he had the dagger in his hand and the Damall's permission.

But what kind of a life was it when you had to kill somebody to keep the place that had been awarded to you? What kind of a world was it where in order to be on top you had to push others under — as if you were pushing heads down underwater — and hold them there until they drowned, and then you could be on top.

Oriel hadn't done nearly as well as he should have and this could have cost his own life, and Griff's, too. *How* that hadn't happened, he reminded himself, was more important than how well he had done. It was more important, if he wanted to continue living, not to let himself lose sight of the truth of things.

They wrapped themselves in their cloaks and lay down on the rocks, to sleep. The sky overhead was curtained with long drifting clouds, through which moon or stars sometimes appeared. Sleeping, then waking to hear the water, see the stars, smell the salty air — then sleeping again, Oriel passed the night.

In the morning, they took off their boots and trousers and waded, barelegged, into the icy sea to pull blue-black skals up from where they clung to rocks under cover of ropy seaweed. Oriel had the tinderbox at his waist. He struck sparks to start a cookfire. When the driftwood logs had heated to coals they lay seaweed in armloads down upon the flames, dumped the skals, and then more seaweed. Steam rose moist and salty, as the skals cooked themselves open.

Each skal had in its shell a few drops of liquid. Each skal opened to reveal a moist nugget of meat. They had searched for stream or spring while the fire took hold, and had found none, but the juiciness of the skals satisfied thirst as well as hunger.

When they were full they lay back in sunlight. "We're too close to Damall's Island still," Oriel said. "I'm not easy, this close. So we'll sail by night until we make the next landfall."

"Is it the mainland we're heading towards?" Griff asked.

"The Great Damall wrote of the Northern Star, and how the Plough points the eye to that one fixed star. Remember?"

"I remember."

"If I know north, I can find south. Knowing north and south, I can find northwest, and the mainland."

"So it is the mainland we are heading towards."

"No other boats sail by night. You can look for rocks. If the night is clear, if we keep well out and away from islands, if the breeze is light and the water not too rough, if our luck holds and my skill is skill enough — It'll be a safer journey by night, while we are still so close to Damall's Island."

"You sleep now, Oriel," Griff said. "I'll keep watch."

They set off after moonrise, sailing into a steady breeze. Oriel headed the boat generally northwest. This meant they had to move among islands, some so tiny they held only a single tree, some large enough for a few houses to cluster about a cove, where fishing boats bobbled on the black water. The dark mass of islands showed clearly against the star-pricked sky. The night air was so cold that both Oriel and Griff shivered, and clenched their teeth against the ague of cold.

After a long time Griff broke into the silence made by the whisper of wind to water and the keel's answering whisper through waves. "I barely remember the mainland."

"Is that where I came from?" Oriel asked.

"Probably, since that's where the Damall went, to get boys. But not certainly. In the books, over the years, one or two of the boys have been just left on the island. Found on the beach. And there isn't anything about you in the books . . . ." Griff's voice drifted off, riding on the sounds of wind and water.

"But you don't know for sure. You can't know. I can't." There was something satisfying to Oriel about this lack of a past. He was as solitary as stone. Because he had no history, he might win for himself any future. He owned all that he was. "I don't remember anything. I must have been young."

"You were. You were a little boy."

"Then, I remember you, and him, too, the sixth Damall."

Griff said nothing.

Oriel had a sudden thought: "What do you remember, how old were you when you came to the island, Griff? Do you want to find where you came from, and go back there? What do you remember? Do you remember anything?"

Griff's face was washed pale by moonlight when he looked back along the boat to Oriel.

"Keep watch," Oriel reminded him.

"I remember you," Griff said, turning back to face the black water. "When I think back, I remember you because — I remember, I was so lonely, I don't even know how long a time it was except I think it maybe wasn't all that long. I just don't know. Except lonely, and frightened. I only remember nighttime, as if it was always night. But I think that I wouldn't have been so lonely, and so frightened, if I hadn't been accustomed to something else. Don't you think?"

"I don't know."

"I think, maybe I must have had brothers or sisters, and I almost remember — but I don't know if I only dreamed this, or if I only pretend it, do you know what I mean?"

Oriel shook his head.

"But the Damall told me, they gave me away to him because they didn't want me. But the Damall didn't always tell the truth."

"Especially not when he thought he could hurt you," Oriel said.

"But he didn't always lie," Griff said, speaking out of the darkness at the bow of the boat.

"I'd not have been like him," Oriel said. "I'd have been a different kind of Damall. Keep watch," he reminded Griff again.

"But he never meant you to be the seventh Damall," Griff said.

"Don't be stupid." Oriel's hand clutched the tiller.

"It was Nikol he wanted."

"No, it wasn't. He told me I'd be the heir, and he showed me where the treasure was hidden, and then he announced it before all after I had won it in the fight. He named *me*."

He could see only the dark shadow that was Griff, sitting, staring out at the water.

"Griff?"

"Do you really think so, Oriel? I never thought so."

"Then why did he name me?" But Oriel was already convinced.

"To make Nikol do what he wanted. Oriel, you know what happened to the fifth Damall, but didn't you ever think who was the sixth?"

No, he never had. The tiller pulled him back to attention and he fell silent, sailing the boat, following the dark sail, thinking about the perfidy of the sixth Damall, wondering about the eighth. *We can never go back, really never can*, he almost said aloud to Griff, but decided not to because he was just as glad to be able to think, *We never have to go back*.

"Should I have killed him?" Oriel asked Griff. His voice floated on darkness.

Griff didn't pretend not to understand. "I don't think so, but because you didn't, things . . . happened. I was glad whenever you didn't kill him. Every time. You could have killed him all the time, and you didn't, and I was proud for you even if it was dangerous for everyone."

The problem was that Oriel deserved to be Damall, because he was the best of the boys, the best of all of them. Nobody had to say it because it was so obvious. Nikol knew it, and didn't question it; what Nikol questioned was whether because Oriel was worthy that meant Nikol couldn't get the prize.

Because Oriel knew about himself that he was worthy to rule. He didn't need to kill anyone to prove it. He didn't need anybody else to be weak so he could be strong. He was what he was: the best choice.

They sailed across the night, in unknown territory now, on unknown waters. The first light showed him an island with a deep eastward-facing cove, and low hills covered with bare-branched trees. He was exhausted by the night's anxious sail. Griff folded up the sail and rowed the boat to land. One of the first things they saw was a creek, flowing down a steep hillside onto the beach and into the sea. No houses could be seen. No smoke rose into the sky. Oriel held onto the bow line but didn't even think of tying the boat, or anchoring it, until he had put his head into the sweet water of the creek and drunk his fill, lying flat on his stomach, sucking up the shallow water where it ran over cold stones.

He rolled onto his back, suddenly helpless against his exhaustion. "You sit watch," he said as his eyelids sank to his cheeks.

He awoke to the warmth of sunlight on his back and the sense that his feet must have swollen in his soft boots. Sharp edges of crushed shells cut into his cheek and forehead and the smell of soil was in his nose — earth, salt, drying grass, rotting grass, roots. He rolled over onto his back and the light almost blinded him. He rubbed his fingers across his eyes to soothe them.

Griff leaned against the trunk of a tree, his eyes closed even though he was standing. The boat had been tied around that same tree, and its line had then been wound around Griff's leg.

Oriel sat up, then stood.

Griff's eyes flew open.

"You sleep now," Oriel said.

Griff bent to unwind the line and in the same motion folded his long legs and sank onto the ground. Even the sun shining full on his face couldn't keep him awake.

It was midday, the sun high in the sky. Oriel went back to the creek and drank again. Cool, fresh, freshening —

Oriel raised his head and looked across the sea. No boat crossed along the dark blue depths. No danger was in sight among the islands that floated silently and peacefully in the distances. He heard no human voices. He saw no human habitation. He had a net folded up in the boat.

Alone in the bright height of the day, with Griff

sleeping deeply behind him and the water flowing cold at his hips as he dragged the net behind — Knowing that if he chose they could stay in this place, build a shelter, dig a garden, fish the sea — Knowing that if he chose they could go on south, to the cities and the sun-ripened fields — Knowing his own name —

Oriel threw his arms up into the air and laughed aloud. The two fish that he had trapped in the net swam free, as it spread loose and slowly sank to the stony bottom. Laughter burst out of him. He was away from the Damall's island, and he had gold and silver coins, and he had the last of the Great Damall's beryls against great need, and he had Griff safe with him, and he had a name — His laughter was a shout of joy and victory.

He reached underwater to pick up the handles of the net and returned to the task. Fish now crowded in, until he was dragging behind him more fish than even the two of them, hungry as they were, could eat. The excess catch he kept alive by gathering the two net handles together and hanging the now bag-like net off the tiller. Their meal he killed with a stone and gutted with sharp shells, then strung onto sticks to cook over the fire he built. Griff awakened to their smell. "What — ?" he asked. "You — ?"

"I caught some fish."

"I forgot — " Griff's eyes were still confused with sleep.

"The fish is ready to eat. There's more, in the net. I hung it off the boat to keep them alive."

They ate their fill, and then more, to finish the cooked fish. After eating, they sat at the water's edge, watching the little waves lick at the shore, and the little boat bounce gently up and down, and the streaky clouds flow slowly across the sky.

"There is always food to be had from the sea," Oriel said. "Fish, gostas, skals. Blue skals or grey or white, they're there for the taking all the seasons of a year."

"An island? or the mainland?" Griff asked.

"There are wives to be gotten on the mainland."

"The market town?" Griff asked. "You've been there, many times, you know the land and the people."

"It would be dangerous to settle close to Damall's Island."

"Wherever you say," Griff said. "That seems best to me."

"Southwest to the cities beyond Celindon," Oriel said. "We can trade our fish on the mainland."

"Bread," Griff suggested, and smiled. Griff had the guarded face of a man who had much to lose by the wrong choice, although he had never had anything to lose. Griff's smile visited his face like a stranger who was only asking directions on his way through to another town.

"We should sail to the mainland today, and find a farm where we can trade fish for bread and maybe also a bed for the night, and also perhaps hear of a town or a city where two lads might find work as . . ." Oriel had run out of ideas but Griff was already on his feet, ready to go on.

They sailed west along the coastline, the wind at their shoulders, dodging islands and peninsulas and rocky outcroppings. By afternoon they had given wide berth to two coastal towns. The first was the market town the Damall used, the second lay too close to the first. Not much later Oriel pointed out to Griff the double-walled city itself, Celindon, spreading back up over steep hills. Late in the day they came to a broad inlet, where a meadow sloped down to the water and a thick line of trees enclosed it. Just in front of the trees was a little house. They tied the boat to an outcropping of rock and also around a sapling, for double safety. Griff bore the netful of fish.

The solitary house had a lean-to shed at its rear, and a small garden behind it where three fruit trees were in early blossom. A round stone well had been dug outside the doorway to the house. This wasn't a farm but Oriel judged they might as well take their chance. The bucket waiting beside the well made him certain the house was inhabited.

He knocked on the door.

It opened so quickly he thought they must have been watched as they crossed the meadow. The person in the open doorway was short, and wrapped in a brown blanket, a woman, old by her white hair. She barely looked at them. Instead, she looked all around behind them.

"Quick," she said, in a voice as hoarse as if she had screamed her throat raw. One hand held the blanket at her throat, the other held the door.

"Quick," she urged them.

Oriel hesitated on the stone stoop. Griff took the netted fish from his shoulder. Fear welled up and out of the open doorway, like water from a spring.

"You're just lads, just boys," she said. "You don't *know*. Inside it's safe — inside it's — quick!"

They obeyed her. She shoved the wooden door closed behind them and barred it shut.

CHAPTER
7

She gave them no time to think. Before Oriel could begin to consider the advantages and disadvantages of doing as she urged, he and Griff were inside, and the door was barred behind them.

The old woman moved around them. She lit a candle that stood on a table and dropped the blanket onto the floor. Under it she wore what seemed to be a man's shirt, large enough to reach almost to her pale knees. She wore no skirt. Her boots flapped as she moved, for the sole was separated from the foot.

Oriel didn't wish to stare at her but he couldn't

look away. Her hair hung down stringy white, and her face hung down from its bones, and she breathed heavily through an open mouth in which he could see only a few teeth, scattered over the top and bottom, all as brown as seaweed. He didn't know how to address her.

She gave him no time. "Why they send boys, and spring begun. And you *know* better than to come by day. And then to linger on my stoop." She shook her head, and peered up into Oriel's face, and then up into Griff's. Her eyes were yellowed, watery.

Oriel was about to offer her the fish in exchange for food, when she wheeled away. "Almost men, almost full-grown, especially the brown one. Not babies. But what are they thinking of?" She wheeled towards them and jabbed with a pointing finger. "What are the men of Selby thinking of when they send you?"

"Nobody sent us," Oriel said.

"Then how would you know where to find me?"

"We didn't."

"Liar," she mumbled, then answered herself, "and how could a lad not be a liar? The world the way it is."

"Truly, Granny," he said, having recalled the proper address for the old women in the market town. "Why should anyone send us? We came hoping to trade fish for bread, if you have it."

"Because if I don't eat I'll die, so they send me food. Bread, fish, cheese, onions, turnips. It waits on the stoop, mornings. I'm never left to go hungry. Because if I die they don't know what worse will happen to them. They're afraid. That's why I have this cottage," she said, nodding her head, tapping at the side of her head with a crooked forefinger. "They drove me out of Selby, the men of Selby, and they keep me here. Sit down. As long as you're here. You're safe enough with me. I've built no fire, and the shutters hide my light. Should the soldiers come, I know a safe place." She seated herself on the solitary stool.

"We wish to trade our fish for bread," Oriel said.

She didn't seem to be looking at them; or, if she was looking at them she didn't seem to be seeing them. "There's the bed," she said. "There's the floor."

A stool, a small square table, the bed — and the room was crowded. "Have you bread, Granny?" Oriel asked again.

"Not for days. Can you tell them? But you must not name me Granny. For I'm not. There's no one to call me Granny, there never was nor will be," she said. "But you're safe here, I promise. Even if it is spring, now. Spring is the hardest time, when the armies have been emptied by the battles of the year before, and over the winter. Summer isn't easy, for in summer they'll take even a boy to fill up empty places, and he'll never be seen again. A girl, too, poor thing — Don't you think about it. There's no ease in thinking on it. Autumn is dangerous, too, because what's left then's the soldiers who have lived through. Good soldiers fight and fall, as all know — the Captains live, and live, and live forever, while good soldiers die in their hundreds. Those that live — or hide away, as I've heard, in hay wains, or run away, I've heard, I've seen them sometimes, like wolves at the edges of the woods, some days. Winter is best, if you have shelter, if you have food, if you have fuel. Do you want to see my babies?" she asked, hopping up from the stool. "How did you come here? I watch the woods."

Oriel didn't know how to answer. He didn't know

what she was asking, and he didn't think it mattered what he answered. But she was like a clay bowl that had been dropped on a stone floor, and shattered into pieces — and she made him uneasy. She wheeled around, standing in front of the bed. Blue veins stood out on her naked legs. Her hair straggled down over her shoulders. "You shan't have my babies. Not one, not any, not boy nor girl, lass that will be, nor lad. I am their guard."

Oriel looked at Griff, who spoke. "We came by boat," Griff said, his voice quiet. "We came by water."

"Then you must go away," she said, "and by water. Go to an island. The islands are too far, far away, for the armies to reach, they're afraid of water, they know nothing of boats. Go to an island and be safe. I've heard of one, an island all for boys, and the biggest boy cares for the others. The boys live, and farm, and fish, all together. There is no trouble among them. In storms they gather around the fire. The house is of stone, and it has many rooms, room for all the boys. In winter they stay inside, safe, warm, fed. In troubles, the biggest boy settles their troubles for them, the biggest boy decides, and when he gets too old he goes away. Because it's men who make soldiers, and battles," she confided. "Not boys. Would you eat some bread?" she asked. "Sit, let me feed you. There's the bed, there's the floor. Are those fish? Tell the men of Selby, from me, I thank them for the fish."

Oriel tried to tell her, again. "We didn't come from Selby."

"Once the sun sets we can have a small fire, just a little one, just enough to cook a fish over. Meanwhile," the old woman said, "there's bread. It makes you sick to eat fish uncooked, lads sometimes don't know that."

She brought a round loaf down from the shelf and held it against her chest while she sawed off pieces with a long knife. Oriel sat beside Griff on the floor, their backs against the door, their legs pulled in close because there was no room to stretch them out. She gave them bread, which filled his mouth with its taste and its promise of sustenance, and he thanked her.

"Men of Selby keep me supplied with bread. For if they don't, what if I were to return to my houses? When my man left," the old woman said, "he left me with my three houses all in a row, one to live in with my babies and the other two for my keep. He said, he couldn't stand the babies. He said he was sick of the babies. As if he had no idea how babies get into a woman's belly, for all the babies he'd gotten out of my belly? This was before. Before they said I had to leave, before they told me to go away, before they moved me into this house and brought me food. The men of Selby know the soldiers will come here first, whenever the soldiers came this is the first place, and they took my babies. The soldiers came and took them. This, I swear it to you, this the men of Selby knew. I hold them responsible. They can't deny it and they will. But they're afraid. Of me. As much as they are afraid of the soldiers. The soldiers aren't afraid. How did you get here? I watch the woods."

"By boat," Griff said. "We came by boat."

She nodded silently and after a while her eyes closed and her head fell forward onto her chest. The smell of fish filled the room. Oriel looked at Griff. They rose to their feet.

But as soon as they moved she was awake, and standing. "Time for the fire, it's safe now. Come, you — " she pointed at Oriel, "there's tinder ready, you start the fire and you — " she pointed at Griff, "we'll bring the babies out."

They could have left the house, and easily. Oriel knew that, but he chose not to. There would have been no difficulty in pushing her aside, lifting the bar on the door, and returning to the boat. Once they were out of the house she couldn't have caught them. But there was something fearsome to her, and he feared it. What he knew of fear was that you had to know its face, or it would drive you the way it wanted you to go.

Also, he thought, blowing on the sparks in straw to bring the fire to life, there was something in her madness — because he had no doubt that she was mad — that was so weak he didn't want to hurt it. She was like the fish he'd pulled out of the water, gasping for air before he took pity on it and smashed its head with a stone.

An old woman was different from a fish. You couldn't just smash in an old woman's head, no matter how much that seemed the only kindness you might do her. Not as if she were a fish. Not when she was too mad to know what she was.

"It's too soon! Too early for the babies!" she shrieked now. "You can't go near them, I'll stop you!" She beat at Griff with her hands, without even making them into fists.

Griff backed away, his back to the door, and slid down to where he had sat before. The old woman stood panting over him, then turned around to look at the bed, then turned back to the fire.

"Good lads, good lads," she said. "How did you get here?"

Oriel answered her again, his voice calm, as the fire flamed among pieces of wood as thick as his wrist, growing steadily warmer and brighter, "We came by boat."

"Lads are good. I believe. It's soldiers are bad, and men, because you can't make soldiers out of lads. I believe. I wish I were sure." She had hunkered down by the fire beside Oriel and her hair shielded her face like a greasy white curtain. Then she seemed to see the fire, as if she hadn't known it was there. She pushed herself up, her hand like a claw on his shoulder, picked up the netful of fish and dumped it all onto the flames.

The fire hissed. Smoke rose. Fish lay like seaweed over the fire. There were no coals yet, to burn on beneath the layer of fish. The fish hadn't been gutted. There wouldn't be much eating here, unless you had a taste for undercooked ungutted fish.

"Let me show you my babies," the old woman said. "Both of you, good lads both, come — little birds in the nest, my little birds in the nest where they are safe — " As she spoke, she got down onto her hands and knees and pulled out from under the bed a long flat wooden box, covered with a blanket.

"Hush now. You must be quiet for now they sleep. All the pretty little birdies, asleep."

Oriel bent down, looking over one of her shoulders. Griff stood at the other. Kneeling beside the box, she folded back the blanket.

A row of sixteen bundles lay in it, each one wrapped tightly around with cloth, each about the size of a six-month shoat. The old woman reached in and picked one up, cradling it in her arms.

The doll-baby she cradled crackled in her embrace, like a straw mattress. Some of the doll-babies were formed from branches, he saw, and some from field grass, and some — he averted his eyes — looked like human babies, only old and dried up like salted fish. Over the old woman's bent head, his eyes met Griff's.

"Forty-one winters hang off my shoulders now," the old woman said, her face turning from one of them to the other. "Oh but there was a time . . . I birthed my first babe when I was fourteen summers. He was to have my man's basket shop, this son of mine, and the tools, and the withy brakes down by the river, all was to be his when he grew. But he got the summer fever, but there were other sons by then, to have the shop and tools and learn the weaving ways, but one went to be a soldier for Matteus and one to Karle and then, you see, the soldiers would come and bring their armies behind them, and they took the girls. So I hid my babies, and my man built this hiding place for them, this nest. You see them? They never give a peep. They know, my babies, they know this world. Or course, after my man left — He grew tired of the babies, the way men do. And I couldn't stay in the town, with my babies. And they carried me out here in a cart, and gave me this house so that when the armies come south from Celindon there will be warning to Selby. They bring me my food, too. I'm old now. But I used to be — thirteen summers, and I was as young as you, a lass to your lads, and my breasts were round and white and sweet as moonflowers." She pulled the doll-baby in close to her chest. "She's safe now, from all of you," the old woman said, hunched there.

Oriel told Griff, "Something must be done. Something, about this." He didn't know what he meant, but he felt it strongly. There was a fire in his heart. He didn't know what he might do, but he felt — like wings spreading out underneath him, for flight — that he was the man who might do it. "Something."

Griff understood him.

The old woman put the doll-baby back in place, folded the blanket back over the box, and pushed it back under the bed, with so much grunting that Griff and Oriel knelt beside her, to help. The wooden box scraped against the wooden floor, like bone against bone. Then she returned to the fire. She plucked at the fish. The top layer she dropped into a bucket, but those beneath she piled onto a wooden platter. "Eat," she said. "I must eat to keep my strength up, to keep the watch," she explained. "How did you get here?" she asked. "I watch the woods."

"We came by boat," Griff told her.

They picked the flesh of the fish off its springy bones. It tasted of the bitterness of the guts but Oriel, who had lived close enough to hunger to know how little the flavor of things matters, ate until his belly was satisfied. After it was fully dark, the old woman unbarred the door and let them go outside, one after the other — not both together because even in the darkness two might be seen, whereas one could slip through shadows unnoticed — to relieve themselves. Outside, under the starless sky, Oriel thought he could breathe again, and thought he would rather sleep the night in the open danger of the boat than the enclosed danger of the little house. But Griff waited inside, and so he had to return.

They lay wrapped in their cloaks on the dirt floor. The old woman had the bed, and her cloak became her bedclothes for warmth in the night. She talked long into the darkness. There was a Countess who never married, the lady Celinde, whose reign was long, longer than any others. The old woman had the babies Celinde could never have because Celinde never married, even though never marrying meant she could never have the babies a woman wanted. She had her lands, instead of babies. Now her lands were filled with soldiers who came to conquer and take food, and coins, gold, and silver, and copper, came like floods on the river, although some years the lands were spared. She learned to save the baby girls. She learned to control the baby boys, except for those who must go off to soldiery until the men of Selby put her into the cart, and her babies with her, and promised her that she would never hunger if she would keep watch on the woods. Ever since the Old Countess had died these many years ago when this old woman was barely more than a girl.

The old woman's voice drifted like a low mist cloud above the room. Every now and then she would sit up in bed to ask, "How did you come here, lad?" One or the other of them would answer her, and then her floating voice would continue, and there would be names told, or memories of a dance, or memories of long winters under the bedclothes with her man before the soldiers came in the spring.

Oriel drifted into sleep and out of sleep, and then at last deep into sleep. A shriek seized him up out of it, and he was on his feet in the darkness with his throat beating.

Someone moved in the darkness. "I hear them!" The old woman's voice cried like a seabird. "They move. It's time, I must."

Griff now stood beside Oriel, both of them ready for they didn't know what from out of the darkness.

She unbarred the door and stood, a dark shape against a silver sky. "I will protect my own. If I am blooded and thrown down, I will rise again. Tell the people of Selby," she said, and then turned, pulled the door closed after her. They heard the bar fall down into place. "Safe now, you're safe," she called.

The voice moved away, faded away. They were left in silence and darkness. For a long time, Oriel didn't speak, and Griff waited for Oriel to speak first, as if Oriel would have the better measure of their hazards.

Oriel waited. Almost, he thought he could hear the sound of distant chopping, but just as the sound became clear to his ears it ceased. He strained at the ears, to hear.

Griff's soft breathing, his own heart, he heard those. At last he went stumbling through the darkness to where the window was, and pulled at the shutter. But it was sealed, somehow, and he couldn't see to open it.

"What do you think she meant?" Griff asked. "Was it all madness? Some of those babies — " Griff didn't finish the thought.

Oriel struck sparks to light the candle. "I'll be happier to be away from here."

"If any of what she said had any part of truth, and I think some or all of it must have, I'd go mad, too," Griff said.

Oriel pulled the bolt back, and opened the shutter a crack. He could see the deep blue sky of coming daylight, before the sun had appeared but after the night had withdrawn from the field. He could hear nothing except the sniffling of wind. He could smell no fire. He had led Griff outside and pulled the door shut behind them before he understood what it was that he hadn't seen in the emptiness before them. The meadow grasses bent towards the silvery water.

The darkened woods waited on all sides, thick as hills.

"I don't hear her," Griff said. "Do you think there *was* an army? How long since she left us?"

"Long enough," Oriel said. His mind was already busy on the problem, thinking it out, to travel north or south, or inland, what unknown dangers might await in every direction, and what known dangers. He didn't know enough — of the land, of the people, of the times. He couldn't even choose well. But there was no help for that, and no use to regret. Once it was light enough to see, he could at least see an immediate danger.

"Where are we going?" Griff asked. "Where's the boat?"

"Gone," Oriel answered.

"But — ?"

When they had the boat, they were free as birds, Oriel realized. When they had the boat, they could have eluded many dangers. Now, they had only their wits, and their feet, and luck.

"Why would she do that?" Griff asked.

"I think, she will have thought she was protecting us. Because the boat could be seen," Oriel said.

"Now what?" Griff asked.

"West," Oriel said. "Celindon lies to the east — remember?"

"Yes."

"I think she was saying that the armies will stop at Celindon, for its riches. There are gold mines in the hills of Celindon," Oriel said. "So Selby, and south, is the better choice."

"Do we go along the coast or through the woods?"

"I think there should be a path into the woods, if the town brings her food. I think that will be the quicker and safer way."

They crossed the meadow in growing light. The grass whispered like water at their boots. It was Griff who spotted the dirt path emerging beside a fat beech tree, whose branches spread out over the path like an arched doorway.

Oriel, with Griff behind him, moved into the deeper darkness of the wood.

PART
II

THE
SALTWELLER'S
JOURNEYMAN

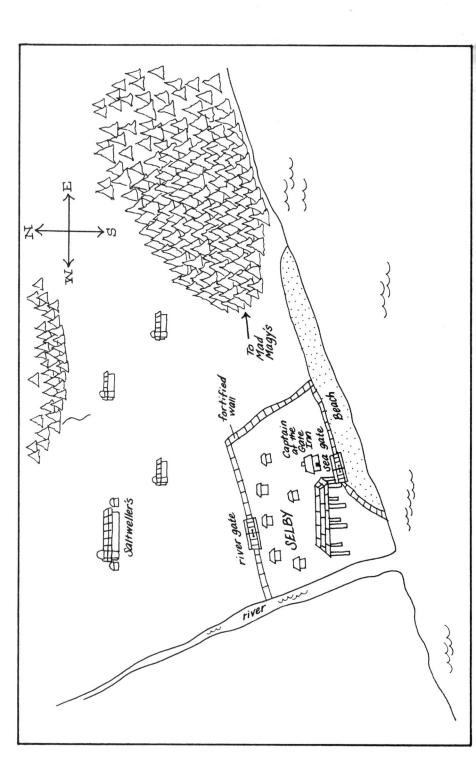

CHAPTER

8

Oriel led and Griff followed far enough behind to stay clear of the back-snapping branches. Although worn down to dirt by frequent use, the path was no wider than a solitary man would need. All around, the woods were crowded with tree trunks, and tangled with undergrowth through which, occasionally, great grey boulders pushed their way. From overhead, sunlight sprinkled onto the little new leaves and flowed down over the long branches of firs to lie in bright patches on the path. It was cool, in the woods, and shady. Their progress was steady. They tramped —

Oriel walked almost into the face of the man.

He was too surprised, almost, to recognize the man as human — as a young man — and then he backed away as there came four faces in front of him. There were four of them, two beardless boys and two men, two short-trimmed beards and two hooded heads. They traveled cloaked and all carried packs on their backs. Oriel hadn't heard their approach.

He backed into Griff, backing away from the four surprised faces. If the four hadn't looked as surprised as he felt — and alarmed — he would have turned and run into the woods, trusting Griff to follow, trusting that as long as he was near to the sea he could never be lost for long. But the strangers backed away uneasily, and if they had weapons, they weren't drawing them.

Oriel thought then that he would see how those four dealt with the encounter. Let them show him what was the appropriate conduct towards traveling strangers. If they were to threaten, he would run. If they were to thrust along on the path, he would step aside without protest. If they were to offer food, he would eat. If they asked questions, then he could learn from their questions what it was one traveler might ask another. If they were to flee from a meeting, he would go on his own way. Of all the possibilities, Oriel thought he would prefer food.

Both of the men were dark, dark hair and dark eyes, although they didn't look alike. The first had a big, square-toothed smile, the second had a squinting way to him, as if the sun shone full on his face. The two lads stood behind in shadows. "Good day to you," the first man said.

Oriel answered, "And to you also, a good day."

"Where might you be bound this morning?"

"Westwards, to a town called Selby. And you?"

"To the walled city of Celindon. Do you know it?"

"I've been to market there, two or three times. I've slept two or three nights there. Perhaps four," Oriel said. "Do you know Selby?"

"Aye, but we're on our way east, up from the southern hills. We've heard there is always work in Celindon, and safety within its double ring of walls. Come you from the east?"

Oriel had thought what his answer to this question might be, thinking it must be asked of him. "From seaward, a small fishing island with not even a village on it."

"At Selby they told us islanders were poor, puny men, but you aren't, and he — " the man's eyes went to Griff, "looks underfed but he's tall enough."

"And I'm strong enough, too," Griff said.

The second man squinted at Oriel, and then at Griff behind him. He put a hand on his companion's shoulder, to speak. "We were about to break our fast. If he knows Celindon, they don't seem dangerous, they might prove useful to us." The first man nodded and the second asked Oriel, "Will you eat with us? What food we carry is simple enough, but if you're hungry, simple is as good as the feast. We can give you news of the south and west in exchange for yours."

"Gladly," Oriel said. "There's a rock a few paces back, where we might all sit down together, and we are hungry — but we can tell you little of the east, and north."

"Little," the first man laughed, "will be double what we know. Come, lead us."

* * *

They ate chunks of heavy dark bread and onions that dripped sweet juices when they were cut. The two lads sat apart. The men faced Oriel and Griff, passing the bread first to their lads, then to the strangers. "We have nothing to eat," Oriel told them. When he was seated and still, he could hear the sounds of the woods — rustlings, and occasional birdsongs, a creaking of branches almost like the creaking of a mast pulled by the windy sail. "We can only offer thanks in exchange for food," he said.

"It's no matter to us if you add nothing," the man said, smiling broadly. He seemed a man more than contented with his lot in life. "We've plenty, as you see, and where we go there is plenty more — if you've the coins to buy. We've the coins, and we've the skills to earn more coins when those are gone — so eat your fill. Then tell us how things stand, to the north and east."

Oriel passed Griff half of an onion and took the rest for himself. He bit and chewed. He had no reason not to believe the old woman and he had heard rumors for years, in the markets. "Things stand at soldiery," he said. "The old quarrels over who will inherit the Old Countess's lands."

"That is as we heard," Griff added. "We saw neither soldiers nor battles ourselves. We were warned, though, and I believed the warning was truly meant."

"And of Wolfers?" The man was not smiling now.

"Wolfers?" Oriel echoed. "What are Wolfers?" He didn't ask Griff. What Oriel didn't know of the world beyond the island, Griff wouldn't.

The smiling man smiled more broadly, but didn't answer. Instead, he rose to his knees, and leaned out a hand to pull one of the lads to him. The boy's cape fell askew to reveal long dark hair, wound tight around itself and fastened close to her scalp. It was a girl, who looked frightened to be so disclosed. "Don't fear, lass," the man said, his voice tender now, and glad. "We'll give them no names, and if they should hear of a journeyman who took his master's daughter with him when he journeyed away . . . How should they know who we are, to set your father on our track?"

The second lad had followed close on the heels of the first. She pushed back her own hood and said, "Don't forget me."

The two girls clasped hands, seated close.

"You give us no chance to forget you," the squinting man said. "If we wanted to. If we dared to try to get rid of you."

"And I've no desire to forget you," the first girl said. "Are we not sisters, in all but birth?"

"I'm not afraid to tell my name," the second girl said. She had a big face, friendly as a dog's. "Jilly."

"Woman," the squinting man warned, "when we're wed I'll teach you to govern your tongue."

"That's if I wed you," Jilly answered him without hesitation. "That's if I find no one more handsome — as this lad is more handsome," and she grinned at Oriel. "Aye, sit still, you great fool, you know I'll likely wed you, and we four will live our lives out together. Here's something a woman knows," she said, leaning toward Oriel in mock secrecy. He leaned toward her, making it a game the two of them played against the others. "A man comes along, he'll come along, and a woman needs only be careful to take a good man. But a companion for the days, someone to be my sister — to hold my hand in the pains of childbirth, as I will hold hers; to come with me to see starflowers when they bloom in the long grass and have the same gladness at the sight; to know the demon-fears that come at night, and not mock them — a man will turn up, as any woman knows, but a true companion . . ." Jilly didn't finish her sentence. She sat back on her heels, with a mocking glance.

They hadn't been playing the game together after all, and Oriel didn't know what to answer without giving her reason to laugh at him, too. He was spared the necessity of speech by the smiling man's impatience. "These two come from the islands, and have never heard of Wolfers," he said to the dark-haired girl. "That decides me. I'd rather live long and thin on the islands than fat in my homeland only to end my brief days at the end of a Wolfer's blade."

"Aye," the squinting man agreed. "But how do we get there? And do we know that the islands have need of a ropemaker's skill? What if they haven't?"

"Then we learn another trade. If you have the time to learn a trade, and live to ply it, there's no trouble to changing the trade you ply."

"I don't like the sea," the man objected now.

"You know nothing of it."

"I've heard. I've heard the sea throws its dead back up into the air. Give me the land, where the dead stay where you put them."

"You great lummox," Jilly said, "the dead have nought to do with the living." But for all that, her words were sharp, her voice was gentle enough.

"You know what I meant," her man mumbled.

"Aye," the first man said, with a smile that showed his big square teeth. "You can have your land, land you can dig your fingers into for planting, but first let me put deep water between us and the Wolfers."

"Who are these Wolfers?" Oriel asked again.

The four looked at one another.

"Terrible," the squinting man said at last. "They are terrible, all men fear them."

"I can tell you what everyone knows," Jilly added. "They live in the north, in a high and barren land, and they know nothing of farming, sowing seeds and reaping grains, or animal husbandry. They are wandering hunters, following the herds of wild beasts. They come south and east, because mountains block them to the north. The mountains guard the Kingdom, people say, if you believe there is a Kingdom. The mountains are real, although the Kingdom they protect is likely fantastical, and the Wolfers can't cross the mountains. So their raiding parties move towards the sea. Trailing blood."

The first girl spoke now, in a whisper, as if she didn't dare to name her thoughts for fear naming might bring them closer. "The Wolfers take children and feed them to the mountains. If they have no children from others they have to give up their own children. They carry off girls of childbearing age, to get them with child, and feed those children to the mountains."

"That's only a story." The smiling man put his arm around her shoulders.

"They eat their meat uncooked," she continued, big eyes staring at Oriel. "The blood drips down, while they eat."

"Wolfers like isolated hamlets, lonely farms." The smiling man's face had grown grim, and his lass took his free hand in both of hers, as if now he needed her to comfort him. He spoke grimly on. "I once lived on one of those lonely farms. Just as I once had parents, brother, sisters, and an inheritance. Before the Wolfers came."

"And what did you do?" Oriel asked. He'd never

had parents, brother, sisters, but he could feel in his own heart the urge to track after their killers, and take their revenge — or die in the attempt. "Did you ever find them? How is it you escaped?"

"I'd been sent out before first light, to gather honey. My brother had found a honey tree, which we thought was great good fortune. Perhaps it was. When I returned in the afternoon . . ." He didn't finish the thought.

"Then how did you identify the murderers when you found them?" Oriel asked.

"You don't think I chased after them? What good would that do?"

Oriel felt it in his heart and his hands, the good that would do — but he didn't know, and this man who did know understood it differently. He tried to open his mind to this new understanding, to give room to it. He had a warning of his own to give. "Among the islands there are pirates. The pirates come seldom but when they do they are merciless. The islands aren't entirely safe. Also, there can be hunger, there is the danger of storms at sea, illness and accident."

"But no Wolfers," the first man said. "Wolfers know nothing of boats and can't swim. They fear water, though they fear nothing else."

"Aye, and so do I," the squinting man said.

"You can learn to swim, learn to use boats," Oriel assured them.

"There's sure to be need of a ropemaker among boats," Jilly said.

"And how do you know we won't be taken to the Dammer's island, and the lasses dropped into the water to drown, while you and I serve our lives out in the slavery of that place?" the squinting man demanded of his companions. "Do you know of that hellish place?" he asked Oriel.

"I think we might," Oriel said carefully.

"Where the only law is the Dammer's law, and all the others serve his comfort, and no women can live. For he hates them. He'll bring in a boatload of women — for his pleasure, and those he sends back decked in jewels, for he has the first Dammer's treasure at his hand, he knows where it is hidden. Aye, the man who could lay hands to that would be a Prince for the rest of his life, but even pirates dare not assault the Dammer's island. They say, the island smokes, the land itself burns, with all the evil done there. They say, you can hear the cries for miles across the water — Aye," he shook himself, "do you know where that place is? I'd not be carried there and die screaming."

Oriel saw no reason to contradict the tales with truth. "Here's what I know: If you hire a fisherman to carry you from the harbor at Celindon back to his home island, you should be safe. If as you approach, you see many houses along a harbor where more boats are tied up, and if the island is large enough for many farms and much woodland, then you can be sure you are safe. The island you fear has only a single house on it, high on a bare hilltop. Only a few boats are moored there, and those no larger than might carry one or two men. No fisherman from the islands goes to that place."

The man took a while, making up his mind, and then he turned to his companions. "I say, we should go to the islands. What say you?" The squinting man agreed and the thing was settled. The four rose to their feet, impatient to get on with their lives. "A season's work in Celindon, to fill our purses, and then we'll to the islands."

"And once there?" the squinting man asked.

"Once there, we'll live long. Live, work, build, breed sons — and learn to swim, too," he laughed again. "It can't be so hard, not if so many can do it. Am I not correct, stranger?"

"I think so," Oriel said. "But before you go, tell us — If we travel south to Selby — "

"The Wolfers have never come as far as the coast before. They've found enough booty inland, westward," the smiling man assured him.

"Those soldiers of the four claimants who fight for rule over the cities of the coast are men like ourselves," the squinting man promised. "No worse than ourselves, no more to be feared."

"Keep your own counsel," the first man said. "That's my advice. For lodging the Captain at the Gate deals fairly. You'll find it just alongside of the sea gate. Other than that, I know nothing of Selby. We slept there only the one night," he said. "And now," he silenced Jilly with a look, "we go on our way."

As she moved by him, at the end of the small troupe, Jilly spoke to Oriel out of the side of her mouth, softly, so none would hear. "They're closer than he's told you, the Wolfers. Go cautiously among those who live in soldiery, for they are accustomed to killing. These are parlous times," she said, and was gone before he could thank her.

When they were alone again, and the woods silent around them, Griff asked him, "Do you go on?"

"For the time," Oriel said. He was thinking over the meeting, thinking of questions he might have asked, thinking of what he knew about the two men and their lasses, and how much of what they had told him he could believe. "For the time, we go to Selby."

Griff didn't protest.

Oriel thought, but did not say, that he suspected now that it would be harder than he'd thought to win their way on the mainland. He would have to be as clever as a river, he thought, to do well. But he could twist and turn like water, and go his own way, however hard the world tried to drive him along another — or, he thought he could do that. "Come," he said to Griff, with such a lightness in his heart at what the day might bring that he could become a smiling man himself. He jumped down from the rock and returned to the path. "Let's see this town of Selby, and its people. Let's try the ale at this Inn. What was the name they gave?"

"Captain at the Gate," Griff said.

"And let's find work," Oriel said. "There is much to be done today." He led the way, knowing that Griff followed.

CHAPTER
9

Selby basked in sunlight. Roofs and chimneys were visible within the walls, red tiles and grey stones, and sand-colored stones. The little houses nestled back against the wall were hung with fishing nets and faced out over the bright blue bay. Boats had been drawn up onto the beach and lay on their sides, as if asleep. The whole scene was washed over with mild spring sunlight.

Oriel and Griff approached the fishermen working around the deep-keeled boats. One man stepped forward to meet them. Bearded and sunbrowned, he wore a bright yellow kerchief tied around his neck. The others, also wearing yellow kerchiefs at their necks, went on with their work. A woman walked out of one house to enter another; a yellow kerchief bound her hair.

"You're strangers here," the fisherman said.

There was no answer needed.

"Where from?"

"The north, and east, a place too small for you to know of it," Oriel answered. "We met an old woman, just beyond the woods. She told us this town would be Selby."

The man nodded. "That'll be Mad Magy."

"Likely enough she was mad," Oriel agreed.

"Or near to it," the man said. "It's been years she's lived out there — "

"And it's been years troubles have passed Selby by," a voice said from behind him.

Nobody spoke for a time. The men on the beach studied the two strangers. Oriel kept his eyes level whenever one of them engaged his gaze, until the other's eyes dropped or turned to look elsewhere. Sunlight fell over his head and shoulders like a cloak. The water rustled along the edge of the beach, and after a while the man before them spoke. "Work, then, is it?"

"We've our livings to earn," Oriel answered. He didn't need to consult Griff, for he and Griff were of one mind.

The man looked at Griff. "Know you anything of fishery?"

Oriel wasn't sure how to answer this. It would be dangerous to spend their days on the same waters where Nikol, or another from Damall's Island, might see them.

The man took his silence for consideration. "If you're a man with the courage to live outside of the walls our merchants have built to protect themselves. A man who likes to keep his eye on dangers, who thinks it wisdom to live beside the dangers, and to know them." His arm gestured to the sea, quiet that day.

"We look for landwork," Oriel decided. "But I would ask you, does all Selby wear yellow neckerchiefs?" If so, and if they didn't wish to brand themselves strangers, he'd have to find some yellow cloth.

"The fishermen are for Karle and wear his color," the fisherman said. "You and your companion wear no man's colors."

"We back no man's claim to the Countess's lands," Oriel answered. The Damall never went into Celindon without first inquiring if it was safe to do so, for there had been twelve years of intermittent warring.

"Karle has the best claim," the fisherman told him. "His wife Eleanore is the eldest cousin of the Countess and has provided six living children. Karle is the man to rule. And tax these guildsmen and merchants their fair share, too."

The fisherman spoke more to his audience of like-minded men than to the two strangers.

"Karle has the better claim, if only the fools would see it."

"Selby seems untroubled," Oriel remarked.

"Aye, it is, or near enough for the time. But as for what will come . . ." The fisherman looked out over the sea.

"If you will direct us to an Inn called Captain at the Gate," Oriel said, after a while, "then we'll leave you in peace."

"Peace you can't leave us, not until the inheritance is won," the man said, "but the Captain at the Gate is easy enough to find." He pointed. "Follow the wall and you'll find the gate open, as it's daytime. Turn to your left hand, maybe two hundred paces along, and you'll see the Inn's sign. What do you know of it?"

"We've heard the cost is fair."

"And that's true. The Innkeeper at the Captain also brews the best ale anywhere on the coast — his ale is clear and sweet, for all that he's a dark-tempered man. You don't want to get to the wrong side of him."

Oriel didn't want to get to the wrong side of anybody, until he knew which way his own path lay. But he didn't say that. He just thanked the fisherman and moved on, Griff at his side.

The sign hung out over the narrow street, so low that a tall man must duck his head to go under it. The name was written out across the bottom, CAP-TAIN AT THE GATE. Oriel reached into the cloth wound at his waist and pulled out two silver coins, which he knotted at the hem of his shirt. That done, they stepped through the doorway.

Tables from the barroom spilled over into a sunlit court. A few men sat at each of the tables, drinking from tankards. At the far right of the low-ceilinged room was a wooden barfront, behind which stood a burly man. He dipped pitchers into a cask, and brought them up filled with frothy ale: Oriel guessed him to be the Innkeeper.

Barrel-chested, thick-armed, the Innkeeper looked strong. His neckerchief was green. He had small, doubting eyes, and when he spoke his voice was rough and full of distrust. "Two is it?" he asked, reaching down two tankards.

"No," Oriel said.

The Innkeeper put the pitcher down, braced his

big hands on the bar top, and waited for whatever lie Oriel would choose to tell, in which the Innkeeper would catch him out, after which he would drive Oriel and Griff out of the barroom.

"We seek an Inn," Oriel said. "We were told — "

The man jerked his head towards a door. "The woman's in there." He had no more interest in them, but hefted a cask of ale into place, as easily as if it had been a babe.

They entered a cookroom where a woman bent over a wooden trough filled with dough, and something savory bubbled over the fire. The woman's grey-streaked hair straggled out from under her green head kerchief. She looked like a round loaf herself. "Yes, lads? What is it?"

"We need a bed for the night, or perhaps longer. We would also eat," Oriel answered, "when you have finished."

"We've time," Griff added.

"You think now you have time, but you'll learn different soon enough," the woman said, although she set back to work. "Can you pay for the bed?"

"We wouldn't ask if we couldn't," Oriel said.

That made her smile, but she argued anyway. "You're the last two honest lads left in the world?"

"I doubt that, mistress," Oriel said.

"I'm no mistress, here. I'm the alewife, not the housewife, not even the bedwife. Not that I'm complaining, for the Innkeeper is fair with me, hard but fair, asking a full day's work for a full day's pay, which is fair." She lifted the dough up in her arms, then dropped it down into the trough.

"Can you offer us lodging?" Oriel asked.

"Aye."

But she said no more.

"I smell," and he sniffed at the air, "a fine soup."

"Aye, if you like fish and turnips. You'll have to wait," she said. But she belied her words by wiping her hands on the apron and turning to ladle soup out into deep wooden bowls. She put a metal spoon into each bowl and cut chunks from a loaf of bread. Oriel and Griff sat on the hearthstone. The woman went back to her kneading, the mass of dough as large as a dog.

"When you've had your fill, you pay me. The soup's one little the bowl, with the bread. The bed's four littles the night. That's six — "

Oriel set his bowl of soup on the stone and rose, to hand her a silver coin. Her hands were deep in the dough, so she told him to set it down on the table.

"You've another trueman, I hope?" she asked him. "Because I know where such boots are made and worn."

Oriel hesitated.

"Aye, you don't have to fear me telling your secrets. I speak only to warn you. There aren't many who'd recognize the Dammer's work, but not all of those who might would look kindly on you. Too many are still jealous, even though the Countess is twelve years underground and the Dammer disappeared a lifetime before she died. Some there were, and many, who wished to wed the Countess, even when she was an old woman, and there might have been an heir of her body and we would not have these wars. And didn't suitors come courting? They say, that when she was a young woman in her beauty, those were the times. My mother told me — the plays, and dances in the open marketplace, feasts and fires. . . ."

"What was the Dammer to the Countess, then?" Oriel asked.

"Why, her true knight," the woman said. "From when she was a child, and however crooked he was to all the rest of the world, the Dammer gave her his heart and his loyalty, and never wavered. Else why would she have given him an island, when all the men he had betrayed were circling around him like a pack of wolves and would have cut him to pieces? He damned them all, always, except for her, everyone except for her. And she saved him in his need." The woman sighed over the dough. "He was true to her, always. And she would never wed any man — they say because the one man she would have taken to bed was of low birth, and landless, and lawless, and the only good thing to be said of him was his loyalty to her."

The woman sighed again, and dropped the dough down into the trough. "A handsomer man than the Dammer has never been seen, or so my mother swore." She wiped the back of her hand across her forehead, leaving a smear of flour, then covered the dough with a cloth.

"You wear a green kerchief," Oriel said. "As does the Innkeeper, as do the men in the barroom. The fishermen, as we learned this morning, wear yellow, for Karle. We know nothing of the kerchiefs, Griff and I," he explained.

"It's green for Matteus," she answered him. "Who married the granddaughter of the Countess's father's sister. Lucia, she is, and a fine lady, they say, although childless. The Innkeeper says Matteus is the man for him, since Matteus thinks that a man who takes his livelihood from the land or sea is no greater — and no less — than a man whose work comes from manufacturage. Treat all equally, Matteus says, tax all equally. The Innkeeper agrees."

"And you?" Oriel asked.

She shrugged. "I am a woman." She picked up the silver coin from the table. "What I think makes no difference, so why take the trouble to think anything? The Innkeeper is no fool, that's what I think, and he's a fair man. He'll show you your bed."

"We thank you," Griff said.

"And we will heed your advice, to find boots," Oriel said.

"I know the man to serve your needs," she told him.

The Innkeeper was a shorter man than Oriel thought he would be from his stature behind the bar, and his beard was so close-shaven that his skin looked unexpectedly soft. He led them across the courtyard to a room just large enough for a sleeping platform. "Privy at the corner of the yard. Does this suit you?" the Innkeeper asked.

"Yes," Oriel answered. The Innkeeper wouldn't look him in the eye, but instead looked all around the room as if searching for mice or the webs of spiders, as if expecting some enemy to come out from under the platform.

"When the barroom has emptied the Inn door is barred," the Innkeeper told them. "Later than that you'll find no entry. It's your loss if you're so careless as to be locked out."

Oriel said nothing.

Back in the courtyard, the Innkeeper faced them. Even though they stood eye to eye, Oriel had the feeling that the man was much larger, and stronger, than he himself was. "I say also this," the Innkeeper said. "I say: I do not like a man who tries to skate through troubled times without attaching himself to any one side or the other. You don't have to be for Matteus to please me — although any man with arms to hold onto that which he has won for himself has to favor Matteus, any man who knows he needs strength to endure hard times. I say no more," the Innkeeper said. He said no more.

His servant gave them the name and street sign of the cobbler, suggested that they go barefoot lest another recognize their footgear, asked how the master bespoke them, and pressed little baked sweet cakes into their hands, saying that she knew how hungry lads always were.

They followed the city wall down to the riverside, to find the marketplace, which was on the river, and the cobbler's shop just off the marketplace. The people paid no attention to two boys, and that was familiar to Oriel, although Selby was not. He wished he could be like a bird, to fly over Selby and see the whole of its shape; but he was earthbound and must note everything, lest the unknown important thing escape his notice and bring him down. "I've seen no slaves," he realized.

"How can you tell them?" Griff asked.

"Slaves wear collars. In Celindon you see many — the collars tell the wealth of their masters. Perhaps the slaves here all serve inside, with the women," Oriel said.

"Must there be slaves?" Griff asked.

"The Damall said so," Oriel answered. "He told me, it was in the nature of men; some must enslave others, some must be slaves. He said it was always so, in all places — " Abruptly, he stopped speaking, and stopped walking. "And unlike you, I never thought to question him."

"I never questioned the Damall to his face," Griff said. "I wouldn't have dared. I questioned only the idea. Why are you laughing, Oriel?"

Oriel could only say part of the reason. "People pick me out, I am the one. They pick me, not you, but they underestimate you. You can deny it, and others might believe you, but I will not. Yet I don't know what they see when they look at me, to loosen their tongues and hearts."

"It's your face," Griff explained. They recommenced walking. "Your face draws the eyes. You look as if — what you will say will be good to hear. What you will do will — whatever it is — be what a man might joy in doing with you, or behind you. Or take pride later in having done at your side. Your face seems to promise something more than ordinary."

"How can a face do that?" Oriel asked, reasonably.

Griff shrugged. "Almost all who look on your face see it in this way," he pointed out.

"But — " Oriel started to argue, then stopped himself. He knew that a man can't ever see himself as others see him. He also knew that what Griff said was true. And he was glad of that, glad to be himself, Oriel, recognized by all who looked upon him.

They had come to the brown river, which here flowed broad and swift into the sea. The people of Selby had laid flat stones along the river's edge and the flowing waters deposited mud on the stones, slippy brown mud on smooth grey rock. They went barefoot across the stones and dropped their four boots into the water. The boots were carried off, sinking as they were swept away. Oriel hoped, without speaking of it, that he and Griff were not going to be so swept away, and lost.

The cobbler wore a green kerchief at his neck, as bright as the one his wife wore around her hair. His fingers were stained brown with his trade, and his palms bore great yellow calluses. The high boots he wore were intricately tooled, and he tucked his trousers into his boots to better display their workmanship. "We cannot pay much," Oriel told him.

The boots the cobbler showed them then were piled up in his fenced yard. "Dead men's boots, which they have no further need of," he said. All were plain, all were brown, some seemed less worn at heel, some few had gashes in the leather. One had its entire toe section cut off. Oriel sat down to try the size of a boot. "There are many men who have died," he observed.

"And what else do you expect when battles rage every year?" the cobbler asked. He passed a pair of boots to Griff, the leather so worn and soft they could barely stand upright. "These may be too greatly worn. This man died in his bed, having stayed at home to till his fields."

"A farmer?" Griff asked.

"And wattlemaker," the cobbler said. "He lived too long. That was his bad luck. With his sons gone to soldiers, the daughters wed, the wife dead, his strength wasted by the years — there was no work he could do, he had to sell his lands away, in order to feed himself. These boots lasted him the better part of a lifetime. It was my father who made them."

"Where do you find these others?" Oriel asked. The boot he now wore showed a pale strip of leather, like a fish's underbelly, where some sharp weapon had cut it open. He pulled it off.

"Women follow their men, their soldiers. I've heard, some even fight beside them, but that — " the cobbler handed out another pair of boots for Oriel to try — "I don't believe."

"Aye, but I do," his wife spoke from behind. She had a child on her hip now. "If the price of your boots would feed my children, I'd not want any other stripping them from your body."

"Aye, but I'm not a soldier," the cobbler said.

"I'll take these," Griff said, "and hope they bring me as long a life as the previous owner." Oriel also had found a pair. "How much for both?" he asked.

"And won't ever be, if I can help it," the cobbler said to his wife. "As I promised you, three years ago when we wed. For otherwise, she swore she'd never take me," he told Oriel and Griff. "Women," he added.

"Life is hazardous enough without a man going to soldiery," the woman answered. "Men," she said to Oriel and Griff, before turning back into the house.

"How much?" Oriel asked again.

"For the two pair? the one soft as a guildsman's gloves and the other barely worn?"

"Aye, the one worn down almost to cloth and the other hacked apart in battle," Oriel said. "How much?"

"Six kiddles."

"Three," Oriel offered, thinking to settle for five.

"Four," the cobbler said.

"Done."

The boots felt stiff but sturdy, as if they could give good protection. There had been little difference between the thin island boots and going about barefooted, but he hadn't known this until he wore good leather. His stride lengthened, with these boots, and Griff stepped out long-legged beside him.

As they returned into the wide marketplace, Oriel looked across to where the city wall came down to the river. There three or four armed men gathered around a doorway under an Inn's painted sign. The sign pictured a mason's trowel laid on a goldsmith's crucible, and named the place THE GUILDSMAN. The armed men drank, and looked restlessly about. Their red kerchiefs hung down over their chests, as if demanding to be noticed. These were dark, rough-bearded men, who kept one hand on the hilts of their swords.

Oriel didn't like their looks, and didn't like the look one man gave them, like a merchant at the slave market. He led Griff along the side of the marketplace, until they could disappear up into an alleyway. They followed winding alleys until they came back to the city wall. They walked beside it, sure of their direction now. At one place it had fallen down and two men, wearing blue kerchiefs, labored to mend it.

"You've hot work," Oriel greeted them.

The two agreed. "But the day starts out cool enough, at this season, and it ends cool," said the man with the hammer.

"Days'll get hotter before we're done this job," said the man who held his trowel over the pan of mortar. "That's if our luck holds, if soldiers don't come down on us before we've finished."

"Why should soldiers come to Selby this summer when they've stopped at Celindon for the last three?" the hammerer asked.

"We can never be sure of peace," the man answered. "Not until one man or the other holds all the cities, and is the Count, named and known." Both of the men looked to see what effect their words had on Oriel and Griff. "And if that were to happen while I was alive to see it," the mortarer went on, "well, that would be a day, I can tell you.

That would be the great day of my life. I can tell you two lads that. You're strangers?" he asked.

"As you see," Oriel answered.

"Then we'll advise you. Won't we? Ramon, whose color we are proud to wear, has joined forces with Taddeus. The two cousins now ride together under a blue banner. They have joined armies, too, so each has more soldiers at his command. Each can bring more men into battle. Each controls more lands. Each has more gold to pay the army with."

Oriel didn't ask how that could be, when there had been no actual increase in men, or acres, or coins. Men who are giving advice wish to be listened to, not asked questions of.

"Ramon and Taddeus together have a larger army. Any man knows the largest army will carry the day."

"A man with the eyes to see what must come next and take his best shelter, even — aye — giving up all he has and starting again, now that's a man," the hammerer added.

Oriel thought of the yellow and green and blue kerchiefs. He thought he would have to be clever as a river to wind his way among these claimants and their colors. "Can you tell me whose are the men we saw wearing red?" he asked.

"Red? Here in Selby?" the hammerer asked, alarmed.

"Aye, in the marketplace, at The Guildsman."

"Those are Phillipe's men," the hammerer said. He turned back to the shaping of stones, and turned his back to Oriel and Griff.

The mortarer explained. "Phillipe has no claim by blood, unless it's the blood of the men he's killed, or had killed by hirelings so he might become Captain. Phillipe claims the cities by right of force." He slathered a layer of mortar onto the walls. "If men with red kerchiefs stand boldly about the marketplace, bad times are coming," he said.

"Aye, and I was beginning to hope that they would settle their differences without Selby."

"I would not be a poor or landless man, should Phillipe take Selby," the hammerer said. "Think you, should we move upriver?"

"Safety lies upriver?" Griff asked.

"Aye, because when armies move, they go along the coast, among the rich cities. When Celindon is beseiged and holds firm, then Selby is safe. But if Celindon falls . . . Upriver are a few farms, a town or two, just villages, perhaps the blacksmith might have a few coins, there is the Saltweller, but his wealth isn't in coins — none of these are worth the effort of an army."

The mortarer reminded his companion, "Mad Magy's hut lies between us and double-walled Celindon, and she's kept fed. So long as Mad Magy lives, they say . . ."

Oriel and Griff walked away. After a while Oriel said to Griff, "I think we may have to choose a man and his color, if we choose to stay in Selby."

"We don't know anywhere else to go," Griff pointed out.

"Tomorrow, then, we find work," Oriel decided. They would wind among the colors, as long as they could, backing no man. They would wind and twist, like a river. "And now back to the Captain at the Gate," Oriel said, "if I can find our way."

CHAPTER
10

They approached the Inn down a sloping street. The cookmaid must have been watching for them because she signaled them from a window, to go around, beyond the building, and enter her kitchen from a side door. "Here," she said, hurrying them to the long bench beside the table, hastily scooping out bowls of the meaty soup. "Before the Innkeeper knows you are back. So he won't charge you the extra meal. But he'll expect to sell you a tankard of ale, before the evening ends, I'll tell you that." She was washing tin tankards in a pot of hot water, hanging them on nails driven into the wall by the fireplace, so they would dry quickly. "He may ask you if you had a meal, for he knows my hunger for children, although he never would give me any, for all that we've lived under the same roof for these many years and all of Selby thinks me his bedfellow. And he not the man to pay enough attention to gossip to deny it, so no other man will think of me for wife. But that's little to complain of, in this world. At least it's not Mad Magy's fate."

"What is her fate?" Oriel asked.

"Set out like a staked goat for the armies. No matter which army it is. Not that it means anything to her, poor soul, since she's lost her children. At least, if you don't have children you can't lose them," the woman said. "Back outside with you now, and not a word — if you value my skin."

"Not a word," Oriel promised.

"Not a word," Griff echoed.

"Aye, you're good lads, anyone looking at you can tell that. How could your mothers part with you? No, never tell me, it'll be too sad a tale. Go now. You must enter the bar from the street. Go, you heard me."

The lowering sun lit up the yellow stones of Selby, and made the city glow. With a bed for the night and a plan for the next day, Oriel stepped confidently through the street door into the barroom.

From where he filled the space behind the bar the Innkeeper stared at the two of them out of pale eyes. Oriel's confidence retreated before that glance. But he wouldn't be driven around the world by such men, he thought. He stood his ground, and Griff stood at his shoulder. The Innkeeper didn't seem displeased to be so faced.

After a time, during which every man in the room turned to stare at them, the Innkeeper spoke:

"Come in if you're coming. Close that door behind you. I'll draw you ale," he said, turning around and reaching up with arms as broad as the thighs of oxen. "Woman!" the Innkeeper called. "Clean tankards! and we've custom here, woman!"

The cookmaid set two tankards down on the table before them, and turned away without a word. As the dark settled, some of the men left, and later the Innkeeper called out for candles. With the candles came moths and other winged bugs. Those moths that found the flames they sought made sizzling sounds in the liquid wax.

Oriel and Griff sat against a back wall, facing the room and the door into the street. The fire behind them burned with welcome warmth. Conversation was conducted at a low level, men with their heads close together. The room wasn't crowded, but it was full, and it seemed that most groups — be they only two or three, or be they a full table of seven or ten — were made up of men who wore the same color kerchief. Sometimes a man would go up to the bar and speak with the Innkeeper. Sometimes the Innkeeper would bellow out, "Woman!" and the cookmaid would emerge to carry a tray of tankards to a table, or carry a tray of tankards into the kitchen for cleaning, or be told to serve a man with soup and bread. The Innkeeper stayed behind the bar.

There was tension in the room, Oriel thought. He sipped at the bitter ale and watched the faces around him. He tried to catch their words, but they didn't speak to be overheard. Words flickered like candlelight. Voices murmured like water. The evening passed by slowly, sleepily.

So that when the door to the street was thrown open and a broad-shouldered man stood in it, his short cape travel stained and his boots muddy, the whole room came to silent attention. The man called across to the Innkeeper: "They told me she was here, my daughter. I ask you, Innkeeper, where is my daughter?"

The Innkeeper greeted this grey-haired stranger with the same pale, wordless glance he had given Oriel and Griff.

"I asked you a question, Innkeeper," the stranger said.

"We have no young woman here."

"And my neighbor's serving wench with her," the man said. His voice growled, roared, was filled with anger.

"Neither have we two young women," the Innkeeper said.

The man strode across the room to lean against the bar, placing coins down in front of him. "Ale," he said. "I've had a long journey chasing after the four of them."

"Now it's four?" the Innkeeper asked, and a number of men in the room chuckled.

"Four," the man said. "My daughter, from my own house, and my journeyman, who still owes me two years of his labor. For I am a ropemaker, well enough known to have need of an assistant. They have taken also my neighbor's serving maid he planned to bed himself, and with them a good-for-nothing lad who followed all trades a little, and in my village we used him for whatever need we had; he was clever enough, in his way. That's four, as I said."

"What's a daughter the less, if you've sons?"

"I've no sons," the man said. "But I've a likely man who'd have wed the girl."

"As old a man as you?"

"No." But his cheeks pinked, and he turned his back to the Innkeeper.

"A young man?" the Innkeeper asked, and the father didn't answer. The room laughed again.

"Aye, make mock," the father said. "I wish you the same sorry fate for your property."

"How long has it been?" one of the customers asked.

"Four days I've been following their trail. Today's the fifth," the father said, drinking again, and putting down more coins to show that his tankard should be refilled.

"Then she's likely with child by now, so why chase any longer?"

"I'll not have him wedding her," the father said.

"No other will have her now," another voice said.

"Nor will that journeyman have what he took against my express desire. The two of them sneaking off together when I refused consent. And there is the matter of my neighbor, too, a man robbed as I have been." At the laughter, he glared around the room, and drained his ale again, and set it down to be filled. "But what would the men of Selby know about such things? You know what the world says of you, don't you? Hiding behind your walls, hiding behind the double-walled city of Celindon, so you'll never have to draw a sword. . . . Do you know what the world calls you?" The ropemaker's sword was drawn. "They're here, aren't they? Tell me, and I'll kill them all. Or I'll have your heart on my blade before you can take another breath to fill with your lies."

Before he had finished the speech, the Innkeeper was around the front of his bar. His body like a barrel on top of legs as broad as tree stumps, his arms huge as he rolled up his shirtsleeves for the work to come, he moved slowly towards the father. The Innkeeper had no weapons but his eyes, with their malevolent glance, and the promise of strength in his arms and legs.

The ropemaker backed away.

The Innkeeper's hands hung huge. His arms looked strong enough to pick up one of the barroom tables to use as a shield. He feared nothing, and nothing that tried to stand in his way would stop him. He rolled like a boulder towards the retreating man.

The ropemaker sheathed his sword. "All right," he said.

The Innkeeper kept moving towards him.

A man moved silently to open the door.

The father didn't dare to turn his back on the Innkeeper. As the father backed into the open doorway, the Innkeeper lifted his huge right arm. He made his hand into a fist and — faster than Oriel could see — slammed it into the father's face, and the man at the door slammed the door shut on the father's heels, and the room erupted into merriment.

The Innkeeper quieted the room by looking around, his face not rejoicing in the victory, nor amused by the event, nor angry.

Oriel was almost sorry he hadn't been given the chance to fight at the Innkeeper's side. He had been half out of his seat, and ready. He had chosen the way he would take across the room, to put himself beside his host.

"Would you then let a daughter of yours choose her husband herself?" a man asked boldly.

"If I had a daughter," the Innkeeper said. Once again, he loomed large behind his bar. "Why should she be forbidden?" He seemed in good spirits now, and gave himself a bowl of wine.

"You should wed, then, and get children, and see if you feel the same easy way," another called.

"After all these years, you should wed your mistress kitchen," another called.

"Let the wench get a child, and I'd wed her fast enough. Woman!" he called, draining his own tankard, letting it clatter down onto the bar. The cook-maid's face appeared in the door. "Did you hear my promise? If you were with child, I'd wed you. I'll not take a barren wife, and why should any man?"

The woman said nothing. Color rose in her cheeks, but she didn't quarrel.

"Aye, go back to your work," the Innkeeper said, dismissing her with more anger than he had shown for the ropemaker. "There's ale for any man here who held his tongue this night," the Innkeeper announced, and the men thronged to take him at his word.

Oriel and Griff rose together and withdrew to their sleeping chamber. Oriel barely had time to feel surprise at the comfort of their mattress, before he slept.

And woke to darkness. He sat up. His heart thudded in his chest.

He didn't know what had awakened him. He was listening to the night outside where the air seemed to be shivering with some echo of sound. He couldn't remember hearing anything.

Griff was sitting up, too.

Oriel's ears rang. "What . . . ?" he whispered to Griff.

"Don't know," Griff whispered back. "Danger?"

"A dream? Don't remember. Did you hear something?"

"Don't know."

They sat in the dark, and listened, trying to hear whatever lay beyond their chamber. Oriel reminded himself that they were within the thick walls of the town, protected.

"Sleep," Oriel whispered. Griff lay back down. Oriel lay on his back and stared up into the darkness until he slept again.

And woke, to what might have been the cry of a seabird. He sat up, and Griff beside him was sitting up. The sound had moved through the room like a flying creature, over whom the walls had no power — He couldn't hold the sound in memory because it had flown before he could fix his ears on it. But at least he knew he had in fact heard something.

"Like the pigs," Griff whispered. "When their throats — "

"I didn't hear," Oriel whispered.

"I heard," Griff said. "Like something human."

"Outside?"

"I think."

They listened. Oriel could hear only darkness. He was relieved that he could hear nothing more than the night.

Griff lay back down. Oriel lay back down.

In the darkness, you would sense rather than see someone creeping towards you. You might hear some faint movement, but how would you know that it wasn't Griff, turning in his sleep?

Oriel didn't know what he was listening for, except that it was danger. He knew that Griff also lay waking, but neither of them risked speech. Oriel lay awake until he saw grey light under the doorway and heard people stirring in the courtyard.

Griff and Oriel had slept fully clothed, like everyone else, so it was simple to rise and pick up their boots. Oriel opened the door, letting in the first pale light of a misty morning.

The cookmaid was hauling up water from the well. They carried the full buckets into the kitchen for her. Her finger across her lips, she let them help her in her work.

"There's only yesterday's bread," she told them, when they were back in the kitchen. "Unless you can eat cold soup?"

"Those would both be welcome," Oriel said, and thanked her for her trouble. Neither he nor Griff sat down to eat. He had a question he needed answered. "In the night, we were awakened . . . ?"

"Those would be travelers, or perhaps lawless people. Folk from other places. The men of Selby know not to come out of their houses at night. Although, they say, if you speak against Phillipe, you may have soldiers pounding at your door in the dead of night, you may find yourself dragged out into the street, and killed there. Many folk will not open door or window, not at night."

"I thought Phillipe had no claim," Oriel said.

"He's a Captain over soldiers, that's his claim. If he can take the cities and hold them against the other claimants, and see the others all dead, then he will have won the Countess's lands. Phillipe says the strength of his right hand makes his true claim, and all who dispute that can do so with their right hands. He's the better soldier, of them all. All fear him, and with reason. They say he's fought against Wolfers and held his own there. Do you know of the Wolfers?"

"We've heard of them."

"We've never seen them, in Selby, but we hear. . . . And there are as many who believe the tales as who doubt them. But Phillipe is no tale, and there are some who say that since Phillipe will win out in the end, being stronger and more cruel, that's reason enough to wear red now. I don't know. The Innkeeper says there will never be reason enough for him to change his colors, but if the city does fall to Phillipe, and he loses the Inn, then what will happen to me?"

Oriel couldn't answer her. He only knew that his decision had been made. He and Griff were leaving Selby, to find work and lives elsewhere.

CHAPTER
11

They left Selby through the sea gate. At that hour only one solitary boat lay keel-up on the beach. The rest fished somewhere on the flat grey water, beyond the veils of misty rain.

The path they followed kept the city walls to their left. It had been marked on the ground by many feet, although on that morning they saw only a few men, and those closely cloaked. As the morning went on the drizzle ceased, and then the mists lifted, and finally the clouds pulled apart to reveal a pale blue sky. By that time they had come to the river gate and could see, under watery sunlight, the countryside spread out before them.

"Upriver," Oriel said to Griff, to identify the land before them, which was also their destination. They stood looking at it.

The river flowed away behind, down to the sea. Ahead, close around Selby, there were many small farms, with gently sloping fields in cultivation, fenced pens for animals, outbuildings to store crops. The freshly turned earth of the fields glowed brown. Upriver, the land became hilly.

Upriver was inland. "I think we should risk inland," Oriel said, but they didn't move.

Their shadows fell towards the riverside, as if urging them in that direction. The path they followed led down to the river's edge and then followed beside the water, going inland. They stood.

"We can live off the sea," Griff said at last. "But those sounds — I think men were murdered last night. I think men are murdered every night in Selby, and the men of Selby wait for Mad Magy to be murdered as her children have already. . . ."

"Is all the world then like the Damall's island?" Oriel wondered.

Griff didn't answer. His dark eyes studied the land ahead.

"It may be, and if it is we know how to live in it," Oriel decided. "We know the island, and we know the cities of the coast. I would go inland, on the chance."

"Then that's what we'll do," Griff said, and he smiled. "Unless, is there a reason that you hesitate here?"

"No reason," Oriel answered. There was a feeling of unease at leaving what he knew, to go into what he didn't know anything of. A feeling was no reason, however, and besides, part of the feeling of unease was eagerness. He was eager to be begun with whatever the land upriver held for him.

They didn't hurry. The morning was warmed gently by a southern breeze. As they walked, the river moved in the opposite direction, sometimes in a slow sweep, sometimes rushing over shallows. The river banks grew gradually less steep. The farms became larger land holdings, and fewer, but they had the same busyness of the year's beginnings. Figures moved about in the fields, a man plowing behind an ox, a man moving a herd of animals from one fenced pasture to another with the dull clanking sound of metal neck bells. Sometimes a woman could be seen, bending over the well. Sometimes children sat looking out from doorsteps, and once a little child stood up, to wave. Oriel waved back. The child stepped forward only a few paces, and waved more energetically. Both Oriel and Griff waved back. The child, its feet dancing beneath its skirt, waved with both its hands in the air in a frenzy of excitement.

The sun was well on its way towards setting when Oriel saw his destination. The farm buildings stood shoulder to shoulder, like companions, with the long green hills at their backs. The yellow stone of house and fences glowed like gold under the lowering sun.

Looking across at the fields that ran up, edged in golden stone, over the hilltops, where sheep grazed, looking down to where a pond had been dug for the ducks and geese that roamed around its muddy edges, seeing a child move among the ducks — Oriel felt peace, deep as a rockbound harbor, fill his belly.

Without thought, without a word of explanation,

he turned onto the narrow path. The farmhouse seemed to await him.

As they came up to the wooden gate, they were halted by the sounds of dogs barking. Two mastiffs came running out of the house and jumped up against the gate, growling low, barking. Oriel and Griff stepped back, to be safely out of reach of the yellowed fangs. The child left the ducks and approached the gate. She called the dogs to silence. They did not obey her. She stood between them, no taller than their shoulders, regarding Oriel and Griff out of round brown eyes in a smooth round face. The dogs barked and slathered and she stood quiet, not smiling, not trying to speak.

Gradually, the clamor subsided. The girl pulled and pushed at the dogs until they stood on four feet again. She put a hand on each dog's shoulder. "Now be quiet, Brownie," she said. "Be good, Faith." She stared up from between them at Oriel and Griff.

Oriel didn't know what she saw to strike her so silent, but he thought he should wait for her to speak first. He wanted to make no careless mistakes here. To be clever as a river sometimes meant moving slowly, letting the land itself guide you.

"Good evening, sirs." When the girl spoke, her cheeks turned pink.

"Good evening," Oriel answered.

"It's a fine evening," she said. Her voice was high and childlike, but so soft he had to listen carefully to hear it. After her first searching regard, she hadn't looked at the visitors.

"Yes, a fine evening," Oriel agreed.

He waited then. The girl waited. The dogs stood patiently.

"Is your father at home?" Oriel finally asked.

"Aye," she said, and continued studying the ground between the toes of her boots.

Oriel waited. She didn't fidget but she wasn't at ease.

"I would speak with your father, if I may," he said.

"Oh, aye," she said. She looked over her shoulder towards the end of the row of buildings, and looked back at Oriel.

Oriel turned to Griff.

"We wonder," Griff said, "if we could ask you to fetch your father to us. Or perhaps your mother?" She shook her head. "We wonder," Griff said, "if your father can be disturbed at his labors? Can we ask that favor of you?"

She looked over her shoulder again, as if for help, but no one appeared. "Aye, you can," she said, but hesitated. Oriel was about to speak impatiently when she warned them, "You mustn't try to follow me, not into the yard, sirs. The dogs won't permit it."

"We'll wait here," Griff promised her.

Then she did go, but she didn't run as a child would. She walked away full of dignity, the way a grown woman would. When she was out of sight they could hear her voice, calling, "Father, Father! Strangers, Father!"

The dogs sat side by side, watching. Oriel and Griff stood side by side, waiting.

Moving quickly, a man came out from behind the farmhouse. He wore the customary loose shirt, loose trousers, and boots. His hair had grey in it, although his thick beard was entirely dark. He approached them without haste and without reluctance. He wore no neckerchief. The girl came along in his wake.

The dogs turned their heads to greet their master, and watch for his commands.

"Good evening to you both," the man said. He was more well fleshed than Oriel and Griff, but not much taller. "My daughter says you wish to speak with me?"

"Good evening to you," Oriel answered. He could think of no way to say what he hoped, except to say it plain. "We seek work."

"Who told you I was in need of workers?" the man asked.

"Why, no one. Are you?" If this was so, it was more luck than Oriel had ever had before.

The man asked, "What do you know of my trade?"

Oriel had to admit, "There are fruit trees here, there are fields and herds. We know how to tend fruit trees, how to farm land, how to fish, how to care for livestock. If you are a farmer, we know how to be useful to you."

"You truly don't know what I am?"

"Truly," Oriel said, and Griff echoed him, "We don't."

"What led you to this gate?" the man asked, mistrusting.

"We were going upriver, seeking work to keep us," Oriel said. "I saw your farm and it looks — "

The man waited.

"It looks a place where I would abide, if I could," Oriel finally said.

The man decided. "I can offer you a supper, at least, and a bed for the night. You want to be indoors once the sun goes down, lads, in case you don't know that. Happens I am looking for help. I may have work to offer you, if you would — abide." The word seemed to please him. He spoke it as if he would like to speak it again and again, as if it were the name of someone dear to him.

When Oriel reached out to open the gate, the dogs snarled, and started. "Quiet!" the man roared, and clouted each across the nose. The dogs sank back. "But until I've opened my gate to you, and opened the door of my house to you, be warned, lads, that the dogs will bring you down. Once you've been welcomed, Brownie and Faith will know you. Unless you seek to harm us, and then they'll be your enemies. Vasil it is," the man said.

Oriel waited for the gate to be opened.

"Have you no names, lads?" the man demanded.

Oriel felt a rush of anger, to be so spoken to. Before he thought, his shoulders stiffened and he answered only, "Aye."

For some reason this made the man smile, and Oriel felt foolish. "Aye," he said again, as the gate was pulled open and they entered, "it's Oriel, and my companion is called Griff."

"I welcome you both," Vasil said, barring the gate behind them. "Come into the house and my daughter will show you where to sleep, and give you water to wash the dust of the journey from you, while I finish the day's work. After we have supped we will talk. Is that well with you?" he asked. "Or have you another manner in mind, to settle our business."

Oriel felt he was being mocked, but not unkindly. "We have no other manner," he said. "We thank you." He needed to learn how to act as men acted. He needed to learn it quickly and cleverly, for there had been no man on Damall's Island to teach him. The Damall had been the master, holding all power over the boys; with all that power, the master had no need to be a man.

The girl showed them to the room where they

would sleep. There, three mattresses lay side by side on a sleeping platform. The room smelled of sweet dry stuff, but she had opened the window to the evening breeze before Oriel could identify the odor, except to know that it was good, clean. She led them around to the back to show them the privy, and looking across the yard filled with ducks and geese they saw Vasil bent over a low pan, as broad as the long roof that had been built over it. Steam rose from the pan. The girl showed them the well and then took them back into their sleeping chamber, where a chest was filled with shirts and trousers in all sizes. "This was my brothers' room," she said.

"You have brothers?" Oriel asked.

She nodded.

"Where are they?"

"Gone," she said. "I have work to — " she said, fleeing from the room.

"The silly child is afraid of us," Oriel remarked to Griff, as they pulled their shirts over their heads.

"Perhaps shy with strangers," Griff suggested.

"No matter. It's her father's good opinion we need, if we're to stay on here."

"Unless she might dislike us for some reason," Griff said.

Oriel's mind was on the more important point. "I hope I know how to get his good opinion."

After a supper of soup and bread served by the daughter, they all sat near to the fire. Vasil had been silent during most of the meal, but now he spoke. "If you were of a mind to try working here, I'm of a like mind. I'm a slow man, usually, but a man should never be slow to wrap his hand around a piece of good luck. So, shall we try one another? For a fortnight, what do you say?" He yawned, and yawned again.

"Yes," Oriel answered, without hesitation.

Vasil laughed out loud, a pleasing sound. "You speak for both?"

"He can speak for me," Griff said.

"Two copper coins apiece for each sennight's work. I offer food, and shelter besides, clothing and whatever is needful, as if you were apprenticed to me."

"Yes," Oriel said.

Vasil smiled, yawned, and rose to leave the room. The girl followed him. Oriel and Griff lingered. Night lay chill outside the thick walls, and quiet lay over the farmstead and hills and river. This was a house where he would sleep deeply, Oriel thought, and rise up strong and rested to work gladly across the day. This was a house where he might abide.

In the grey morning, Vasil took them outside to show them his property. "I'm a saltweller. In fact," he said, his voice ripe with satisfaction, "I'm the only saltweller within a sennight's travel. Salter, Saltzman, by whatever name, the work and profit of the salt spring are mine, as my father's before and his before him, as far back as anyone has heard. My spring produces salt of the finest quality. It was my salt that the Countess, while she lived, must always have. In her own great house at Celindon, the bailiff knew that only one salt was fine enough. Mine. When the Countess traveled, she always took a cone of it with her, and never for visit-gift. She would never part with Vasil's salt, except to offer the saltcellar to a guest in her own house."

He expected Oriel to say something, so Oriel obliged. "That is a great honor."

"Was, lad. Was." Vasil shrugged. "Since the death of the Countess — But I don't complain. Times for a salter are never as hard as for other men and I'd be a fool not to be grateful for that. But times haven't been the same as they were in the Countess's day. Or her father before her, when the Old Count ruled the cities. But," and he clapped his hand across Oriel's shoulder, "there's no use in regretting what has gone, is there? Since change is the rule, and things once lost in the changes can never be regained. Any more than lives once lost can ever be regiven. What do you know of a salt-well?"

"Nothing," Oriel said.

"Then to start with," Vasil said, "you should know that what I show you here is not negligible, however much it doesn't look like riches. There are farmlands with the property, as you know, and woodlands all around, but the heart of it is here."

Oriel looked where Vasil indicated. He saw two huge, flat, shallow metal pans, each one large enough to hold a man lying down with his arms outstretched. Each pan was filled with a blue-green liquid, which steamed because of the fire beds over which the pans — now that he looked more carefully he could see how the arrangement worked — hung suspended by chains from each corner. The chains were attached into the roof beams. The pans were not hung at equal height from the ground. One pan hung a handsbreadth above the other. All around the pans, the ground was crusted with white.

A row of cone-shaped baskets hung above the pans, a pile of small wooden boxes, of a size to hold a house's valuables, occupied a corner of the covered shelter, and now that he noticed it, Oriel saw that the liquid in the higher pan came dripping down from a sluice. The sluice led back up to three shallow wooden boxes, lined up like steps.

A shallow basket mounded with white snow had been set down beside the wooden boxes. Oriel didn't know why the snow hadn't melted.

Vasil watched their faces, and pulled gently at his short beard. "All right now, lads, you listen while I tell you what's what here. This," he said, leading them out beyond the roofed structure to a tiny puddle of water that was not clear and clean as a spring should be, "this is the brine spring. It's belonged to my fathers since before anyone remembers, and nobody knows how it was found, how the saltworks began." He hunkered down and dipped his fingers into water that bubbled up gently at the center. "Taste it."

Oriel crouched down, and Griff followed his lead. They both tasted.

"Salty. You'd know it now. When you taste that, it's a saltwell. Stronger than salt seawater, you can't mistake them." Vasil went on, in loving detail, explaining how the brine was elevated up the stepped boxes, then flowed down the sluice into the pans. There the water was removed by heating. "First it looks like scum, on the top. That sinks. When it sinks, you want to move the mother liquor down to the next pan, because what you've got from this spring is basket salt, and Vasil's is the finest basket salt anyone can buy. Cleanest. Purest. You take it up from the bottom of this pan, when you've tipped the mother liquor into the other. From the other, when it cooks out, we take fishsalt, for salting the barrels of fish. It's too strong for table, but some farmers also use it for their cheeses, if they can't get the finer."

151

"How do you know when to tip the pans?" Oriel asked.

"Aye, you can taste it. You'll learn the taste soon enough. For now, if you know the look, the color, and thickness, and call me to determine, that'll be good enough." Vasil stood up, and faced Oriel. The man's face had turned to solemnity. "But I'm not sure it's a wise man who would take two unknown and untutored workers on at the same time."

Oriel didn't know how to deal with this. Griff waited by his side. "Last night you said differently," he reminded Vasil.

"I also said last night that I'm a slow man. It takes me a time to think things out. This morning, I'm saying to you that there may be only one man's work here."

It didn't have to happen that just because a place suited him, he would suit the place, Oriel thought to himself. This house and its saltwell, and its fields and herds pleased him, although he didn't understand why. But that didn't mean there was a place for him here. Moreover, he argued silently, the chances of another pleasing choice were greater on the mainland.

"I am sorry for that, Saltweller," he said, concealing his disappointment. "We thank you for the night's lodging."

"You're a hasty lad," Vasil said. "You, Griff, is it all the same to you, if you stay or if you go?"

Oriel hadn't thought of Griff staying on here without him. He had only thought that he wouldn't stay on without Griff. "Stay if you choose," he said.

"I don't choose," Griff said. "But if you do, I'll not be angry."

Oriel spoke to the Salter. "We need a place where there is work for two, together." Vasil already knew that. The daughter now came to stand in the kitchen door, across the farmyard. She watched them, wiping her hands on her apron, her hair wrapped around with a white head kerchief. "But tell me, how is it you wear no man's colors? You must be the only man of Selby so undecided."

"That I'll explain as we sup," Vasil said, "having noticed that you yourselves wear no colors."

"Aye, but we are not men of Selby," Oriel told him. "And we must make our farewells, and be on our way upriver."

"Aye, but I don't think that is necessary," Vasil said. He laughed, pleased with himself, pleased with Oriel and Griff. "You didn't think of it? You didn't think of a test?" He clapped Oriel on the back, and clapped Griff on the back. "I was testing your loyalty, lads. To know if you were loyal to one another."

"Why should we not be?" Oriel asked.

"Loyalty isn't convenient, much of the day," Vasil answered. "But tell me, you will stay, the two? For a trial period?"

Oriel didn't like being tested, and he thought of saying No. He thought he'd had enough for a lifetime of this way men had of testing lads, to determine if the lads were fit for manhood. But he did want to abide in that place, and he thought that a man living alone with his one daughter would need to be sure his workers were loyal men. So he said, "Yes."

"You speak for both?" Vasil asked, as he had the night before.

"Oriel can speak for me," Griff answered again.

CHAPTER
12

Over that evening's supper, the Saltweller began the tale of how he came to be no man's man, in the question of the Countess's heir. This was a slow-told tale, with no main pathway but only a maze of byways through dense woods — and no apparent destination. The telling of it took up many evenings. Vasil unfolded the story step by step, step after step — and often step upon step, step across step, steps all the way around.

At first Oriel waited impatiently for the end but then, as he grew accustomed to coming back to the low, heavy-walled house, which seemed — every evening — to welcome him, he grew accustomed to Vasil's slow telling. And he was glad as he listened that he could hear the story in pieces. There was more sorrow in the tale than Oriel would have liked to hear in one night.

Sometimes Griff was present, to hear whatever part of the tale was told that night. Sometimes it was just Vasil and Oriel. Sometimes they were walking up to the pasture, where a herd needed care. Sometimes they were waiting for the mother liquor to taste ready, sometimes moving faggots onto the fire, sometimes packing conical baskets for draining or wooden boxes for drying. Sometimes they would be sitting at the fireside after the day's work, or sitting on a bench beside the door watching the day's light fade. The Saltweller's voice would begin: "In the days when the priests had returned to the land, and I was a boy, and my father was Saltweller . . ." This grew into the story of Vasil's oldest son, who would have studied to be a priest had the priests not fled the wars, the son who had supported — as had the Saltweller — Karle. The son wore his yellow neckerchief proudly and did what any boy of spirit must do when he had chosen his leader, and died in a battle before one of the cities up along the coast, where — since Karle's army had fled from that battle — his body was lost to recovery.

The second son, as his father had at the time, supported Ramon — this being before Ramon had leagued himself with the scoundrel Taddeus. But the weakness in armed strength that led to the ill-chosen leaguing had led Ramon previously into ill-conceived battles, in which he was outnumbered, during which any number of men's sons were slain, and their blue neckerchiefs stained with their own red blood.

And so the stories went, for the Salter had a son dead in every man's color and he would no longer wear any man's. He had lost wives also, but they had died of fever or the bloody flux or childbirth. For all the uneasiness of present days, the Saltweller pointed out to Oriel and Griff and his daughter, any man alive had known worse, since the Countess died. Selby was lucky in being out of the way, off the main roads between the greater cities. The citizens of Celindon, for example, were eaten with envy for the peaceful life in Selby.

The daughter's name was Tamara. There were older daughters, two of them still living, married to neighboring farms. So all of the landholdings along the river belonged in the Saltweller's family. "For they were pretty enough girls for the purpose. Who weds Tamara will be Salter after me. That's if the armies come to peace. If these wars don't kill off all of the men. If in the division of the spoils the saltwell doesn't fall to some stranger's gift. Because there is only so much a man can do, to secure his child's future, Oriel. And what of my little Tamara, do you find her pretty?"

Oriel didn't find Tamara at all. He didn't look for her. She brought food to the table, kept the house, cared for the fowl, cultivated the kitchen garden and orchard to produce foods that she gathered, and set out on the table, and preserved in woven baskets or salted kegs against the coming winter; also she first sewed and then kept clean the clothing of the men of the house, and the linens. Griff seemed comfortable in Tamara's company but Oriel couldn't be. She was a child, of only ten summers.

When her chores were done, she played with her doll, or tied cloths around the dogs' tails saying they had been hurt in battles and she was caring for them.

Griff could chatter on with her, and listen to her stories. Tamara must always be imagining, and Griff's attention encouraged her. She spoke of a land she named the Kingdom, filled with beautiful ladies and brave lords who lived adventurous lives, and met up with giants, and true love, and of Jackaroo, a man who was — as far as Oriel could tell by the hearing — little better than a pirate, for all that Tamara described his mask and cloak and deeds with sighs of admiration.

Oriel didn't know how much of this Griff gave credence to, and he didn't ask. He had real questions to ask of the Saltweller, questions about the length of time packed salt needed to hang over the salt pans — the general rule, since the dampness in the air, and the temperature of the day, and the wind, and the heat of the faggots under the pans all also affected the exact time the packed salt had to hang over the fires, drying.

One autumn evening after Tamara had babbled tirelessly while sewing the tabbed waistband for a pair of trousers Oriel could wear in winter cold, Oriel asked Griff as they climbed onto their beds, "Is this Kingdom actual, do you think? And the great impenetrable forests under ice mountains?"

In the candlelight, Griff had smiled. "The Kingdom is more real than the golden city of Dorado, I think, but less real than Celindon. Vasil says there used to be merchants, before the death of the Countess, who traveled great distances. Now the journeys aren't safe, but at that time travelers told strange tales."

"But, Griff," Oriel protested, "the child says that her mother, dead these many years, has gone to the Kingdom."

"Just as she denies the death of her youngest

brother, who stole the purse of coins Vasil kept under the hearthstone to give to Matteus. Except she says he has gone to the Dammer's island."

"So it's false," Oriel agreed. He pulled his bedclothes up for warmth against the chill of night. "Her mind is filled with fancies. She weeps over the princess whose lover came back from afar with a foreign witch for a bride, who carried him away and he was never seen again, and the princess died of a broken heart. And this story brings tears down her cheeks."

Griff didn't comment.

Oriel blew out the candle. "I believe in Mad Magy, and her babies — but not in a princess who dies of a broken heart."

"I think they may be the same story," Griff spoke across the darkness.

"No, not at all," Oriel told him. "The child said — did you hear her? — that she will teach us to dance. As if I had time for dancing." He was smiling to himself as he fell asleep.

It was early in the first winter of the three Oriel spent as the Saltweller's man that he gave his master the truth. He gave it unwittingly, but in the end it turned out to have been wisdom that he didn't know he used, to have been truthful.

The cold had closed in with the darkness, and the windows were shuttered against rain. Snow came rarely to Selby, the Saltweller said. It was not unknown, just uncommon, but meantime the rain was cold enough. They were all four seated close to the fire. The Saltweller was reckoning up his stores and his coins.

"Remember that for me," Vasil said to Oriel after he had named the number of saltboxes that the Innkeeper of Captain at the Gate had purchased for his winter stores. "To which I add — Tamara, do you remember what the summer purchase was?"

"For the Captain?" Tamara asked. She was sewing a sleeve onto a shirt for her father. The needle went in and out, as she wrinkled her brow. "Was it four? That seems so few, so was it fourteen? You told me, I remember when you told me. I just can't remember *what* you told me, Father."

Vasil sighed. He scratched lines on the hearthstone. Oriel, like Griff, was fitting together pieces of wood for saltboxes. "How many of the summer's boxes did he take credit for, when he placed his winter order?"

Vasil didn't ask this question of anyone in particular. Oriel had taken no note of the number at the time, and neither had Griff. They hadn't thought it was necessary.

"Every year at this time, Father worries that the spring is producing less salt," Tamara explained. Her needle, pulling its long train of thread, moved in and out of the thick cloth.

"Aye," the Salter laughed ruefully. "But I can never remember exactly the last year's numbers. It's enough for my poor head to recall whose bills are paid up, and whose owing. I am probably being cheated out of a good profit."

That thought didn't call forth any laughter.

Without thinking, Oriel asked, "Could you not keep record books?"

"Aye, if I had books, if I had quill and ink. If I knew how to read and write. Aye, I could do that."

Oriel could sense Griff's wary stillness.

He could almost feel the Saltweller's eyes on the back of his neck. "It's time you were in bed, Tamara," Vasil said at last.

"Yes, Father," she answered, folding her sewing

together and setting it into its basket. She was almost out of the room when he called to her. "Tamara?"

"Yes, Father."

"If you were to wed, would you take one of these lads?"

"Yes, Father."

"Which one would it be?" the Salter asked.

"Why, you would tell me which," she said. In the light of the candle, her face seemed more solemn than ever, her eyes larger. The cloth around her hair made her look not so much a child.

"But if I were to ask you your own preference?" her father asked.

"I prefer Griff, Father."

"Why him?"

"Because he likes to talk with me. Just as Oriel likes to talk with you. So we get along. Griff doesn't mind when I am stupid."

"Go now, Daughter," her father said.

"Good night, Father," she answered, and left the room.

There was a long time of silence, while Vasil stared into the flames and Oriel stared at his knife blade, and Griff patiently scraped a flat surface smooth.

"Is it not time to speak the truth?"

Oriel didn't move. But inside of his head, all was movement, like a river running over rapids, searching for the way through, trying routes around rocks and over shallows, a turbulence of thought more rapid than he could follow. Griff, he knew, would do and say nothing until he heard Oriel's choice.

After waiting a while, the Saltweller's rough voice queried quietly, "Have you not learned over the seasons that I am a man to be trusted? Can a man throw his sons alive to those wolves who care only

160

to win the rule of cities to themselves — can he do that and not learn to question common wisdom?"

Oriel looked up at Vasil, to answer, "Aye, Master, I think a man can." Oriel knew that trust between man and man had its own fields of honor, and even if one of the men was a lad and the other the master, still there might be honor between them.

"And have I not seen," Vasil went on, "how your feet mold themselves to the very shapes of the hills and fields of my lands?"

"That I did not know," Oriel said, choosing not to acknowledge that he had suspected it. He couldn't know how much the master had guessed of the desires he warmed his heart before.

"Can you not give me the truth? Oriel? Griff?"

Griff watched Oriel, to give away nothing Oriel chose not to give away, to deny nothing Oriel should speak.

Oriel asked, "Tell me what you guess. It might be that the truth is dangerous to us, and should not be told, but if it is already known we will acknowledge it."

The answer pleased Vasil. "I think that you can figure with numbers. I think perhaps that you can write with letters, and read them. These are skills the Dammer's boys are trained in, before they are brought to the slave market at Celindon."

The Saltweller spoke cautiously, as a man fishing in a river plays his line out. Oriel didn't respond in any way. He didn't look away and he didn't allow any expression onto his face.

"I have heard of such slaves, who are bought at the highest price for the promises the Dammer makes about how useful these boys will be, especially to the great guildsmen of Celindon. But I've heard also that these boys make trouble among the other slaves, with the proud airs they take for themselves, and they care more for the fullness of their bellies than for the well-being of their master, or his house. These boys can see no farther than their noses, or so it seemed to me, hearing the tales; since their own well-being depends on the well-being of the house. Do you agree?"

Oriel answered, after a hesitation to consider, "Aye."

"These boys have taken coins to falsify the names or numbers. Such coins are often offered by one who wishes the great house ill — and there are always some to wish a great house ill. These boys will try to be masters among the slaves, and slaves to the masters — spiteful to the one and fawning to the other. The Dammer has starved out of them their courage and loyalty, until they are ruined. Even women make better slaves than the Dammer's boys because a woman will be loyal to her master, if he once gains her heart. The best use for the Dammer's boys, to my mind, is to use them to teach you letters and numbers so that you can keep your own record books, and then sell them to the mines. Lest they undermine your house with their cowardliness."

Oriel nodded slowly.

"I think," the Saltweller said, "that if you can speak of keeping records then you can write numbers, and letters."

Oriel nodded slowly.

"I think," Vasil said, "that you must be from the Dammer's island."

Oriel took a breath and said it. "Yes. I am."

"And I also," Griff said.

Unsurprised, the Saltweller rose from his stool. He went to the cupboard and took out a jug of wine. He poured out three bowls and gave one to Oriel, one to Griff, keeping the third himself. "This I believe," he said. "Not everyone can be ruined by evil experience. There are some who cannot be ruined. And there are others who find themselves in company with such men, and have the wisdom to know their fortune. I would ask you both to stay here, as my men. Tell no one else whence you come, deny it if asked, I will put my word behind you should it be needed. I would ask you, further, to teach Tamara the understanding of numbers and letters." He raised his bowl of wine to promise, "I will keep my faith with you."

"We will keep ours with you, Master," Oriel answered, and drank.

As the wine slid down his throat, happiness flooded up like rivers to meet it. For the time it took to swallow the wine happiness was the very bones of him, over which his flesh was wrapped.

He was learning to work the goodness of the property and he would work it well. He could bring to the house his knowledge of the sea, and how to take the goodness of sea and river for the benefit of the house. He felt also, in himself, that he might become the kind of man the Salter was. Oriel had frequently accompanied his master to the market in Selby, and once to the inland city of Belleview, and once in the fall to double-walled Celindon. When they had been in Celindon, that city had been held — with smoke still rising from the ruins of the embattled streets — by Karle and Eleanore; but what heir was in power made no difference to the Salter. Vasil wore no man's color, but all men knew he had given a son to each cause, except Phillipe's. If Vasil was no man's follower, then he followed no man's enemy. Vasil had earned the right to move independently, and he kept that right to his house

163

and all within it. Oriel thought he also had the strength to move so independently; he thought his was the same kind of strength his master had. Oriel thought he would make a worthy saltweller.

He must, then, wed Tamara. Given her own choice, she would take Griff, but she was only just approaching eleven winters and it would be two more before her father asked her to take the man he wished her to wed. Oriel was fairly sure he could win Tamara's heart, when her heart was ready to be given to a husband.

Griff himself said, at some time that first winter, "When Tamara chooses, as the Saltweller will ask her, she will choose you, Oriel. How could she not?" Griff asked.

Oriel knew that you couldn't tell a woman what to do with her heart. He had seen that from the first, that being one of the things Mad Magy had to teach, if you were wise enough to learn from her. He had seen it also in the cookmaid at the Captain, who would never leave her rough-handed Inn-keeper, however little he gave her in return. Oriel thought that if he were a woman he would choose himself over Griff. That first winter he sometimes tried to see past his companion's face, into Griff's heart, to know what was there — because he would not like to take from Griff any of the little that Griff might desire for himself, he would not be such a man, not unless urgent circumstance or urgent need drove him to it. He tried to see if Griff would have liked to be the man to husband Tamara, and he saw none of the lingering glances that gave a man away, just as he saw no hunger when Griff's eyes followed the line of hills over the farm's rising and falling lands.

Over that first winter, when the weather was too

rough for any army to move through it, quiet spread over Selby. Day followed day, bringing sunshine or sleet, rain, cold, and great chunks of ice floating down the river from the hills. Day followed day, bringing daily chores, until the stools and tables were all mended and a pile of woven cones was stacked in the storeroom, until all knives and daggers were honed to razor sharpness and a stack of saltboxes stood beside the cones, until shirts and skirts and especially trousers were mended. Oriel divided the Damall's coins into two equal parts and sewed them into the hems of his trousers. The beryl he kept in its own hiding pocket, beneath one of the waist tabs where its bulkiness wouldn't be noticed.

It was a mild winter. The herds could be left in the fenced pastures, where the two mastiffs would gather them together and drive them in at the first sign of a storm. There was mildness among the factions, also. When Oriel went into Selby and wandered among the market stalls, or sat with his master over bowls of stew, slabs of bread, and tankards of ale at the Captain, talk turned as often to the weather as to the movement of armies. A man wearing Ramon's and Taddeus's blue neckerchief might ask to escort a maid home who wore the green head kerchief of Matteus and Lucia. And that man might try to steal a kiss. And the maid might let him, knowing this would be no occasion for bloodshed, because Selby lay under the peace of winter.

CHAPTER
13

They had a summer of peace. This was the third such summer the people of Selby had enjoyed and they made the most of it. For with every year of peace, the likelihood of war closing in upon their fruitful fields and orchards in the next year became greater, and the fear of it also. On some nights, distant lights would burn along the northern horizon, or the western. During some days smoke would rise, like faraway clouds. The people of Selby would stare off into the distances and await messengers. Over the second long summer no messengers arrived.

The town built its walls thicker and taller, and cared less what color neckerchief a man wore than how honestly he dealt in his trade and how lightly he danced on the square after market days, and how straight he could stand after an afternoon in one of the Inns, and how fair his daughters were. The people of Selby cared more for Selby than for any victories among the heirs.

On market days, after the companionship of the morning's labor of loading a wagon and selling the wagonload of salt, after the companionship of beer and bread, Oriel and Griff and their master walked home through darkening air in a different companionship. Tamara watched for them, to offer hot food and demand the news of the day.

Tamara was growing into her womanhood. Oriel could see that. Anyone could see the roundness of her, and the care with which she wrapped her head kerchief around her hair, and pulled two or three locks out from under the kerchief, to be admired. Oriel didn't know if everybody could see the new way she looked at him, from under her eyelashes as if she were a little afraid of him, or the little smile that let him see the tips of her teeth, and seemed to make sport of her own seriousness, and seemed, somehow, also to make sport of him. Despite the woman's work that kept her busy, Tamara found time and energy for more. She made Oriel and Griff teach her numbers and letters. She asked, looking at Oriel from under her lashes, if they might not have a boat. With a boat they could travel on the river, quicker than walking, and Oriel had once built a boat by himself — hadn't he? he'd told her about it — so he could do that again. She looked down again to remark how handy a boat might be, for

167

catching fish also, and to remark that she might be useful in the building, if Oriel and Griff would let her help with it.

"I can work, and work hard, can't I?" Tamara asked Oriel, who agreed. "Even if I'm not as pretty as some, I am a strong worker. Does a lad care for that as much as prettiness, think you?"

"How could a lad not care for you?" he asked her.

The game between lass and lad required neither of them to answer this kind of question, so that both could imagine what an answer might be. But Oriel knew what he thought: Tamara was dowried with the saltwell and its lands, she was skilled in housekeeping and husbandry, she was a round, neat person with hair that shone in the sunlight when she let it hang down to dry after washing, and she often had thoughts about him that made her cheeks pink, when he caught her staring at him.

It was a good year for rain and sunlight, and each farmstead had full barns, grains stored, and roots, and its animals fed to fatness, their young plumping up at their sides. All of Selby counted its luck that second winter.

This made it seem the more cruel — or perhaps made Selby feel the more lucky — when spring brought the news, from the villages upriver and the cities to the east along the coast, and the cities to the west. The news was dangerous. The news was the more dangerous for being contradictory. There were too many stories afloat on the spring air for any man's peace.

Celindon had been taken, its double-walled fastnesses breached and its houses burned to ashes — some said by Phillipe, some said by Karle, all disagreed about who had defended it, and one or two of those who brought news from the north reported nothing changed from earlier years except a citizenry more closely cloaked in hunger. The walls of Celindon stood, others claimed, the guildsmen counted their coins in safety, the slave markets were full, and the gold mines produced richly. Eleanore's children had all died off in the poxy fever, rumor said, and Lucia was — at last — with child. Taddeus had taken his troops over to Phillipe, leaving Ramon weak as a beached fish. Phillipe had had his wife murdered so he would be free to marry Eleanore, and he was willing to take her sons as his heirs, over any sons he might get from her.

If you could believe Phillipe. If you could believe rumors of him. If you could believe anything you heard.

Danger was in the air, the very air the people of Selby breathed into their bodies.

The men of Selby were fearful, and undecided. A few remained staunchly loyal to their colors, but most were not. All hoped that Selby was small enough, distant enough, a poor enough prize that no Captain would desire it.

And then there came word from inland, word of Wolfers. Where Wolfers passed, they left nothing standing, not farmhouse nor any growing thing, not tree nor animal, and not man nor woman, nor child. They spoke a tongue no man could understand, baying like wolves. They ate the hearts of the enemies they killed in battle to take into themselves the courage of their foes.

Mad Magy was given the best of the vegetables, and sweet cakes; the most tender meats were put into buckets of soup for her, just in case there was truth in the old saying. Selby remembered the old saying, that spring, and hoped. Selby will stay safe as long as Mad Magy lives on its borders, they said to one another.

"Not in the spring when there's little to take," the men of Selby said to one another, glad of the distance Selby lay from other cities. "Not until the crops are grown and worth the taking," said those of cheerful disposition. "Perhaps never," the most hopeful said. "Perhaps there will be battles elsewhere, perhaps these tales of Wolfers are untrue, perhaps we'll have another year of ease."

And the blues would no longer drink ale among the yellows, the greens spat on the reds, who had no claim under law except the law that the strongest takes what he can get and hold, and the reds mocked any man who gave his life merely because a cause was just.

Fights became more frequent and they were welcomed. At least, Oriel thought, while the blood hammered in his heart and his closed fist hammered against some man's jawbone, and he didn't know if the blood he wiped from his face was his own or another's — at least he wasn't sitting in his fear, just waiting for danger to strike.

The Innkeeper of the Captain at the Gate tolerated no brawls within his doors and heaved any quarrelers out no matter whose color they wore, so his was the place Vasil chose for a measure of ale and news, at the end of a market day, after which the three would go home the longer, safer way, around the town walls. Tamara would be watching out for them. Alone, she was forbidden to leave the farmyard, forbidden to take their boat out onto the river, forbidden to greet strangers. She had no desire to disobey and no sympathy for Oriel's bruises. "It'll be knives and daggers soon," she worried, "and then what is the difference between the men of Selby and armed soldiers? I'm not so much a child that I don't see the seriousness of things. Color turns against color, and the walls that should protect us cannot. If the armies come in the spring there will be no crops planted, and we will go hungry, if we live. If they come in the summer, our labor will go for nothing, and we will go hungry, if we live. If they come in the autumn — "

"Enough, Daughter," her father said.

"And I'm no longer a child, at twelve," Tamara insisted.

"She has the right of it," Oriel said. Until Tamara had said it, in those words, he hadn't understood the deep senselessness of the situation. "And it's wrong."

"We still have time," Tamara said, encouraged by his sympathy. "We could take ourselves inland, upriver, until danger passes."

"And abandon all we own?" Vasil asked.

"With our lives safe, we can reclaim our property."

"And be called cowards?" Vasil asked.

By the readiness of the Salter's objections, Oriel knew the man had thought the same thoughts.

"Nobody would ever think any one of you a coward."

"You don't fear Wolfers inland?" her father asked her.

Tamara's round, serious face turned scornful at the suggestion. "I think these Wolfers are — stories, to frighten us with. Are you frightened of stories, you three? I don't believe these Wolfers are real. Oriel, do you?"

Oriel was distracted by admiration of Tamara's resolution. All over Selby, he thought, women must be talking thus to their men. "Yet you put faith in the Kingdom, Tamara."

"There were merchants who traveled there."

"None for years, none since the wars broke out, and many years before," her father said.

"But they had been there. You've heard such men, Father. I think there must be such a country, hidden away among the mountains, where every city isn't the prey of armies, where every farm isn't endangered. I could live happily in such a place, whatever — "

"Never mind the Kingdom, or the Wolfers, Master," Oriel interrupted her.

A sudden thought held him in its talons and he could think of nothing else except to tell his master the shape of it.

"If Selby could protect itself. Then it would need the aid of no armies, it would have no four-colored affrays. If the people were men of Selby, and no other man's men. Then the town could stand. Why should the people of Selby give their coins to four foreigners, to supply and outfit armies, when they could gather the coins to outfit themselves for battle? Or to pay tribute with, if they decided that was the wiser course?"

"Could the men of Selby fight?" Vasil asked.

"We see it every market day, now," Oriel said, smiling. "I could fight, and more bravely for the place where I live than for some man ambitious to be Count over cities I'll never see."

"But we have no Captains," the Saltweller said. "Although we might find a Captain for hire, to train us in soldiery."

"Would you not prefer Selby's color to any other man's?" Oriel asked, although the question didn't need asking.

"That isn't what I meant," Tamara objected. Her eyes filled with tears that spilled onto her cheeks. "That isn't what I want."

"Aye, Tamara," Griff said. "But we must make what's best out of what we have."

"Can the men of Selby forget their old quarrels, to act as one?" the Salter wondered.

"I could follow you, Master," Oriel said. Griff agreed. "Or the Innkeeper at the Captain, he's a man bold enough to follow." Griff agreed. "So there's two alrea — "

Vasil's deep laughter broke out, and cut Oriel off. Vasil looked at Oriel, and laughed, and laughed.

Oriel flushed. He felt a boy again, and a small stupid boy, and as if he were back on Damall's Island. He felt his cheeks grow hot and a desire fill his heels, to turn and run away from the mockery. He felt in his fists a clenching and a desire to strike out at this mockery.

"Why do you laugh, sir?" Oriel inquired. He heard how stiff and cold his voice was.

The Saltweller seemed not to hear that, or, if he did, he chose not to take offense. "Aye, you'll laugh, too, when I tell you why."

Immediately, Oriel understood that there was something here Tamara should not know. Immediately, he was at ease.

"If Selby were to stand for itself, and not for any man else." The Saltweller turned to his daughter. "Like you, I have heard too much of the Kingdom to disbelieve, although I have a hard time believing what I have never seen with my own eyes. I think, if all is lost here, we might do well to search for your Kingdom. But I will do all I can not to be driven from my land, and I like your thinking, Oriel. I could wear the colors of Selby, and I think I know many

173

who feel the same way. The Innkeeper at the Captain," at which naming a huge smile cracked his face in half, "among others."

Almost every man of Selby attended the meeting at the Captain at the Gate. Those who couldn't fit into the barroom stood craning their necks at the door and passing the words that were being spoken back along, out onto the crowded street. Vasil presented the idea: "Why do we offer our loyalties to strangers? Why do we wear the colors of men we don't know, and hope never to meet?"

Voices challenged him, from all corners. The Innkeeper growled deep in his throat, and called for silence. Gradually, silence fell, so that the one protester who called out could be heard clearly. "Selby has no soldiers, Saltweller."

"And why should we not be our own soldiers, if needs must?" Vasil answered. "I'd trust you, more than your sworn master Karle, to fight well for my land and daughter. Wouldn't you so trust me, more than some soldier hired to do your killing, who if he doesn't live won't enjoy the profit of his hire?"

"Or the booty he seizes," a voice called.

"Just because I will fight, that doesn't mean I can," a voice called.

"Will outweighs Can," the Innkeeper answered. The crowd fell silent again. "We can hire one of these Captains to teach us to fight. Lads aren't born knowing how to be soldiers, are they? Soldiers have learned the use of arrow and spear, sword and dagger. I already know how to use my fists and feet, and I believe I can learn all the rest, and I believe I can learn it quickly. I believe you can, too — we all can — if we would all choose to be men of Selby, and no other man's men."

"Without the protection of the Count — whoever he is — where would we be?" a man asked.

"Aye, look around you, where are we with it?" the Innkeeper called back. His cheeks were red, with heat and excitement, and his eyes sparkled. His fist pounded the barfront, for emphasis. "There was a dead man four mornings ago, a man whose only error was taking too much to drink on the same night when those who wore another man's color at their necks had also had too much to drink. I name no names, but I have one companion less in this world, and I have not so many men I call companion that I can spare any. I name no names, and bear no grudges, for we have grown to be this way — but when I think it could be otherwise, when I think we could stand together, stand for Selby, and stand strongest that way — my heart rises," the Innkeeper cried out.

"There's truth in what he says."

"We must be stronger together than divided into four. That's only sense."

"But when there's a victory decided and a new Count, what will happen to us?"

"No harm, for we'll have sided with none of his enemies."

"Why should there ever be a victory, when there has been none yet, not even at the start when men were fresh and well supplied?"

"If we stand all together, then at the worst we will fall beside friends."

"And never serve any Count again? I don't think I can imagine that."

"Imagine it," the Innkeeper advised. "Have you forgotten the Countess's stewards, when they came to collect her taxes? Have you forgotten what it was to give over to her luxury the coins or fish, the grains or barrels of ale, the steel blades or cloth or shoes that you had made for your own family's keeping? To be spent on some great rope of pearls to hide the wrinkles on her neck?"

"Also for houses where the poor might find food," a voice protested.

"For the keeping of priests, who fled the land as soon as she died," another voice said.

"For the Countess's long peace," someone reminded them.

Those words, and many more of like import, were spoken over several meetings. A meeting was called, men spoke and listened, and at the end there were always more men than there had been at the meeting's start who were convinced that it was time for change. More and more men arrived at the meetings as did the Salter and his two lads, wearing no man's color.

Rumors came to Selby, all summer long. Rumors came closer and closer, but still Mad Magy lived in her little house and was fed by the city, the men taking in turn the responsibility for carrying food out to her. While rumor tightened like a noose.

The men of Selby met together. Why should they not bind themselves by oath to one another, as they would be bound by oath to any man who ruled over the city? Let the common rule be the master, and the common weal. The men of Selby would rather choose one of their own number to be their Governor than give that honor to a man chosen by a Count.

After one of these meetings, Griff suggested to Oriel that the Governor's place might be filled not by one man but by a pair of men, or four, or five. Or that the Governor should be first man for only a limited run of years. So that, Griff said, there would never be danger that one man would try to rule as Count over Selby.

"Bring this before the meeting," Oriel advised, ignoring the envy nibbling at his heart. Griff owned the honor of the idea.

"No," Griff answered. "You should bring it forward. For when you speak men listen, and they want to hear the truth in what you say."

Oriel did what Griff wished, and brought the idea forward as his own. Oddly, it was the Saltweller's objections that rang out loudest and quickest. "What man can serve more than one Governor? How can a council exact obedience?" he demanded.

"What one man have we obeyed these last years?" a voice answered him. "And I do not see the city walls crumbling, and I do not see the men of Selby unable to feed their families. I tell you what men I could follow — the Saltweller for one, and our host here, for a second, and this lad to make three. The Saltweller for his wealth and the wisdom to conserve it. Our host for his courage. And the lad to keep us honest, and show us where the new ways lie. Am I the only man here would pick out these three?"

"Oriel's too young. He owns no land. He has no trade," Vasil objected. "What does he know of governing?"

The same voice put Oriel to the test, by asking how Oriel would see the oath to Selby was kept. Oriel's answer was that paying a fine seemed enough to keep a man true to his word. Who would impose the fine, he was asked, and who would enforce it upon a reluctant citizen, and who would judge the question, and how would that man be recompensed for the time sitting in judgment took from his labors, and where would the fines be kept and to what purpose would they be kept? Oriel thought that all the men of Selby should contribute to a common fund, into which also the fines would be paid, in coin or goods, field fruits, and labor, too. The city itself might choose a man of proven judgment, to render justice; out of its own wealth the city might pay this man for his services to it, and other men also, for didn't the citizens of Selby often complain about those houses whose waste was thrown out into the streets, houses that emptied their nightpots over garden walls into a neighbor's yard? Did the wives of Selby not often suspect that such filth was a breeding ground for sickness, and did not everyone know it was a breeding place for vermin? What no man could do on his own, a town of men banded together could accomplish with ease — to determine a manner of keeping itself clean and sweet smelling. Common rules of conduct might easily be decided upon, as those that most men agreed to follow, and when written down, all might know what was expected of the citizens of Selby.

Oriel looked around at all the attentive faces. There was some fear in their silence but he didn't know why they should fear his words — and just as he knew his mistake Vasil named it.

"Aye, he can write. Aye and read, and figure with numbers." Vasil had the room's attention now. "Aye, what you're thinking, that's what the lad is."

Oriel knew he could fight, fist against fist, or with cudgels, against his master. He thought he might just win, given his youth and quickness. Oriel's heart rose at the anger in his master's eyes because he knew, as surely as if words had been spoken, that the Salter wished him ill.

"Are you from the Dammer's isle, lad?" a man asked.

"Yes," Oriel said. He owed no man any explanation.

"You, Griff," the man asked, "you also?"

"Yes," Griff said. He added, "We escaped."

"Escaped?" the man asked.

"Yes," Oriel said.

"You never told me that," Vasil protested.

Oriel said nothing.

The man who had questioned him made up his mind then. "A lad clever enough to escape the Dammer's tricks and true enough to resist his temptations? and he can read and write? That's luck for Selby," he said. "I call Oriel luck for Selby."

As they walked home, the Saltweller at first strode on alone, but then he gradually slowed until the three walked abreast. The master said, "Look out you aren't too clever for your own good, Oriel. For all that you can convince most folk, aye, and rightly, too. Aye, lad, I never thought to turn against you."

Oriel didn't know what the Salter might do. But here, under the open sky, he was as good as any man of Selby. As good, he thought, and better.

The Saltweller spoke slowly. "And I'm not glad of my jealousy. So if you can win my daughter's heart . . ."

"He can," Griff remarked. "He has it already."

"Then you'll wed her, and be as good as a son to me, and be a son any man might be proud to claim," Vasil said slowly, working it out. "An honor to the house."

No armies came to Selby in the fall, but the men continued on a common way. They gathered a part of all crops and stored them, grain, onions, turnips. The people also stored weapons, purchased by the town of Selby and paid for by taxes. They hired to their own use a Captain the smith and cooper had found in Celindon; this Captain taught all the lads and men how to use daggers and swords, arrows and spears, axes and scythes, for defense and to attack. He taught them how to consider the defense of the city. He taught them how to fight together and listen to orders, how to trust their officers and fellow soldiers. He drilled them, day after day. After the long winter in Selby, the Captain wanted to make his home among them, but they sent him off, each man at a meeting casting his vote on the question as he thought best for the well-being of Selby.

They told the Captain, paying him, that they would be glad to see him in two or three years, if he was still minded to settle with them. They were too young in soldiery, they explained, to take in a man so experienced. Such a man must assume the role of leader should it come to battle, and they wished to lead themselves. If he ever needed a refuge, Selby would welcome him, they said.

The Innkeeper escorted the Captain on the first part of his journey back north to Celindon. It was not until he watched the two broad backs walking away, both giving an impression of great strength, although the Innkeeper stood no higher than the Captain's shoulder, that Oriel remembered to ask Vasil, "What was that thing that made you laugh, sir? Remember? Last winter, when we first spoke of Selby protecting itself, and I said the Innkeeper was a man I would follow."

Vasil turned to face him, not smiling now. "You'd never tell?"

"You have my word."

Vasil took a time to think it out, before saying, "He's no man, our Innkeeper. I don't think anybody but me even suspects it. He's a woman, and always has been."

"Why should a woman pretend to be a man?"

"To keep possession of the Inn. There was a son and daughter when the Inn's people came down with the swelling fever. The story goes that when the doors were opened and the survivor came out, it was the son alone who survived. The other three bodies were burned in their bedclothes, as is the way of destroying the disease. The son took possession of the Inn. Except he never grew a beard and all suspected that he couldn't play a man's part with a woman, as can happen after the swelling fever. It was because of this, we thought for years, that the Innkeeper was so fierce in his quarrels. Fiery and ill-tempered, quick to use his fists or cudgel on you, that was our Innkeeper, until finally it took only a look from him to stop a man in his tracks. Because nobody wanted to go against his great arms. Only look at them, Oriel."

The Innkeeper was walking back toward them then on his massive legs. His arms bulged with strength.

"Then how do you know what he is?" Oriel asked Vasil, not convinced, although he could see no reason for his master to lie.

"His skin, which I've never seen less than freshshaven," Vasil answered quietly. "Then, more, I saw him squatting one day, to relieve himself."

"Men do that sometimes."

"Aye, but they don't leave behind them buried in the leaves of the woods such cloths as women use in their monthly times. A woman may dress as she will, but she will still have her monthly times. Except when she is too young, or with child, or nursing babes, or too old — a woman bleeds, in harmony

181

with the moon's phases. Do you know this, Oriel?"

He didn't, but he didn't admit it. He shrugged his shoulders, as if to say, of course he knew.

"And you know how children are begotten?" Vasil asked, not deceived.

"Yes," Oriel said, for he did.

"Yes what?" the Innkeeper asked then, having come close enough to hear their talk. "Yes what, in that voice, which says its owner will be happy to quarrel if he has to."

Vasil answered. "I'm just making sure the lad knows all a lad needs to know about women, if he's to wed my lass."

The Innkeeper laughed, a brief, barking sound. "You'd have him wise before he is old, then? As long as a lad knows how to get sons, he knows enough. What needs he to know more? Aye, and what more is there to know?"

Oriel believed Vasil, that this Innkeeper was a woman beneath the clothing, and voice, and words; but he had difficulty remembering that, when the Innkeeper spoke so.

"Aye," the Innkeeper said, "and if the armies close in on Selby, there'll be many lads who never will get sons. Many sons who never will know their fathers. Those of us who have no sons, no children, may be counted the lucky ones, if armies close in, and our hopes of ourselves prove false. But I don't think I'll live to see that day. I think I'll have fallen in battle. Think you so, Salter? For I find I have an appetite for self-governance. With all its drawbacks, I find I prefer being my own man."

CHAPTER
14

The third winter Oriel and Griff spent at the Saltweller's lasted long. Winter's grip on the coast was like a mastiff's: His teeth closed, and he held the land and the people, and he did not let go.

Stores ran low. At the meetings talk varied between the governances Selby's men would place upon themselves and whether or not need was great enough to open up the warehouses. These were the stores against famine or seige, for times when starvation — more than mere hunger — was the danger. Ground grains and salted fish filled the warehouses, enough — they had measured it — to feed all the people of Selby across an entire season. The aim was to have a full year's supplies in store. No army would spend a year to take such a small prize as Selby; the booty and lands weren't enough to reward so much of an army's time.

Before winter reluctantly slunk away northward, all had agreed on an oath, sworn by every man. The citizens swore loyalty to city and fellow citizens, swore obedience to the ordinances of the city, swore to defend the city, its people and lands, with their lives if need be, and swore to tithe to the town, in coin or kind. The Innkeeper of the Captain at the Gate, speaking in a single voice for Selby itself, swore to the citizens in return that each would be treated as an honorable man would treat his own son, or his own father, never letting them want, never denying them justice, never putting the profit of one man before the profit of the whole people. "Until death releases me," the citizens swore. "Until death releases you," the Innkeeper swore.

Oriel remarked to Vasil, as the two returned from one of these meetings in the late winter, that it had been good fortune for Selby to have such business to occupy its attention. "Otherwise," he said, "these stories from inland would breed panic."

"Do you think, then, that they are no more than stories?"

"I only hope so," Oriel admitted.

"I, too," the Saltweller agreed. "But since the world so often plays hope false, I will not have my daughter left alone."

For across the winter, as if the season itself were not dismal enough to keep men's spirits down, refugees came to Selby — not many, two men, one woman, two boys of perhaps six and eight. All had the blank faces of those who have seen what they cannot bear to remember and still cannot forget, waking or sleeping. The first man scurried through, silently accepting food before he ran off to the south, as low to the ground as a whipped dog. The second man came to die by the Inn's fire, speaking disjoint-edly of longhaired longbeards, of flames, of swords that sliced a man's head off as if it was as easy to kill a man as a fish. He had burns on his body that oozed green and his flesh stank like carrion. He lifted himself up by the fire and cried to an empty doorway, "Wolfers! There's no hope for us! Ice-cold eyes, oh, I cannot bear — !"

The woman, who arrived at the dead heart of winter so starved that her bones jutted out of her face, ate hastily as she crouched in a doorway, then fled. She spoke little, but what she spoke was sen-sible. "They are quick and cruel, and their long yellow hair they tie back, and their beards they pluck from their cheeks until they hang down long only from their chins. They fear water. I will rest when I have put water between me and the Wolfers. Then I will rest, and grieve. If a fisherman were to take me to the islands in his boat, and leave me . . . I have no coin to pay but I will pay in the coin every woman has for a man."

Seeing her, no man would take her payment, but a fisherman took her in mercy out to one of the inhabited islands, when he sailed out on a trading journey, and she kissed his fingers, he said, as if he were a Count when at last she came to the water-washed shore. She kissed his fingers and she wept, as if she didn't understand that she might well starve before winter eased its grip on the stony land. She kissed his fingers and smiled, as if her own danger didn't matter, he said. He spoke in a voice that vibrated with fear, because she was one of those women that life batters against without ever bringing them to their knees, he said. "And these Wolfers have brought her down," he said.

The two boys shivered by the fire at the Captain at the Gate and would answer no questions. They shivered in silence and broke the darkness of night with screaming. On the third night they ran out of the Inn and across the sands to the sea, either pursued by some dream or still in it. They were returned to the beach, days later, by a falling tide. They lay side by side there, no more silent in death than they had been in life. All around their pale bodies seabirds circled on outspread wings, and soared, and cried out.

Oriel found that he could never forget the fear that hovered in the darkness, waiting; but he could usually work at his tasks, and speak his mind, and sleep the night through, because there was a plan being shaped and worked out, a way to defy dangers. More than once he said to Vasil, as they walked the long road back from city to saltwell, "It is good fortune for Selby that there is so much to do in becoming our own masters."

"Aye," his master would answer.

"I do not think these are all stories we hear, and false," Oriel said. "I am afraid — "

"Aye," Vasil said.

"Master, we are too far from home for the dogs to hear us."

"Do you know my mind so well?"

"Griff would guard Tamara's safety," Oriel reminded Vasil. "They will go to the boat and flee by water, if need be; that is the plan."

"And even if the buildings were burned and the animals slaughtered, still the saltwell would give us wealth to rebuild with," Vasil answered.

"But it will be good to arrive, and sit warm and safe within."

"Better, right now, to hear the dogs give warning and know that all is well."

As if they could hear their master's wish, the dogs belled out, and were turned loose. Hearing which way the dogs chased, Griff opened the door, to light their way home.

"If all the farmers take refuge within the town walls," Oriel said, as they hung up their wet cloaks and went to stand by the fire and drink down the mugs of warmed ale Tamara brought to them, "what about the animals? Fowl, goats, those at least could be kept, for the food they give, and would it not be wisdom to have orchards within the walls, and gardens?"

"What, build new walls?" the Saltweller asked, unbelieving. "With these just completed?"

"Not build new," Oriel said. "Or, mostly not. These walls could be moved outward, which would also bring the fishermen's houses within the walls, for their safety, and also that would strengthen the bonds between fishermen and city."

Vasil drank deep and said no more, but at the next meeting he proposed that very plan, and he did not name Oriel as its source. Oriel knew it would be useless to argue ownership of such a thing as an idea, but he felt as if something had been taken from him. He understood that Vasil would like to keep him down, as a father does a son, so that the father can maintain the authority of his own higher position. But he thought, in his private mind, that Vasil would not be so concerned to keep him down did he not fear how high Oriel might fly, once Oriel moved on his own wings. That thought kept Oriel patient. He would have Vasil's lands, and a place in the city that was higher than Vasil would ever be able to claim. If it came to battle, Oriel would prove the best man. Also, if it came to peace. Also, Oriel added silently as Vasil accepted the praise and admiration of the meeting for his farsightedness, if it came to preparations for battle, or preparations for peace, to rebuilding and refortifying, or even merely enduring. In any chance, he knew himself the better man.

As if to make up for its tardiness, spring came suddenly. One morning spring thrust itself up from underground, loosening soil, loosing flowers into an air that overnight had become so sweet you could almost taste the summer berries ripening within it. The shoulders of sheep were heavy with wool, and everywhere young were being delivered, dog and cat and goat, fowl and swine and sheep.

Oriel awoke in darkness, but as if the sun had already risen in his heart. All in the house seemed made glad, even as they busied themselves wordlessly in the dark for the day's long labors to begin, once the sun had lightened the sweethearted world.

The labors themselves seemed light, although they were hard: Oriel alone watched over the salt pans, gathered and hung to dry the cones, and then packed the salt into the wooden saltboxes. Griff and Vasil worked the fields behind an ox, harrowing up, plowing to fineness, bending to remove stones that appeared like the wildflowers, every year; then while Griff held the ox to the track for a final plowing, Vasil walked behind to sow the seeds. Tamara meanwhile dug over her kitchen garden, and planted it with onions and turnips and parsnips, as well as the less sturdy garlic. She watched over the birthing of pigs and goats, and was sometimes called to one of her sisters' houses for a sheep or ox because her hands were strong and knowledgeable to pull out the young, when the dam was too tired to push any longer. Meanwhile, she baked breads and cooked up stews made out of fish she had caught in the earliest light, trolling a net over the boat's side. Meanwhile Tamara opened the shutters wide and washed over every surface of the house with hot water. She hung linens and bedding out in the fresh air. Oriel worked with her when he had the time, when he knew he had time while the salt pan steamed its water away.

As if there were not enough to keep men busy, Vasil was called away to a meeting in the town every second or third day. Oriel could not be spared in the rush of spring, but Vasil must answer the knock on the door at dawn or the exhausted runner at midday. Rumors rode up from the south on the soft winds, or in from the western hills. Rumors flowed down from the north with each evening's cool air. Phillipe was on the move, he had taken Celindon last autumn and held it over the winter, his soldiers were closing in on Selby.

The men of Selby nervously wondered if they should sue for peace, surrender without battle, or send to Karle who, rumor said, had an army encamped west of Celindon. Now, rumor said, Karle had taken Celindon but found it more in ruin than richness. The men of Selby feared choosing sides and they feared not choosing sides. They met together, and reaffirmed their choice to be independent. They wore neckerchiefs of all four colors, cleverly cut and sewn by the women, who bordered all the kerchiefs, including their own head kerchiefs, in a border of white.

The people of Selby wore their colors bravely,

but their hearts often failed, and then they would call Vasil from his fields. They called Oriel, too, but Oriel couldn't be spared. The land couldn't spare both of them so it was the master who went, and spoke calming words to uneasy men, and led them in the drills of soldiery.

No sensible Captain would attack, once the seeds were sown, once the young were birthed and fattening. If he didn't attack when his chosen victim was weakened by winter, all agreed, then a sensible Captain would wait until the harvest. Why should he starve his soldiers when, if he only waited until high summer, he could bring full-bellied men into the quarrel, and know that the countryside would feed them, and know how much damage he would do to the countryside by waiting and burning what the soldiers couldn't eat or carry away. Men who watched their year's labor destroyed and knew that winter would find them unready surrendered more quickly than men who knew they already had nothing.

Every day that passed without alarm raised hope that the city was safe, at least until harvest. Every farm labored long and hard to plant its crops. The Saltweller's house was no exception. After the day's labors all slept deeply across the ever-shortening night. Oriel thought he had never been so tired, as day followed day and sometimes, if the fires under the pans burned too slowly, he stood alone into the night waiting the time when he could scoop up the clotted salt, hang it to dry, and go at last to his bed. On such nights, in early spring, it often happened that a messenger would arrive from the city. The dogs would bark and Vasil would be at a dark window. No man of sense opened his door at that hour, and the fire of the salt pans was hidden behind the house, in comparative safety. Oriel stood in firelight, straining his ears to hear in the darkness beyond, first the baying of the dogs and then whether Vasil would shout them down to silence or shout for assistance.

The Saltweller's house had its plan, just as the city had its plan in these uneasy times. The city planned to use the fisherboats to transport those who could not fight to an island, where they had food stored and shelter built. There was refuge for those who might need it, children and women and helpless old, or ill, and also those wounded in battle. The Saltweller planned, should need arise, to flee to their boat and go downriver to safety.

Plans were made; and rumors poured in as fast as seeds poured into furrows. These were rumors of bands of Wolfers and sudden raids that left no survivors, that destroyed for no more reason than a love of destruction. The cruelty of the tales brought tears to Tamara's eyes and robbed her cheeks of color. The Saltweller kept a bold front: "If there are no survivors, who spreads the stories?" he asked. "Aye, if there are such Wolfers, and as many of them as the tales say, even so they are no more than men. They can die, can they not? Especially when those who face them are trained in soldiery. As are the men of Selby," he finished proudly. "I will not worry overmuch about the Wolfers. If they come so far to find us, they will find us ready."

Oriel couldn't but admire the man's courage. His own courage was equal, he knew, but still he admired the Saltweller's.

Spring grew into summer, and the land prospered under sunlight and warmth and rains. Selby, at the Innkeeper's suggestion, named runners, who would carry warning from town to farmstead, so that the people might come quickly into safety. There were also runners named at the outlying farmsteads, who would bring to Selby early news of approaching danger.

The wheat swayed golden in its fields, fields of rye ripened, and the men of Selby began to say that no sensible Captain would take his armies to battle now. He would wait until the harvests were in. Oriel thought that the men of Selby secretly hoped as he did that this might be a fourth year of peace. Whenever hope grew too strong, however, there would appear distant smoke, dark on the horizon, as if from a giant's chimney, and people would look to it and wonder if Celindon was in flames.

Oriel lived in a state of constant alarm. He kept his coins, and the glowing beryl, always with him, hidden in his trousers. Whenever the dogs barked he reached for his dagger. He slept uneasily and was always conscious of his unprotected back as he bent over the salt pans. He was glad of the house and the companionship of its inhabitants; without those, he doubted he would have slept at all, under the constant threat of danger, under the constant promise of excitements. But all four could work together and all trust the others. They were bound together, for the well-being of all. One summer night, as they sat together on a bench by the door to watch the final fading of light, the Saltweller remarked, "We know who you would choose for husband now, Tamara, don't we?"

"How do you know?" she demanded. Her cheeks were pink and pleased, her eyes sparkled, and a little smile like waves playing at the foot of a boulder played around the edges of her mouth. "You can't know my mind. They say," Tamara said, choosing

Griff to smile teasingly up at, "that a maid's mind has more twists and turns than a fish fleeing the net. Griff told me that, didn't you, Griff?"

Oriel noted the smile that passed between the two of them. The girl was causing him to doubt what he was sure of. Then Griff looked to Oriel over her head, and it was as clear as if Griff had spoken the words aloud. *What girls get up to, how is a man to trust them? But you and I know one another*, Griff's look said.

"I would not have you be a minx, Daughter," the Saltweller rumbled.

Tamara looked up, immediately solemn.

"I would have you name your choice," the Saltweller said.

"Now?"

"Not if you are not yet ready to make it," he said. "But otherwise, yes, I'd have his name."

"I am ready, if this is the time. You are correct, Father, you do know, you all know it."

"Oriel," the Saltweller said.

"Him," Tamara agreed.

Oriel's gaze was on the black sky, and the sight of the stars appearing; he felt the rightness of everything.

"If he will have me," Tamara said, practically whispering the words.

Her voice recalled Oriel. "How could you doubt it?" he asked her. He had never doubted it. "Do you doubt me? You need never," he promised her. "But I would ask as your father did in that earlier year," he said, teasing her now, "why? Why would you choose me?"

He thought her cheeks flamed red, but in the dim light he couldn't be sure. He knew her eyes looked at him with a fire that struck him in the belly. "Oh — you know perfectly well," she cried, and jumped up from the bench to run inside.

The three men sat on, peacefully watching the approach of night. "Sooner is better than later for this wedding," the Saltweller said, as he rose to go inside to his bed.

"Aye," Oriel answered.

In a little while he asked Griff, "Who will you marry?"

"Someone," Griff said. "When you are wed and settled, then it will be time enough to look. When these dangers are past — "

"They may not pass so quickly," Oriel warned him.

"Aye," Griff agreed. "So I'll wed when . . ." He could not say. "Whenever the time and woman are right," he finally finished.

Oriel thought that if he were to be wed, he would want Griff also to be a married man. "We must watch out for a wife for you," he said. In his mind, he ran over the girls of the city, selecting the few among them he judged might suit Griff, and serve him well. Aye, and be faithful to him, as Oriel had no doubt Tamara would be faithful.

Rumors rode in by sea and land, and the Saltweller was called in to another meeting of men swept by the fears those rumors fueled. Summer was full upon them, the salt pans were newly filled with brine, which had just begun to steam, so Oriel worked beside Griff to pull the weeds out from the young onions. Tamara brought them cheese and bread at midday, and all three sat under trees at the edge of the woods, overlooking the bending river. The sun beat down and they were in no hurry to return to their labors. Insects were buzzing and birds —

194

The dogs at their feet growled.

Stood up to bark, baying —

Oriel was on his feet and had thrust Tamara behind him, had turned with Griff to face the woods before he saw that the dogs watched in the other direction, off across the field.

Oriel turned again. The woods were at his back. The dogs clamored and he drew his dagger, as did Griff beside him.

"We'll make for the boat," he decided. The two dogs bounded off across the field, low and belling.

Oriel had never seen a Wolfer and was not sure he even believed in them, any more than, say, any other fabled thing, any more than the Kingdom. But these were Wolfers. He knew it without question, as the three stepped out onto the field. They were tall, lean, sun-browned. Their long yellow hair was tied back, and thin yellow beards hung down from their chins. They held short swords ready and seemed to have their mouths wide open as the dogs attacked.

Oriel was so busy watching the dogs attack, and listening to catch the sounds that came out of the Wolfers' open mouths — like pigs at slaughter, like the cries of men in flames — as they without hesitation stepped up, and ran their swords into the dogs' great bodies, as if the snarling teeth were nothing to fear — so mazed by surprise that it was almost too late when he heard Tamara's whimpering cry and turned — Griff at his shoulder — and saw five more such men — shrieking, blunt swords raised in both hands to strike down into his heart. He barely had time for the thought: Someone must stand against these Wolfers, and delay them.

"Tamara, run!" he said. "The boat!"

Sounds rushed by his ears and the events swirled

in front of his eyes. He had his dagger in his hand.
Tamara protested, he didn't remember her words.
Faces with blue eyes, bright blue and cold as a
winter sky — He thought they must pluck the hairs
from all of their faces except eyebrows and chins,
to have such beards.

"You must — !" he cried, and she ran — he
thought those were her stumbling tumbling steps
he heard — down the hillside. To the river. To the
boat.

The open mouths made sounds like wolves with
the prey in their sight. The sound rose up howling
out of the dark throats.

Griff was at his shoulder. "Back to back," Oriel
said, remembering the Captain's teaching. The
Wolfers moved in close, and there were the three
now crossing the planted field. They had no hope,
he and Griff.

Oriel heard now, as if she were only now speaking
it, what Tamara had said in protest. "I'm not worth
it."

They didn't rush into the fight, these Wolfers.
They wore leather vests, like protection, and leather
sleeves on their arms. They spoke briefly, but Oriel
didn't understand the words. They weren't speaking
to him, in any case.

Cruel faces, they had, narrow and smiling with
pleasure at the fight, with the odds eight to two.

"She's right," Oriel said, over his shoulder to
Griff. They were circling now, he and Griff, drawing
towards the woods, where they might take flight.
"She isn't worth it," Oriel said, and he laughed out
loud. He had chosen this course of action, whether
Tamara's life and safety had equal value with his
own or not. He alone chose his own course of action.

"She has the boat untied, and oars in the water," Griff reported.

The Wolfers smelled of sweat and urine, filth, blood. Their leather, from boots to shoulders, was stained in dark patches. At some signal Oriel couldn't see, or some word he couldn't understand, they closed in.

With that wailing sound they had broken from the trees with, the three Wolfers raced to join the fray.

"But she *is* worth it," Griff told him, the familiar voice at his ear.

Oriel felt his feet moving delicately on the earth. He felt how the muscles of his thighs were braced against shocks. He felt Griff's broad back at his back.

Fear burned through him, like a flame. Fear coursed through him, like icy water. He threw his head back and raised his dagger, to strike — and cried out wordlessly, as if the great cry could gather all his fear together and set its swelling course behind him, to add it to his strength.

He heard Tamara's voice, rising up, thin, to call out his name. "Oriel!"

Two cold-eyed Wolfers came closer to him, swords raised towards his throat. Their swords were longer than his dagger and he would have to move past their blades to set his own blade into at least one throat before theirs — in a rush of blood — his own blood — sank into him.

The blow that felled him came from the side.

197

PART III

THE WOLFGUARD

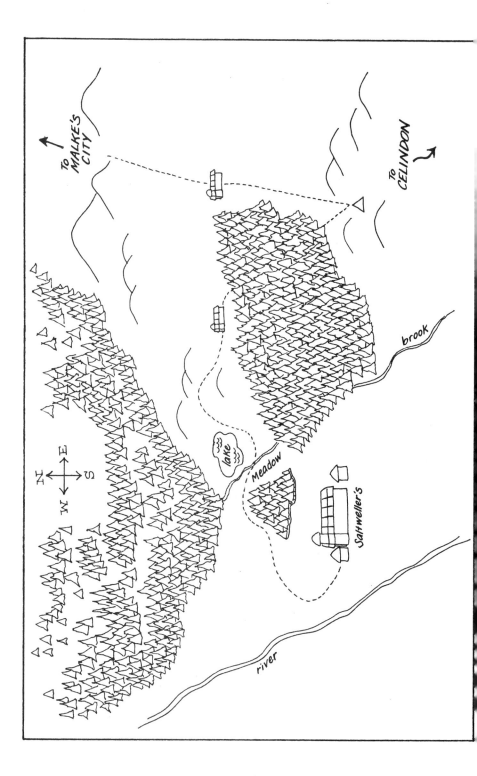

CHAPTER
15

There was only pain.

Oriel opened his eyes, but the brightness of the sky jabbed through them, into the swollen bloody mass behind. He lay in the darkness of his closed eyes, trying to move beyond the geography of pain to find his hands, or feet. He listened.

He heard rushing in his ears, as if he were being dragged along behind a great wind. He heard nothing but the rushing, as if he were being swallowed in the sea.

But the unyielding ground lay under him.

Pain was black, and had spread — pooling out

like spilt wine — and it beat against his brain bone. The way he was lying, on his back, the sun burned at his eyelids. Light burned the darkness away.

Pain shrank like a puddle under sunlight — red and swollen now like a deep wound. He didn't know —

Griff. Where was Griff? Oriel opened his eyes and sat up. Pain sliced at his head and he couldn't move his arms so he bent his neck, to ease pain. The rushing had gone but now it was a beating hollow sound he heard, and beyond it the musical silences of a spring day — birds and insects, breeze and the distant river. He opened his eyes again and lifted his head.

Griff sat beside him. With a glance and an almost imperceptible motion of his bloody mouth, Griff warned Oriel to keep silent.

They were under a tree at the edge of the woods, with the field they had been weeding in front of them. His hands were bound together at his back. A Wolfer watched him out of icy blue eyes.

The Wolfer sat apart, his sword across his knees, one hand on the sword's hilt. Oriel didn't know what danger the Wolfer expected from him — every time he moved his head he became dizzy, and it looked for a while as if there were two armed Wolfers seated across from him, one slightly behind the other. Oriel's wrists were jammed against one another in a way that twisted his hands and he wasn't sure that his legs would hold him upright, if he tried to stand. Griff, too, had bound hands, and one of his eyes was swollen shut, his lip was split and bleeding, there was blood drying around a cut that had gone through the cloth of his trousers at the thigh, and into the skin.

Oriel remembered that he must have been

knocked unconscious. He almost asked if Tamara had made it safely away, until he remembered Griff's voice telling him that she had untied the boat, and he remembered her voice calling his name, floating up over the river's bank. He wondered if Selby had been warned in time to put up a fight. He wondered how that battle had gone.

Under surprise attack it was the outlying farms that were in the most danger, although each householder had been advised to make a plan for escape, in case of surprise attack.

The Saltweller's house had had such a plan, and one of three had been saved.

If Oriel turned his head slowly, the pain was less. He looked over the house and yard, fields and woods, into the distances, and saw dark smoke billowing up here and there. He looked southward along the river, and did not see smoke where Selby might lie burning.

The sun had moved along the sky into full afternoon; he must have been unconscious for a long time, Oriel thought. Griff's eyes were closed now, although he still sat up; Griff had folded himself down over his bent knees. The Wolfer did not move. His cold glance stayed locked onto them.

Oriel didn't know what would happen next. He met, and held, the Wolfer's glance for a long time, thinking. Then he shrugged, smiling — and saw that he had surprised the man — and closed his eyes again. Whatever happened, it would be better to be rested.

The sun was not much farther down in the sky when a wailing call awakened him heralding the approach of a ragged band of men. The Wolfers were easy to recognize, with their long yellow hair and long narrow beards. Longhaired longbeards, they were rightly called that. The ragged band came closer — five men, none unbloodied, and they carried two over their shoulders. The fall of arm and head suggested that those two were lifeless.

Oriel and Griff remained motionless on the ground, but their guard rose and spoke to the tallest and broadest of the Wolfers. This man answered the question, then spoke briefly to all of them, with gestures towards the two bodies, now lying on the ground.

Oriel looked at Griff in alarm. He couldn't hear their words, not clearly enough to distinguish what was being said. He could hear only a garbled mass of sounds as the Wolfer spoke. It was as if Oriel's ears were full of thick blood that distorted sound, and made speech meaningless. He thought suddenly that he might be deaf.

The big man came towards them. Oriel ignored his dizziness and the throbbing of his head to climb up onto his feet. Whatever was going to happen to him, he wanted to meet it standing up. With his hands behind him all movement was awkward, and every smallest gesture of his head almost blinded him. The worst was when he was almost up into a kneeling position, getting his feet under him and his face thrust down towards the ground, as if he were doing obeisance to this Wolfer. The thought of being understood to be kneeling before the man gave Oriel the strength to push himself up, until he stood.

His legs shook. He leaned against Griff. Griff was steadier but leaned back against Oriel for balance.

The Wolfer watched. His eyes were cold as knife blades. As soon as they were standing, the Wolfer spoke. He spoke to Oriel, who would not look down, look away. Oriel was afraid and he was in pain, but he knew he could conceal that from the Wolfer.

He couldn't understand the Wolfer's words. Without moving his glance from the man's face, where dirt and sweat and blood streaked together, Oriel asked, "Griff, do you understand him?" At the corner of his vision he saw Griff shake his head. Griff looked pale, wide-eyed.

Oriel took a breath. "We don't understand you," he said, and was glad that his voice didn't quiver, and didn't rise high as a girl's.

The Wolfer studied him.

The man was an enemy. That fact was in his hard face and cold eyes, it was in the stance of his body on heavy legs. The man felt enmity for Oriel and would kill him without a qualm, unless Oriel was worth more to him alive. That was the simple truth of the situation.

Oriel could no more alter the Wolfer's enmity than he had earned it. He was just going to have to live with it. Unless, of course, the Wolfer killed him, which would be — in a way — the easiest way, and perhaps would even come to seem the best way. But if Oriel had to live with the Wolfer, as enemies, then he was going to have to be as cruel as ice. Sharp, cold, unfeeling — a memory of the way icicles hung off the Damall's eaves was in Oriel's mind, and a memory of the numbing killing coldness of the river in early spring, when great chunks of ice floated down it, and a memory of a boat left at the dock in Selby when the freezes came, its wooden ribs crushed by the swelling of the ice, its thin leather skin punctured by the sharp ice, destroyed entirely by the unconcerned ice.

"Speak," the Wolfer said. "Little." He pointed

at his own chest. "Rulgh," he identified himself. "King."

Oriel kept his face expressionless, although he thought of laughing. His eyes must have given him away because the Wolfer narrowed his own cold eyes and looked dangerously close to anger. Oriel shook his head, hastily trying to repair the damage. "King rules over all men," he said. "Wears crown, sits on throne, all kneel before King." He tried to act out his words, not an easy task with hands bound behind him. The Wolfer looked puzzled. "Rulgh not King. Rulgh is — " Oriel thought of the most accurate word — "Captain. Captain fights — " he moved his shoulder as if an invisible arm held a sword before him. "Captain leads his men," Oriel said, looking at the silent group of Wolfers behind Rulgh. "Captain takes prisoners." He looked at Griff and turned to show his own bound hands.

Rulgh grunted, and seemed to understand.

"Oriel," Oriel named himself. "Oriel prisoner. Oriel prisoner of Rulgh. This is so," he said, for emphasis.

Rulgh smiled, and revealed many black teeth. "Is so." He made a grunting inquiring sound, and pointed at Griff. Hoping he understood the man, Oriel said, "Griff."

"Pri-so-ner," Rulgh said.

"Is so," Oriel said. "Say it," he muttered to Griff.

"Is so," Griff said, watching not Rulgh but Oriel.

Oriel saw Rulgh raise his foot and saw his intention, but he didn't warn Griff. The Wolfer hooked his boot behind Griff's knees, and took Griff down. Griff gave a surprised cry of pain, but made no further complaint. He had been trained on the Damall's island.

Oriel didn't flinch away from the foot when it was

directed at him. He clenched his teeth against a roar of pain when his head hit the ground. He made no sound when Rulgh kicked at his rib cage, but he curled up to protect his head.

Rulgh said something and Wolfers came up. They pulled off his boots and then untied his hands to strip off his shirt, leaving him clothed only in trousers. The man who found the coins sewed into the ankle hems put one silver coin down into each of his own boots before calling Rulgh over to show the find, and exult over the coins.

Rulgh put his hands out and the man let all of the remaining coins fall into the cupped palms.

Rulgh looked down at them, smiling. His smile didn't change as he looked at the man. It stayed on his face as he stared down at Oriel, who stared back at him. "Him take?" Rulgh asked.

Oriel said nothing. He glared back at Rulgh. He, too, had been trained on the Damall's island.

Rulgh said something to the other men, who held their comrade captive while they examined his clothing, and the sheath of his sword, the inside of his mouth. They pried open his hands. The man held out, briefly, but then they bent to his boots and he talked quickly, his voice apologetic and resentful. Rulgh didn't answer. He added the two silver coins to his own purse and then took out a dagger — Oriel recognized his own dagger in the Wolfer's hand — and cut a nick out of the man's left earlobe.

The man kept his head bent, to show submission or to conceal whatever might have been read in his face. The little chip of ear dropped onto the ground, a little blood dripped down, and Rulgh turned away, finished with the event.

Oriel lay on his back. The beryl dug into his spine

like an unhappy memory. He thought they wouldn't think to search for any more coins on him, and he wasn't surprised when they ripped open with their knives the hems of Griff's trousers, and he didn't dwell on his memory of Tamara bending over the cloth, to stitch a hem or sew on one of the tabs that tied the waist, beside a fire over which a pot of stew bubbled fragrantly. The beryl dug into his spine like a prodding finger, to keep him alert.

His hands were tied again, this time in front and not so tightly. Griff's hands also were retied, also with a leather thong. The Wolfers pulled them up to their feet. They were shoved and dragged down towards the Saltweller's house, with the Wolfers close around them.

At the end of day, the two dead men were placed side by side on the floor of the house, before the fireplace. The house and outbuildings had been torn down wherever possible, and the salt pans had been emptied over their fires while the trough had been torn down with axes and cudgels. All was mounded around the bodies, anything that might burn and that the Wolfers didn't want — linens, fodder, shutters and bedsteads, boxes of salt, those portions of the livestock that weren't roasting over the open fire the Wolfers made and tended, with a barrel of wine waiting beside it.

As the flames rose in the house, the band of men moaned in a kind of a song. Oriel and Griff had been placed between the chanting band and the doorway. The sun was sinking into the horizon and the sky looked as hot as the house felt, burning.

"I hope — " Griff said, softly under the sounds of fire and chant.

"Hush." Oriel, too, hoped that they were not going to be forced to march into the burning house, but to name his fear would only give it more power. It was all Oriel could do to stand still and stare unafraid into the growing flames.

It wasn't that he was afraid so much as that fear crowded in close around him, like ice closing in on a boat at its mooring, and it took all of his strength to hold fear at a distance. And all of his courage.

The Wolfer band began what seemed almost a dance, as the flames consumed the house. The smells of burning flesh — manflesh and animal — mingled with the smells of burning wood and cloth and grains. One man beat at the barrel of wine with his sword, in a rhythm like marching feet. The others formed two groups, facing one another. They were miming some action, Oriel thought, as he watched the story.

The smaller group, led by Rulgh, rushed at the larger, who held their arms out at an angle, as if they were straight sticks or a line of spears. Rulgh yelled something at those straight-armed men. Oriel heard a single word, *fruhckman*, repeated over and over among Rulgh's words. Rulgh's followers, in the miming that moved back and forward like a dance with swords, echoed this word. The encircled men didn't step out of their formation and didn't respond.

One of Rulgh's band rushed forward, leaped up — as if overleaping a wall — then fell back to lie motionless on his back. Another followed him.

Oriel understood now, he hoped: They were telling the story of the battle. He also understood that the city had stood firm, and held its walls. Even though the Wolfers told the story to honor themselves, and their dead, it was clear that Selby had defended itself. He was glad of that, for the Saltweller and his daughter, and the land itself. He had no hope for himself, or Griff.

"*Fruhckman*," Rulgh sang out, like a final curse to the straight-armed men as the reenactment ended and he left the scene, alone. The flames roared as the fire ate its way up the wooden walls and into the roof beams of the Saltweller's house. The drumming ceased. The play was over. The silent Wolfers all watched the flames, as if Oriel and Griff were invisible. Then they went to their meal.

Oriel and Griff stood wordless. They watched the Wolfers eat, and drink. They listened to their voices. Oriel and Griff stood motionless, sweating with the heat of the fire, coughing with the smoke. Behind them, night darkened the sky. The Wolfers ate, and drank, and when they were finished they gathered up whatever meat was left and threw it onto the burning house. They heaved the barrel and whatever wine it still held into the flames.

Oriel knew it would be of no use to ask for food or drink. He didn't know what purpose his life offered the Wolfers, but he had no doubt they had some use for him. He thought they might sleep then but, in spite of the dark, the Wolfers moved on, and Oriel and Griff were led off, away from the Saltweller's house, inland.

Every step was pain, so much pain to his head that he didn't even feel the sharp sticks and stones that cut into his bare feet. They stumbled but they didn't cry out, he and Griff. If they seemed to be slacking or slowing, a sharp jab in the back from the sword of the Wolfer who walked behind sped them on. At last, when it seemed that morning was so long overdue that a man might think she had turned her back on the world forever, the band arrived at a meadow where bonfires burned, and many Wolfers were gathered. Shapes on the ground near other Wolfer bands were, Oriel assumed, other captives. He heard moaning and complaining in a language he recognized. His head pounded so badly that he could barely see, even in the dim light. His back stung from the pricks of the sword that had cut into his flesh. His legs shook with tiredness. But he stood.

Griff shivered beside him. When Rulgh came by and said something, Oriel just stared at his captor. He was relieved when the Wolfer lifted up a hand to clout him on the shoulder and knock him to his knees — this was permission to rest.

He barely had time to fall into exhausted sleep before he was shaken awake under a morning sky. A man was talking to him, someone he knew slightly, one of the fishermen, a quarrelsome man, swift on his feet and brave in attack, a man quick to see an advantage and take it. The man had crawled over to Oriel.

"You fool," Oriel greeted him.

"What are they going to do with us?" he asked. "I've a wife, and a child on the way, I've family will ransom me. Can you talk with them?" His voice was high.

"Don't talk," Oriel said. His head was bad, but not as bad as yesterday. The throbbing was like a knife, cutting into his eyes, but no worse than that. He couldn't find this man's name in his head.

"You've got to do something," the man said. "What are you going to do, Oriel? I tried to get to the boats, I tried."

Simson, the man's name was Simson.

"How far are we from the river?"

"Fool," Oriel said again, seeing the dark shape of Rulgh rise up behind the man.

Rulgh pulled Simson back by the hair. There was nothing Oriel could do. He couldn't understand what the Wolfers were saying, and Simson made things worse by pleading, "Don't hurt me, please, don't kill me," over and over. One Wolfer took out a short sword and put it across Simson's throat, two held Simson down on his knees. Simson protested, "I've never hurt you!" and wept, and called over to Oriel that he was worth a good ransom. "Ransom, coins in plenty!" Simson cried out to the man holding the sword, and then twisted his head to cry up to Rulgh, who held him firm, "Ransom, in sovereigns and truemen, and necklaces and rings, I have friends, Selby will — You have to understand — "

Rulgh spoke a word and the sword cut across Simson's throat, cutting off his voice. Blood spurted, poured.

Oriel sat silent.

The Wolfer with the sword, bloody now, said something to Rulgh, and they both laughed.

Rulgh looked at Oriel over Simson's body. "*Fruhckman*," he said, and sounded disgusted.

Oriel knew what that word meant, now. *Coward*. It was the first word of the Wolfer's language Oriel learned, and he learned at the same time that among the Wolfers, cowardice was a quick way to death.

CHAPTER
16

There were several bands of Wolfers, each under its own Captain, that gathered together. The Wolfer bands had come down upon Selby from different directions, Oriel guessed, and now the Captains talked, scratching with sticks on the bare ground. If success was counted in surviving warriors, Rulgh's band was the least successful, by far. If it was counted in the number of captives, also, Rulgh had made a poor showing in the raid. But if it was counted in booty, Oriel thought there would be none to match Rulgh's handful of coins. When the Captains finished their conference the bands traveled on separately.

Rulgh led his men on for a day and the better part of a night. The captives weren't fed, weren't given drink, weren't allowed to speak. Oriel's legs and feet felt like blocks of ice, or stone, and they moved only by blind habit, not by any choice or strength of his own. His head — his head ached, and throbbed, until he thought it would be a comfort to die and lie painless on the ground.

He could do little more than force himself to continue breathing. He didn't know why he should take the next breath, take the next step, keep up with the band of Wolfers as they moved through trees, up hillsides, across streams and never even bent down to take just a mouthful of cool water.

Oriel could almost taste how it would feel to have his mouth full of cool water.

When the band finally stopped moving, it was still the dark of night. Oriel and Griff were shoved down onto their knees. Hands pushed their faces into dark water, and held them there. Oriel gulped water down, then raised his head. "Not the sea," he said to Griff, who lay on the grass beside him. "Do you think we're back by the river?"

If it was the river, they might wade into it, and float downstream. He knew he didn't have the strength to swim but he thought he might be able to stay afloat.

Griff shook his head. "Don't know," he said. Griff's face was a patchwork of shadows. Oriel didn't know that face.

"Why are we the ones drinking?" Oriel asked Griff, and he was pulled up, back from the water. He was hoisted up onto his feet, to face Rulgh.

By words which Oriel couldn't understand and an

openmouthed gesture that he could, Rulgh asked if the water was safe to drink.

Oriel ran his tongue around his lips and said, "Mmmnnn. Good," he added.

Rulgh peered into his face and then looked down to where Griff lay, still drinking, his face still in the water. *"Googht?"*

"Is so," Oriel said.

Rulgh spoke to his men, and then spoke to Oriel that same incomprehensible phrase he had used the night before, before he had knocked Oriel down. Oriel didn't understand the phrase and lacked the means to ask. Rulgh hit him, this time more gently than before, but hard enough to knock his legs out from under him, and knock his head against the grassy ground as he fell onto it. The phrase, Oriel thought, shoving himself wormlike back towards the water, to drink again, must be the Wolfer word for *Do have a seat*, or *Why don't you rest?* He filled his mouth and his belly with cool water, and then he and Griff crawled into the grass to sleep.

They were strong, these Wolfers, he thought the next morning. His head continued to feel clearer and less painful. The sun didn't hurt his eyes. Griff slept, and Oriel pretended to be asleep. The Wolfers were content to leave them so, for the time.

Oriel was strong, but nowhere near the Wolfers' strength. He and Griff stumbled behind the band that day, driven from the rear by whichever of Rulgh's men had the job of keeping the captives moving. The pace was somewhere between a walk and a run — hard and unceasing. He could hear Griff gasping for breath, even over his own labored breathing, long before the Wolfers took one of their brief rests. He no longer knew how long he had been moving, or in what direction — whether it had

215

been a journey of days, or of a single morning, whether towards the sun or away from it. Oriel was lost.

So even if he had found himself unexpectedly free, he would have had no idea which way the sea lay. He couldn't have found the sea again.

They carried no food, these Wolfers. They carried nothing but their weapons and whatever booty they had seized. They didn't seem to need food — Unless, Oriel thought, as Rulgh gave him permission to lie down at the end of another day, the journey had been only one day and not — as he thought — many. He didn't know how he had managed the days. How did men stand such things? he would have inquired of Griff, but they were both already asleep.

They were beside another body of water when he awoke. But perhaps, he thought, lying still, feigning sleep, he had dreamed the time between. His hunger was real enough, and he wondered if the Wolfers knew how to catch fish. It was a grey day, with rain near enough to smell. He woke Griff and they stood up together.

"Weak," Griff said, and sounded it.

"Don't let it show," Oriel advised.

Rulgh rose from the fire and came towards them. Oriel's head was clear, despite hunger, and he could see that Rulgh was a man with the marks of years on him. Not that he was so old a man, just that the years had treated him harshly.

Oriel lifted his bound hands to his mouth and mimed chewing. Rulgh shrugged, shook his head, and held out empty hands. Oriel said, "Fish. In water?" and indicated the water, which was not the sea and not a river.

"*Lackh*," Rulgh said.

"Fish in *lackh?*" Oriel asked, his hands together miming the swimming motion of a fish, the sounds of the Wolfers' language clumsy in his throat.

Rulgh let him know how difficult fish were to catch.

Oriel let Rulgh know that he and Griff could catch fish, with just their hands, but better with spears. He didn't think the idea of a net would be familiar to the Wolfers.

Hungry men would always fight more desperately, Oriel realized. Perhaps there was some wisdom to the Wolfers' way. For men who wandered the countryside, destroying and looting, what need was there of the skills of fishing, hunting, gathering? Oriel wondered where the Wolfers wintered, and if they had wives, children. He wondered if there was a chief over all the Wolfer bands. He determined, if he lived, to learn enough of the language so that Rulgh could tell him these things.

It was little enough to desire, just the knowledge of a language.

If he lived, he repeated the thought.

"Griff and Oriel catch fish?" he asked Rulgh. He mimed eating, as if he were tearing the flesh off the springy bones of fish. Rulgh gave permission, "Is so."

Oriel held up his hands. Rulgh cut the leather thongs, first Oriel's, then Griff's.

Without boats, without a net, with only their bare hands and sticks scraped to points with sharp stones, it took a long time to catch enough to feed the seven Wolfers. The band waited until there was enough to feed all of them before any one man cooked himself a fish. The strength a bellyful of water had given Oriel and Griff was gone, and they were sitting back

217

from the fire and the eating men to gain whatever good the rest would give them, when one of the Wolfers came towards them. Rulgh, it was, and Oriel climbed painfully to his feet, and Griff got up more slowly beside him. Rulgh handed Oriel a fish — still warm from the fire, its skin crisped. Oriel inhaled the aroma of cooked fish, and handed it to Griff.

Rulgh took it away from Griff — who was too wise and weak to protest — and returned it to Oriel.

Oriel gave it to Griff. He held out his hands to ask for another. Rulgh shook his head, and held out empty hands.

"That's the last," Oriel interpreted.

Griff peeled some flesh off one side and passed the fish to Oriel, who peeled off some meat and jammed it into his mouth. He almost spat it out, it was so strongly flavored. He almost couldn't swallow, he was so hungry.

Rulgh watched them.

"Small bites," Oriel advised Griff, who nodded.

Rulgh stayed watching until they had picked the bones clean. It didn't take long. He said something that Oriel didn't understand and walked back to join his men. Oriel and Griff went to the edge of the *lackh* to drink again, and sat beside the still water, away from the Wolfers. "We can talk," Oriel said. "I think it's permitted, for now. Has it been days?"

"I don't know. I have a beard started. How long — ?"

"Until we die," Oriel said.

Neither spoke for a long time.

"Unless we escape," Oriel said.

Behind them the Wolfers were getting up, gathering together their packs.

"Do you see any way to escape?" Griff asked.

Oriel shook his head. "We should have all three run together," he said, bitterness on his tongue.

"Then Tamara wouldn't have gotten away," Griff pointed out.

"You still would say she was worth it?" Oriel asked, surprised.

"Of course."

There was no point in arguing since there was no way Oriel could undo the choice he had made. He wondered if, knowing what he now knew, he would make the choice differently. If he hadn't ordered Tamara to run, if he and Griff had also run and she the slowest — Capturing Tamara would have slowed the Wolfers down enough so that he and Griff could have escaped, at least to swim to the deep, safe center of the river. It surprised him that Griff saw the event so differently from the way he saw it. He had never thought that Griff might see things differently.

"You chose right," Griff said.

Oriel shrugged. "If I had chosen to run away, you would have come with me?" he asked.

"Of course," Griff said. "But it wouldn't have been the better choice. She couldn't fight them as we did, to delay them as long as we did. So Tamara carried the alarm to Selby and Selby is safe, and only a few people — we two among them — are taken. A better choice," Griff said again.

Oriel didn't disagree, partly because he discovered that he desired Griff's good opinion, and hoped to keep it. The other reason was that they were called to the day's march at that time. Before he was lost to all sense except for the pounding of his heart and jerking his bare back away from the pronging sword behind him, Oriel thought about Griff.

Griff was like his own hand — and when Griff disagreed with him, Oriel felt as if his own hand, even while it obeyed his wishes, had desires of its own, or ideas of its own. It was like watching his own hand walk away free, on its five fingers, and knowing that he had kept it bound to his wrist to serve his own convenience.

That was no way to treat his own hand, he thought. He thought also, That was no way to get the best service out of his hand.

He had used Griff ill.

But he had saved Griff, too.

Midday brought them to a farmhouse high on a rocky hillside. More hills rose ahead of them, some entirely bare, others raggedly overgrown. The Wolfers left Oriel and Griff in a gully, bound now with thongs at the ankles as well as wrists, and gagged. Oriel was so exhausted and thirsty that the cries of the human and animal inhabitants of the farm barely entered his ears. He could think of nothing beyond his own belly and sleep-seduced brain. As he slept, the sounds of the Wolfers' attack disturbed him no more than a bad dream.

The sight of the bodies disturbed him, however, and he had to draw ice like a blanket up and around his own body, pull it down over his eyes. Griff gasped for air, and gulped, moaned as if the pain had been his own, and asked, "Oriel?"

Their guard watched, enjoying their fear. Oriel saw his wolfish face as if through thick ice.

Inside the farmhouse the seven Wolfers had spread out around the main room. The smell of ale was in the air, and the smell of meat roasting over the fire. A boy of about ten summers was tied up beside the doorway and two women served the men — the housewife and her serving woman, their dark hair hanging loose, as if the head kerchiefs had been ripped off, their dark eyes wide with fear, tears staining their cheeks. The housewife, her skirt of a finer fabric, her apron not so stained with labors, moaned and mumbled to herself as she turned the meat on the spit. The first glints of madness shone out of her eyes. The serving woman was made of sterner material and had had, Oriel guessed, no children. He thought he knew what the women's fate would be, and he became a man of ice.

The gags were removed, and Rulgh brought Oriel a chunk of bread, a chunk of meat. Oriel took a bite of the meat — roasted goat, rich and pungent in flavor, it filled his body with strength — and passed it over to Griff's bound hands.

Rulgh snorted, amused. He stood over them, to watch the comedy.

Oriel took a bite out of the bread, and passed it to Griff. Griff had taken a bite of the meat and was chewing it. He passed the meat back to Oriel. One bite at a time, each in his turn, they ate, and Rulgh watched them, amused. "*Tewkeman*," he said. Oriel thought he knew what the word meant. He was beginning to understand these Wolfers, and their language. They were cruel and strong, fearless as animals. They took women and food wherever they found them, but carried no supplies and left — as Oriel guessed — no creature living where they passed. Somewhere in the night the door burst open and a man stood there just long enough to hear his son cry out "Father!" in relief and hope and terror, before the Wolfer sword gutted him. Oriel and Griff were given the job of taking the father's body out to the pile, which with their bound hands was a hard task.

The housewife had kept hidden among her linens a golden brooch, which Rulgh held in his hand when he spoke to Oriel in the morning. The farmhouse burned behind him. "Gold," Oriel told the man. Rulgh took from the purse at his waist the coins he'd taken from Oriel and asked, "Gold?"

While Rulgh kept Oriel, Griff dragged the bodies into the burning house. Oriel concentrated on Rulgh's lined face, and concentrated on keeping his own face icy smooth, icy cold. Rulgh asked, with words and gestures, where the gold came from. Oriel answered, drawing with a stick in the dirt, what he knew: There were gold mines, in the hills behind Celindon.

"Celindon?" Rulgh repeated.

Oriel drew a city on a peninsula, and put in the two rings of walls. Rulgh recognized that. He made signs that Oriel understood to mean soldiers, and battles. Rulgh raised his right hand, with his forefinger and the little finger both extended, while his thumb held his two middle fingers in against his palm. In that gesture, Rulgh's hand resembled the head of a horned animal. Oriel understood — this was the sign to mark, and to ward off, dangers.

"Gold mines," he said, copying at the same time — as best he could with bound hands — Rulgh's gesture of danger.

"Is not so," Rulgh said.

"Aye, is so," Oriel said. "Soldiers," he pointed at Rulgh's scratchings, "guard mines. Slaves," he indicated his neck, where the band that marked a slave was worn, "work mines, carry," he mimed hands full, "gold out. Brand," he said, and sketched a long curved line, like a crescent moon, on his own cheek, the mark with which the slaves of the mines were identified.

"Brand," Rulgh said, and pushed up his shirt to show a white and puckered patch of flesh on his arm.

"Yes," Oriel agreed, "fire makes brand." Behind them Griff heaved something heavy through the farmhouse door.

Rulgh went away and Oriel turned to help Griff, but later in the day — when the Wolfers were exhausted with drinking and eating — the Captain returned. Oriel sat with Griff, who hadn't spoken a word all day. Griff kept silent and as if mindless. The boy was with them, weeping and complaining and mourning. Oriel was not concerned about the boy — except to silence him when possible. He was concerned about Griff. Griff would not know how to turn himself to ice.

Rulgh returned to say — if Oriel understood him — that the Wolfers wanted to attack the mines and take gold.

Oriel advised against the attack. He made the sign for danger. "Many soldiers. Few Wolfers. Steal," he said, "be thieves." He mimed stealing a purse from his own waist, while he looked the other way.

"Wolfers not stealers," Rulgh said. "Wolfers fight."

"Wolfers fools," Oriel said, impatient, and too worried about Griff to guard his words.

"Fools?" Rulgh asked.

Having risked the remark, Oriel risked the answer. He didn't have any hope, and he didn't care all that much anymore. He thought he understood more of the Wolfer tongue with every day that passed, but he wasn't sure of the words. "Fool," he said, "*tewkeman*."

Rulgh's light blue eyes glared at him, like sun off ice, briefly, before Rulgh showed his teeth in a smile. "Is not so, Oriel," he said, and then got up to fetch Oriel more meat and bread, and a bowl of ale. "That man fool," Rulgh said, pointing at the boy.

"What about me? why don't you give me any food?" the boy asked Rulgh. "I'm hungry, Oriel, will you give me — why doesn't he give me any?"

"You man fool," Rulgh said when Oriel pulled at Griff's naked arm, trying to rouse Griff from his stupor to eat. *"Tewkeman."* Oriel ignored Rulgh.

"Mines?" Rulgh asked the boy.

The boy turned to Oriel. "What is he saying? What does he want? What's he going to do?"

"Do you know where the gold mines are? near Celindon?"

"Not really," the boy said. "I've heard stories, but like the Kingdom, it's only stories. I've never been — "

"King-dom?" Rulgh asked.

"Stories," Oriel said. Rulgh didn't understand. Rather than give the Wolfer occasion to be angry, Oriel said, "Away north," with a wide gesture of his arm. "Over mountains."

"Ah," and comprehension shone out of Rulgh's eyes. He said a word Oriel didn't know, but assumed meant Kingdom, and then repeated "Kingdom. You see?" he asked, pointing to his eyes, a mocking smile now on his mouth.

"No," Oriel said. "Stories," he said, and waggled his fingers in front of his mouth, to show words, only words. This Rulgh understood. *"Brautel,"* he said, waggling his fingers by his mouth. "Not so."

Then he turned back to the boy. "Mines?" asked again. The boy shrank back, and only stopped himself from weeping because he was more afraid than miserable. "Gold? Mines?" Rulgh demanded.

"Say yes," Oriel advised the boy.

"But — "

"Say yes and try to lead him there. He'll kill you if you get it wrong, but I think he'll kill you anyway so you might as well give yourself a chance."

"Yes!" the boy cried. "But I have to eat first."

Oriel put that into what he thought was Wolfer words, and Rulgh understood. One of the other Wolfers brought the boy food. After they had eaten, the seven Wolfers and their three captives rose, and walked away up the stony hill. They left behind them the smoking ruins of a farmhouse, inhabited after them only by the dead.

CHAPTER
17

The heat of fires, the heat of blood, the heat of fear and fighting — Oriel never remembered how many farms they had taken on their way to the gold mines. He was a man of ice, against the heat.

Griff moved beside him like an animal sickening to its death. Half of the time when his glance fell on Oriel, bound nearby, it was as if he had never seen Oriel before.

The boy clung close to Oriel, when Rulgh did not have him at the head of the band of Wolfers, leading them back southward and seaward. Oriel never asked the boy's name.

Warm sunlight, warm rain — it was not always easy to be cold as ice, cruel as ice, in every thought and desire. Always before, Oriel realized, there had been a prize for the winning. The Damall's island, the Saltweller's lands: Those were what he had desired and won, before. Now the prize was life. To live through the day was his highest hope.

What Rulgh must not know was how closely Oriel's strength was bound to Griff's needs. For that reason, Oriel shared what food he was given equally between the nameless boy and Griff. All three shared equally the little they were given, except that Griff ate less than either of the others.

When Rulgh searched Oriel's face, as if to know what was in his mind and heart, Oriel thought if it weren't for Griff he might become a Wolfer. Only Griff held Oriel to the life he had known, and Oriel was not always glad of that. He could become, he thought, a Captain of a Wolfer band, aye, and even one of the foremost Captains, were it not for Griff.

The morning they arrived at the mines, sounds gave them warning that the mining camp lay ahead. The Wolfer band, and its three captives, crept up unobserved, sheltering behind boulders.

There were twenty or more soldiers visible, but only six of the slaves, with iron collars around their necks and red crescents on their cheeks. There were hobbled donkeys and a wagon piled with chunky stones. A yellow flag flying over the doorway into the hillside told Oriel these were Karle's men, and the path that disappeared into the darkness within the hill led to Karle's gold.

Some of the soldiers were gathered into groups, gambling for coins on the fall of the bones, while awaiting their meal, a spitted animal that rotated over the flames as a slave turned the handle of the spit. All the soldiers were armed, but none were wary.

Why should they be armed? Oriel wondered, and then he wondered if — if he were to betray the Wolfers' presence by a warning shout, and were the Wolfers to fail to kill him, and were he to survive the battle that would follow — he wondered if he would thereby gain for himself any fate other than to become one of these slaves. Their beards were ragged, around the scarred cheeks. They moved slowly, as if weak and stupid, like men accustomed to slavery.

Oriel thought that such slavery must be his lot, should he betray his captors.

Because Griff, Oriel thought, would not last a day in the mines. He himself, Oriel thought, would last for several seasons. Whose would be the worse fate he couldn't have said.

The sky overhead was cloudy, under a growing wind. The wind picked up dry earth and blew it in gusts, in circling whirlpools. Even the sound of wind favored the Wolfers. Oriel waited to hear what plan of attack Rulgh would devise. The opening to the mine shaft was a little ways up the hill; if the guards could gain it, like a small doorway it would be an impregnable position. If it were his battle, Oriel would lure the soldiers away from the mine, down into the gully. The armor plates the guards wore would be heavy to carry, so Oriel would tell his men to attack, then seem to retreat in disorder into the hills and then, when the enemy had carried his heavy armor up and down a few hillsides, turn to fight. The difference in numbers — more than three soldiers to each Wolfer — put the Wolfers at great risk.

The risk was so great that Oriel would choose to arm his captives, if he were a Wolfer.

All of these thoughts passed through Oriel's mind in the time it took Rulgh to gather his men around him, and talk urgently to them. At the end of Rulgh's speech, the Wolfers unsheathed their swords and raised them up into the air.

"No," Oriel said, keeping his voice as quiet as the looming danger permitted. "Rulgh, don't — "

The Wolfers shouted out a great shout, and then another.

Rulgh looked at Oriel.

"Fool," Oriel said.

"*Fruhckman*," Rulgh said, cold-eyed.

Oriel, as cold-eyed as his captor, drew himself up tall. "Not so," he said, and turned his back.

The Wolfers shouted again and again, as if each shout made them braver, stronger, more ready for battle.

Above the Wolfers' shouts, a horn sounded.

The Wolfers, in a line of seven, scrambled up the hillside to meet the enemy. At the top of the hill they ranged themselves in a line of seven, howling now. Oriel left Griff behind a boulder with the boy and crept up to watch.

The soldiers had drawn back to the mine door and stood ready, behind a barrier of slaves. The slaves knelt, making a wall three kneeling bodies deep in front of their masters. Their hands were manacled, their necks circled with iron; they had no weapons, no defenses.

It was only a brief battle — the Wolfers bloodied their swords on the slaves, giving the soldiers time to reach across the human wall with their spears and longswords. Oriel could see immediately that it was hopeless —

But he admired the blind courage of the Wolfers. He watched one man, his sword hand sliced off, held by the beard while an armored soldier drove a sword into his belly and pulled it up towards his heart: The Wolfer showed no fear, not before pain, not before death, not before his enemy.

The Wolfers were doomed. Oriel turned around, to flee with Griff and if their strength held, and they had any luck, they might make it back to Selby —

Once again the sound of a horn cut through the noisy air. This horn sounded from a distance, and distracted the guards. There was the sound of marching feet, there was a distant calling of voices, there was a cry come up among the soldiers at the mines, "Form up. It's Phillipe's army. Never mind these — " There were the cries of the wounded, and moans, and the sound of the wind. "Get the wagon inside. You, man, pile the bodies here — you heard me, let the dead take the blows for us."

Rulgh and two of the Wolfers came away on their own feet, and they supported another man whose blood poured down over his face. The soldiers didn't even watch their flight.

Horsemen in armor, two carrying red guidons, rode up onto a hill facing the Wolfers, and stopped there. Behind them the tips of spears carried by marching men became visible.

"Surrender, we would be fools not to surrender!" some of the soldiers at the mines cried loudly, making the argument. "We'll be slaughtered where we stand. There are a hundred of them for sure."

"But where is Karle's army? Sound the horn again!" another soldier answered. "He swore to protect us. He swore — "

Oriel advised Rulgh: "Go now, if you would live." He made the sign for danger, then pointed to the mine entrance. He pointed urgently in the opposite direction.

Rulgh reached down and hauled Griff to his feet, then hauled the cringing boy up. The boy struggled, and pulled back, and cried out shrilly. Rulgh roared at him, then ran him through with a sword, then shrugged him off the blade as if he were a loaf of bread. Oriel took the warning and pushed at Griff's back. "Go, Griff, where he leads."

Griff's blank face showed no response.

Oriel shoved at Griff's shoulders, as hard as he could. "Go now. Follow me. You must."

Griff obeyed him.

Oriel couldn't remember — when — in what direction Rulgh led them. He couldn't —

The Wolfers ran steadily, even burdened as they were by the injured man. The injured man had received no attention to his wound, but still he forced his feet to rise, and fall, in the slow unvarying pace Rulgh set, and maintained.

Griff stumbled, and when he did Oriel punched him hard between the shoulder blades. Griff's bare back was swollen with red cuts and scratches, and if he had had the strength Oriel would have been sorry to have hit him so roughly on his back.

The line of men moved up hillsides and tumbled clumsily down them. It snaked among trees and around boulders. It splashed across streams without ever bending to refresh its mouth with water.

It was hard to run like that with hands bound in front of him, Oriel noted. It would be hard, also, to run like that supporting a man who could not count on his own strength. But the Wolfers made no complaint.

Sometime in the darkness Rulgh stopped. With

groans of relief they all collapsed where they were. The night air was mild. A pale golden glowing in the sky showed where the moon hid behind clouds. They were among trees.

If he had had to run, even walk, for another day, without any rest, Oriel knew —

The Wolfers could have done it. They were not weak as other men were weak. They needed little to eat and drink, needed little rest, less than others. That was their secret strength; and Oriel thought that somehow, in the northern lands where they came from, their fathers must long ago have taken wolf-women as wives, to breed such sons.

Oriel, his legs collapsed beneath him, slept suddenly.

Rulgh's cold eyes looked into Oriel's face, and Rulgh's hand slapped Oriel. Once, across the side of the head, and Oriel's ears rang like bells. Again, on the other side.

Oriel would show no feeling. His head cleared.

"Go," Rulgh said. "Bring," he pointed down at Griff, who still slept, where he had fallen in the night.

Oriel could never remember much of the first day, anything of the second night, the second morning — Morning and afternoon and night all blended together — he thought he must have been asleep, but he knew he had been awake, and moving.

When the sun was high in an empty sky the band rounded a hill and looked down onto a solitary farmstead. A wooden-sided house, a lean-to beside it, garden behind and fenced yard, and human figures in the garden bent over, working at the soil. Behind, a forested line of hills rose. Beyond that, at the distant edge of the world, a jagged line of white clouds lay along the horizon.

Rulgh approached Oriel, where he leaned against a tree trunk. "Oriel. Come. After."

Oriel nodded, to show he understood.

"Bring Jorg."

By the time Oriel realized that Jorg was the wounded man's name, the three Wolfers were bounding down the hillside, their voices raised in a howl, or shout, in a sound that made the hair on Oriel's neck stand up. Their swords were out for the attack. Oriel could have attacked with them. He could have found the strength.

It wasn't long at all before a Wolfer called up, and waved. Oriel and Griff, with Jorg between them, took a slanted easy path down the hill to the garden. The woman was on her knees, weeping, with two little children hiding in her skirts. Her belly was swollen out with a third child. Her hair, and that of the two children, was black as a moonless night, softly black like night clouds. The woman's hair, neither bound nor combed, flowed over her bent shoulders like a nighttime river.

Rulgh reached down to lift a lock of her hair from her shoulder, and to rub it gently in his fingers, as if it were a cloth of wonderful weaving.

The woman looked up at Oriel, and at Griff. Her mouth was slack with fear and trickled blood. "Help us," she asked. "Help me. These children, my children — "

Oriel had seen too many women, heard too many women's cries, to feel anything. Still, a sickness gripped his belly.

Watching his face, the woman ceased her weeping. "How can I save their lives?" she asked, almost in a whisper.

"There is no way," Oriel answered her. "Nor your own," he said, although she hadn't asked that.

233

She nodded, and rose up, gathering her children under her arms. "Then tell me this: How can I ask him to kill us quickly, and at once?"

Oriel had thought he was beyond where pain could touch him. "There is no way," he said again, and in anger. He turned to Rulgh, speaking in the simple language they had developed between the two of them. "*Fruhckman*, to kill children. *Fruhckman*, a woman — aye, and so great with child — "

Rulgh's face grew red. "Not so. Is not so."

Oriel looked into his captor's eyes briefly, then turned his head to spit onto the ground. Rulgh would know his meaning. Oriel hoped only that, in the slaughter that would follow, he would be the first on Rulgh's sword.

"Aye," Griff's ragged voice came from Oriel's shoulder. Griff hadn't spoken in days. "Is so," he said now.

Rulgh raised his sword over his head and howled, like a wolf. At the sound, the children whimpered into their mother's skirt, and one of the Wolfers moved to pull a child loose, but Griff let Jorg fall to the ground so that he could stand between the man and his prey.

"Not so. Rulgh not so, not *fruhckman*," Rulgh cried aloud, telling the news to the empty sky. "Feed us," he said to the woman.

She was afraid again. She looked to Oriel. "Tell him, can you tell him? The armies have destroyed the good of this farm."

"Are you alone?" Oriel asked her.

"My husband went to battle — for the silver piece they give to every man who joins an army."

"Which army?"

She shook her head. It made no difference to her,

which banner he fought under. "He gave me the coin, but I buried it. Should — ?"

Oriel shook his head quickly. "Don't — "

She understood him without explanation. "My man will be dead by now, I think. And I will be glad to join him. But for the children, here, I'd — "

"Can you feed us?"

"Poorly."

"Do so. Can you wash this man's wound?"

She shrugged. "Why should I?"

"For your children's lives, as may be," Oriel said.

"You said there was no way."

Oriel shrugged, and wondered at her stubbornness to have no hope. "Perhaps even among the Wolfers there is."

Rulgh had hovered impatiently over the talk. "What?" he demanded now. "What?"

"Woman will feed you," Oriel answered him.

Rulgh glared at him but did not ask why it took so many words to say so little.

The Wolfers gave Jorg the straw mattress and then dropped to the floor. Even the Wolfers were tired out. They talked among themselves in low voices.

The farmwife made a pot of watery turnip and parsnip soup, and brought out half a round of bread. Oriel kept close, should she need an extra hand as she served the Wolfers. Griff stayed outside with the children, who seemed to recognize him as one who would not push them away.

From what Oriel could understand, there were two things bothering the Wolfers. First, their dead. He couldn't tell if it was the loss of the men or if it was that they had been abandoned at the site of the battle. Then, second, something about gold troubled them. *Malke*, that was a word they kept using

235

next to the word for gold. It was Malke that really worried them.

The next day found the Wolfers rested and ready to go on. Jorg, however, couldn't leave his bed. The farmwife fed him water from the stream, and cooled his face with damp cloths. They would stay, Rulgh said, until they knew Jorg's fate. Meanwhile, their eyes often went to the wife, and Rulgh's hands often went to her mass of black hair, but he forbade any man to take her for his desire.

On the second day, while Jorg sweated and mumbled on the bed, Rulgh sent his two men off to the west, to search for game or food, and himself took Oriel into the hills east of the farmstead. They soon found, and ran down, a goat that had either been turned loose to wander in the woods, or had escaped into the woods. But the point of the hunt was for Rulgh to take Oriel's opinion of how the Wolfers might get the gold they had failed to win in battle.

Oriel tried to explain to Rulgh how he might have fought the battle at the mines. Rulgh asked Oriel what the chances of a second attack might be and wasn't angered when Oriel said it would undoubtedly fail. "Go like a thief," Oriel advised again.

Rulgh was reluctant. Wolfers were bold. Wolfers weren't like foxes, to steal in and steal out in the secret parts of night. Wolfers were warriors.

Oriel shrugged, and turned away from his captor.

Rulgh asked if one of his Wolfers, or he himself, could disguise himself as a slave, and betray the mines from within.

Oriel asked if the man was ready to be branded with fire, and — should the plan fail — live out his life as a slave in the mines.

Rulgh shook his head. He would not use a Wolfer so.

Oriel shrugged, and turned away.

Rulgh said, they would take Oriel, sell him to the soldiers, let him then betray from within.

Oriel knew who he would betray.

Rulgh watched his face and said, No, they would take Griff, sell Griff.

Oriel hid his feelings.

Rulgh watched Oriel's face and said that Oriel would stay with the woman and Jorg and children. When Rulgh returned with the gold, then they would deliver the year's booty to Malke.

"Malke?" Oriel asked.

"King," Rulgh answered. He waved his hand in the direction of the white-clouded horizon. "Days away. In city, Malke waits. Wolfers give King," Rulgh held up his two hands, then gathered the fingers of one hand into the opposite hand, "from two, one hand."

Oriel understood now. "Take me to the mines. Not Griff."

"No." Rulgh turned away.

"I am stronger."

Rulgh turned back. "Yes, stronger. Strong to keep here, or Griff — " He made a chopping motion with his hand.

Anger burned at Oriel's belly. "If you harm Griff — if anything — I will have revenge," he told Rulgh.

Rulgh didn't know the word. "Revenge?"

"Aye, revenge." Oriel raised his bound hands to his own throat and drew them across, like a blade. "I am dangerous," he said, and made the sign.

Rulgh laughed out loud.

The three Wolfers, and Griff, left the next morning. After that, Oriel awaited their return day after empty day. He worked the garden and snared rabbits when they had picked clean the goat carcass. Rulgh had untied his hands, knowing that as long as there was a question of Griff's safety Oriel would do Rulgh's will.

When Jorg died, Oriel and the woman carried him to the hillside, and buried him. They left Jorg his clothing, and his boots, too, lest Rulgh should accuse them of robbing the dead Wolfer. The woman thought Oriel should at least trade his trousers for Jorg's heavier pair, but Oriel — mindful of the beryl he wore hidden at his back — refused. Day followed long day, and still the Wolfers, with Griff, did not return.

The woman knew better than to try to escape, or send her children away; for Oriel must stop her. But he promised her, "If they return and all is well, if you can stay behind when we go north, then take your silver coin and go south. Go to Selby, on the coast," he told her. "Find the Saltweller. Ask for help from his daughter, Tamara. Tell Tamara, it is Oriel who sends you, and Griff."

"Griff with his sad eyes," the woman said. "You, Oriel, who seem kind but you are cruel. Which of you was this girl's sweetheart?"

Oriel had no time for such questions. "Can you find your way to the sea?" he asked the woman.

"I can try. For the children." She turned away, to return to the garden, where the weeds grew abundantly. Her great belly went before her like a sail filled with wind.

"He has spared you," Oriel reminded her.

"I understand," she said, her back to him. "I would be a fool not to be grateful. Or to you, also."

"It would be dangerous to be grateful to me," Oriel said. He looked away to the south, where long days ago the Wolfers, and Griff, had disappeared into the trees. He looked away to the north, where those clouds lay — as always — along the horizon. "Those clouds, do they never move closer? Do they never bring rain?"

"Those are the mountains, not clouds. Farther away than even the Wolfers' realm, they say, and impassable. The mountains are covered in snow all the year round, so high are they, if you can believe the stories. If you can believe the stories, a man who crosses the mountains, and lives, will find himself in a land where the soil is rich and the law is strong, under one King, and the people prosper, for they work year after year in peace."

"I've heard of a Kingdom," Oriel said.

"Aye, there are always tales," she said.

The thick long arms of the onions waved in their rows in the garden before the Wolfers, and Griff, returned. Four had gone and four returned, one bent over with the weight of the sack he carried on his back, and the other three walking upright.

Rulgh made his proud greeting to Oriel. "We are stealers, and have gold. We have no men dead. Malke not complain of Rulgh, not with much gold. Now we eat."

Griff twisted his shoulder to let the heavy bag roll off, and Oriel turned him around. Griff's back was crisscrossed with scars. The crescent on his cheek Oriel had been ready for, but these puckered lines — as if he had been whipped until the skin began to peel away from the meat beneath. "What is this, Griff?" he asked.

Griff shook his head.

"No, tell me," Oriel said.

Griff wouldn't speak.

"If slave," Rulgh explained, still smiling. "A slave is whipped."

"The soldiers whipped you? Why?" Oriel asked.

"It doesn't matter," Griff said. Griff moved now like a man who knows his own strength and knows his own strength is enough. His eyes, as the woman said, were sad, a dark sad brown.

"Not soldiers. Wolfers. I," Rulgh said. His eyes were bright with his own cleverness. "To make soldiers *tewkemans*. To believe Griff slave. Slave run away from master."

Oriel was a man of ice, burning cold. "I warned you," he said.

Rulgh ignored him. Rulgh didn't even dismiss Oriel, he just ignored him. It was all Oriel could do to keep his heart and eyes icy cold because he couldn't even make good his own word.

Rulgh had taken from Oriel even the power to keep his own word. He had whipped Griff hard enough to leave ruts in Griff's back, and counted himself clever to do that. There was another reason why Rulgh had whipped Griff; he wanted Oriel to know that Oriel was powerless.

But Oriel would never accept that knowledge. It was false, and Rulgh was false, and Rulgh would come to understand that.

"It's done now," Griff said. "Finished."

"We eat," Rulgh said, and clapped Oriel on the shoulder in celebration of his victories. "We rest, one day, two, and then go home. Jorg?" Rulgh asked.

"Dead. We buried him," Oriel said. "There," he indicated the forested hillside. Rulgh looked at the trees, then back to the house, and decided to think of his dinner rather than the dead.

Oriel and Griff served the Wolfers stew made of

small animals Oriel had trapped, and bowls of honey mead, mixed with herbs and water. Then he set out food for the woman and Griff and himself. But the woman breathed in gasps, and had no hunger. "It's my time," she said, and she left the room. All through the summer evening they could hear her. The children slept. The Wolfers slept. Oriel and Griff sat close together and the woman moaned rhythmically. "Can we ask them to leave us here?" Griff asked Oriel.

"If Rulgh takes us with him he has booty and captives and gold. My guess is, it's shame to a Captain to lose so many men," Oriel said, "so he has to take us with him."

The woman cried out, from the grassy hillside beyond the garden.

Oriel knew that his face, under the faint moon, must look as pale to Griff as Griff's face did to him. "I know nothing of childbirth," Oriel said, "and she has had two children already."

"Aye," Griff agreed.

They slept, and well, and when they awoke in the morning the woman had finished with her work. She lay in a pool of blood, with a bloody babe in her arms. Her lower lip was ragged, where her teeth had bitten down into it.

Griff spoke. "When they held me down, and branded me, I cried out, Oriel. But," he held up his hand to stop whatever Oriel was going to say, "no more than that. Not with the fear of knowing what was to come, nor with the pain that came after. Only with the pain then — as any man might," Griff said. He bent to pick up the bloody babe. The woman's eyes flew open, alarmed. "I will wash him, as the dams do their kids," Griff said.

When Griff returned with a squalling babe, Oriel

had helped the woman move from the soiled birthing place to a clean, grassy spot. Rulgh came with Griff and the woman took the child to her breast, to hide it from Rulgh's eyes.

"It's born?" Rulgh asked.

"Aye," Oriel said.

Rulgh stared down at the woman's pale face and sweaty hair. He looked at the blood on her hands, as she held the naked babe.

"We leave at sun-high," Rulgh said. "Eat now. She serves us?"

Oriel didn't need to answer.

"Agh, leave her," Rulgh said. "Woman, children, slow Wolfers down. Tell enemies where we are with cryings. We eat now, Oriel. Griff," he said. "Serve us." Anger grew in his voice.

They hurried to obey him.

CHAPTER
18

They journeyed northwards, with Oriel and Griff sharing the burden of gold. Hills led them up to flat high grasslands, beyond which sharper hills rose. Food was scarce, because there were few settlements to raid; but at least Rulgh elected to fight no direct confrontations. It seemed that once he had learned the ease of thieving, he preferred it to the Wolfer way of blade and fist and fire, of arrow, cudgel, dagger, of teeth and fingers if all other weapons failed.

Summer flowed away under their bare feet and left Oriel and Griff trudging the hard ground of fall.

The rain that came down over their bare heads and bare shoulders fell colder and colder. Oriel used his strength to keep moving and had almost none left for speech or thought. He and Griff huddled close together across the nights. The Wolfers had no fire, nor needed any.

One day white specks appeared in the grey air, floating down, dancing on the wind. "Snow," Oriel said.

Beside him, Griff grunted under the weight of his burden. A few pieces of snow rested on his dark brown hair and gleamed, melted, on his shoulder. He asked, "Remember the stars, when we sailed at night?"

Oriel remembered nothing of that sail, except the dangers to which he had sat alert.

"Snow is, like being there, among those stars," Griff said. "This snow."

"I don't remember," Oriel said, with regret.

The air grew grey as sword blades, and tasted metallic. Slowly, the mountains came closer, rising up white into the air. On a clear day the mountain whiteness was enough to set Oriel's heart racing and make him feel, against all reason, hope.

They followed no path, but gradually they were joined by other bands of Wolfers, until they became part of a great army, all with the same destination although each Wolfer band kept itself separated from all the others. They shared neither food, nor fire, nor words.

Over the silence of the moving mass of men, the wind blew.

Oriel and Griff had their hands bound again with leather thongs. Oriel was tied with a leather rope to one of Rulgh's men, and Griff was so bound to another. All captives, Oriel saw, traveled so. His feet were so thickly callused that he could barely feel the cold. His belly was so empty he was almost glad for the numbing icy pain of cold on his naked skin, because it distracted him from the seizing sharp-toothed pain of hunger. When he slept, he dreamed of fires and warm soups.

They climbed hills and saw the mountains still distant, ragged-topped against the sky. The bare trees gave no shelter. The frozen ground gave no comfort. At last, through another sky filled with falling snow, Oriel could see a dark mass, along the rounded top of a hill. The army of Wolfers approached the mass, and Oriel saw that it was a wall, twice Oriel's height, stretching away to two sides. The wall was made out of wooden stakes, bound together with leather straps. The arched double gate was closed.

Rulgh was not surprised to be so welcomed, and neither were any of the other Captains. The Wolfers seemed to have no intention of entering the city behind the gates. Instead, they rested at last, and built campfires out of stacks of wood that waited beneath the walls. Nobody seemed surprised when a line of men, wrapped in fur cloaks, walking on fur boots, emerged from between the gates to hand out furs from the wagon that accompanied them. Meat also came out in wagons, and bread, and a frothing drink.

Stupefied by the warmth of furs and the fullness of his belly, and the blinding drink, Oriel sat dumb beside Griff, both of them shivering themselves back to warmth within furs, and stuffing themselves to nausea. His shoulders and back ached now, and his fingers and feet hurt, down into the bones. His belly throbbed painfully with the work of eating. It wasn't until the next grey morning, the lightening sky colorless, that Oriel had the thought to wrap furs around their feet and tie them with thongs, and thus make boots. He had no hope that their condition would become easier. He had no confidence that they would be allowed to keep whatever comforts they had unexpectedly been given.

"Malke's Feast," Rulgh said, leaning over for a quick word before he lurched away to join up with the loud singing, boasting, jeering, and storytelling of the Wolfer Captains. "Three," he said, squinting at the four fingers he held up. "Then Malke comes. Then Rulgh — great man, with gold."

After two days of the feast and two nights of full-bellied sleep, warm under furs beside a fire, Oriel almost couldn't remember the hardships of the journey here. The Wolfers were filled with rejoicing, and excitement, too, and Oriel thought he understood the purpose of Malke's Feast: Oriel was not even an honored guest, as were these Captains, and he had no place of his own at the feasting tables, as the Captains did. He brought no booty to place at Malke's feet. In fact, he *was* the booty. He had no reason for gratitude, yet he felt gratitude to Malke, for the feast.

So whatever resentments and angers these raiding bands might have been carrying with them — for the sacrifices they had made and pain endured — would be less after three days at Malke's Feast. Even Oriel, after only three days of feasting, found his desire to take revenge on Rulgh less urgent, even when the sight of the red cicatrix on Griff's cheek reminded Oriel of the red stripes that scored Griff's back, and reminded him of how Rulgh mocked his helplessness.

* * *

246

It was a pale northern midday when the great gates split, and opened wide. A line of fur-cloaked archers emerged; they knelt down, arrows notched. The Captains and their bands gathered together, facing the archers. Spearmen came out, marching two by two, and behind them a great figure of a man, tall and broad, with a black fur like a long cape over his shoulders and a great worked golden chain on his chest that shone no more brightly gold than did his hair as it flowed down loose over his shoulders, and the gold of his narrow beard, flowing down over his chest. His eyes were blue as ice. Malke, the King.

Many pale-haired women came next. At that sight, the Captains made a noise in their throats, as if they were a single man. The women gathered behind Malke.

Malke stepped forward, although he stayed behind the archers and spearmen. He spoke to his raiders, a speech of welcome, as Oriel understood. Malke wore leather gloves on his hands, and rings on all of his fingers. He wore gold bracelets up his arms. When he was finished speaking, four men carried a carved wooden chair up to him, and Malke sat in it. He raised one ringed hand to point with as he called out a name. A Captain stepped forward. In the cold air, Malke's breath smoked.

Invisible in the throng of Wolfers and their captives, Oriel and Griff watched the ceremony. Oriel counted fifteen Captains, some with bands of twenty around them, none but Rulgh with so few as two. All the bands stood behind piles of booty.

The Captain faced the King, and his band stood behind the Captain. The Captain presented his booty, carried forward and spread out either by his captives or by his men. He told the story of his campaign, while the King and the women attended.

Afterwards, Malke sent a man forward, to take up shares of the booty. Then he called out a name and the Captain beat with a closed fist, once, upon his chest. Malke called out another name, and the Captain responded with the same gesture.

This was the end of the ceremony. Malke gestured with his raised right hand, and one of the women came out from behind him, to greet the Captain, and a child followed her, who was handed into the Captain's arms despite its cries and reachings for its mother.

The day stretched on. At the third band, with whose booty Malke was not pleased, one of the men stepped forward. He told a tale that differed from his Captain's tale. Oriel listened carefully. Was he saying that the Captain had run away from an enemy? Oriel thought so, but couldn't be sure. Malke asked for corroboration from the rest of the band, who stirred uncomfortably under his eye, but kept silent. Malke studied the Captain and turned the rings on his fingers, silent, brooding.

At last the Captain could stand it no longer. He began to speak, his palms facing outward. He started explanations and excuses.

Three arrows flew into his throat.

Oriel looked to Malke, whose left hand was just settling back into his lap.

The Captain's body was dragged away. The man who had made public the Captain's cowardice was named Captain over the band. One of the women brought two children forward and set them at the foot of Malke's chair. He took each by the hand, and then gave them back to their mother. She knelt before him, her lips on his right hand. Malke placed his gloved and ringed left hand across her bent neck, and then sent her away.

Malke called out another name.

It was not a dignified ceremony. The crowd before Malke was often noisy, responding to a Captain's tale of exploits, advising the King, calling out to the women, who often called back. Men walked around. Malke was often restless in his chair and sometimes rose, left the scene, returned shortly. The ceremony went on without him. Only the bowmen and spearmen maintained an unmoving, watchful silence.

The second time a member of a band spoke against his Captain, it was the Wolfer the King punished. He was not executed, however, but his hands were bound as Oriel's and Griff's were, and he was shoved roughly over to the side of the waiting crowd. His Captain ignored him, as did the Wolfers he had run with. He had put all at risk with his perfidy, with his desire to gain the Captainship that was the reward for denouncing a coward or thief.

Oriel studied Rulgh's sharp profile. Oriel had the beryl at his back. He didn't think he could buy their freedom with it; he didn't think freedom was one of the choices he had. But he could betray Rulgh with it, or make the attempt. If he could show the stone — and he could — and argue that Rulgh had been too stupid to find it, or say that Rulgh had let him keep it so that Malke would not get it — and Oriel would not stop short of a lie, if it would serve his ends. Then Rulgh would be executed and lie in his own blood on the frozen ground, and Oriel would have the revenge he had promised.

But Oriel and Griff would still be captives, and probably move into Malke's possession. Within the walls of Malke's stronghold, Oriel didn't imagine there would be many chances for a captive to escape. Moreover, even if he and Griff could escape from the Wolfers, this was not a land where food was plentiful to find, and this was not the season to be wandering homeless. Moreover, Oriel didn't know how far he was from the sea, or in what direction the sea lay. The mountains blocked forward progress, like an ice wall, impassable.

It would be foolhardy to make a move now.

It might well be, Oriel thought, that looking backwards he would see this as his last chance, the last time when they might have attempted escape. But he could only follow his own judgment.

Rulgh was called forward. When the Captain and his two men stood before Malke's great chair, the King made a mockery of peering at the band, peering around behind Rulgh as if looking for something he couldn't see. Rulgh called Oriel and Griff forward, to set down their booty. The lumps of gold and the handful of coins were the best of it. The rest was weapons — among which Oriel saw his own dagger, and Griff's — and some cloths woven in rich colors. The gold lumps were abundant, and Oriel used them as a shelf over which to display the rest. Rulgh started to tell his tale.

A woman came up to Malke's left hand, and Oriel thought this must be Rulgh's wife, because of the way she flashed her eyes at the speaking Captain. For his part, Rulgh addressed the tale of his exploits to her as much as to his King. She listened, and cast the glance of her eyes like a spear from under the fall of ashen hair, most often at Rulgh but sometimes at Malke, who turned his face away as if to conceal that he had been watching her as she watched Rulgh.

Rulgh came to Selby. Oriel heard the name, hissed like something hated, "Selby, Selby," by some of the other bands. He stood with Griff at his shoulder and wondered how this day would turn out.

Malke was pleased by the gold chunks. His greedy eyes measured their number. But when Rulgh had told of the battle at the mines, and the band's return there as stealers, Malke's expression shifted abruptly to displeasure. He called out a name, and Rulgh beat once with his fist on his chest. Malke called out another name, and another. Each time Rulgh made the gesture to say, *This is a dead man*. As the list went on, Rulgh grew stiffer and stiffer in his pride and shame. At the last, Malke stood up, crossed his arms before his chest, then opened them wide, in a gesture of refusal.

Oriel watched Rulgh. The Captain would have spoken, in the heat of his anger, but he dared not. Rulgh stared at the woman. She looked only at the ground. Malke pointed, at various men around the fires, at Rulgh, at the mountains, and Oriel understood the order: Rulgh was to lead a band of men into the mountains, and over the mountains; if he returned with sufficient wealth, then he could kneel again before his King.

Rulgh swallowed his anger and attempted to persuade the King. The season was unfavorable, no man had ever returned from beyond the mountains, Rulgh was a Captain proven by many successful seasons who had had the misfortune to have one poor year. Malke demanded to know where were the riches of Selby. Rulgh gestured at the mound of gold. Malke would not be persuaded, he would not sit down, he would not give over the woman who now stood at his side. He ordered his servants to come forward and take up all of the booty Rulgh had laid before him. "Bring," Oriel heard the order given, and then the Wolfer word for "captives."

This was a danger he hadn't thought of.

Rulgh moved to stand before Oriel and Griff. "No," Rulgh growled, deep in his throat. "These are mine."

The crowd fell silent, and Oriel could see Malke measuring the situation. The King didn't know if his power would hold in this quarrel. He didn't know whether the other Captains might stand with Rulgh, against their King, when their right to booty was the issue. Malke was unsure of his own power, and Rulgh knew it. Oriel could sense the pull back and forth between Rulgh and Malke, to be the victor in this contest of wills.

Oriel had no part in the decision. He could do nothing to affect the outcome of the contest.

But he could almost see the understanding rise up in Malke's eyes: If he gave way to Rulgh in this, then Rulgh must obey whatever Malke's will was in the other thing. By winning the captives, Rulgh had handed over all else, and must obey Malke's orders.

Malke smiled and waved his hand in a gesture, brushing Rulgh away from before the great chair just as a man brushes a fly out of his hair. He looked at the woman in triumph; and she was watching his face, to catch his eyes when they fell on her. She knelt before him and her long hair fell down, hiding her smile, and Malke's hand dropped onto her neck.

Rulgh turned on his heels and paced to the back of the crowd. He pulled Oriel and Griff behind him.

CHAPTER 19

By moonrise, a small band of men had gathered around Rulgh, where he stood at the rear of the throng. The white moon sailed up into the sky. Oriel waited in the shadows. Rulgh would be Captain of this Wolfer band, but the band was made up of men Malke had found wanting in service. Malke's judgments were made swiftly, without hesitation.

In the white, warmless light of the moon, his people's fear rose up like a tide towards Malke, and it seemed to Oriel that the King drank in that fear, as if it were wine to give him strength and rejoicing.

It seemed to Oriel also that Malke was a fool, not

to know that fear was a thing that could turn, like a snake; and what a frightened man might do, in his fear, no man could know. It seemed to Oriel that if he were King over the Wolfers, he would rather have their hearts filled with courage than fear.

Sitting in the shadows, with Griff at his side, it seemed to Oriel that he could be King over the Wolfers, and that he would be able to command obedience from these wild and war-loving men.

At last Malke rose to lead his party back within the gates. The booty followed, including Rulgh's mounds of gold nuggets, and all the crowd followed. Last to leave were the archers, who pulled the gates closed after them. The sounds of celebration began, within.

Rulgh walked away from the bonfires. Without a word, he turned his face to the hills, where they lay white as bones under moonlight. The band fell in behind him, ten men. Six captives trailed the Wolfers, tied together into pairs and each pair led by a member of the band. Rulgh set a quick pace.

When they were three nights from Malke's city, the Wolfers settled around a fire they had built in the forest but forbade the captives to lie down. Rulgh, in the first words he had spoken since Malke had announced judgment on him, pulled Oriel and Griff out among the leafless trees, and tied them back to back to one of the narrow straight trunks. "Wolfguard," he said.

Oriel was too tired to ask, too stubborn to speak. When they were alone he asked Griff, over his shoulder, "Are we sentries?"

"I can't stay awake, Oriel," Griff answered, in the voice of a man at the end of hope.

"Then sleep, as you can. I'll watch. Later, I'll

wake you and you can watch while I sleep. As we have done before, Griff."

Thus they passed the night, sleeping and watching over one another. Sometime in the night, Oriel heard a distant howling sound, and understood that they were watching against dangers out of the darkness, and that there was especial danger of wolves.

Thus they passed also the next days and nights. They moved always northward, and fed off what the Wolfers stole from the farmsteads they passed. They ate on the run, and lit only small fires against the bitter cold of night. Each night, the captives were staked out around the Wolfer camp, to give warning.

Oriel and Griff were fed enough to keep them alive. They wore furs over their shoulders and furs around their feet and legs. They had been toughened by their summer of captivity. The other four were not so fortunate, although each huddled within his own fur. The others wore leather boots and often stumbled, and fell, and had to be dragged back up onto their feet.

The first pair of Wolfguards was lost because of exhaustion, and the inability to understand that two bodies huddled together under two furs would be warmer than two men, each in his own fur. This was after snows had fallen, and one of the men's hands had turned black with frostbite, and had been cut off by Rulgh's sword, so the smell of blood called the wolves down on them. When it happened, it was Griff's turn to sleep; Oriel heard cries from across the circle of Wolfers. Oriel would have thought the cries would waken Griff, who leaned against him for warmth and support; but Griff slept through. Oriel listened — as the Wolfers awoke and considered what they needed to do for their own safety, as the cries became more desperate, beating like the wings of birds against the barren hillsides, as silence fell again.

The mountains came nearer and the hillsides grew steeper, and the little streams had frozen where they ran. There came a grey, low-clouded day, when the band came upon a farmstead nestled in a hollow, with snow pulled up around it like bedclothes.

The four captives were left where they had fallen in the snow, while the Wolfers attacked. Griff dozed off, but Oriel could not. The sounds of what little resistance the householders offered seemed to come from far away, and he looked about himself. There were few trees and the mountains took up much of the sky here. The clouds pressed down upon him and the air was thin in his mouth. The wind came howling down from the mountains. He wondered how much longer he would live, and if he would bring Rulgh down before he died. He wondered what kind of farm this barren land could support.

They were dragged to their feet and driven into a gated yard, under a rising wind. Rulgh and his band were the only occupants now. The farm was provisioned against winter, and so the blizzard that came down over them found them safely housed.

The Wolfers' way of getting through was to eat and drink themselves into a stupor, and then to sleep until the stupor wore off so that they could eat and drink again. The four captives served them, and cleaned up after them. Outside, the wind howled.

Rulgh acknowledged to the band, there, that they were going to the Kingdom, as Malke had ordered. When he named it, the Wolfers stirred unhappily where they sat. They demanded more ale, and wouldn't look at Rulgh. Oriel listened attentively, and found his understanding much increased, as if his ears had suddenly been cleared and he could now hear the Wolfers' language.

Rulgh spoke to the men of golden streets, and of rich stews, and of breads baked with nuts and fruits. In the Kingdom, Rulgh said, all men drank ale as freely as if it were water, and they drank wine as if it were no more costly than ale. And the women, Rulgh said, were dark-haired, and warm, not like the yellow-haired ice-women the Wolfers had known.

One man answered him: They were being sent to their deaths, and were fools to obey. No man had ever crossed the mountains and returned to tell the way. "It's not," the man said, "that I mind dying. But I would like to face death equally, and know his name."

The others merely called for more drink.

When the storm had blown out, and the snow had settled, the band moved on. Now they wore wooden boards strapped to their feet, narrow boards they had carved to rounded tips. The boards were as long as their arms, and rubbed smooth, so they could move as much on top of the snow as through it. Oriel and Griff were clumsy with these extended feet for a day or two, until they learned how to imitate the Wolfers' gliding movements. Without the boards, they would have sunk down into snow as high as their waists and been unable to move. They would have been trapped in the snow.

The captives were laden, now, with stores. They trailed behind the Wolfers up long sloping hillsides. Wolves followed the band by day and encircled them by night. When Oriel stood Wolfguard, with Griff leaning sleeping against him, he could see the eyes of the wolves, glowing red. He heard the quarrels of the other pair of captives as they pinched and poked one another to be sure both were awake and on guard. The captives lay down to sleep only at the turnings of the day, from light to dark, dark to light.

The trek was long, and it was many successive nights that Oriel and Griff stood Wolfguard, each trusting the other to wake while he slept. They were too exhausted by the endless uphill trudges, by the search for shelter as the brief day slid into the long night, by unpacking fuel and building tiny fires, too exhausted to speak to one another more than the waking words, "It's my turn to sleep." They needed no talk to perform their tasks, and if they had, Oriel could not have offered it. The air was thin and icy on his skin and lips. His breath feathered out before him, as did Griff's.

The Wolfers, who carried nothing but their weapons, because Wolfers weren't beasts of burden, and who were familiar with the use of the boards, moved more easily, but still the long trek wore them down. The stores were almost entirely gone and the second pair of captives had been dragged off, their screams mingling with the wolves' snarling, before the band came to another fenced farmyard, high up against a hillside that rose into the shoulder of a mountain. No smoke rose from the chimney.

"Blizzard," Rulgh announced confidently. In the time they had been traveling, Rulgh's beard had grown in roughly all over his cheeks, and his voice had grown rough-edged, and his long hair hung down ragged and filled with ice-droppings. Griff, too, looked rough, by which Oriel knew that he himself looked as much bear as man.

The gate stood open, and they crowded into the undefended yard. The door to the house stood open to the cold. It was as if the inhabitants had risen from their meal, with only half of it eaten, and fled the house. But where would they have gone? Rulgh had no question about *why* they had fled.

Neither had Oriel, and he had just enough strength left to be glad that the inhabitants of this vast northern land had some means of warning one another when danger ranged, before he and Griff were set to work, while the Wolfers fell onto the floor by the fire and slept.

The Wolfers slept so deeply that Griff could ask Oriel, "If we ran away?"

Outside, in that white wilderness, Oriel and Griff would have no chance to live. Oriel couldn't find the words inside his head to push out through his mouth, but Griff understood. He sat down beside Oriel and closed his eyes, to sleep until their masters called them awake.

Before the blizzard lifted there was rest, and food, days and nights of howling winds, and the Wolfers sleeping like winter-fat animals in their caves, or waking to quarrel. As soon as the sky cleared they moved on, the boards once again strapped to their feet.

The mountains rose like a wall, high and white and sharp.

At night the wolves crowded closer, bolder — Oriel was wakened by Griff to drive them off with the boards.

It was only Rulgh's voice that made it possible to continue moving forward, only knowing that Rulgh would jab the point of a sword into his back — cutting through the fur he wore wrapped around his body — or into Griff's back, if they faltered —

He wondered if they had moved at all, some days, so slowly did they move up the mountain's side —

Only the promise of more pain if he halted kept him moving.

They followed a shallow ravine between two tall hills, until the ravine became broad enough for two or three abreast, moving swiftly now with the boards along level ground. When Oriel looked up, the mountains rose all around him.

They were trapped among the mountains.

Oriel didn't even know what direction would lead them out.

He didn't think Rulgh knew, either, except that there was a plume of smoke far ahead. Oriel pushed his legs forward, pushing the boards through the snow. Beside him, Griff breathed.

Downhill, he thought, downhill would be out. They were moving steadily uphill, and he didn't know when he had last seen a tree. Bare white-grey rocks, whole hillsides of only rock, where the wind had blown all the snow away. White fields and hillsides of snow, and a white-blue sky above.

Oriel couldn't hear his own breathing.

When they came to it, the smoke seemed to rise out of a tiny hill of snow, up against bare rock. The Wolfers pulled at the hillside with their hands, and a man crawled out — bareheaded, wearing cloth; his face was pale but his eyes were dark under thick white eyebrows, and his long white hair blew in the wind. He beckoned them to enter the mountainside, and he held back a doorway made of skin.

The ten Wolfers entered and when they were safe inside Oriel and Griff could follow. They leaned the boards against the stone. The man urged them all to sit close around his fire. He gave them thick hot food. He rubbed fat into their feet and hands and faces. The firelight moved over the one room, like sun running over water.

How long he slept, Oriel didn't know. There was a time when his fingers and toes ached, the bones of his body pathways of pain; and he thought he heard men moaning.

Oriel knew it wasn't Griff's voice. So he could sleep again, since when he slept the pain of his bones went to a distant place. From that distant place, the pain had trouble reaching him.

He awoke to see Griff's face, shadowy in firelight. Griff looked as wild as a Wolfer, a stranger's face. Except for his eyes.

Oriel struggled to sit up. Sitting, he saw the white-haired man feeding someone across the small room, on the other side of the fire. "He wakes," Griff said, and the white-haired mountain man answered, "Good. Do you want to try him with some porridge?"

It was not until he had eaten, and slept, and wakened to eat again that Oriel realized what he had heard: his own language.

Rulgh lived, and three of the others. The rest were gone, as if they had never been. The mountain man's room was in fact a cave that ran back into the mountainside for forty or fifty paces before it ended at a damp stone wall. The man had filled the back of the cave with branches of wood and great mounds of ground stuff — it looked like a mixture of leaves and nuts. This, cooked with melted snow, made his food. The wood burned for his fire. The mountain man had supplies to keep himself, and guests, too.

When Rulgh could speak, he demanded to know who this man was. The mountain man understood his question, but had no words to answer it. "Why does it matter who I am?" he asked Oriel and Griff. They couldn't tell him. "Come," the man said.

He led them outside, where the sun reflected off fields of snow, to warm the air. The white peaks rose all around them. In the bright light, the mountain man's eyes were blue, with flecks of brown in them, like bits of ice floating down a river in the spring melt. "Ask him where he is taking you," the man said to Oriel.

"To the Kingdom," Rulgh answered.

"My homeland," the mountain man said. Oriel put this into Rulgh's language.

Rulgh demanded, "Where is the pass?"

"Why do you go to the Kingdom? Ask him," the mountain man said.

Rulgh took a breath to answer but was interrupted by a sound that filled the air, as if somewhere nearby a giant had been punched in the belly and expelled a bellyful of air, "Mhhuummphh." Or perhaps, Oriel thought, looking around to find the source of the sound, it was as if the mountain itself had belched, gently, like a girl at a feast.

The mountain man didn't seem alarmed, but still Oriel moved next to Griff, for better defense should they need to defend themselves. Rulgh looked around, at peaks and sky, and almost as if in answer to the question he hadn't asked, the sound came again, "Mhhuummphh."

"What's happ — ?" the Wolfers asked.

"Hush," the mountain man said. "Listen."

Oriel signaled Rulgh and the others to quiet.

There was no sound in the great icy silence of the mountains. They waited. Then Oriel could hear a distant waterfall, rumbling.

But no water could fall, not in these frozen wastes.

The noise was gone so quickly, he couldn't be sure he had really heard it.

The mountain man waited for a long soundless time. Then he spoke again. "It's over now, the avalanche."

"Va-lanish?" Rulgh echoed.

The mountain man shrugged. "The snow falls over the hillside, like a landslide. If you are caught, and if you aren't smashed, and you make room to breathe before it freezes over you, and settles down on you, and if you dig your way upward and you are lucky, if you are a lucky man, then you live."

Oriel started to translate, but Rulgh waved him to silence. "The pass," Rulgh insisted. "The Kingdom."

"Who are you, to him?" the man asked Oriel.

"We are his captives," Oriel said.

"You don't have the look of captives. You wouldn't be captives in the Kingdom. Mightn't they be servants, though?" he asked, and listened to his own question as if it had been spoken by another.

"He knows the pass?" Rulgh demanded.

"Now we go inside, to eat, and then sleep. Tell your man that," the mountain man said to Oriel.

Rulgh didn't want to cooperate, but he gave in, grudgingly, with an eye on the white disk of the sun, which was sinking towards the tallest of three spiked peaks. "All right," he said.

"The pass lies there, just below the sun," the mountain man said. Oriel told this to Rulgh. "Tell him, the sun goes through the pass every night, he goes between the middle and right peaks and into the Kingdom, where he sleeps in the arms of his beloved. For the women of the Kingdom are beautiful."

When Oriel told Rulgh this, the Wolfer burst into harsh laughter.

"Tell him that later — he will see it — the moon comes searching for her husband, but she does not know where the pass into the Kingdom is."

"*Tewkeman*," Rulgh answered. "*Brautelman.*"

The mountain man turned his two-colored eyes to Rulgh and stared for so long that the Wolfer became uneasy. Still the mountain man stared at the Wolfer, until Rulgh made the sign of the horned animal, to protect himself. Finally the mountain man spoke. "Yes, I think so. Come inside, before you freeze, for if you freeze here there is no other person but me to find you, and save you again."

When they had dipped their fill of porridge out of the pot with their fingers, for there were neither bowls nor spoons for them, the mountain man said, as if no time had passed since his last words, "and I will only save you once."

"*Tewkeman*," Rulgh muttered, but without conviction.

"She was my sister, and she carried his child, and the soldiers came to kill her. And they killed her, as it was the Lady Earl's wish and order, and so I wanted to kill the Earl, they said so, so I had to run away, because it was the Lady Earl who should die. Not that boy. It wasn't the boy's wish and order. He couldn't order, nor wish, neither, I think; for when I found him he lay there and didn't blink or breathe, all the time I asked him for my sister."

The man leaned his head close to Oriel's, as if what he said now was spoken in secret. "I came through the pass, when he rescued me, and brought me here, and he drew the mountains up behind me."

"Who rescued you?"

"Jackaroo, he carried me along in the palm of his great hand, and set me down — so gently — so I

would live safely here. Not for your profit and service!" the man cried out at Rulgh; but then he
winked at the Wolfer with a friendly smile.

That decided Rulgh. Oriel could see him make
up his mind. So Oriel was not surprised the next
morning to have a pack strapped onto his back, filled
with the mountain man's dried porridge. Griff carried wood.

The mountain man seemed untroubled by their
departure. He hung around Oriel's neck the curled
hollow horn of a mountain goat. "If you are in need,
call on this. I will answer you, or I will send a mountain to your aid."

"What now?" Rulgh demanded.

"Tell him, he knows where the pass is," the
mountain man said. Oriel told them this. They all
stood outside the skin doorway, under bright sunlight. The mountain man pointed off to the east,
where the sun hovered over a distant line of peaks.

"This is not what he spoke before. I believe nothing," Rulgh muttered. "Follow me." He moved off.

They followed, with long gliding steps on the
boards. With every step, Oriel and Griff fell behind.

By midday, it was as if they had never found
shelter with the mountain man. Rulgh drove all of
them forward, always uphill. Oriel kept the triple
peaks in his view — because he could remember
them, not because he had faith in the mountain man.
Also because when Rulgh's voice called them forward, faster, unless Oriel thought of the triple peaks
he would have refused to move.

Griff would refuse, if Oriel refused.

They would both die, then.

That night, as they stood guard, Oriel tried to ask
Griff. "He meant an avalanche," Oriel said. "With
the horn. To call one down, if I hear . . ."

"Ah," Griff said. His voice sounded so thick with sleep that Oriel almost didn't tell him, but he thought that Griff also had a part in the choice, since he had a part in the danger. He had never given Griff a part in the choice before, but now he thought he had owed it to Griff.

"Wake up, Griff. Listen. If I call down an avalanche, if I can do it, we may be swept into it."

"Yes," Griff said.

"To our deaths," Oriel said.

"Yes," Griff said.

"And there may well be no pass," Oriel said.

"I know," Griff said. "But he gave us no food tonight."

"He'll let us die," Oriel agreed.

"If you can do it, then you must," Griff said.

The next morning they moved along a sloping field of snow, going up slantward. They were heading towards the lightening sky, although the three peaks Oriel watched for rose at his left shoulder. There seemed to be nothing but bare rock and snow-fields by the three peaks, which loomed close above them. Oriel didn't try to persuade Rulgh. He could barely persuade himself to take the mountain man's word. He could see no shadowy cut across the triple peak, just stone and snow.

But he had chosen to believe the mountain man, and he kept that belief frozen in his mind, like ice. When he heard the mountain rumble, hummphing, he looked up. It seemed to him there was a ridge of snow, on the peak that Rulgh had chosen to struggle up; and it seemed to him the ridge moved a little to one side.

Griff and Oriel were half a hillside behind the four Wolfers. "Drop your pack," Oriel said to Griff. If there was a pass, and they were to find it, the packs would slow them down. If they were to have any hope — if they survived the avalanche, if Oriel could call it down with the horn — then that hope lay in moving as quickly as they could. There was half a day's light left to him.

The mountain hummphed again, and the Wolfers stopped, worried. Oriel raised the horn to his mouth, shoving Griff off to the side, in the direction of the three peaks. Oriel blew into the horn, and followed Griff, still blowing into the horn. They struggled sideways along the slope, as the Wolfers turned to see them.

The high calling of the horn curled around the ragged peaks, like a bird's cry, as Oriel hurried clumsily out of the way, and Griff climbed beside him.

The mountain rumbled, and then roared. Oriel halted, and lifted his eyes to the three peaks ahead, and the high central peak, and the blue sky beyond the ice mountaintops, in case he would never see anything again. He felt Griff standing at his shoulder. He turned, and blew the horn again, although he could barely hear it now, in the roar of the mountain. The Wolfers raced back down the slope, on their boards. The mountain followed them. Rulgh looked for his captives and his mouth was open, on a cry or a curse, and snow was tangled in his yellow hair.

Even the Wolfer's war cry was drowned out by the sound of the mountain, falling.

PART IV

THE SPAEWIFE'S MAN

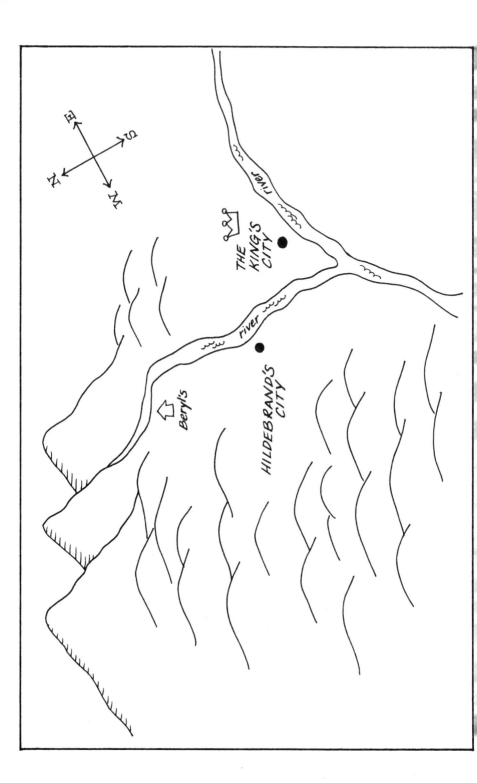

CHAPTER
20

It was as if the Wolfers had never been. It was as if in the whole world there was no more than the stone mountains, cloaked in snow, and the blue sky, and the two of them, himself and Griff. All that moved were mists of snow, raised up by the rushing avalanche, and caught now in the tireless winds of the high mountains.

Griff's teeth showed in his face, and he was smiling broadly. "We lived, Oriel."

Oriel stood, silent, dazzled by the brightness of the sun and the memory of the mountainside, moving.

"And now which way?" Griff asked. He sounded untroubled by what had gone before, or what might come.

Cold rose up around them, as heat rises from a fire. Boldly, as if all of this coldness couldn't reach it, the sun shone down. "To that middle peak, where he said there is a pass," Oriel said. "That's my thought," he added. "What's yours?"

"I follow you," Griff said.

"We will have, I think, no chance for another choice," Oriel told Griff, not wanting to conceal the danger.

"We haven't much time, either," Griff said. "Since without food or shelter, if we rest it's likely we'll never rise again."

"Don't you mind?"

"Of course I mind. Do you think that I don't value my life? But I'd rather meet death in your company than alone, and I'd be dismayed to be in a world where I couldn't follow you. So," Griff said, with the same smile, "while I mislike death, aye, and fear the journey I must one day make at her side, I can't be low-spirited."

As they climbed up the slope, their steps were long-footed and awkward on the boards, their progress slow and sideways.

"If there is a pass, and we can find it before dark catches us, we may live," Oriel said to Griff. "The man named this place first, when Rulgh demanded. Although later he said that Jackaroo carried him through it, and Jackaroo comes out of Tamara's stories."

"Is it not good to be free of the Wolfers?" Griff asked. "It was near a year they had us."

"And four years ago the Damall had us — and here we are again, only the two, heading we know not where." At that thought, Oriel smiled as broadly as Griff, letting the cold scrape against his teeth. "Only now it is full day. And now we have nothing to eat. And then I knew where we were going, but you did not, and now neither one knows."

"Now we know the same," Griff said.

They pushed on. What seemed a violet shadow formed by afternoon shadows became a narrow ravine, as they approached it. It was a cut into the mountain's neck that ran neither up nor down, to Oriel's eye. He looked into it, and hesitated.

Griff awaited his decision.

Oriel took a breath of the thin air. They had one chance, and this looked to be it. His singularity didn't cause the sun to creep along the horizon, gathering clouds around his head for protection. There was only one sun, and he traveled high and bold across the sky. If Oriel hoped to live — hoped to make his way across these mountains to whatever land lay beyond — then he must try the high way and boldly. He must risk the one chance.

His feet on the boards slid over the surface of the snow, as did Griff's. Sometimes the boards made whispering sounds in soft snow. Sometimes there was an icy crust, over which the boards crunched. Griff was behind him, as they followed the narrow ravine. The shadows grew milky blue. The air was suddenly colder. They pulled their furs close around them, and went on.

Oriel let the land give his feet direction. He could not think to choose a way: Darkness had descended, and to inhale this high mountain air was to breathe in an ice sword. Cold came at them from the stones of the mountain below their feet, from the wind that swirled around them, blowing from all directions, and only their own movements kept them warm. As the night grew colder, and longer, those movements became slower, and more difficult. Stars sprinkled the black sky, like a distant snowstorm.

They slogged on, having no other choice.

The white disk of the moon sailed out from behind a mountain peak, sailed into the sky. The moon came so sudden and bright and bold into the sky that Oriel had to greet her with a lifting heart. If, after all, they were going to die in the cold of the mountains, still they were not yet dead, and he chose not to despair.

He didn't hope — that wasn't it. It was that he refused despair, while he lived. And they lived.

His legs moved of their own will, now, and he didn't even have a guess as to how much of the night remained. If they could live through the night then they could live through another day, before hunger and thirst joined with cold to bring them down.

He thought the sky must be lighter, but didn't know where east was, and did know how his eyes would try to deceive him.

But then the grey of a lightening sky paled the snowfields rising around him, and he looked up, to find the middle peak and be sure of their direction. The peak was gone. For a heartbeat, he was afraid — afraid that in the darkness of night and the foolhardiness of continuing to go forward, he had undone them. Then he stopped, and slowly turned around, until he could see Griff behind him, and behind Griff the middle peak, rising up into a cloudy sky.

The narrow ravine twisted on, and the way grew easier, and then the ravine opened out.

Oriel halted. Ahead, steep hillsides gradually became filled with trees, like black bones set up in the snow. Ahead, under a pale cloudy sky, the land sloped downward. In the far distance, a single column of grey smoke hung suspended, visible, now, in the muted light between dawn and day.

That smoke was the only sign of life in the whole wide landscape. It was too far away to be reached by nightfall. As soon as the sun rose, the smoke would no longer show up against the sky.

If this was the Kingdom, then it might be that they had come at last to the Kingdom, so that they might die here. Even if it had been summer, and they well fed and well rested, the source of the smoke would lie a day's hard journey ahead.

Oriel looked to his right, where the mountain's face rose steeply, and giant icicles cascaded down it, and to his left, where snow slopes rose. The wall of mountains lay behind them now.

Griff stamped his feet in the boards, and Oriel followed the example. His mind felt as sluggish with cold as his body. Or perhaps both mind and body were sluggish with fatigue — because within the Wolfers' furs he was warm enough, and he had traveled beyond hunger.

He lifted his feet and stamped them again, but they slid out under him. He balanced, fingers clutching the furs, flying downhill for three heartbeats before he tumbled off sideways into the snow.

Griff, his own boards slipping on the snow, hurried after.

Oriel took the hand Griff held out, and pulled himself upright. They stood, breath smoking. "If only my legs were strong enough," Oriel said, "I could ride the boards downhill. See that smoke? It's too far — I couldn't hold the boards under me all that steep distance. Could you? You go ahead, if you're strong enough."

"I'm at the end of what little strength I had left. I'm sorry, Oriel." Griff looked around him. "Icicles, Oriel. Look. Can we break one off? If any are small enough to break, and keep in our mouths until they melt. For drink, Oriel."

"A waterfall," Oriel whispered.

"Aye, it could be, when the ice melts," Griff agreed.

"No, Griff, listen. A waterfall means a flow of water, a stream, going downhill. If we follow a stream downhill, or follow its bed, then it will come to a river, and rivers also always move downhill. And people live beside the rivers."

"But how do we find the stream, under this snow?" Griff asked. "And wouldn't the river be solid ice?"

"Ice is easier to move on than snow, with the boards," Oriel argued. "The stream — that we must hope to follow, because it will be cut into the ground, as water does. And Griff? If we take the thongs from our feet and tie the boards together, if we sit on them, instead of trying to stand, because if we sit we can't fall over as easily, and we can wrap our furs around both of us — can you see the idea? — like a raft."

Griff had already sat down in the snow and was struggling with the leather thongs. Oriel sat beside him. When they were seated close on the bound boards, Oriel's back up against Griff's chest and the furs held tight around them like a tent, he said — before they pushed themselves loose from the holding snow, and rode this chance down — "The midpeak is at our back, and see? — where the smoke rises? there are two rounded hills to its right and three sharper ones to the left with one overlapping the other? We'll be able to see the peak and perhaps the hills, long after we have lost the smoke. Will that guide us, do you think?"

"We can try," Griff said.

They pushed with their hands into the snow, breaking through the crusted surface. Beneath them, the snow raft started to slide, slowly. They pushed again, and the boards moved more easily. They pulled their hands back under the furs, and leaned forward.

They were in flight. The wind whistled into Oriel's face, blew snow up into his eyes, and they were flying down the mountainside. Oriel had never dreamed of moving like this. He thought this must be the way birds felt, crossing the sky. He thought they might in fact be flying through clouds of snow. He thought that he wanted the ride never to end — his heart was soaring into laughter, and beating fast with the excitement of it, and the speed of it. He couldn't see anything, he had no idea where they were heading, he couldn't choose, or hope, or regret — all he could do was ride along, as a bird high in the air rides along on its wings.

The snow-covered mountainside seemed smooth to look at, but as they rode it they discovered it was filled with bumps, and curvings. Sometimes Oriel thought they might tumble off the boards, and sometimes he thought they might be flung off, and sometimes — as they jounced along in tooth-jarring fashion — he thought the boards must break up and drop the riders into the snow, as a boat breaks up and drops its sailors down into the sea under battering of waves.

They followed what Oriel hoped was the stream, descending. Certainly it was the land itself that steered them, and dropped away under them. The land itself carried the boards, and the two riders, down from the mountains. The journey took no time at all.

When they came to rest, Oriel's cheeks stung and his knees were stiff with having been braced to meet the unpredictable shiftings of the boards. He rose even more stiff than he had sat down, although that stiffness passed in the excitement of looking back — to see the three peaks, with the tallest at the center, rising in the distance behind them. "Look how far we've come, Griff," he said.

Griff's cheeks were bright and snow hung off his head and beard. "I could wish to do that again," he said.

"Not to walk up, though," Oriel pointed out. Griff turned and saw how the snowfield they had ridden sloped up, and up, and still upwards, before it turned into a steep shoulder. From where they stood the waterfall was only visible if you knew what you were looking for among the rocks and snows. The pass had disappeared back into the mountains.

"Not to walk up," Griff agreed. "Not if I had any hope to live. But still . . ."

"We need to get the boards back on our feet," Oriel said, bending to untie the thongs and separate them again. "We need to keep moving." The excitement of the ride had strengthened him, as much as warm food might have. "We need to be sure we're on the streambed. And wrap our feet again."

The frozen stream lay almost directly at their feet, as if its bed had been the path they had ridden down the mountainside. The snow lay deep here, but not so deep as on the mountains. The air was cold, but not so cold. They followed the stream, and whenever the view ahead cleared, Oriel stood with the middle peak at his back and the five hills ahead to sight their direction.

The stream seemed to be widening under their feet as they glided along, but darkness also seemed to be overtaking them from behind. Oriel wasn't sure, and he couldn't tell from the usual clues of light or hunger, if they had traveled a full day, or if the days were pitilessly short on this side of the mountain. All he knew was that the energy of the wild ride down the mountain had long since left him when flakes of snow started to flutter in the air, like moths, and then like a cloud of white moths.

There was no need to talk of it. Griff moved along steadily at his side. They were among hills, and trees; they had a wide stream for roadway; if the snow came down thick before they found shelter, then they probably couldn't survive another night. If night fell upon them out in the open, they wouldn't see a dawn, Oriel thought.

They moved slowly, and ever more slowly. The snow fell thickly and they moved through it, as good as blind. He was more relieved than surprised when they rounded a broad curve of the stream, where it ran between two sloping hills, and saw the dark shape of a house. Smoke rose out of its stone chimney.

They had no strength to be glad. They barely had the strength to leave the windblown surface of the frozen stream and make their way, leaning upon one another, up to the doorway of the house.

Snow rose almost to the windows but the stoop had been brushed clear. Griff leaned against Oriel, as if they were once again Wolfguards; and Oriel leaned against Griff to keep his balance, while he raised his hand to pound on the wooden door.

The door was pulled open, just enough so one eye could see out. There was someone, but he couldn't see clearly. There was no way to speak it, except the bold truth. "Please, help us."

The door opened and the boards on their feet caught on the lintel so they fell, wrapped in furs, onto the floor. Oriel crawled towards the fire. Sleep fell down on him, like an avalanche.

He struggled to swallow, struggled upwards: He lay on furs by a warm fire, and she raised his head so she could spoon something into his mouth —

Her eyes were blue, dark blue, like the sea on a cool clear summer morning. Her hair was the color of leaves in autumn, as much brown as red, a jumble of curls. "Drink this," she said.

"How long — ?" Oriel couldn't remember his question.

"Not long." She spoke softly, as if he might be easily alarmed. "The drink will fight fever and ease sleep. And your friend also, I've given him tisane also." She tilted the bowl and he drank it down. Warm liquid filled his stomach, gently, and spread out from his belly to his chest and loins, sending warmth from the inside to meet the fire's warmth that comforted his naked skin. He felt her hand on his forehead, and along the side of his face, as if her palm and fingers sought to know the bones underneath his beard, before he slipped back into the warmth of sleep.

In his dream, his only hope was to fight his way through the storm. He moved blind and bent into the white winds. But there was a warmth that wished to pull him back, pull him down, wrap around him. He knew that to give way to the warmth would be his death, but he longed to turn around and be gathered into her arms; so that every step he forced himself to take, with naked shoulders in the snow, and he couldn't see Griff —

Oriel sat up.

He was in a small room. A fire burned in the stone fireplace. He was on a low pallet on a straw mattress. Two simultaneous thoughts alarmed him. But Griff lay on a similar pallet. And Oriel wore the trousers where the beryl was still safely sewn in place, at the middle of his back.

Those things known, Oriel thought he might lie back down, to sleep again, but he had no will for sleep. He looked about him. The room had rough wooden walls, and shuttered windows. Griff slept on his back, his chest rising and falling, and he had been shaved, the scar on his cheek a white crescent. Oriel's hand went to his own face and he, too, had been shaved. Oriel thought to wake Griff, and then thought to let him sleep on, and then his belly thought of food. He got off the bed and went on bare silent feet to the window. When he opened it, he saw only fields of white, and tall firs covered with white, and falling snow that filled the air with a windless silence. The cold air bit at his chest. A door, when he cracked it open, revealed a large room, where a table and stools were set out in front of a broad stone fireplace, and another table rested against the opposite wall and a girl sat there. She turned the heavy pages of a book. Beside her, a cupboard went from floor to ceiling. Its doors were open to show rows of dolls. A pot hung over the fire, and there was a food smell in the air.

She turned around. Her eyes were as darkly blue as the sea under a clear summer morning, her hair wild curls. "It's you," Oriel said. "You gave me drink. How long have I slept?"

"Just the afternoon and night and into the morning," she told him. "I'll show you the privy, then you'll want to eat. Aye, and drink, too, I'd guess."

"Yes, please, thank you," Oriel said. The top of her head came about to the level of his eyes, and she wore a red shirt and blue skirt, with heavy black stockings on her feet. She led him through a storeroom behind the fireplace and opened a door to show him a farmyard, and the privy across it. When Oriel returned to the light and warmth, the girl looked up, red-cheeked, from the soup pot. "You've no shirt nor boots, not even stockings. I should have — "

"No matter, lady. No harm, as you see. I'm accustomed."

"I'm not a lady," she laughed. Oriel would have made some response but by then the bowl had been set before him, and a spoon put into his hand, and he was spooning thick meaty soup into his mouth, and he could not think to do anything but eat. Griff entered the room, barely awake, and the girl gave him stockings and a shirt, then showed him the privy, and served his bowl. She cut chunks of bread from a long loaf and dipped mugs of water from a bucket. She brought a green shirt for Oriel, and thick knitted stockings.

Oriel pulled the shirt on over his head. "It's been a year, nearly, since last we wore shirts," he said, moving his shoulders under the cloth to become accustomed to the feeling.

"Do you feel as if you want to vomit?" she asked. "Eat slowly," she advised Griff — who halted his spoon halfway up to his mouth, and looked dazed as he stared up into her face. "How long has it been that you've gone without?" Griff returned to his food, and it was Oriel who told her that it was perhaps two or three days since they'd last eaten, or not much longer.

"You'll find plenty to eat here," she promised.

"But you know nothing of — " Oriel said. "But we — "

"We'll have plenty of time to tell our tales," she said, and smiled at them. "Or did you not see the snow falling? So eat now — although, be careful not to overfill yourselves, or you will be ill. I promise you."

"Do many starving folk wander here from the mountains that you know this so surely?" Oriel asked.

"You're the first," she said.

Two candles burned on her table, and two more on the shelf above the fireplace. Their light, and the light from the fire, moved all over the room, revealing shelves filled with bowls and mugs, cheeses and bread. The dolls in the cupboard were brightly clothed people of all ages and conditions. Griff wore a blue shirt. The rafters overhead were brown wood, with dark shadows behind them. The firestones were grey, with black stains on them. The wood floor was scrubbed to a pale sandy color. Until he saw all the colors, Oriel didn't realize how he had become accustomed to a colorless world, a white world. And cold, where this room was warm, welcoming. He would have thought they were long-awaited visitors by the welcome the room gave them.

He rose to see what book she read. The page had drawings of plants, with the words beside the drawings. He read slowly, for some of the letters were strangely formed. *Peppermint, to soothe the belly, and chamomile to give ease in sleep.*

"That's what it was," he said.

She looked up at him. But why should she decide *now* to fear him? "What do you mean?" She closed the book.

"It was chamomile, in the drink you gave me, when you woke me. I remember. I recognized the aroma, that's all."

"You read letters?"

"Aye, as you must also."

"Are you a lord?" she asked, wary.

"Lady, I don't know what I am."

His confusion didn't concern her. "Reading is dangerous knowledge, for those who are neither lords nor priests."

He'd forgotten danger, in this house. But then it must be dangerous knowledge also for her; and for him to have of her, and for her to have of him, that, too. They would have to trust one another, then. The thought, he noted, didn't alarm him.

"I thank you for the warning. As for all else you've given us, without our asking. Oriel, that's my name," he introduced himself, "and he's Griff. We've come from over the mountains," he told her.

She didn't doubt him. "It was a long journey, by your beards. And not an easy one, by the marks on your backs. And the crescent on his cheek," she said. "Griff."

Griff lifted his head and smiled at her. "Not an easy way at all. Best forgotten, now that we've arrived safely," Griff said.

So Griff also felt welcomed in this room.

"Won our way, too," Oriel reminded Griff. "Griff also reads," he told the girl, "and we know numbers, but we've been in danger before — all of our lives, haven't we, Griff? When you think of it." Oriel's spirits were rising within him, like a bird moving

284

into flight. "Where are we, lady? And what are these dolls? and what is your name? Are we in the Kingdom?"

"Yes, of course," she said. "Where else should you arrive, when you cross the mountains?"

"The world is so large," Oriel explained, laughing, "that I might be anywhere at all, lady, once I cross the mountains."

She rose from her stool and brushed her hands down over her apron with dignity. Her cheeks were still pink. "I ask you, don't call me lady, for I'm none. What you call dolls are puppets, most of which my grandfather made. Have you never seen puppets?"

They hadn't. Now it was her turn to laugh at ignorance, but she kept it to a mischievous smile. "My grandfather came from the lands south of the Kingdom, and he brought the puppets with him. Here, Oriel, sit with Griff and I'll — It's better to show than to explain. Besides, the snow has us trapped, or, it has *you* trapped — Do you wish to travel on, have you some destination?"

She brought out a three-paneled screen, with a window cut into the central panel. Over this window, a curtain fell. Then she fetched two of the dolls from the cupboard, and Oriel saw that strings tied to the dolls led up to wooden crosspieces. She disappeared behind the screen and he heard only clatterings.

She had shaved them, and bathed them, too, he thought. She had fed and clothed them. Why should she do such a thing? Was the Kingdom a place where strangers had no power to harm you, and thus were never to be feared? Where life's necessities were present in such abundance that nobody begrudged giving them to another?

Could there be such a place? Oriel doubted that, although he had no doubt that this was such a place. He would have turned to Griff with the questions, except that the curtain rose up, pulled back by some invisible hand, and he saw the dolls, standing upright, now, in front of a painted city — and the dolls spoke.

The dolls not only spoke, they also moved. Each moved in his own way, and each spoke in his own voice. They were a countryman — plain and simple, in dress and words — and a city man — who spoke and dressed with more fancy touches. Each thought the other a fool. Each thought he was getting the better of the other. They met and quarreled and parted, and the curtain was lowered again.

The girl came out from behind the screen, holding one of the dolls suspended by its crossed wooden pieces in front of her, and by movements of her hand she made the doll precede her. It was the countryman. He went up to Griff's stockinged feet and placed a hand on Griff's leg, as if to attract his attention. Griff reached down to shake the hand, as if the puppet were a living man.

"That's what puppets are, that's what they do," the girl said. She could have no doubt that she had surprised them. "And I am the puppeteer's granddaughter, and the puppeteer's niece, and I'm the puppeteer, too." She curtsied mockingly. Oriel stood and reached out a hand to lift her up, as he bowed to her mockingly. Griff took the crossed wooden pieces and tried to make the countryman walk, as she had, but he failed.

"There are puppets for all stations of men and women, even the highest born. My grandfather made most of them, my uncle made others, and I have built one, but not well. There is a book, with the words for the puppets." She stopped briefly, then hurried on. "I am clever with my voice," she announced.

"Aye, you are," Oriel agreed.

Her blue eyes watched his face.

"My name is Beryl," she said then.

Again, Oriel laughed aloud, just for the joy of it. If this wasn't the house of his good fortune, then fortune was a cheat. Again she turned away from his laughter, but this time he thought he understood her feeling, although he didn't understand her reason. "No, lady, why do you turn away?" His hands at his back, his fingers worked at the waist of his trousers.

"Why should you laugh at my name?" she demanded, angry, "when my name is no odder than yours."

"I am not laughing at your name. I am not laughing at you. I am laughing at fortune, or luck as I think, for — " Oriel had worked the beryl out of its hiding place and brought his closed hand around. "Look," he said, and opened his fingers.

Beryl picked the beryl up in her own fingers. "What is it?"

"A precious stone, called a beryl. You see? It's all we have left of what we started out this journey with. So when you tell me your name is Beryl — You seem to me a great good fortune, Beryl."

She looked up, pleased, startled. "I would like to be that," she said, as if he had asked her for a solemn promise and she were giving it. "What do you know of the carving on the back of this?"

"It's a bird," Griff said.

"It seems a strange thing to do to a precious stone," Oriel said. "To carve into it."

Beryl looked from one of them to the other, and

then returned the stone. "It was my grandfather who named me," she said. "But he died when I was young. He had white hair, I remember, and his fingers were bent — " She made her hands into claws.

"Are there no men for the house?" Oriel asked.

"My uncle has gone to the southern Kingdom," she said.

"When do you expect him to return?"

She shrugged, and didn't answer.

Oriel tried another approach. "Do you fear us, Beryl?"

"No," she said.

She told them, "You are right to wonder about me. I have lived alone here the year and more since my uncle traveled to the southern Kingdom. And this spring I'll take the cart to Hildebrand's city by myself, to the spring fair, to try my fortune as puppeteer, which is not what a woman is supposed to do. Because I think if my uncle didn't return after the first winter, then he won't. Whether of his own choice or because he has been cut down, I may never know."

"Are you safe here, alone?" Oriel wondered.

"Aye, safe enough, so far. I am a full two days' journey from the nearest dwelling. The people — " she stood straighter, her dark blue eyes looking directly into his, "might say they feel unsafe so close to me. Distant as I live, I live too close for some."

Oriel was puzzled. She was perhaps sixteen or seventeen summers, and a girl, and of laughing disposition, and willing to care for strangers in need. "Why should anyone fear you?" he asked.

She stood before him as the Wolfer Captains stood before their King. "They say I am a spaewife," she said. "Which I am not, not as they mean it, although

I know herbs to heal with. But that is only because the Herbal was my reading. And would they have me deny my own knowledge, when my knowledge might heal them? But, you see, I gave advice, when I was asked, most often to girls who wished to wed — and they asked what I saw in the future, and I answered — as I should have known not to. I have no powers. I only thought, when I thought of the girl's nature and the man's nature, what would be likely to happen. I only thought, and spoke my thoughts. But it came to pass and so — They call me spaewife, when they are afraid of me. They call me by name when they need my help."

She stood before them.

"So you may wish to leave when the storm lifts, and make your way to a village or to Hildebrand's city."

Oriel looked briefly to Griff, to be certain they were agreed, before he answered. "And why should we, when we have still to learn how to work these puppets, when you have saved our lives? Is it not so, Griff? When this is the best place I have ever come to, in my whole life? The best we have ever known, isn't that so, Griff?"

CHAPTER
21

This good place, where the girl Beryl lived alone, was a small farm at the far end of a narrow valley. Hills rose around it, like a cupped hand. The house lay close to the river, on rising ground, with its farmyard and outbuildings spread out behind. The house had four rooms — the big room for cooking and eating, with its shelves for cookware and food, with the cupboard where the puppets and a few books were kept; a bedroom off one end for Beryl; a bedroom off the other end for Oriel and Griff, and beyond that a storeroom, which had once been another sleeping room but was now crammed full — with

scraps of cloth and wood and string, painted back-
drops, with baskets of onions, milled wheat, parsnips, and apples, with dried herbs in clusters
hanging from the rafters, with a mattressless bed-
stead on which lay boxes of clothing whose wearers
had died, or gone away.

Outside, there was a barn, where fowl roosted in
straw and goats gathered, where a small horse
munched hay in its stall, where the winter feed was
stored. In a back corner, draped over with a heavy
brown cloth, stood the cart. Its long narrow shafts,
between which the horse fit, rested on the dirt floor
of the barn. Oriel and Griff insisted on seeing the
cart, and admired the way it folded down upon itself
to make a protected place for puppets and supplies.
When the lid of the cart was unfolded upward, it
became a puppet stage and the floor of the cart
became boards where the puppeteer stood, hidden
from the crowd, to work his puppets' strings.

Winter wrapped the farm and valley up in snow.
The three of them were isolated at the back of this
valley, at the back of the Kingdom. It seemed as if
there were no other living persons in the world, and
the world was improved by that.

It was not very many days before Oriel felt as if
he had always lived in this place, with these two,
and the snow piled high beyond the door, and the
warm hearth within, and the smells of bread and
stews, and the chores that needed doing. Beryl
showed them how to work the puppets. "The people must never know that the puppeteer is there,"
Beryl said. "The coins are paid to the puppets, not
the puppeteer." Oriel's hands couldn't learn the
knack of the puppets. He couldn't disguise his
voice, either. If he spoke high and soft for a woman,
he only sounded like a man making fun of a woman's

higher voice. If he creaked and groaned with age, Griff and Beryl laughed aloud. He could do any man, soldier or King, slave, lover, highwayman, goatherd, traitor, but it was the words he spoke that changed, not his voice. Griff was quick with the puppets and he could speak convincingly in a child's voice as well as the voice of an old person. But it was Beryl who gave the puppets life. Her hands enabled all of their moving parts to work as if of their own wills. Beryl could speak in anyone's voice, in everyone's voice, and in the voices of animals, too, if animals could speak. Once Beryl walked a young man onto her stage. In the way he strode across the stage, in the set of his shoulders and chin, Oriel recognized himself; the puppet stepped without hesitation to the front of the little stage and looked into the room. He picked out Oriel where he sat. "You know me, don't you?" the puppet asked, as boldly as Oriel himself might have.

Beryl talked freely but asked no questions of Oriel or Griff; in fact, she would not let them speak of themselves, and whenever they started, she would quickly begin some other tale, of her family, of the Kingdom, of Jackaroo, of the healing powers of herbs, of anything it seemed, just not to know their past.

Her own past made a long tale. Her grandfather the puppeteer had come to the Falcon's Wing, the Inn at the southernmost point of the Kingdom, stepping out of the forest on a journey that began nobody knew where, with only an idiot for servant and companion. "Like us," Oriel said. "You're the idiot, Griff."

Griff pointed out, "I'm the one who can work the puppets. That makes me the puppeteer and you the idiot, Oriel."

Beryl's grandmother lived at the Falcon's Wing. Beryl's eyes grew moist as she told this part. The grandmother saw in the first glance that this stranger was the man for her, and her heart never faltered for all of their long lives together. This was the way of the women of her family, Beryl said, to love immediately and always. Beryl was the only child of the couple's youngest daughter. Her own mother had seen the man she wanted and gone with him unhesitatingly; only to return alone, great with the child she gave birth to before dying. "I had grandfather and uncle for mother and father," Beryl said. "I didn't lack anything."

"Why did they leave the southern Kingdom?" Griff asked.

To get away from the Lady Earl's soldiers, Beryl said. The last Earl but one in the south, Gladaegal, Earl Sutherland, had died too soon, leaving two young sons and a third unborn. His lady was made regent, until the oldest son could be named Earl. Only this lady was cruel, and greedy, and perhaps angry to be left so young without a husband. When her eldest son died of a stomach sickness, tongues wagged. Tongues wagged about how he had come to be so sick, and how long the second boy would live — for it was well known that the lady preferred the infant who was at her breast to the boy who was already training at soldiery. This second son drowned, and tongues wagged. Then stories arose of a lost Earl, the true Earl, who had gone away into the southern cities, beyond the Kingdom, and become a great man there — or died young there, in a duel, over a lady's honor; the stories were not certain. "You can imagine how hard it was to know the truth," Beryl said. "You can guess how uneasy people were, under the heavy rule of the lady. My grandfather feared that if the Earl's Lady knew of him, he would be taken by soldiers. Those whom the soldiers took away were never seen again. So my grandfather, with my grandmother and their two youngest children, my uncle and my mother, came away into the north. My grandmother grew herbs, for eating and healing — she wrote the Herbal, which I read in — and shared her understanding of sickness with any who asked it of her. My grandfather was the puppeteer at the fairs, and although he would never perform in any of the lords' great houses — although he was asked, and asked again — he earned enough. My life has been an easy one."

"Why did your uncle go away south?" Oriel asked. "Has the danger passed? Is the Lady Earl dead?"

"She died, but — " Beryl continued the tale. "After her two older sons died, she was regent under the law until the baby grew to a boy of twelve, the year he would be named Earl Sutherland, and then — as she and her priests changed the law, and none dared deny her — until the boy was eighteen summers, and wedded. But the young Earl died soon after his only child was born, and she a daughter, Merlis. With the young Earl dead, his mother again ruled, all through her old age. Thus there is no Earl Sutherland, and has not been for many years. Any man who hopes for the title and lands courts the lady Merlis, in whose inheritance they lie. And she, for the last four of her twenty years, has lived at the King's court, while priests and stewards rule her lands. While her people learn to fear and hate the priests and stewards, and the lords, too, mistrust them. While the priests and stewards, I think, learn to desire the land for themselves. But now the King has declared a tourney, for all the men who would try for the Earldom. They will fight for the title, and the man who is champion will be Earl."

"Then why," Oriel insisted, "did your uncle go away into the south? Leaving you here alone."

"To find out his brothers and sisters. The Falcon's Wing and its village lie far from Lord Yaegar's walled city, which is the southernmost city of the land, so they might be safe. My uncle wondered how they fared in the dangers."

"Why," Oriel asked her again, not many days later, "did he leave you behind alone?"

"Because he knew I would be safe, here in this holding. He knew I could keep the farm and flocks, and if I wanted to, take the puppets to the fair. Because," she looked Oriel right in the eye, "he had started to look at me as a man does at a woman, and so he had to leave, because my uncle is a good man. Because," Beryl said, and her dark blue eyes were steady, "when a man and a woman share a home, when they are together from one day to the next, day after day, desires grow between them."

Oriel thought of Tamara, and understood. A father must be careful who he takes into his home as apprentice, he thought. "When we were at Se — " he started to say, but Beryl raised her hand as if to ward off a blow, and said, "No. Don't tell me anything."

This was not the first time she had silenced them. Griff said that he trusted Beryl to have good reason not to want to know, but Oriel wondered. This day he asked her, "Why do you not let me speak, and tell you my history, and Griff's?"

"Where *is* Griff?" Beryl asked, standing up quickly, putting on her cloak. "He may need help finding eggs, and I need eggs to feed us," she said, her back to Oriel as she hurried out the door. Oriel stayed by the fire, with only the puppets for company, and wondered what was in Beryl's mind.

He found it out, as he thought, that night. Griff had gone to his bed and Oriel rose to follow. Beryl, still seated at the warm fireside, looked up into his face. Her eyes were as dark as a morning sea, and she asked him into her bed.

"Do you know what you offer?" he wondered, and Beryl laughed, although her face had more of anxious hope than laughter in it.

"I've lived among farm animals, all my life," she told him, "so there is little I don't know." Oriel had suspected that she had given him her heart and he was certain of it, after the night. But she said nothing of that to him. He could share her life, he thought, and he knew it would be a gladness to be Beryl's husband; he wondered what Griff would say to that possibility.

In the morning, however, after they had greeted Griff and sat down together, pink-cheeked and contented under his gaze, and after they had all broken fast with bread and cheese, Beryl asked if she might see the green stone again. Oriel gave it to her. She wrapped her fingers around it, as if trying to squeeze it into another shape, and when that failed she opened her hand and set the stone down at the center of the table.

"The falcon," Beryl said, "is the sign of the Earls Sutherland." She looked at Oriel, long and deeply, as she had often looked at him in the night, in the light of the candle that burned by her pillow. "I have wondered how this falconstone came into your hands."

"It belongs to him," Griff said in a quiet voice.

"I don't doubt it," she answered. "But I have wondered, you see — Griff? Do you know what I'm thinking?" Griff nodded. She went on. "I've wondered what it signifies that you bring the falconstone into the Kingdom with you. At this very time."

Oriel saw it all, at once.

As soon as he had seen it, it seemed to him that this destiny had always been waiting here for him. He needed only to go boldly forward. He needed only to try his chance.

If he might be Earl Sutherland —

There was no further thought of husbandry in his head. If he was to be Earl, and win the hand of the lady Merlis, then he could not have a wife. This they all three knew, and didn't speak of, although Oriel and Beryl lived together in her house as a man and his wife would live, sharing chores and bed pleasures, sharing also the forming of the plan that would bring Oriel before the King.

So that Oriel might try his chance to become Earl Sutherland.

They must rehearse until each of the three players knew his parts and the others' parts also, so well that all three played together flawlessly, whatever random line or event the particular occasion might add. Then they must costume Oriel so that he would look a showman, who might be also a lord in secret disguise. He could wear the showman's cape that Beryl's grandfather had worn, and he wore it easily; but beneath the cape, what shirt and what trousers, and how high his boots, were matters of great importance. All must be suggested, but nothing claimed. "It is well you go clean shaven," Beryl said. "It's lords who always have gone clean shaven, as it is lords who know how to read," she said.

"You read also," he protested. "I learned letters at — "

"We need to play the soldier's tale again," she

said. "Come on, both of you. Sluggards," she called them. "Babblebrains. To the field, soldiers!" Her voice rang like a horn. Oriel and Griff obeyed her, laughing.

Rehearsed and ready, they set off for Hildebrand's city, to join in with the fairing throngs, and crowds of entertainers, and also to practice the playing out of their parts before a city crowd. Beryl knew the ways and chose their routes. She skirted the villages that lay between her valley and the city, and when Oriel asked her why, she said that the spaewife could never be sure of her reception in any place where people lived and talked together. So they slept out under the open sky, or under the protection of trees, and one day's journey outside the city Beryl sat by the fire, putting tallow into her autumn-colored hair until it straightened and lay flat. She braided it then, into two long braids, which she coiled around her ears. With her hair so mastered, she herself seemed tamed.

The next morning, Oriel saw for the first time the people of the Kingdom, traveling towards Hildebrand's city for the spring fair. The men were bearded, the women wore their hair coiled around their ears, men and women and children all wore brown homespun. When they were among the crowds, Beryl let Oriel speak, to ask for food or drink at the Inn, or to offer assistance to a fellow traveler. If she needed to say anything, she spoke hesitantly. She explained it: It was dangerous to seem too much the stranger, among strangers. As spaewife she was already feared. As puppeteer, because she was an entertainer, she could live by rules that ordinary folk envied and avoided, but didn't fear, as long as she seemed not much different from everyone else. "If my tongue is as bound as my hair, it behooves you to study for the meaning of my words," she warned them. When she moved among the people, she must seem one of them, lest they notice her and become frightened by her solitariness, and strangeness. Her grandfather had advised her in this.

"Why did he leave his home?" Oriel asked, thinking of how he and Griff had made their way to this place.

Beryl didn't know.

"I think you don't know much about the man," Oriel observed.

"I know what he wanted me to know," she snapped at him. They were naked under the bedclothes in the privacy of their room at the Inn where they would stay, for the fair days. Oriel gathered her to him then, his lively bedwife, who might greet him with a kiss or a challenge, and he couldn't be sure which.

The fair field, for the three days of the fair, was transformed by booths and tents, and the crowds of people, into a small city all of its own. A busy market for livestock was held at the same time, in a fenced ring behind the tents of the merchants and entertainers. Merchants sold wool and skins and blades and paper, woven cloth and leather boots. The smells of food filled the air, breads and sweets and roasts and ales. Voices argued, quarreled, sang, begged, haggled; animals brayed and barked. What struck Oriel, looking about him, wandering about, even more than the sameness of the people's appearance and the contrasting colorful elegance of the lords and ladies when they appeared, was that there were no walls around Hildebrand's city. There was no guarded entry into the city, no way of assuring the inhabitants their nightlong safety.

Beryl told him that the border cities, where strangers might approach the Kingdom in number, did have high stone walls, Northgate's to the west, and Yaegar's in the south, and Arborford, up against the forest in the east.

Did Beryl think of herself as a southerner, Griff asked.

"Nay," Beryl said at last, "when you are the puppeteer, you belong nowhere."

"Nowhere and everywhere," Griff said.

Beryl smiled at him, across the firelight, from within Oriel's arm.

There were four puppet plays to give, one after the other, and then a short rest before beginning the round again. On the first day, before the first play, just before Oriel would emerge from behind the puppet stage, he pulled his showman's cloak close around him, and doubted himself. Beryl and Griff had no time for him, being busy with the puppets as they settled themselves into place over the small stage. Oriel was alone with his own unsureness.

But why should he doubt himself, he wondered, who had been always a man to be reckoned with, even when he had been a boy. That thought gave wings to his spirits. Bold as sunlight, he had promised himself, and so he would be — and he turned his face to the sky and loosened his fingers from the cloak's edge. For if he did not dare to be showman, how could he dare to try for Earl?

He stepped out. The small audience barely noticed him, so intent were they on the lowered curtain. He stood, and waited, watching the figures and faces. He recognized, as they gradually turned their faces to him, the wondering, hopeful eyes — which was what he had been accustomed to see, all of his life, except for those rare occasions when, like Nikol, the eyes had held a dangerous stillness. Even Rulgh had looked wonderingly at him.

Oriel opened his cloak out, like the wings of a falcon, and smiled, and bowed his head to his audience, and greeted them. "We have a tale to tell," he said. His voice, his gestures, his face, something about him gathered the crowd together, and gathered in also those who had thought to walk by without stopping to see the puppets. Oriel sat down on the edge of the cart, with the stage at his left shoulder. "Once there lived a woodcutter," he said.

That was the cue. He heard the curtain draw up behind him. The faces before him moved their attention to the stage. "Who went out early in the morning, to chop the wood he would take to market." Behind him the puppets clattered, as the woodcutter bade his wife good day, shouldered his axe, and marched off. This was the story of the woodcutter who caught the dragon's tail, and so won the wishes, which his wife used to get more wealth, until finally she wished herself King. When she became King, she drove her woodcutter husband away, and he went back to the forest, and freed the dragon from where the axe held him pinned. The wife was left in her plain rags before the proud lords and ladies of the court, and in her plain wits, and they drove her out of the palace. She made her miserable way back to the woodcutter's cottage.

This point of the story, as the puppet wife returned to the little cottage painted onto a cloth, was where Oriel needed to be more than showman. He turned to the audience. "And how shall the husband greet her?" he asked.

A man's voice cried out that her head should be

taken off, or maybe she should be driven with sticks far into the forest and left to fend for herself if she could and to die if she couldn't. Another man's voice said she should be forgiven, for women couldn't help their greed. A woman said she should be made to be a servant to the woodcutter and never again a wife. At the harsh judgments, the puppet herself stepped forward to persuade the audience to mercy, and to harangue them for their pitilessness. "I'm only a poor old woman," she whined. "What would you have of me?"

Then the woodcutter came home, with his day's labors on his back, and she set meekly about being his wife again. "And so they lived the rest of their days in harmony," Oriel ended the tale.

Afterwards, as the plays went on, the thought flew about in Oriel's head, like a bird trapped in a barn: The crowd had answered the puppet's questions, so they would let her have her own life. He could hope now that when they trailed their net in the King's city, they might snare the King. There was good reason to hope.

Hope, and the soaring sense of the crowd that wished him well, and opened their purses to him gladly, was not strange to Oriel, or unexpected. But to have his boldest hopes confirmed — he could have leaped up to a mountain's peak and laughed into the sky with it. For if he could have the chance, he could win the Earldom. He was the man to be the Earl Sutherland.

At the dance that evening, with the fiddlers and pipers playing music that bubbled like water under his feet, Beryl would not dance with him. He chose, then, girls whose hair fell loose down their backs, going boldly up to such a one with his hand held out, to lead her into the dance. And she would always take his hand, and follow him into the circle of dancers, and follow him with her eyes when the dance was over and he led another partner into another circle of dancers.

At last Griff stopped him, to take him back to where Beryl stood. Beryl told him that those girls were only wed that morning and unless he wished every bridegroom at the fair to seek his blood, he had better become one of the circle of watchers, aye, and best to stand apart from her. For he should not become known as the Spaewife's man. Not if he would be Earl. If he would be Earl, Beryl advised him, then as showman he had best be seen to be alone, to stand apart from all other men. "As you do," Beryl added. "Is it not so, Griff?"

Griff was there in the shadows with them. "It was always so, lady," he said. "From the first — "

"Aye, don't tell me," Beryl said, and held up her hand to Oriel as if it was he who had spoken.

Then, one afternoon, Oriel was challenged. As the puppets bowed behind him, and in front of him the people laughed and clapped their hands together and reached into their purses to drop copper or silver coins into the basket, a man's voice called out. "You, Showman. Show-peacock."

Oriel stepped forward, searching the crowd for the face that voice might speak from. A rough-bearded man stepped to the front of the crowd, with two companions. All had dark hair, and they might have been brothers. "You, Showman. Have you a name?"

His was the voice of a man eager for the fight. "Aye," Oriel said, but said no more. If there was to be a fight, it would not be one he asked for; neither would it be one he feared.

The crowd subsided, whispering, watching.

"Are you too proud to give it out, this name?"

"No," Oriel said. He could have laughed aloud.

"See him, people," the man said. "He goes unbearded. Would you wonder what his name is, when he goes unbearded, and colors his shirt, and his boots are up to his knees?"

The crowd's curiosity was raised, and Oriel thought he might satisfy it. But he was careful to toss his name out to the crowd like a girl's laugh, not to give it up to the man like a surrendered weapon. "Oriel." He called it out clearly.

A ripple went through the crowd, and for the first time Oriel was uneasy. He didn't understand. But the man did, as his smile showed.

"Rik's my name. Although you are too proud to ask for it. Or-i-el," Rik said, dragging out the letters. "And you came from the south, I'll wager, that's what you'll say, if I ask you."

Oriel was opening his mouth to agree, when the murmurs warned him. The language was the one Oriel spoke himself, but Rik's tone was a Wolfer tone, the way a Wolfer with his blade at a man's throat spoke, and stood, and smiled.

"You'll say the south, Showman, Or-i-el with your high-stepping name, aye, and your fancy clothing, like a lord, isn't it? Isn't the creature made to look like a lord?"

The crowd murmured behind Rik, now nearly convinced by him. Griff stepped out from behind the stage. "What is it?" he asked quietly.

Oriel shook his head, without taking his eyes from Rik's face. "Don't know. Wait."

"For we all know what the girl is," Rik called.

He said that, as if that was what he had been waiting to give voice to. The sigh of fear that rippled like rising water among the crowd greeted these awaited words.

Rik turned to the crowd, but his two companions stayed facing Oriel, and Griff. "I know what I think she is," Rik said. "I've heard of women who can take the bones of dead men, and the blood of living babes, and stir them in a pot. When such women say the words, they draw on the power that threw stars out into the sky, the power that cracked open stone mountains to let out rivers — They say the words and a living dead man steps out of the cauldron."

Oriel watched the faces. They were unsure, and in their fear ready to be convinced.

"Aye, Rik, she's only a girl," a woman's voice called. Rik turned to see who had spoken, but could not catch her. Once the woman had broken silence, a man asked, "Aye, and how has she harmed you, Rik?"

The man meant well, meant peacefulness, but the question inflamed Rik. He didn't answer the man, but wheeled around to pour his hatred out onto Oriel. "I ask you again, who are you?"

It was not the time for a soft answer, nor for a coward's answer, whatever Beryl might have advised. Oriel would choose his own way, and he would take it boldly. "I am the Spaewife's man."

This was not the answer Rik had looked for. It was not the answer the crowd had expected. It displeased Rik, but the crowd saw something to like in it.

"I am the Spaewife's man, for her goodness, and her honor," Oriel said.

"And I also," said Griff at his shoulder.

"So you had best tell us in what way she has

harmed you, Rik," Oriel said. By naming the man, Oriel isolated him from all the rest. Rik had to answer alone, now.

"Aye, and she gave a charm to the girl who was to be my wife, and she refused to wed me then, and she wed another. Until then, the girl had been mine, as her father and her brothers agreed, and the holding that her father gave with the girl would have doubled my lands. Aye, and I am a man of broad lands and fat flocks, and the girl had never said nay to me before, until the witch charmed her. On the day we were to wed, friends," he added. This the crowd sympathized with. "Her father came, and her brothers, and they brought her there, but the girl would not say the words. Aye, and she had been found at the Spaewife's cart."

Oriel didn't know what the crowd was thinking. He only knew what his own choices were — to fight, with whatever chance he himself had against Rik's bulk, and he thought his agility made chances even; to call Beryl out to speak for herself; to make the fight general and then flee at the first chance, when the melee grew wild enough; or to say his thoughts and trust the crowd to prefer him. He thought they might, he thought they already did if he could give them good reason. He thought, if he made that choice and it failed, he could then choose among the others, so he had little to lose.

He angled his head to one side, waited for silence, then asked, "So the great harm is she took away your wife-to-be from you?"

"Aye," Rik grumbled, and his companions echoed him.

"I think she did harm you, then," Oriel said. Rik smiled, seeing a victory. Oriel went on. "To take not just the girl, but also her dowried lands, despite the word her father and brothers had given to you. Great harm to you," Oriel said again, and some of the crowd — who suspected his thought — grinned up at him. "But I wonder if it wasn't a great good for the girl."

Rik turned red, from chagrin and embarrassment, as the people behind him laughed at the trap Oriel had set, and called out agreement to Oriel, and women's voices called out approval of what the puppeteer had done for the girl, if she had done it, whether she had done it by charm or spell, or merely good advice, as sisters might speak to one another. Rik turned pale then, and his hands clenched at his side, but even his two companions had slipped back away from him. Besides, there was something he saw in Oriel's face that he didn't quite dare challenge any further.

Rik turned his back on the puppet stage and the two men who stood before it. He shouldered his way out through the crowd. The crowd finished what they had started earlier — fishing into purses and drawing out coins; people came forward to drop their coins into the basket. They stared hard at Oriel while they did this, although they asked him no questions.

Each day, each hour, the audience before their stage grew larger. Oriel and Griff carried purses heavy with coins by the time the days of the fair drew to a close. It seemed that everyone who had come to the fair spoke of the mysterious showman, and wondered who he was, and where he had come from.

When the fair days at Hildebrand's city were done, Oriel and Beryl and Griff traveled with the entertainers and merchants on the King's Way to the King's city, where they would try their scheme to catch the King's attention. Oriel had at his back, safely hidden, the beryl. It was on the Damall's beryl, with the falcon carved into the stone, that the scheme rested.

CHAPTER
22

The King's city overlooked the joining of two rivers. The King's palace was at the tip of the peninsula formed by those rivers. Behind the palace, and around its spreading gardens, lay the city itself, its buildings of stone and wood, its twisting streets, the spacious gardens behind the houses where great lords lived, and the open squares and markets. There were no walls around the palace and there were no walls around the city. The fair field, where for five days tents and booths would be crammed with people, lay just beyond the city.

In the crowds that came to see the puppet plays

there were more lords and ladies, more servants in livery, bands of soldiers, and occasionally a priest or a pair of priests. It was to the priests that the puppet first whispered, "Take me to the King. I have something to tell."

The puppet whispered this as if he had a true life of his own, and had seen the priest out of living eyes, and chosen to speak out of a living will. But in fact Oriel gave the cue, if there was a likely man in the audience. "Let the play commence," he would say, with a showman's upward lifting of the arm; and Beryl, hearing him say *commence*, not *begin*, would know that at some time during the story, a puppet should come forward to whisper to the audience.

Oriel gave the cue twice for priests, in the five days of the fair, and once for a man in purple livery, with a crown stitched over his heart in silver threads, whom he took for one of the King's household servants. So that was three times the whisper had been started, before the rest of the entertainers went on south, following the fair to Sutherland's city and then on to the other two smaller cities of the south before the final days at Yaegar's city, with its tall stone walls to defend the forest entry into the Kingdom and guard the River Way. The rest of the fair, merchants and entertainers, beggars and cooks, moved on under the care of a troop of soldiers. The puppeteer and her two men stayed on in the King's city, performing in Innyards and beside fountains, and when a likely messenger stood among the watching crowd, one of the puppets would come to the front of the stage to whisper across the audience, "Take me to the King. I have something to tell."

Oriel watched his audience when this happened. He could see the questions in their faces. Was this a jest or was it a plot? Was it done merely to make a mystery that would draw crowds, and draw coins from purses? Or was there some urgent message the King must hear, and these bold puppeteers, and the handsome showman, too, him especially, were they heroes for the Kingdom? For all knew of the unrest in the south, and all knew how precarious was the temporary peace among those ambitious to be named Earl Sutherland. All hoped the King's Tourney would produce a strong champion, a man who could gather up the reins of the unruly Earldom and win obedience from its willful lords, and let its people till their fields in peace, and raise their herds without alarms, and pay taxes to only one lord, only at the customary times of the year. But what could a puppet know? And was there not some story that the puppeteer was a girl? Aye, and spaewife, too, who could read the future in a woman's palm, and knew what spells would cure, or cause, disease? And who was this showman who seemed to gather all of his audience together into a single heart?

The crowds flocked to Innyard and fountain square, and Oriel — who could gather them together with his voice, and hold them attentive — thought it was only a matter of time before one of the whispers reached the right ear, and the puppets were summoned to play before the King.

That time came, and the summons came, and Oriel stood at last in a long, tall-windowed hall, bathed, fresh shaven, on Beryl's advice wearing a green shirt. Before him sat the King, with his Queen beside him, and their children around them. Also present were the lords and ladies of the court, as well as a few priests and soldiers and ministers. Servants waited patiently at the rear of the hall, just as Oriel did at its front. It was the middle of a long, late spring afternoon, and sunlight the color of jonquils blew into the hall. Oriel looked at the young women of the audience, to recognize Merlis among the ladies. He saw a brown-haired girl in a golden dress, her hands folded in her lap and her face serene, and knew her for the lady who would win his heart, the lady Merlis. He saw her, and named her, and was content.

They had chosen their three plays carefully. Two were taken out of the old puppeteer's book, which was also the source of the third, but the third had been added to until it had to be called a new story. The first was a tale of a Prince who fought a dragon, to save his land and win the hand of his Princess. Oriel and Griff had carved and painted the dragon puppet, which always drew gasps of alarm and admiration from an audience. At the end of this play, in the silence after the clapping had ended, the King leaned across his sons to say to Oriel's golden-gowned girl, "Doesn't it make you wish our land was troubled by a dragon, Daughter? that such a Prince might come forward, to save us?"

If she was not Merlis, then, as she could not be if she was the King's daughter, Merlis must be some other young woman. Oriel looked again, and saw a lady sitting proud in a green gown, with gold ribbons worked into her long dark hair. This, he thought, was the lady before whom he would lay down his heart. This was Merlis.

The second puppet story was one the people told, about the old farmer who wished to wed a young wife, so he disguised himself as he courted her. On their wedding night when he changed into his nightshirt behind the screen, the old farmer flung over it his false hair and binding corset; unable to see that his young wife, undressing behind her screen, was flinging over it her own false hair and binding corset. This was the cleverest puppetry, and the King's court responded wholeheartedly. The lady in green rose up at its end, and went to stand behind a young courtier with her hand on his shoulder, as a wife does.

Oriel looked around again, while his audience talked among itself and smiled up at him. Would Merlis smile so, he wondered, if she were the daughter of an Earl? Might dark-rimmed grey eyes mark this smiling lady as of Earl's lineage, with the white fur trimming her gown as a lady of wealth must wear. Oriel readied himself to give this lady his heart.

However, the third tale began what he must succeed at in order to set about winning the heart beneath those grey eyes, and the lands she brought with her. Oriel concentrated on his showman's part, to make the puppet play work; for the story was too complicated to be told without a showman. It was the story of the Emperor's stolen daughter, and of the loyal soldier who spent his life seeking for her, despite the perfidy of courtiers and the enmity of kingdoms, despite year after year of failure. At the last, the soldier found a child and in a dream was told that this child — if he could rule over the Emperor's realms — would bring lasting peace to the land. The soldier returned along the ways he had come, to take the child to the Emperor. Some people helped him, some sought his death, some tried to take the child and either put him under their power, or kill him. The loyal soldier persisted, but was overcome by treachery. He died on the gallows, asking for word to be taken to the Emperor. But the Emperor was dying then, on his golden bed, under silken bedclothes, still mourning his lost daughter. And the soldier's dream-named child was lost in the crowd that watched the hanging. "They had only hope," Oriel said, as the curtain slowly lowered, "that the child would live, and find his way, and become Emperor, and bring peace to the people."

Pale tears fell out of her dark-rimmed grey eyes and down over her soft cheeks. The King sighed, and turned to his Queen to say, "I wish Merlis would have come to see these puppets. For all that she protests, I think she would have found them worthy."

Then the lady was not here. Oriel would have laughed at himself if he had been alone, would have laughed at his own hopes; and he was sorry to lose the grey-eyed lady, for he knew she had a heart that the puppets could touch.

"Not trivial at all, are they, Gwilliane?" the King asked.

"Not at all trivial," his Queen assented. "They should be generously rewarded, don't you think?"

"Indeed so." The King rose from his heavy chair, a man of middle years and of middle height, of a certain plump dignity of carriage, and with a pleasant expression on his round-cheeked face. The King had the face of a man to whom life has always been a pleasing affair.

A tall, spare man, whose face seemed carved from pale wood, so much did it refuse to bear any expression, leaned forward, to speak into the King's ear. He wore a red shirt, high-collared, and carried a sheathed sword at his waist. "Yes, one must inquire," the King said, and both watched Oriel.

Oriel thought this must be a soldier, and one of high rank, since he could speak so closely to the King. When he stepped forward, with a clanking of the metal of his sword and a creaking of the leather of his boots, Oriel moved to meet him. They faced one another. Oriel thought he ought to be uneasy, but he was not. He had no weapon, nor plan. He had only his own words and his own self, but he felt well armed.

"The King wonders, and I wonder, what might be the meaning of the whisper, the reports of which have been often brought to his attention," the soldier said.

A black-robed priest, who wore a heavy gold ring on his right hand, joined the soldier. "My priests heard of it."

A third man, clothed like an ordinary lord except for the heavy silver chain he wore upon his chest, joined the other two. "It reached my ears as well," he said, in a voice as pleasing as song.

Oriel answered all of them. "I would tell the King alone."

"Not possible," the soldier said, without hesitation. At the same time the King said, "We can go — " and the smiling man objected, "It is customary to have others present when — " and the priest asked, "Is it safe?"

The Queen asked, "Is a man who rules ever entirely safe?"

"Please be seated, sire," the soldier said to the King. "I think that this showman must speak before us all."

"Yes," the King acquiesced. "That must be so. What then is the news your puppets wished to be brought to me, Showman?"

"No news, sire," Oriel said. Now, facing the King, he felt uneasy. He could pass it all off as a jest they had thought up in order to draw crowds to the puppet show. This King would not punish him for such a jest. Why should Oriel, after all, think he was a man to try for the Earldom, the lands, and the hand of the lady?

The question made him smile, and gave him confidence. Because he was such a man, and more. He looked over the crowd, briefly, and saw that few of them were interested in the events at the front of the hall. Aye, but they would be, and soon, he thought, reaching into a deep pocket that had been sewn into the hem of his shirt. He held the beryl out to the King.

Puzzled, the King looked to his Queen, who smiled. The King held out an open palm. Oriel dropped the green stone into it.

The King recognized it immediately, and the Queen also. Both looked intently up into Oriel's face. The King's face, in its kindness, was troubled. "I will hear this young man privately."

"Yes, but with your closest advisors present," the Queen said. She rose from her chair then. "Let us withdraw," she announced to the court, which followed her out of the long hall. The King and the three men remained.

"Is there not another behind the screen here, one who works the strings of the puppets?" the smiling lord inquired.

"There are two," Oriel answered, and then turned to the King. "They companion me, and advise me. I ask their company, sire."

He did not need Griff and Beryl with him to bolster his courage, but he wanted the two behind him, so that he might be understood to be not a man alone. Oriel's mind worked swiftly, calculating the expression of each of the four men, calculating his chances, looking for sources of enmity and measuring its strength. Here, were subtle dangers. Oriel had led a troop of boys out into shelterless places and brought all safely home, he had sailed night seas, and he had faced wild men in hopeless battle. He had chosen to fly down the steep mountainside in risk of death by catastrophe rather than take the known way in risk of death by privation. But the present adventure was the one, the only one, that he had chosen for himself. These subtle dangers he had sought out.

"Is there any reason to refuse his request?" the King asked his attendants. "What do you advise?"

The three consulted together before they gave assent. Oriel called his companions out. Griff stood at his left shoulder, a little behind, and Beryl at his right. Both Griff and Beryl wore the brown of the people. Beryl had her braided hair wound around her ears, and the only way Griff differed from the men of the people was in his clean-shaven face, and the crescent scar.

"Your names?" the smiling man demanded.

"This is Griff, who has traveled with me from the first," Oriel said. "This is Beryl," he introduced her.

"A woman," the soldier said.

"As you see, my lord," Beryl answered. "As befits a land where the King attends to the words of his Queen and consort."

"And so I do," the King assented. "You're right to point that out, Baer, and I am glad to think that my people know me so well."

Then the King and his advisors waited for Oriel to name himself.

Oriel knew that, and let the wordless time grow, until at last he broke the silence to demand, as boldly and discourteously as it had been demanded of him, "Your names?" He looked at the courtier, who did not smile now, and at the priest, whose eyes narrowed under grey eyebrows. It was the soldier who answered him, with an approving nod, "Haldern. First Captain, Lord Haldern. First Minister, Lord Tseler," he waved a hand at the courtier, "and Lord Karossy, First Priest as well as Custodian of the Books of Laws and History." Lord Haldern bowed stiffly, from the waist. When he did that the other two had to follow his example, or make their quarrel known.

Oriel and Griff imitated him, while Beryl curtsied.

"My name is Oriel," Oriel said then, speaking to the King.

"Oriel?" The King studied him, as if he recognized something about him. "What do you want of me, Oriel?"

"I would ask of you the privilege to enter the Tourney, and to try my chance to be Earl Sutherland. No more than that," Oriel answered.

"Do you think," Lord Tseler inquired, "to purchase that right with the stone?"

Oriel understood what the First Minister was attempting to discover about him. He answered boldly. "I have no desire to part with the stone, unless the King will take it as a gift — For it is mine to give — or to spend — as I will — or to keep. I show the stone, sire, to claim my right to ask a place in the Tourney."

"Do you not overreach yourself?" Lord Karossy asked.

Oriel thought there was no need to answer that, which was not a question. He stood patiently until a real question might be asked him, or an answer might be given to his request.

"Your name is Oriel," Lord Haldern said, "and you are not, I think, a man of the Kingdom."

"That is true," Oriel agreed.

"What land do you come from?" Lord Tseler asked.

"From countries to the south," Oriel answered. "As far back as I remember, I come from an island far to the south of this Kingdom."

The three advisors conferred again, until Lord Tseler inquired, "Who is your father and what is his station?"

"I cannot say," Oriel said. "I never knew, and had no way to discover. Nor mother, neither."

"Your age?" the King asked abruptly, as if curiosity had caused him to speak out of turn.

"Not less than eighteen winters, as near as I can count," Oriel said.

The King shook his head, as if that was not the answer he had hoped for. He turned to say to Lord Karossy, "You know the story I am thinking of. You know the book."

Lord Karossy had a fleshless face that sloped forward to his long, sloping nose. Oriel couldn't have said whether he was an old man or a man of moderate years. He was thin as a tree in winter. "Surely he is too young," Lord Karossy protested.

"Just fetch the book," Lord Haldern said, impatient.

The King was a comfortable man, even as he sat in a chair that he made a throne by sitting in it. He merely nodded his approval when Lord Tseler leaned down to say, softly enough for privacy but loud enough for all to hear, "If you give Karossy your word that no one will ask the man any further questions while he is out of the way, then I think he'll do your bidding swiftly."

"You have my word, Karossy," the King said. He turned back to Lord Tseler, who was pulling straight his white overshirt and brushing smooth his long vest. "I would remind you, Minister, that the man has a name. Oriel."

The minister took the correction humbly, or so Oriel thought until he caught the expression in the man's eyes. "I beg your pardon, Oriel," Lord Tseler said, and his eyes begged nothing of the kind, would beg nothing of Oriel.

Oriel answered on a laugh, giving his pardon as if he were accustomed to having it asked by the great men of the Kingdom, as if it were not possible for someone as insignificant as Lord Tseler to offend him.

They awaited Lord Karossy's return in a silence of occasionally cleared throats, and shuffled feet, and questions almost asked. "Did you — ?" "No, did you — ?" Lord Karossy brought back with him a large, leather-covered book, which he carried before him like a babe. The King held out his hands to take the book, but Lord Karossy gave it instead to Oriel, with a sharp glance from under the grey eyebrows, and terse instructions. "The section the King remembers is twenty-six pages back from the center."

By the expression on Tseler's face, and the consternation on the Captain's, and the displeasure on the King's, Oriel knew Lord Karossy hoped to snare Oriel somehow through the book. He couldn't know exactly how the snare worked, but he knew how he planned to elude it. First he asked the King's permission to read. That given, with Lord Karossy mumbling apologies to the King, Oriel opened the book to its center. Silently, he counted back twenty-six pages. Silently, he stood and read.

The page told part of the Kingdom's history, not as a story is told, but as if the writer wrote down notes of the significant events for later reference. Oriel read slowly, to understand why the King had sent for this book. A name caught his eye, written in fading ink on the heavy paper. He read the writing: "Sutherland's heir slain, leaving eldest son Orien." Later, the name reappeared in the small script. "Orien gone, rumor says run off — murdered by brother? — to wed his southern Princess."

Oriel questioned the King. "What would the writer mean when he spoke of a southern Princess, sire?"

"There are no such southern Princesses in the Kingdom," the King answered, which was what Oriel expected to hear. "I think it must mean a Princess from the lands beyond the great southern forest, beyond the Kingdom, where maps picture a sea, and stories describe a watery world as endless as a forest."

Oriel nodded calmly, although his heart raced. He thought he knew the King's mind in this. "Orien's year gone. Gladaegal sworn Earl. Dry season in the north but generous crops in the south, so doling rooms fully stocked. Queen brought to bed of a son."

Oriel passed the open book to Griff, ignoring the expressions on the faces of the King's advisors, and pointed with his finger. Beryl studied the stone floor of the hall, avoiding his glance, and he judged that her own skill in reading must be kept a secret.

Griff read, looked at Oriel, closed the book. He said nothing. He returned the book to Oriel, who returned it to the King, who passed it back to Lord Karossy.

"It's the story of Orien I was thinking of," the King said to Lord Haldern and Lord Tseler.

"That was long ago, in your father's time," Lord

Tseler said. "Was it not? If I remember correctly, for my memory is not as fine as yours, sire."

"Do you think of some magic, sire?" Lord Haldern asked, and the thought troubled him. "Do you think to explain the falconstone? By what, an ageless sleep?"

The King answered neither of them. "Step forward, you, man. Griff? It is Griff, isn't it? Step forward."

As if they had often played this game together, Griff first asked Oriel's permission, and only when he had it did he approach the King. Even concentrated as he was on winning his desire from the King, Oriel understood how fortunate he was in Griff's quick understanding, and his unwavering loyalty. The King reached up from where he sat, to pull Griff's head down, and then turn it to one side, to show the scar on his cheek.

Oriel thought to protest, but chose to keep silent a little longer.

"There was a story, was there not? about the lost Earl. That he had been scarred on his face, in a battle with pirates?" The King asked these questions of his advisors, and then released Griff, who returned to Oriel's side.

"You wish to let the man try his luck," Lord Haldern spoke. "You think — and I agree, sire — that there are too many coincidences."

"What coincidences?" Lord Tseler demanded.

Lord Haldern answered. "The name. The scar — never mind that it's on another's face. He comes as he says from lands to the south. He brings a falconstone. These are coincidences enough for me. You, Griff, where did you get that scar? Come on, man, speak up — or shall I whip it out of you?"

Oriel couldn't have held his tongue if he had

wanted to. "You'll whip no one, unless it's me."

He needed to say no more. His word was good, and every man in that room knew it. Moreover, by the expression deep in Lord Haldern's eyes, he saw that the soldier had hoped he would answer a threat to Griff in just that manner.

"Baer?" Lord Tseler asked. His voice was rich and soft and pleasant, but it was dangerous.

"Sir?" Beryl looked up. She feared these men. Oriel didn't know why she should fear them, when she stood under his protection.

"I think you are a subject of this Kingdom?" Lord Tseler asked.

"Yes."

"Who is your father?" he asked. "Who are you, that you come here with this man?"

"I am the puppeteer's granddaughter," Beryl answered, "and my father was a soldier, who left my mother behind. She, dying, left me behind, a newborn babe. Now, I am the puppeteer."

"What do you know of these men, Baer?" the King asked.

"Sire, they came to my door in a winter storm, and that is all I know. Hildebrand gave my grandfather a holding which stands alone at the western edge of a narrow valley, far beyond any other village or habitation. My uncle had it from my grandfather, and now I keep the farm and flocks. If you follow the river backwards into Hildebrand's lands you will reach my uncle's holding. Beyond me to the west are only empty forests and bare hills, and the mountains."

"Was it this last winter when they came to your door?" Lord Karossy asked.

"Aye, it was, sir. In a storm. They wore wolf skins over bare shoulders, and wolf skins wrapped around their bare feet. They had boards tied onto their feet in a strange manner. They were starving, thirst tormented them, they were exhausted. They said they had come over the mountains."

"Did you believe them?" Lord Karossy asked, as if he intended to credit Beryl's answer.

"Aye," Beryl said. "I believe them."

"It will be you," Lord Tseler's voice said, "who hatched this scheme to bring Oriel before the King."

"Aye," Beryl said. "When I saw the green stone, with the falcon carved," she said, and hesitated, looking at Oriel, before she went on. "All know that the falcon is the sign of the Earls Sutherland. All know of the Tourney, to name the next Earl. I thought the King should know of the stone, and the man who owned it."

"How do you know he owns it?" Lord Tseler asked, sharply now, as if at last he had caught her out, as if at last now the truth would be told.

"Aye, he told me so, my lord," Beryl answered him. "He is a true man," she said.

"But does that make him worthy to be Earl?" Lord Karossy asked.

"I can't answer that, sir."

The King interrupted. "That's not a fair question to ask, when there is one man in the room who is entered in the Tourney himself, and two of us who have sons contending. Do *you* think you are worthy to be Earl?" the King asked Oriel.

"If I did not think so," he said, "I would not have come before you."

Having answered that, and all the other questions, he judged it time to require an answer of the King. He looked at all four of the men's faces, wondering how he should put the question. He could choose one of the three advisors to be his sponsor, and trust in that man's influence with the King. He could ask all three, one after the other, which might join them together in his support, but might insult the King's pride by seeming to put his advisors before him in importance. He could make his suit to the King — but the King never seemed to determine anything without taking advice — and moreover he might thus risk offending the other three by seeming to put the King before them in importance, and risk further that they might band together against him.

The King, he thought, wished to say yes to him, for the fact of the stone, and the nearness of the name, and Griff's scar. For the King, those were reasons enough. So it was the King he asked, and he went down on his knee to make the request. "I ask permission to try my chance to win the Earldom, sire," he said.

"You must meet the lady," the King said.

That was answer enough for Oriel. He rose, satisfied.

But the King's advisors were not satisfied. "Do you grant his suit?" Lord Karossy asked.

"We don't even know if he can fight," Lord Haldern said. "If he can't, it's only a cruelty to let him try. Can you, Oriel? With sword, and lance? On foot and on horseback? As to words, I think we have seen already how well you fight with words."

Ignoring the question of lance and horse, Oriel spoke from confidence. "I have some training in soldiery, sir. I have fought for my life, and I think I will fight as well for an Earldom."

"He has time to learn what he doesn't know," the King said. "The Tourney isn't until the autumn fair."

"But he's a stranger, and knows nothing of our laws," Lord Tseler objected. "I can't permit this, sire."

He had gone too far. "But I can, and I do. As long as I am your King," the King said.

PART V

THE
EARL
SUTHERLAND

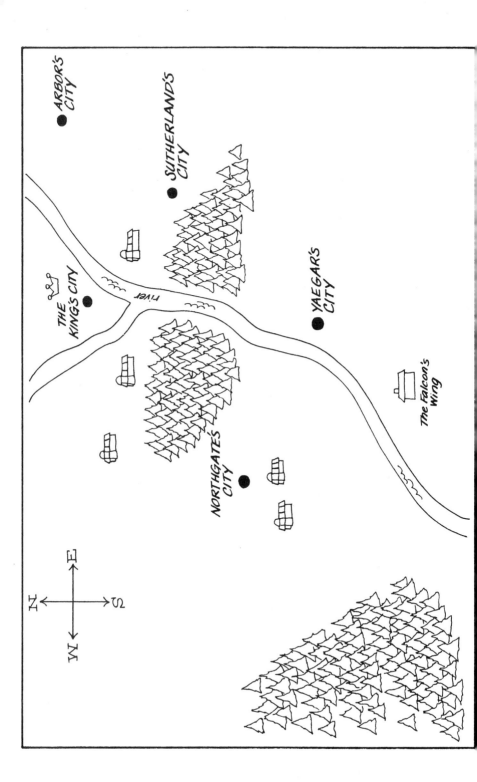

CHAPTER
23

Oriel would be the King's man in the Tourney. "If you agree to stand in my sponsorship," the King said, "then no man will deny you the right to take your chance. Who is the victor of the Tourney, that man will be Earl Sutherland. He will wed — you aren't married, are you?"

"No," Oriel said.

"The victor will wed Merlis, only child of the last Earl. Thus he will join himself to the ancient house of Sutherland, and insure that his children will have the blood of Earls in their veins. In direct line," the King added. "There are many who can claim the lineage, including my own family. I have two nephews in the lists, and one son. Tseler has his eldest born entered. Haldern is himself a contender, for he has long been a widower. Many lords have sent also their sons, and grandsons."

"Many of the southern lords," Oriel guessed.

"Also the northern houses," the King told him. "For every house has younger sons ambitious for a higher place than birth gives them. I think there is no house that is not represented."

"Arbor's," Lord Haldern spoke.

"That's so," the King said. "Arborford sends no man, although the lord Arbor has two sons here as pages, and neither one of them is the elder son, and both are brave lads. He will not give them permission to enter the Tourney."

"Why is that?" Oriel asked.

The King didn't know. He looked to Lord Haldern, who answered, "Arbor says, he will not have his sons fighting one another to the death, brother against brother."

Lord Tseler had something to add. "Arbor says also that he will not have younger sons dreaming that they might supercede the elder. He says, he is master in his own house and he will serve his Earl, and he will serve his King, and both willingly, but he doesn't think he could accept service to his own son."

"Or," Lord Haldern added, "service to any man who had slain his son."

Oriel needed to be sure he had understood correctly, so he asked, "The Tourney must be played to the death?"

"To the death," the King echoed sadly. "That is not my will," he said, "but my will has been overruled."

There was soft whispering behind Oriel, and then Griff spoke in his ear. "Ask, if you can, how a King's will might be overruled." It was good advice, and he guessed that Beryl had given it. He guessed also that Beryl couldn't give her own voice to her own question. He gave his voice to it, thinking that if a King couldn't work his own will, then a man who would be Earl should know why, for his power was more limited than the King's.

The King didn't answer him. He looked at his First Captain, and then at the First Priest, where they stood beside Lord Tseler.

"The King's will cannot, of course, be overruled," Lord Karossy said, the words formed precisely by the thin lips. "That is the law. A wise man, however, knows his own limitations and takes counsel when it is needed, for every man, even a King, can profit from counsel."

Oriel looked from one man to the other, thinking his own thoughts. The King's sad expression said that a King must stand by his own rulings.

"A man who has seen a chance to increase his own wealth, lands, power," Lord Tseler began. He spoke the words slowly, as if they were addressed to one who might have difficulty understanding what men of greater understanding comprehended without explanation. "If he has seen his chance and then lost it, he will in his bitterness be a great danger to the man who has won it from him."

"If you defeat a man in trial of arms, or battle, and let him live," Lord Haldern warned, "you'll have an enemy in him, and probably in his sons as well. That's common sense."

"For you have taken something away from him," Lord Karossy explained, "and he will feel the need to take the thing, or something of equal value, away from you."

They were convincing, but Oriel wasn't convinced. However, the argument of it wasn't what concerned him, not at this time. "Do you mean then that at every contest there will and must be a man left dead on the ground?"

"Yes," Lord Haldern said, with a resolution that seemed strange to Oriel, until he remembered that Haldern himself was a contender.

"Not the spoken contest," the King pointed out. "And if your opponent is unhorsed with the lance, and cannot rise up, there is no need to slay him."

Lord Haldern ignored the King. "You must go to the Tourney as if you went to the chance of your own death. For that is what you do."

Oriel, who had lived months as captive to the Wolfers, knew enough about facing death to measure Haldern's courage. But by the same token, he knew too much about facing death to wish to be the death-dealer.

"Griff?" he asked. If Griff thought as he was thinking, then Oriel knew the right of it. For he knew the truth of Griff.

"For myself," Griff said, after thought, "I would choose the risk of making a friend out of an enemy. If he were my enemy in a fair contest. A fair contest," he amended, "fairly fought. For I don't think I would become an enemy to a man for the reason of him proving more able or more worthy than I am. I don't think you would do that either, Oriel. Although, we have known some who would hate a man for just that reason."

It was decided, then. And if Oriel was going to lose this chance, then he would lose it now, and absolutely. If he was going to give it up, he didn't wish to prolong the giving. "I cannot enter such a contest," he said. "Sire," he added, wishing to show no disrespect.

"You fear dying?" Lord Tseler asked, to make the accusation.

"No," Oriel answered. "I fear killing."

All four men stiffened at his words. The King turned around, and then stood up from his chair, awkwardly, with his hands outflung like a woman when the Wolfers attack. It was Lord Haldern, however, who laughed out loud and said, "So might every man. So ought every man. And I think, if memory serves me truly, the law says the same. Does it not, Karossy?"

Lord Karossy answered cautiously. "The law will hang a man, if it must. But it does not — " his long pointing finger silenced Lord Haldern's protests — "require that a man be killed."

"I thank you for the honor you have done me," Oriel said to the King. He bowed, and felt Griff and Beryl behind him doing similar courtesy. He needed to leave the hall quickly, for if he did not his courage might fail him, and he might agree to fight to the bloody death anyone who stood between him and the object he desired — aye, and slay their whole families, too, so that he might be Earl. But this was not the way he wished to take the prize — as if he were a gryfalcon, bloody with the hunt. For Griff had spoken truly, as Oriel had known he would, and Oriel would be wise to follow Griff in this. "I thank you for the honor, sire, but — on these terms — I can't accept it. I leave the falconstone in your possession," Oriel said to the King.

The King turned irresolutely to face his advisors. "Surely — "

"You are the King and your will rules," Lord

333

Haldern said now. "But I stand with Oriel. I would have you know this, sire: If this young man comes into the lists, I will withdraw my own candidacy and support his. If Oriel will stand for the title, I will stand with him, and say he is worthy. Also, I can teach him the skills he may lack, for not having been raised a lord's son. I would be glad to be Oriel's teacher and his advocate, and not his enemy. If he were in the lists. That is, sire, if the terms of the contest were altered and if Oriel agreed to enter."

The King didn't hesitate. "Done," he said. "I so rule," he said. The other two spoke brief syllables but the King cut them off. "There will be no more talk on the subject."

Oriel thought he saw now how the King's will was governed.

"Let the notice be written and read aloud to all, let the contenders each be informed by messenger. The Tourney is a fight to surrender, not to death. It is done," the King said, and he raised his right fist up into the air.

This must have been a ceremonial gesture, like the bringing out of the whipping box, for all three advisors bent their heads and responded as if in one voice, "As you command, so it shall be."

The King, his crown a gold circlet resting lightly on his forehead, said again to Oriel, "You'll let me sponsor you in the Tourney, I hope."

"Yes, gladly," Oriel said. "If I win through, I will serve you to the best of my strength, and honor, all of my life."

"I believe so," the King said. Oriel had pleased the King, and won for him something the King had been unable to get for himself. The King was for Oriel. "I believe that of you. And now what would you have me do with the falconstone?"

"I would ask you to present it to the Earl Sutherland, when he is named," Oriel said. "And hope I will be the man."

He wished to be excused, now, from the company; he wished to be allowed to go with his companions and consider his plans; he wished he were free to clap his hands in the air and dance his feet on the ground, aye, and shout out his joy. But he judged it not the time to ask for anything. He would let the older men govern the day.

But he hoped they would let him glimpse the lady of the lands.

CHAPTER
24

Oriel had never before lived such days. He had so much to learn and he was so eager to progress that he had almost to forget himself, Oriel, or else he could not concentrate on winning all that he, Oriel, had the promise of winning. It seemed as if time was chasing him from behind, to trip him up and hold him down with a foot on his neck, for all must be accomplished by the autumn fair. But it seemed also as if his heart raced ahead of time, and time was a weight his desires dragged behind them. He cared little for sleep, and less for food. Nothing tired him, nothing discouraged him.

At first, Lord Haldern taught him the skills of the sword in the privacy of his own courtyard. For those lessons, Griff also was a student, so the two could duel while Lord Haldern called corrections, and corrected positions, and positioned their hands and shoulders. He taught them how to move their feet, in attack and defense, in concert with the use of the long blade for attack and for defense. Also during those days Lord Haldern had both Griff and Oriel mounted on horses, until they could both ride the great beasts with confidence, and dignity, too. During those days, Oriel's arms ached from sword fighting, his legs and groin ached from riding, and his heart ached from the continual desire to improve more quickly.

When both Oriel and Griff could present themselves well in these two most important areas, Lord Haldern asked them how things stood between them. Oriel was slow to understand, but Griff was not. "I serve Oriel," Griff said, "as I have from the first."

"For what reason?" Lord Haldern asked, his eyes narrowed. They were all three refreshing themselves with goblets of cool red wine after a training period; sweat ran down their faces and dampened the fine cotton shirts they wore.

Lord Haldern's question puzzled Griff. "How could I not?" he asked, so Oriel answered for him. "I think he chose me when I was a boy, and because he is so true a man he has never wavered."

The answer satisfied Lord Haldern. He suggested to Oriel, then, that while Oriel prepared himself for the Tourney, Griff might be better used as a student of the laws and history of the Kingdom, and especially the southern Earldom. Oriel didn't have time to undertake both those studies and his own contender's skills; and since Oriel trusted Griff as much as he seemed to — "Aye, with my life," Oriel interrupted — then Griff could store the knowledge that Oriel had no time to acquire but would find immediately needful, should he win through to the Earldom. "When you win, that is," Lord Haldern said. "For you are already almost as able as any of them, except Verilan, and we have weeks yet left to practice."

This was the first Oriel had heard of his skills relative to the other contenders. He didn't think he was satisfied to be equal, but he didn't trouble Lord Haldern with this thought.

So Griff went daily to the libraries Lord Karossy kept, and sat reading among the priests. He would sometimes bring back two or three new acquaintances to dine with Oriel, and they would discuss the kind of authority the King held over his Earls, its history, its rights, its points of overlap and conflict and how such points had traditionally been settled. There was one day when Lord Karossy accompanied his priests to Haldern's table, and the First Priest found occasion to remark privately to Oriel, "The King is easily influenced, and there is no need for any of his chief men to lack of anything. This is a time an Earl's power might increase greatly, and his wealth, too, and his honor among men."

Oriel worked at his skills of horsemanship and sword fighting, and at his understanding of the thorny points of law — those were his activities across the mornings and into the afternoons. In the late afternoons he went to the palace, where the Queen taught him the dances, taught him the courtesies of palace life, taught him the songs and stories that had for generations been known to the Earls Sutherland and their people.

It was Lady Gwilliane Oriel asked about Merlis. Gwilliane answered that Merlis had fled to her own castle, two days after Oriel arrived. "Why should she flee?" Oriel asked.

The Queen brushed her long-fingered hand across her forehead, and brushed away her distraction. "The King makes you his man in the Tourney, even though Lilos, who is his own son, also aspires to the title," she said.

"And to the lady," Oriel said.

"Yes, the lady. I concur with my husband's judgment," the Queen said, "although I know that the woman Lilos weds will be glad of him. So when I say what I am about to say I hope you will understand, Oriel, that — I hope you understand. But I think the girl might be permitted to select her husband herself. She's not even a girl, she's nearly twenty-one summers, so it is the more insulting to her to be given away in marriage to the man who can win the court to his cause with pretty speeches, who can knock others off their horses most efficiently, who can use his sword better than the others. Is this how a husband is chosen?"

Oriel didn't know. It was how Merlis's husband was to be chosen.

"Why not let the girl rule as regent, and let her first son be Earl in his proper time. For if she chooses the man herself, there must be many children, and sooner or later there will be a son, and he will be of the blood. So all will come right."

"I had been told that the troubles in the Earldom began with a woman's regency," Oriel said. They were walking in the garden at the lady's pace, walking and talking as lords and ladies often did in the warmth of a late spring afternoon.

"I can't deny that," Gwilliane sighed. She turned

to place a hand on Oriel's arm, where the green cloth was woven across with silver threads. "Her husband, they say, could govern her — while he lived. But our Kings have lacked Gladaegal's strengths."

They walked on. Her skirts brushed over the grassy path.

"You should think of this, if you think of becoming Earl Sutherland," she advised him. Her long dark hair, streaked with grey, hung down her back. "For my husband will be your King."

"He will be my King, lady, whether I am Earl or not," Oriel said, and caused her to smile.

Sometimes Lord Tseler walked with Oriel from the palace back to Lord Haldern's home, the two striding off together into a setting sun, or a star-crowded night. Tseler liked to talk about the anthill nature of life in the King's service, the many toiling bodies who did the work that enabled the Kingdom to exist. "When the King is weak," Tseler confided, "then all those around him become greedy, and must be watched. A minister knows his King's weaknesses and he guards those very points, much as soldiers guard the palace gates."

"But there are no soldiers at the palace gates," Oriel said.

"Just so," Tseler said, nodding wisely. "If men don't fear their King, then they will dare to betray him."

Oriel was not so sure of this, but he held his tongue. "Why do you tell me this?" Oriel asked.

Lord Tseler raised his nose, as if he were sniffing the direction of the wind.

By that time, Lord Haldern had taken Oriel to join in the practice of swordplay among the others who sought Merlis's hand. Their numbers had increased to fifteen or more when the terms of the contest were altered. It seemed that more wished to wed the lady of the lands than were willing to die for the chance to attempt her.

At first, Oriel was among the least skillful of the contenders, but he improved rapidly. The men, young and older, said of him at first that he would never give up, and then complained of him that he would never give in. Oriel enjoyed the contests, enjoyed an equal opponent, enjoyed a superior opponent, and — as they gradually appeared, then grew in number — enjoyed playing an unequal opponent with his ringing steel.

Lord Haldern also took Oriel riding about the countryside, to practice horsemanship and to develop endurance for long journeys on horseback. It wasn't many days, Lord Haldern told him, before they would go off with a troop to collect taxes for Sutherland's house. The King's troops had for many years now made those collections. There were those, Haldern guessed — although he didn't know it for a certainty — who would be sorry to give up the task, for they would have found ways to take private profit from the public duty.

"I will be glad to be the one to ride the southern lands beside you," Lord Haldern told Oriel, speaking privately. "And I'll be glad to introduce you to Lord Yaegar's sister, who has lived in her brother's city at the southern boundary of the Kingdom for all of her life, under her father's hand before and now under her brother's hand, for neither man would part with the dowry that would have brought her a worthy husband. I tell myself, perhaps she has waited unwed so that I may propose for her again."

"Again?" Oriel asked, too surprised to hold his tongue.

"I courted her, but the lady's father refused her anything in dowry. Even so, I almost took her then, as she was."

Half teasing and half curious, Oriel asked, "Without any dowry?"

"What's a dowry when a woman's heart makes her willing in bed, and glad to welcome you into the home? Now my fortunes are such that I don't require anything from a wife — only her heart, only her presence in my days and nights."

"Yet you would have wed the lady Merlis?" Oriel asked. "You would once again have given up — has she a name?"

"Rafella," Haldern said, and Oriel knew that if Beryl had spoken that way through a puppet, it would have been intended to tell an audience that the man's heart was in the woman's keeping. He thought of Beryl with a quick pang, wishing for an hour of her company, a night in her bed. He hadn't thought of her for days, hadn't even remembered her, for weeks now. The pang stung him, and was gone.

"You would have given up the lady a second time to marry Merlis?" Oriel repeated the question.

"When the King is weak," Lord Haldern said, "his Earls must be strong, and true."

Lord Haldern and Oriel rode out into the lands of the Earls Sutherland, as the days moved into summer. Oriel came to know the slow rising slopes, and the sweet taste of the waters in the lazy streams. His heart rose to that land, as they rode over a hill and he saw the plain spread out before him, farmsteads and villages and sometimes in the distance the lazy curl of river. His heart rose when his horse stepped into an ancient forest, and the thick-trunked trees whispered overhead. His heart rose every time he dismounted and felt the land under his feet.

And when he thought of the lady of these lands, he almost couldn't breathe, so high did his heart rise, like wings to carry him terrifyingly high into the air. He was impatient to be introduced to her but impatience did him no service, so he mastered it. The present gladnesses were enough.

As he played against other contenders for the lady's lands and hand, winning and losing in rehearsals of strength and quickness and words and courtesies, he found some good companions. Lilos, the King's younger son, was one of these, and also Wardel from Hildebrand's house, Lilos for his willingness to see the good in others and Wardel for his refusal to let any other take advantage of him. Both of these men were young. Garder, who was Lord Tseler's second son, was a cautious man, too cautious for wiving so that although he had almost thirty summers on his back he was still unwed. Tintage, the fourth of Lord Yaegar's sons, refused to take anything seriously, not winning or losing, not another man's pride or dignity or privacy. Tintage was a mocker of things; yet he had eyes as dark and secretive and soft as the skin of a mole, seeking blindly for the safety of his den under the earth. Verilan, as quick as a springing birch, was Oriel's favored opponent at swords, for his quick feet and clever hands, for the inventiveness of his fighting. A man who could keep Verilan at bay could hold his own against any swordsman.

These six, with Griff and Lord Haldern, often gathered of an evening in Lord Haldern's wide gardens, or they went together to an Inn. When they were together they spoke of sword skills, they spoke of points of law, they spoke of the history of the Kingdom and the breeding of horses. They spoke of the hunt, and bed pleasures, gaming, and the truth of men and the truth of women. They spoke of all subjects but two. They did not give voice to their common ambition. And they did not speak of the lady Merlis except — sometimes, late in the evening, when the sky was black overhead, someone would propose that they all drink together, to the lady.

All would draw a breath solemn with hope, raise goblets to the stars, and drink.

Then Tintage would break the mood, turning it once again away from serious thoughts — for the prize was great and they all desired it with full seriousness. Each intended with full seriousness to win it away from the others. Thus, Tintage's mockeries were welcome to them. "I know how my father would speak to this occasion," Tintage might say.

They had all heard much about Yaegar, a thick-headed heavy-fisted man, who communicated with his sons in clouts and curses. "What's that?" someone would ask.

"He'd tell me to use poisons," Tintage would laugh. "Poison their cups," Tintage would roar, mocking his father. "Nobody'll be the wiser, and dead men can't complain, so you'll have the place." Or Tintage might slide down into his seat as if he were afloat on a sea of wine, his eyelids falling down over his eyes, to remark in a roaring voice, "I'll drink to any woman as long as she's female."

Lord Haldern privately admitted, "I never could like Yaegar. He's too lazy to keep his word, and he's a bully when he can be," Lord Haldern said. In the morning he would seek Oriel out, to say, "I speak out of turn, in the company, in the drink."

Oriel kept his own counsel. It seemed to him that Haldern would not speak falsely, drunk or sober, just as it seemed to him that Tintage — who made lighthearted any room he entered, any occasion he took part in — would never speak entirely true, sober or drunk. That is, unless the truth served his own purpose.

Only Tintage spoke of Lady Merlis by name, and then only to mock her tallness, or her prides, or her attempts to act Lady Earl. Lilos would turn pink-cheeked to say, "How should a woman be more, when her grandmother had the raising of her, and her grandmother — well, everyone knows what was said of that lady. I am sure the Earl's daughter is as good as she is pure."

Tintage would wink at the others, who joined in his mockery of Lilos's chivalry, and Lilos's pink cheeks.

Verilan would ask, "Do you impugn the lady's honor?"

"Do you hear him?" Tintage would say, dancing away from danger. "Impugn," he repeated, echoing the dignity of Verilan's voice. "Impugn. Impugn." Each repetition of the word he accompanied by a different noble pose, and a different noble face, until even Verilan joined in the laughter.

"I keep you safe from pomposity," Tintage told them. "For which reason, I am the most important person here. I keep us from killing one another. For that's what we all were willing to do, isn't it? And still would, if we must."

Tintage's nonsense had enough of truth in it to scrape the skin of every man's conscience, and reduce all to uneasy silence.

Oriel spoke out, with a smile to add to his boldness — bold as a smiling sun, he thought to himself — "Not I, I have no wish to kill anyone. Not even you, Tintage. I desire only to beat the hearts out of every one of you, and leave you licking at the dust, and after that to collect taxes from those of you who pay your taxes to the house of the Earl Sutherland. But as to killing — Who then would I drink with? who fight with? Don't sulk, Tintage," Oriel said, paying special attention to the mole-eyed young man. "I think they are laughing at me, not you. I don't know a one of us who would dare to laugh at you." Tintage flushed with pleasure. "You're too sharp for the rest of us."

"Not for you," Tintage answered, with a little mocking bow.

"That's what Griff and I hope," Oriel said. "Isn't it, Griff?"

Oriel intended to make his farewells to Beryl before Lord Haldern, with a few of the contenders and a troop of soldiers, rode into the south to gather taxes. Oriel wanted to tell her that he must be away but that Griff remained in the King's city, if she needed a friend. Now that he remembered Beryl, he remembered he hadn't seen her since that first day before the King. He only guessed that Griff knew where she was, however, since when he was with Griff it was either with a group of people and the subject of Beryl didn't arise, or they were alone and the subject didn't arise because they were discussing points of law, or plans for how to repair damage the Lady Earl's long regency had done in the Earldom.

Oriel intended to seek Beryl out. He told himself that if she had needed anything from him, any help, or desired his company, she would have known where to find him. Since she hadn't, he assumed she had chosen not to. But he didn't like to leave on such a long journey without telling her that he was going, and doing her the courtesy of bidding her farewell. He knew how much in Beryl's debt he was.

Oriel intended, but day followed busy day and somehow, as he drifted into sleep, he hadn't remembered to ask Griff where she was lodging. He had forgotten, and he reminded himself to remember, and in the morning he forgot again. So that when Beryl was brought by a servant into the room where he sat alone, breaking the night's fast with a meal of bread, cheese, beer, and new onions, he rose to his feet at the unexpected pleasure. A full summer morning's light poured into the room and bathed her in its glow. She was dressed plainly, as a woman of the people, but her dark blue eyes were eager to see him, and her hands — as she accepted his offer of a seat, and food, and drink — moved in the familiar gestures, taking a knife to cut a mouthful of cheese, tearing off bites of bread, holding a goblet. It was good to see her face.

"How is it with you, Beryl?" It was good to speak her name. Those nights were done, but he remembered her hair unbound, and the gladness of her naked soft flesh. "You'll like the yellower cheese, I think. It's sharper."

Her mouth answered his smile but her eyes didn't. Obedient to his wish, she tried some of the yellow cheese, and Oriel asked, "Are you well? Have you been keeping well? How came you to arrive this morning, at the very time when I've been thinking of you?"

She looked him full in the eyes, but didn't speak.

"We're riding into the south, to collect the taxes due to Sutherland, and I wished to take my leave of you. And to ask if there is any message you would like delivered to your uncle, if I can find him. And to ask," Oriel now realized, "where I might find him, if there were any message you wanted to send."

"No message," Beryl said, and slid more cheese from the knife into her mouth.

"I wish you could see me now," Oriel told her. "I'm almost indistinguishable from a lord."

"I know," she said. "I often hear about you."

"From Griff?"

"Him. And others, too, the people of the city. Do you want to know what they're saying about you?"

"No." Oriel shook his head. Then he admitted, smiling, "Yes, I do. Since I know you'll report truly."

"At first, they doubted you. They thought you had some hold over the King, to be marked by so many favors." She gestured with the knife to silence his protests, cut off a chunk of bread, and went on. "Then, they liked to hear of how you learned to fight so well, with swords, and to ride. For you weren't born a lord, so what you can learn any man might hope for. That's what they now think."

"And you, what do you think?"

"You already know. But if you would hear it again," Beryl said, her eyes like seawater dancing under a bright sun, "I think that everyone who looks on you sees a man who will make a true Earl. More and more, the people of the city say the same. They give you honors you haven't even tried for. Many ladies' hearts they give you, and victory in argument with the wisest of the priests, and an eye to see when ministers waste the King's wealth in their own rivalries. Not to mention your great prowess at the hunt."

"There is no great prowess," Oriel protested.

She emptied her glass and said, "But I do believe the story they tell of a man who stood unmounted to fight off a boar, when another had fallen from his horse into the boar's path. A man who beat the beast senseless and then slit its throat, and then gave the prize to the fallen man, who is his rival for a great prize."

"That was Tintage," Oriel said. "He'd flushed the boar, and then had the bad luck to be knocked off his mount. It was his kill, by rights."

Beryl grinned at him, then made her face solemn, then grinned again. "It was his kill, by rights," she mimicked him in his own voice. Oriel heard how happy and careless that voice was. "Aye, Oriel, you have so much awaiting you, as you deserve, that you can give honors away like baubles. Aye, and it is good to be in your company again, Oriel," Beryl said. Then she rose from her seat and folded her hands in front of her, and said, "I must be going now. But I came to say to you, I am with child."

"You don't look it," Oriel said. He rose also, wondering if this was good news for her, or bad.

"Not yet," she said. Beryl seemed to be just herself, her ordinary self. She seemed content.

"What will you do?" he asked her.

"Do?" and she looked at him again. They stood face to face now. "I'll leave the city, perhaps before I start to show, but I thought — there should be someone else who knows about the child."

She didn't need to remind Oriel that her mother had died giving birth. He felt a sense of his own strength when he made her the promise: "Yes, I will see to the child, should there be need."

Then Beryl was gone and a servant had come to take away the plates and it was time to strap on his sword and join Haldern. There was no time to ask Beryl the questions he only thought of after she had left him: When will it be born? Can a woman keep a farm while she has an infant child? Have you need of coins? It is my child you are carrying, isn't it?

When he saw Griff that evening, he planned to ask those things of Griff, but there was time only to say, "Did you know Beryl is with child?" before Griff had to rush away. By the time they met again, a couple of nights later, Oriel had other news on his mind. "We ride out the next day but one to go into the south."

The horsemen rode out of the city and followed the King's Way east until they reached a ford; there they crossed the river and headed south. Lord Haldern led them. In his troop were twenty picked soldiers and six of the young men who would contend for the title of Earl Sutherland. Oriel was one of the six.

He alone wore neither hat nor helmet. He alone lacked stitching or sign, in gold or silver, to name the house he belonged to, or the lord he served, or to identify him as a King's man. His shirt and cloak were the green Beryl had recommended to him for his chance before the King. He had not thought by his simpler dress to single himself out, but he was not displeased to have done so.

Near the King's city, the land prospered. The fields bloomed with crops and the orchards with leaves and budded fruit. Fish leaped up in river and pond. Oriel saw between the rows of leafy onions how rich and black the soil was. In the green stems of rye and millet and in the honey-colored heads of wheat, he saw how the soil fed everything that grew on it. This was a prosperous land.

As the troop moved farther from the King's city, however, things changed. The people welcomed the soldiers but all bewailed that the protection was only temporary. For a farmer didn't know when he planted his crops if they would be left to grow, and young men refused to work, without the promise of a harvest. Why should we labor to dig into the ground what will only be burned away when it breaks through the soil? they asked. Better to take the pleasures we can find now, while we live.

So each village and every lord welcomed Haldern's riders, and looked with hope at those who were contenders for the Earldom and the hand of Merlis. All pitied Merlis, who must keep within her castle for her own safety, and was thus unable to help her lands and her people.

Haldern's riders passed this castle at a distance. Oriel saw its tall towers rising up into the rainy sky, and he wondered if the lady stood at one of the windows, looking across to the troop of soldiers and suitors as they crossed her land, to collect her taxes.

One evening, after they had been many days on the roads, they came into a village by the river's side, one of the villages in the Earl's granting. There, several people had collected around a man who stood with his fist raised over a woman who knelt on hands and knees in the dirt before him.

Oriel recognized the event. Without thought of asking permission or advice from Haldern, he leaped off his horse and shoved through the crowd to grab the man's arm from behind.

The man was tall and thickly muscled, but surprise gave Oriel temporary advantage. Memory of the whipping box burned in him. The man would have had to have been even more tall and even more heavily muscled than he was to shake off Oriel.

"What — ?" the man grunted. "Who — ?" Oriel pulled down sharply on his arm.

"She's a woman," Oriel said. "Why should you — ?" The man turned, to shove him.

Then the man pulled himself free of Oriel's grip, and stepped back, on braced legs. "Who are you?" he demanded.

"Oriel. By what right — ?"

But the man had undergone a complete change of expression and attitude. He dropped to one knee and took Oriel's right hand into his. He bent his head over the hand, before he rose to stand before Oriel. "I'm Major of this village, my lord," he said.

Oriel wondered why the man's spirit should so suddenly shrink at the sight of a shaved face, and high boots. Unless it was the sight of the sword that conquered him.

"The woman is a widow," the Major said. "By custom, she must give back the cottage and boat that were her husband's holding."

"By custom?" Oriel asked. It seemed an odd custom that would require a widow to give up her livelihood.

"By custom and by law. If he has a brother — "

Oriel interrupted, speaking loudly. He had watched men lie before. "Not by law, I think." If the man deduced that Oriel had read the law, so much the better.

"I spoke hastily," the man admitted. "Custom is as much as law, for us, my lord. By custom alone, then, the man's brother is given the holding."

Quick to sense her advantage, the woman knelt in the dirt again, at Oriel's feet. "Help me, my lord," she said. "And my children. Help us, we implore you."

Oriel didn't pity her, and he wished she wouldn't

kneel so at his feet, with a hand on his boot as if she were a dog. "Why were you about to strike her?" he asked the man.

"According to the custom, she must relinquish the holding, as the village asks her. She has been told she must leave the cottage, and she disobeys. So we have told her she must leave the village. But she won't go. There must be punishment, or who would obey my word? I don't misuse her. She doesn't bend barebacked, my lord, and I have neither stick nor thong."

"Aye, and you use your fist well enough to break flesh and bones, and you use shame," the woman cried. "Save us, great sir!"

Oriel didn't know how to proceed. If the people were encouraged to go against customary usage, then the village would be at the mercy of whoever proved strong enough to force his will upon the people. So obedience to custom, especially in parlous times, gave the village the safety of numbers banded together. But the woman had children to care for, and the village should take care of its own in times of need — or what did the village have to offer its people in exchange for obedience?

This question was more complicated than the whipping box.

The men on horseback waited quietly for him, to let him play out the scene he had entered. "Who is the brother?" Oriel asked, thinking that the man might be compensated with coin. For he knew how fierce a woman could be, for her children. "Which man stands to lose the use of the holding if the woman keeps the cottage and keeps use of the boat?"

Faces were amused, and before he turned back to the Major of the village he had guessed why. But he waited until the Major spoke it. "I am that man."

Then Oriel let anger flow into his shoulders and his voice and his face. He knew that he seemed now as dangerous as an unsheathed sword and that might cause trouble he wished not to have, but still he judged that fear would serve him best here. "I have no time for this," he said. "Let the woman be, let her live in the holding and fish with the boat." The woman clambered to her feet, still pale, but now satisfied.

"Thank you, my lord," she said, and bowed her head.

Oriel looked around at the men and women, who had gathered first to see a beating and then whatever fight ensued, if they were lucky enough to have a fight to watch. They were, he saw, glad enough for what they deemed justice. Their glances were on him as he walked back to his horse and remounted. He spoke to the watching eyes. "You need a new Major I think." He turned his mount away before any answer could be given. Let the village know that it must be ready to protect itself and every person in it.

An Earl, Oriel thought as he rode behind Haldern out of the village, with the purse of tax money in the soldiers' care, was an idea as much as a man. The idea of the Earl, the idea of the Earl's justice, would be enough to govern men's behavior, most of the time. The certainty of the Earl's concern and action was all that was needed. The Earl didn't need to be a daily presence to keep order. He needed only to be known to be in his castle, in his power.

CHAPTER
25

The lands of the Earls Sutherland pleased Oriel, more than any other country he had seen. Often, as they rode, he would stop his horse, dismount, and walk, trailing farther and farther behind the others. He did this just for the pleasure of walking the southern lands, the sense that when he put his foot down on the land it became his. He did this under the strong southern sun and the fat plopping southern rains. The others stopped mocking him when they saw that mockery didn't affect his good humor.

He taught them to swim, on a dare. The bolder ones — like Wardel — chose to be rowed out onto the river so they might jump into the deep water, learning to float on top of it by necessity. The more cautious ones — like Garder — he led into the water from the shallow banks, giving them time to learn to trust their ability to float. Some he teased and led laughing into the knowledge. Some he challenged and led quarreling. Some he persuaded. Haldern declined, saying he was too old to learn anything new, and Oriel let him be. Lilos said he was too skinny to learn, and too afraid, and would have to put it off until a later, fatter, braver time, and Oriel didn't argue with the Prince because he thought how tender his pride must be. So the two of them went off one early dawn — the sky as pink as a girl's mouth — to teach, and to learn, where none but the two might see any panic, humiliation, or failure. Lilos had, as Oriel had foretold, small difficulty learning.

The horsemen were welcomed into the great houses of lords and fed well, and entertained with music and dance. They were welcomed at towns and entertained with the best foods the Inns could produce. They were welcomed into villages and offered shady shelter, and cool water. But why, Oriel wondered, were the people so quiet and, he thought, anxious. The people and their lords were anxious to please the riders, anxious to welcome them and to wave them on their way, anxious, and wary, too, he thought. Why should these people — with their guarded smiles and low-pitched voices, with their way of listening before they uttered an opinion so that the opinion they uttered never varied from the opinion they heard — be the inhabitants of this prosperous land? The people of this land should be gladsome, openhanded and openhearted, boisterous.

The people of Yaegar's land were at least boisterous. Yaegar's great house had been built out of
wood from the forests, and as they rode up before
it, its doors and windows were flung open, and servants rushed out to take the horses from them, and
more servants rushed out to demand that the riders
follow them into the house, where the steward
clapped Tintage on the back and laughed into his
ear, and offered great cups of ale to all of the riders.

Tintage drank his down, and the servants cheered
him, and he ordered them to fill his cup again. "I
welcome you to my father's house," he said to the
company, "which belongs to three brothers before
it comes to me. It is mine insofar as they give me
permission to inhabit it. I call them Mumbo, Jumbo,
and Gumbo. They are giants of men, and they take
the one brain they have between them around in a
box. No, you laugh, but I speak truly. My father
dotes on them. For no one else in his whole broad
demesne can down a tankard of ale as rapidly as
Yaegar, or any of his three older sons. They are great
men, those four." Tintage downed his second cup
of ale, and clapped the steward on the shoulder.

Lord Haldern, Oriel noted, stood at the rear of
the company, although he must be — Oriel
thought — eager to see the lady. Oriel was eager
and impatient for the lady Merlis and he had never
even seen her, much less courted and won and given
her up years ago.

The horsemen were taken to a large hall filled
with sleeping couches, and bade to table with Yaegar. The steward told Lord Haldern that Yaegar
regretted that their stay must be so short. Yaegar
had their tax purse ready for them, and he remembered Haldern well from years earlier, the steward
told them.

"Take care," Tintage warned Haldern. "I wouldn't trust the man, and especially when he seems to show goodwill."

"I'll deal courteously with him, since he has spoken courteously to me," Lord Haldern answered, "and since moreover he has in his giving that which I desire."

"All the more reason not to trust his words, however courteous," Tintage said, filling the air with flourishes of his hand as he mocked a courtier's bow to Haldern. "Since he doesn't fear you. I think I'd be a contented man if my father feared me."

Tintage stood still, as if listening to his own words. "Or," he added, "if I had no father. Are you contented, Oriel?" he asked.

Oriel thought perhaps he was. "But don't think it's because I have no father," he said. "The father has nothing to do with it."

"I wouldn't let Yaegar hear you saying that. He'd clout you all the way into tomorrow, and then he'd stomp on you when you landed."

Oriel laughed. But he was curious about Yaegar, and watched for him when they were led into the dining hall. Lord Haldern and Lilos and Garder were seated at a long table with Yaegar and his three older sons, and so was Oriel, which honor did not escape him. The rest of their party was scattered among the lords and ladies, stewards and squires and their wives and sons and daughters. Food was plentiful, platters of roast meats, plates of pastry, rounds of bread. Their wine goblets were kept well filled. Yaegar ate in great devouring bites. He let his three sons lead the conversation, to speak of the hunting season and the births among the hounds and the births among the horses, to speak of the amount brought in by taxes. Theirs was the only table at which no women sat.

When mention was made of the Tourney, Yaegar at last looked up from his plate, and seemed surprised to see he had guests. Yaegar was a thick man, thick necked, thick shouldered, his head set as square as a rock. His great hand wrapped around the dagger he used to cut off chunks of meat. "I've a son in this Tourney," Yaegar said. "Don't I? Yes, I see him here, across the room — Look, boys, it's our dancing master. Stand up, Tintage, and let me see if you've grown to any size yet. Welcome home," Yaegar said, mocking.

Tintage rose, to bow in mockery.

"No, you're still a wee mite, just like your mother. She was a fair dancer, too — Do you remember her pretty ways, boys?"

The three looked away at this public shaming of their brother.

Yaegar had no such soft feelings. "You made us a promise, Dancing Master," he said. "You promised us you wouldn't be back until you had the Earldom, and we would all bow down to you. Or until you were dead," Yaegar said. Tintage alone stood, his moleskin eyes helpless and angry. "You break your word now, too. That leaves you honorless, doesn't it?"

Tintage for once had nothing to say.

Yaegar laughed out loud. "But you know I'd never have let you enter the contest if there was any danger that you'd win. The rest of you," and his eyes rested on Oriel, "you've nothing to fear from Tintage. If I hadn't thought he'd be outmanned at every chance, I'd have tossed him into my dungeons, and kept him there. Can you imagine? If this dancing master were my Earl?"

He ripped off a chunk of bread, and chewed it, and washed it down with a long drink of wine. Then he noticed Tintage. "Sit down, nobody told you to keep on standing there," he said. He turned to Haldern to ask, "You can tell whoever becomes the Earl that my forests are full of outlaws and he'd better come here first when he rides to restore order into the south. Will you carry this message? You were a reliable messenger, if I remember correctly."

"You remember correctly," Lord Haldern said, expressionless.

"But wait." Yaegar slapped at his forehead. "Didn't I hear that you were a contender? But aren't you old for the contest, and if you win, old for the lady?"

"We won't ever know that," Haldern answered, with apparent unconcern for Yaegar's barbs. "I have chosen to back Oriel, and that is now the extent of my part in the Tourney."

Then Yaegar turned his attention to Oriel, as if this were all news to him — which Oriel doubted. The dark eyes glittered. Oriel knew that he was expected to feel fear, and that he was expected to be all the more courteous to Yaegar, because of his fear of the man, and because of his ambition to be Earl over Yaegar.

Oriel didn't think he cared to do what was expected.

"Why does he back *you*?" Yaegar asked Oriel.

"Perhaps I'm the best man," Oriel answered carelessly, and went on with the much more interesting activity of eating a fowl's leg.

Yaegar thought about that. "You can't help but be better than Tintage," he said. "But I wonder why Haldern gives up his own hopes, for your advantage. What are you, some by-blow of the Earl's?

Did one of his whores manage to smuggle her child into some lord's house and have you brought up as an imitation lord? What are you, a bastard heir?"

"What I am, I have no idea," Oriel said. "I only know who I am." He chose to say no more.

Yaegar couldn't stay silent long. "Can you fight?"

"Yes."

"You're not too dainty for it?"

"No."

"You've a fine face on you, a little too dainty looking for rough work, Oriel," Yaegar insisted.

Oriel looked into the hard black eyes, and a smile was his only response. He didn't fear this man.

Lord Yaegar smiled back at him. "Yes, I see what you mean, Haldern," Yaegar said then. "I see it indeed. I'd wish you luck, Oriel, if it didn't mean offending these two nobly born lords."

Again, Oriel answered with a smile, but this time because he couldn't think of any response that wouldn't offend Lilos and Wardel, without at the same time belittling himself to Yaegar. Yaegar was not a man he would want to belittle himself before.

But Yaegar, he reminded himself, kept order in his lands, protecting his people; and he also saw to it that his people paid their taxes, to him and to the Earl. Other southern lords had neglected the Earl's share, especially in these Earl-less times.

Haldern put down his knife, put down his goblet, cleared his throat. "I'm sorry the lady Rafella isn't dining with us," he said.

Yaegar's smile was like the hunter, when his dog has flushed an easy target. "That's right. I forgot. You and my sister have an unhappy history. You must wonder where she might be, and if she might prefer to avoid you. Unlike you, Rafella never wed."

Haldern said, "I am once again free to marry."

361

"I'll be sure to tell Rafella, when next I see her," Yaegar said, and turned his shoulder to Haldern to ask Lilos, "And how is that estimable woman, your mother?"

Fury flamed up into Haldern's cheeks.

Before Haldern could offer offense, Oriel said, "I would like to be introduced to this lady, who has been so long remembered."

Haldern wasn't pleased to have Oriel interfere, but Oriel went on regardless. "Can you summon her? Or does she follow only her own wishes?" Oriel asked Yaegar.

"It's my wishes govern her," Yaegar said. "As they always have, even when suitors came sniffing like foxes to a henhouse, thinking if they got the hen they'd also get the house."

"That's good news," Oriel said cheerily, "for it means that I can have the pleasure of the lady's acquaintance. Unless you will refuse me that honor?"

Yaegar no longer had the choice to refuse, and he knew it. He gave the order. Lilos — no stranger to courtly machinations — chose that time to present his father's greetings to Yaegar, and to bring out a golden plate that the King had caused to be sent to this mighty lord, whose lands prospered even in these times. Lilos presented the plate with many fine words. Yaegar had to respond with the formal words of honor for the King, and respect to the King's son, and pleasure in the King's gift.

During this time a small woman with fading red hair entered the hall. Oriel was watching for her. She had not, apparently, been warned of visitors, for her hand went to her throat in alarm when she saw Lord Haldern at her brother's table. She seemed altogether small and quiet and pleasing, and her eyes filled with tears to see the King's Captain.

She moved to her brother's side.

The ceremonies of the King's presentation completed, Oriel was introduced to the lady, as he had requested. He rose, to bow over her hand, and she spoke his name in a voice as soft and deep as the moving of water around boulders at the sea's edges. "I think you have an old acquaintance with Lord Haldern," Oriel said, and led the lady to where, now, Haldern rose to give her greeting.

"It has been many years, Captain," the lady said.

"They have been kind to you, lady," Haldern answered.

"Oh ho! In your presence, the soldier turns courtier, sister," Yaegar said. "His wife must have polished his manners. But she's dead, as I heard, years ago. Do you wonder if he's finally coming back to you? I would, if I were you. Are you hopeful, sister?"

Haldern's temper rose again. "I have come for that purpose. I do ask that honor, if you will grant it to me," he said to Yaegar.

Yaegar answered lazily. "You got the granting from my father years ago, if you remember, but she had no dowry. You remember that. For which reason you left her and wed another. As did all her other suitors, so it isn't any particular shame to you to have done so. She has no dowry still," Yaegar said.

"I ask no dowry," Haldern answered.

A brief buzz of conversation went around the listening room, as if a single bee had flown in the windows.

"He has you now, Father," Tintage's mocking voice called.

Tintage would ruin it, if he wasn't careful, Oriel

thought. He tried to catch Tintage's eye, to warn him.

"She'll be taken from you after all," Tintage crowed. "And who will keep your house for you then?" His laughter bubbled up and he turned to the woman seated beside him, to share the joke.

"Rafella has nothing," Yaegar warned Haldern. "She has nothing of her own. Everything she has belongs to me, pillion and pillow, horse, jewels, the shirt she sleeps in, bed and bedclothes, all are mine. So if you would still have her, Captain, you take her naked. Now and naked . . . unless you change your mind again, and ride away again, for which no man of sense would blame you."

Yaegar was counting on the lady's shame and enjoying her humiliation. Haldern could say nothing without risking her further.

Silence hung over the room like a sword, until Yaegar's eyes shone with victorious laughter, and he raised his right hand to wave his sister away. But Oriel walked around to stand beside the lady, and the sound of his steps rang out in the silence.

"I have a cloak to cover you, lady," Oriel said. "I have boots, to protect your feet from the rough ground. I have a shirt, soft enough to wear against your skin. For I think Lord Haldern will welcome you as wife in any garments."

"Yes, and with all my heart," Haldern said.

Oriel wrapped his cloak around the lady, who was no taller than his shoulder. The cloak covered her entirely. He lifted his green shirt over his head and then he sat to pull off his boots. As her dress rustled to the floor beneath the cloak, Yaegar spoke.

"I haven't granted my permission," Yaegar said.

Rafella looked to Haldern, hope already fading from her eyes.

"I think you have." Oriel faced the thick-shouldered man. "I think you said that she could take nothing of yours with her. That means that if she takes nothing, she can go. That is the granting."

"I didn't intend that. I deny it. Who would contest me?" Lord Yaegar rose from the table.

"I would," Oriel answered. He was naked but for the trousers and his sword. But he didn't feel naked. He felt clothed in the quickness of his youth, and in the skill of his arm with the long sword. He felt armored against this man and he felt almost eager at the chance to bring Lord Yaegar to his knees. What he didn't feel was in any way afraid. "I would contest you and I would say that you have not given your word with honor."

"As will I," said Lilos, moving to stand at Oriel's side.

"And I." Wardel joined them, then, along with Garder and Verilan — who would be the best ally if it came to a fracas.

Lord Yaegar watched, and then he took his hand from the sword hilt, and then he sat down and then laughed aloud. That would be the only sign of Yaegar's concession, the laughter.

Then Tintage arrived from across the hall to stand with them.

"Last, always last," his father observed. He pushed his wine away. "You've got what you came for, Haldern. By which I mean the coins. If you choose to take Rafella with you, then you can have her — I'll give her in exchange for taking this — dancing master. Now what are you waiting for? Don't you have more errands to run for the King, Haldern? In some other place? For I've had enough of you. Go now."

They left the hall, with the lady walking in their

midst like a prisoner under guard, for safety. Oriel went last and he turned at the doorway to look back at Lord Yaegar. Yaegar rose to his feet and raised a hand in salute. Oriel would have chosen to make no response, but Yaegar was a man the Earl could depend on, at his southern borders, if the Earl was strong enough to master him. Oriel raised his own hand in answer to Lord Yaegar, who had saluted him as if he were already Earl Sutherland.

They rode back to the King's city across the long summer days. Their route followed the River Way and they splashed the dust of the day's travel off in the river each evening. Lord Haldern had hired two girls to serve his lady, from the first village they had come to after leaving Yaegar's city; Rafella rode beside her betrothed during the day, and slept nights beside her serving maids.

Now that the time of the Tourney drew closer, Oriel felt that he must meet Merlis. Why that desire should become so urgent now, as the slow summer twilight left a purple world behind it, and bats swooped down to take the humming insects from the air, Oriel didn't know. He just felt his ignorance of the lady like iron chains at his ankles, holding him down.

The others had all known her from childhood, except for Tintage. They all, except for Tintage, found her surpassingly excellent. "She's pretty enough," Tintage said, "she's prettier than most, and I've never danced with any lady more easy on her feet. Merlis would dance all day and all the night, too, if she could. She's proud, and many might find her cold, but I never have. I've heard from others that she seldom smiles and almost never

366

laughs, but they don't know her as I do. Perhaps. She is no more vain than any other woman, but that is vain enough. Would I find her so very desirable, I wonder, if she didn't wear the Earldom on her finger?" he asked. He looked around at the firelit faces. "Would any of us?" he asked.

The others murmured some response, neither disagreeing nor agreeing. Only Oriel could say with perfect honesty that he couldn't say, never having even laid eyes on the lady.

"And there are many other ladies at the courts who will be glad to see Lady Merlis married to her Earl. Many of them fair ladies, as we know," Tintage said.

"You are a dancer," Garder said. "If you watch Tintage among the ladies, Oriel, you will learn much about how to please them. They flock around him like flies to honey."

"Oh," responded Tintage, laughing, "say flies to the spider's web. I think I am more bitter than sweet."

Lord Haldern promised Oriel many days during which entertainments and feasts would be given, many nights for dance and music to celebrate the Tourney. Lady Merlis would be there, and Oriel would meet her, and dine at her side, and dance with her.

Riding homewards, with Rafella as their common charge, the troop seemed a band of comrades rather than opponents, each of whom must seek to defeat all the others in a day not far ahead. But Oriel, who knew his own desire to defeat each of the others and take the prize to himself, assumed that the same desire was in each heart. But none, Oriel thought, had a measure of desire to equal his own. None knew what it was to have and lose everything, then have and lose it again, and now find the better chance within your grasp.

Lady Rafella would stay in the Queen's care until her marriage day, it was decided, and the Queen wished to give her the trousseau appropriate to a lady of her birth. Oriel and Haldern returned to Haldern's house, satisfied. Oriel hoped to meet Griff there, but he was disappointed. There was a message asking Oriel to call on Beryl, at an Inn just to the north of the city, but no word from Griff, and there was a message summoning Oriel and Lord Haldern to an audience with the King, on the first morning after the return of the company, to hear the King's pleasure.

The King's pleasure, spoken with Lord Tseler and Lord Karossy at his back, was that the battles of the Tourney must be to the death. He had reconsidered his previous decision, and retracted it. Any man who wished to leave the contest under these terms might do so without loss of honor.

The King's pleasure left Oriel — and the others — wordless.

"Men whose advice I respect had concerns," the King said. "Also, a superfluity of contenders have come forward, and some are men of lesser birth. The lady, I have been told, feels devalued by the lower risk to her suitors. I have decided."

The audience chamber was crowded with men, many of whom Oriel had never seen before. Those who had traveled together into the south avoided one another's eyes.

"In three days' time," the King said now, "we will give a reception, to welcome Merlis, and to do her homage, and to let her greet those from among whom her husband will come. For now, go to your houses and apartments. The audience is concluded."

So dismissed, they couldn't stay to argue, if any had so desired. Oriel couldn't read in any face what the thoughts behind it were, except for Haldern's, which revealed concern, and except for Tintage's, which showed amusement at the vagaries of Kings and fortune. Oriel almost wished he could have Tintage's ready laugh against any occasion. He wished for Griff's return.

Haldern fumed at the King, as they left the palace, but he judged that the King, having changed his mind twice, would not change it again. "Twice might pass as wisdom," Haldern said. "Thrice admits indecision. You must set your heart to it, Oriel."

At Haldern's house, Beryl awaited him. She waited with her cloak gathered around her. She waited without sitting down. She greeted Lord Haldern courteously enough, and did not ask after Griff, but asked instead — in a lifeless voice that belied her eyes, which seemed to burn like dark blue coals — if Oriel would grant her a private audience.

Oriel thought it was luck to have Beryl there. He wished to talk with someone uninvolved, and someone other than Haldern, who had spent so many years in the King's court that he was in the habit of believing that the way of the court was the world's only way. He asked Beryl to take off her cloak, and offered refreshment — did she prefer fruit or cheese, water or wine? — and welcomed her. "I need advice," he said, as the door closed behind him.

But Beryl held her cloak close. "You shamed me,

Oriel. To send Griff, so. Aye and you shame him, too."

Oriel at last saw that there was something amiss here, but she gave him no time to think.

"You made no response to my message, so I came to see you here, and tell you. To say, you shame your friends." Her face was pale with the fury that burned in her eyes.

"Griff asked you to wed," Oriel guessed. She nodded impatiently. "You have refused him?" She nodded. "As you would refuse any man?" She nodded again.

Beryl had told them that the women of her family gave their hearts but once, and Oriel was sorry now to have taken hers so carelessly from her. He might have stopped her, he thought; but he wasn't sure a man had that power over a woman's heart, to forbid the gift of it. In any case, it was too late now. He made her the only promise he could. "I've seen women with their babes, Beryl," he said. "I've seen what women will do, for their children. I would wish that you find a man who takes your babe to his heart, for then he may have your heart also."

She shook her head. "You know — nothing, nothing of me — " she said, and then shook her head again, as if to empty it. When she spoke then, it was in a cool voice. "I wish you well, Oriel," she said. "I wish you success, and the lady. I take my leave," she said, and left the room.

Oriel studied the door she had pulled closed behind her. He wondered what Griff was thinking of, to ask Beryl to be his wife, and he determined that he should never speak to Griff of it — lest the answer be what Oriel hoped it wasn't, and the question an unkindness to Griff. But he wasn't surprised to find at this measure of Griff's worth that Griff was beyond all price.

And there was so much he wished to speak with Griff about. He sent one of Haldern's servants to call Griff from his books. When he looked across the table to see Griff's bony face, and his brown eyes, and saw what pleasure it was to Griff to be once again in Oriel's company, Oriel thought that the world had come right again. They shared a loaf of round bread and a roasted fowl, only the two of them dining, since Lord Haldern was paying court that evening to his lady. Oriel told Griff, who listened with interest and admiration, and curiosity, the events of the journey. Then he said, "It is once again a contest to the death."

"Will you fight?" Griff asked. "To the death, I mean."

"The land needs an Earl to govern it, the lords need their Earl over them, the Majors, too. So there must be an Earl, and he must wed, and that quickly — to get sons, since there must be an Earl to rule and his sons to inherit."

"As with the King and the Kingdom, as with the lords and their land grants," Griff agreed, "and even the people and their holdings."

"Do you ever think that there might be another way?" Oriel asked. "There was another way for Selby."

"What are you thinking of?" Griff asked him.

Oriel shook his head; he didn't know how to shape his thoughts.

Griff's thought had a hard-edged shape. "I think, you might wish to fight, Oriel, to the death."

Oriel studied the familiar face. He remembered how it felt to dismount from his horse and stand with his two feet upon the ground, to walk along and feel under his feet the land that might be his own. There was something that hurt him in the way the hills rose so gently from the broad, rich southern plain. Something painful in the lazy curves of the river, golden under a sinking sun, shadowed by the trees that grew along its edges. He thought of the dark soil and fish-filled streams, of flat plains and muddy river edges, of houses built on the gentle hillsides. The land nourished all. If he would be Earl, he must be as nourishing as the land.

"Oriel?" Griff interrupted his thoughts.

Oriel raised a hand, for silence.

After a while, Griff spoke again. "There are other countries than those we've seen. We could try our fortune elsewhere."

Of course Griff understood that if Oriel was not Earl Sutherland then he couldn't stay in the Kingdom. There was never anything Griff hadn't understood.

"Might there not be another way?" Oriel asked.

"Yes, but what?" Griff asked, and Oriel couldn't answer. For there would be an Earl Sutherland. And that man would be wed to the lady Merlis.

CHAPTER
26

He saw her first from the distance. She stood beside the Queen. She was welcoming guests and she drew his eyes just as a layer of high mountain snow, shifting, would draw them.

Her green gown was dark as summer leaves, and a falcon had been stitched in gold across the skirt. Her hair hung long, and straight, white gold like the sun in early spring. He came closer, to see that her face was as calm and carved as ice in winter, and her eyes the grey of the sea at autumn's end. Her slender white neck rose out of the jeweled necklace that lay upon her dainty collarbone, and her slender white hands were clasped together in front of her. Her shoulders sloped gently, her arms were gentle curves, under the gown there was the suggestion of more curves, at breast and waist and hip.

Oriel thought, if he could serve her in any way, he would give his life gladly. He thought — with desire like a knife at his belly — what it might be like to have her naked in his bed. He thought he would like to wind her silky hair in his hand, and hear her laughter, dance with her, and watch while she dined to see how she fed herself. He wondered what was in her mind, to keep her face so still, and secretive.

In its perfect beauty.

One by one, her suitors were brought before her. They must formally declare their desire to wed, here before all the guests, and answer whatever question she might put to them. There were fewer suitors than there had been, for many men had left the contest under its renewed terms, but several yet remained. Lilos, raised in the court and at ease with the courtly ways of thought and conduct, had explained his decision: "Until I fight, I may always choose not to fight. And what if I dropped out, and then all the others did, too, all of you as well, and left the lady to some churl, whose only deserving lay in his having outwaited the rest of us? I can't abandon the lady Merlis to such a chance, nor the southern lands neither. I'll wait, and watch."

"And if," Wardel inquired, "the one man who was left was more worthy, what then?"

"That I don't know. But I will know when the time comes upon me," Lilos answered, so readily that Oriel knew he had already asked himself that same question.

Now Oriel waited to be presented to the lady, and feel her eyes on him. It seemed now, watching her as she held out a long slim arm, so that a suitor could bow over her hand, that it might be worth a fight to the death, for the chance of having her, if there was no other chance.

Yet he couldn't wish to kill any one of them. When he thought of driving his sword into Garder's belly, and pulling it free while red blood followed after, he turned cold. His spirit refused the idea of smashing the shield back into Verilan's face, so hard that the metal helmet Verilan wore to protect himself would be driven into the bone of his narrow nose and, when that broke, the bone of chin and forehead. Or hearing the snap of bones breaking, as Lilos fell to the ground, or Wardel, and being glad of it.

And yet he could imagine it, and imagine himself being glad, now, when he thought that these men stood between him and the lady. He could imagine stepping over their bleeding faceless bodies, to claim for his own the lady and the lands she was dowried with.

Oriel didn't know what to think, and he was so dazed by the closeness of the lady, and the smell of flowers in the air around her, that when she asked him a question he barely heard her words. He had to answer — raising his face from her tiny hand, with the single ring on her finger, the little pearls in a neat row on the golden band — and seeing how her eyes were stormy grey, and cold — and he answered stupidly, for all sense of himself had fled when he held her fingers in his fingers —

"I'm sorry — ?" he said.

He heard laughter behind him and the lady was

not pleased. He drew himself upright, that she might see he was worthy of her and meant no mockery to her.

"I asked you, Oriel, King's man, as I have asked each of the others, if you would have me without the lands. If you would wed me yet not be Earl Sutherland."

Oriel would never tell her anything false. She must always know the truth of him. "Lady, I can't say."

Again laughter, and he heard now how witless his answer had sounded. Even his voice had been swallowed back nervously, as he spoke. "How could I answer that truly," he asked her, "when no man who weds you can do so without taking your lands also. You are the Earl's daughter, lady," he said.

If she knew how much he honored her, and treasured her, she would not look at him that way.

"You are alone among these suitors to speak so," she scolded him. "Do you claim to be the only honest man among so many? For all the others will have me as I am, even landless."

Oriel could not answer. He thought he had been a fool not to prepare an artful speech, as he thought now the others must have. Then he thought she was too good and beautiful for the smallest falsehood, and so he did not speak, that he might not dishonor her.

And that, too, angered her. Her face told him nothing, as a puppet face revealed nothing of the puppeteer behind it. But her eyes, and the voice in which she spoke to him, both told him more scorn than her words carried. "You are the King's own man in the Tourney. I must welcome your suit," she said.

And that pricked him. He would not have her

think little of him. "Your words do honor to the King, as they should," he said to her. "Have you no honor or grace for me?" he asked.

"Yes," she said, and then stood icy angry, for she had lost her composure. "As much as you deserve."

These were words used like swords, and Oriel didn't know why she should hope to wound him.

"You may find, lady, that as much as I deserve is more than you think," he said.

"You know what I think, then? and on such short acquaintance?"

"I think," Oriel admitted honestly, "that I might know you all my life and never know your mind."

"Now you call me false!" she cried. "I have no more to say to you!" She waved him away.

Oriel obeyed her wish. He thought, too late, that he might have said he would call her fair, fairer than any other. He thought, too late, that he might have sworn to her truly that he would be content to use his life in service to her.

Later, although how much later he couldn't have said, there was dancing. Between the time when he held her fingers in his hand and the time of the dance, there was wine, and food, and many people talking and laughing together, and candles burning in the hall; but he could remember only her voice, and her face, and the way she had of holding out her hand and at the same time drawing back as she stood there in her green gown with the falcon sewn into it in gold threads, welcoming her suitors.

Later still he approached her again, to claim a dance from her, and she did not see him and so turned her shoulder to him as she went off on Verilan's arm. He came up to her again, where she stood with Tintage, who had somehow caused her to laugh. Tintage was telling the story of Rafella's rescue from Yaegar's house. Oriel thought that the lady might think well of him, for Tintage told the tale unsparingly. "As always, in my father's presence, I was the fool," Tintage said. "I dared not go to the side of my friends, for fear of my father's hand; I dared not stay back from the event, for fear of my father's mockery — and my brothers ready to follow his lead — and Rafella, who had been like a mother to me, to comfort my fears and failures, to speak on my side of a question, to find me worthy of a place in her heart. And I could not move to her side, to aid her, not even to stand beside the better man."

The lady spoke gently to Tintage's unhappiness. "Is it better, then, never to know doubt? never to fail? Stones have such lives, do you say it is better to be a stone than a man? Do not speak of better men, Tintage. I know what you have had to endure."

In the lady's presence, Oriel lost much of his quickness, but he understood from the gentle way she spoke to Tintage that she might not admire a man only for the deeds he had done. She must also see the testing of his heart. Oriel thought his own heart had been tested; but he was not sure. His strength had been tested, and his courage, his cleverness and his loyalty, his boldness, endurance — but where was his heart in all of that?

This lady touched his heart, and painfully, as no other had done; just as her lands — and he thought of her lands, looking at her as she spoke generously to Tintage — touched his eyes, and the soles of his feet, and the palms of his hand as he ran the rich soil through his fingers.

"Lady, I ask the honor of the dance," Oriel said. The heart he wasn't sure he had thudded in his ears.

She held her hand out, with a smile, but held it out to Tintage.

"Merlis, it wasn't I who asked the honor," Tintage said.

"Ah, but it is you whom I choose," she answered. After a pause she added, "for the dance."

"I can't be so churlish as to refuse," Tintage said, but he looked ruefully over at Oriel. "Don't be upset, friend. It doesn't matter who the lady wants, since she goes to the Earl."

Her cheeks turned pink with shame; and Oriel wished to punish Tintage for that; and he saw in the dark mole eyes that Tintage had chosen his words carefully, and now measured their effect. But Tintage should not, Oriel thought — his heart like a clenched fist to see it — give the lady pain.

Merlis drew back, and drew her hand out of Tintage's. "I'll have neither of you!" she cried.

Her voice was such that people nearby stopped speaking, and turned to see what caused her to speak so.

"The choice is not yours, lady," Tintage reminded her.

"Leave her," Oriel said to him. "Let her go." Maugre the shame of it, he would fight Tintage here, before all of the assembled guests. "Can't you see how you offend her?"

"I am the unhappiest of women," Merlis said, her voice soft again now — and Oriel thought she might be, and he wished that she might live to say of herself that she was the most fortunate.

He wouldn't trouble her again, he thought. It would be gall to a proud spirit to know she must marry whoever proved strongest in the Tourney, whoever was most willing to slaughter men — men who were perhaps his friends — for the prize of her hand, and her lands. Oriel couldn't blame Merlis if she felt bitter to the world, and betrayed by it.

He thought, watching her walk away from him, that he could be nourishing as the land for her, and patient, too, and let her grow into a life with him as a garden would grow — slowly, greenly, into its own flowering.

All soon knew how things stood with Oriel. Only Tintage dared to front him with the knowledge, but he felt the laughter in which the others joined when he was absent, and he almost admired Tintage for his forthrightness. At practice, Oriel had only to think of his opponent as winning Merlis's hand to have grief and despair and a desperate anger added to his strength and skill. For he couldn't long deceive himself: The lady liked him least of all the men who sought her hand.

He wished to understand what he had done wrong, that he might do right. In his confusion — in his longing for Merlis — in his need of her advice, he sent for Beryl. But she was nowhere to be found in the city, and even Griff didn't know where she might be.

The ladies of the court counseled him instead. Some thought he should find a landed lady who would know the luck she had in such a suitor. Some thought he should pretend to think another more desirable, and then, they said, Merlis would seek him out. Others maintained that a woman spoke most sharply to the man she most desired, as if a woman feared to give a man her heart and therefore tried to drive him away before he could see the danger she was in. "Merlis doesn't know her own heart," they all agreed. "If you win her, she will be glad," they promised him. "If you persist."

Oriel persisted. The desire he had to be in her company, if he couldn't have her smiles, for the sight of her if he couldn't hear her voice — unless she was nearby, he had no peace, and when she avoided him all around the hall his longing burned like a flame in him. When — and it happened thrice; on three occasions that shone like bonfires on a dark plain it happened so — during an evening of dance and song, the lady looked around to meet his eyes and summon him to her with a smile, and speak fair to him — then he was dazed, dazzled, and filled with hope. He was unsurprised that Merlis at last had chosen him. He was no less joyful, and his longing did not abate, but he was unsurprised. Unsurprised, but as glad as the land itself must be, to feel the warm spring sunlight falling at last upon it after the cold of winter, and to feel its own richness stirring within it, to feel the grass and flower swelling out, tree and herb and grain, all growing things.

Thrice after such occasions, his sword was like a bird in its quickness and flight, and no man could stand against him. Joy was a more potent weapon to him than grief or anger. Joy made him invulnerable. After such occasions, he would go eagerly to the next meeting with Merlis — and she would turn coldly away, scorning him.

Gwilliane was worried. "Merlis is not the woman to play so coyly with you. There is some deep feeling there."

Oriel could not speak, for the hope that the deep feeling was for him.

"We have deemed her ill," Gwilliane said. "We have measured her in her own lands, never in herself."

Oriel could make it all up to her, in the devotion of his heart that would never weaken.

"Poor child," Gwilliane said, and Oriel understood that it was the lady Merlis whom she pitied.

"Tell me," he said, because he wished to know all that he might of the lady, and because to be talking of her both eased and fueled his longing.

"Merlis was raised to great pride, and in the bitterness of the inheritance she could never have. And what have we done for her? I think, Oriel, that no woman should believe that a man might think death a fair exchange for the chance of her hand."

When Oriel saw the lady thus, in herself and removed from his desire for her, he knew what her perfect lover would do:

Her perfect lover would win the prize, and then lay it at the lady's feet. He would give to her the governance of her lands, and of her own heart. He would give it freely, knowing the chance that she might not give her heart, and hand, and lands, to him, even though he was the most worthy. Even though he had proved his worth in the battles of the Tourney, and then again in the gift, she might prefer another. But even knowing this, the perfect lover would serve his lady rightly.

Oriel understood this, but he knew his longing for Merlis was too strong. If he could win her, he would take her, willing or no. He wished her willing but if she could not be, then she could not. He would keep her, willing or no, in the castle he had won away from her, in his bed. If he could just win her, he would not let her go.

But he longed to find her willing, since she must come to him through the blood of men he admired, at the price of their lives, since she must come only at risk of his own life, since she was so beautiful and proud and had his heart.

At last, but it was only the ninth day after he had first seen the lady, the day of the Tourney arrived. By the end of that day there would be an Earl over the south. That man would be wed, and would then have the task of bringing order back to his lands. The day that dawned pink and gold would end in blood for many, and Oriel greeted it with relief.

For soon the game would be played out. He would have death or the lady, but he thought he would likely have the lady. He had measured his opponents — had he not taught them how to give themselves to the water, and seen which part of them fear touched first? and how each reacted? He knew their hearts, every one.

He knew his own heart, and his own desires. In what he had been, he saw what he might be. He dressed himself in green — shirt and trousers — over which the light armor would gleam silver. He pulled on high boots and strapped on his sword. He thought of the lady, and then drove her from his mind and heart, until the day should be done.

Only Griff was with him. Haldern had gone on ahead to stand with Rafella among the royal party at the Tourney. Oriel felt gratitude, that morning, for Haldern, and for Griff, and even for Rulgh and before him the Saltweller and the men of Selby. He thought that it might be said to be the sixth Damall who had started him along the path that led him to this day — and he laughed aloud.

The morning air was crisp, winy. It seemed to Oriel that with every step, every time his foot went down on the earth, his strength increased. It seemed that with every breath he drew in, he became more clever, and perhaps wise, too. He stepped out, glad, and Griff was beside him.

The Tourney had three stages. For the first, the contenders would present themselves to the King and the lady Merlis, to argue their suits. For the second, they would ride against one another, to unseat with lances and — if lucky — bruise one another or — if very lucky — break another's bones, which would lessen the opposition in the third and final stage of the Tourney, duel with swords to the death.

Oriel was ready for the risks. He was trained for them, trained against them, and he welcomed the contest. He and Griff walked up the winding streets. The sun rose up into the sky. At the Tourney field, warm sunlight fell down over everything, and the leaves shone on the trees as bright as the jewels of the lords and ladies.

An open tent had been set up to shade the dais where the King sat with his Queen, and the lady Merlis with them. The long greensward, edged by ancient trees, spread out before the dais. Grooms held horses, which nudged and nuzzled at one another, unknowing that they must soon thunder down upon one another like enemies. Lances stood propped together, all holding all the others erect, like brothers. The contestants stood together, each with his attendant.

Oriel approached and saw immediately how the day's work — even before it had been begun — isolated each man, each one away from every other. Each man's face was a mask, and Oriel felt the mask that was his own face. He turned it to the masks of the men who had — until this day — been his comrades. For there were only six left now in the contest.

He went up to the dais and bowed before the King, the Queen, and the lady Merlis.

That morning was one on which the lady smiled at him. To see her smile — at him — his heart rose, leaped, tumbled over. His legs nearly trembled. None, to look at him, would have seen this; but Oriel knew it.

He turned to the other suitors and it hit him like a glove in the face:

He must kill each man, to win the prize.

He almost wheeled around on his heels to challenge the King, or to beg the King to once again change the rules of contest. Lilos, who was the gentlest of men, was the King's own son, and did a King care less for his sons than other men did? Tseler also had a son to lose here, dignified and astute and an honor to his father. All but Oriel had fathers to give them up. And these sons, did these sons care less for their lives than other men? Oriel did not.

Must the Earl come to his title at the price of such men?

Oriel stood among the silent suitors as the thoughts rose up in his mind, like trees pushing their way full grown up out of the generous earth.

Must Oriel come to the title at such a price?

Beautiful as the lady was, and proud, and as needful of happiness to ease her sad heart, and rich as the lands were, and wide: Was there no other way to make an Earl?

He wished he had time to talk to Griff on the question. For there surged up into his mind a way to try that would not soak the earth in blood. But he would risk all in trying it.

Aye, and even if he won the Earldom, if he won

in this manner he would have lost too much in the winning. Better to risk all than to lose such men, wasn't it?

If he risked so, and won, he might even give the lady back her own hand. He well might. He didn't have to. He ought to, he hoped he would, he hoped he could when the time came.

Looking around at the mask faces, Oriel said to them, "I ask the privilege to be the first to speak to the lady."

None protested, for each had privately decided, as Oriel had, that the man who spoke first must of necessity be in the weakest position. The others, following him, could mimic and echo his words and ideas, should they be fine enough, or they could avoid the errors of thought and voice they saw him make. Moreover, the present event was most vivid, and thus the most recent speaker would seem most convincing. The last man to speak, therefore, had the strongest position.

Although, Oriel had thought without saying it, and thought that each suitor had had the same thought, since it came to blood anyway, it mattered little when or how well you spoke or thought. Since a dancing bear — if he but stood living at the end of the day — would have the lady, and be the Earl.

When the trumpets blew into the air, and the suitors stood in a line on the green grass before the King's pavilion, Oriel drank in the winy air and stepped forward. He bowed to the King, and to the Queen. He went onto one knee before Merlis. "Lady," he said.

Her grey eyes were cold on him. Her hair shone pale gold.

Oriel stood, to speak. "You of my heart."

She did not smile, or show that she heard his voice.

"I have sailed in the dangerous night across the sea to come before you," Oriel said. "I have climbed the stony sides of impassable mountains, to stand here. I have endured servitude and slaughter, cruelty and cold, to come to you. Always, I have left the place I held to come to you."

The lady Merlis was not impressed by such things, her face said.

"Lady, I would assay a dragon at your behest," he said. "I would go without food or sleep until I had called the moon down from the sky, to please you. I would make walls with stones dug out of the earth with my bare hands, to keep you safe. I would spend every waking hour of my entire life waiting for you to smile upon me."

This pleased her more. Given time, Oriel knew, he could have won her, without an Earldom in the offing, without anything more than his willing heart, he could have won her. But he had not been given time.

"For you are the bright gemstone of the world, lady. I give you my heart, and gladly, and my service, gladly, and I would gladly give you my life."

He waited briefly, for her to be sure how much he would give for her before he added, "But I will not give the lives of these men."

He had puzzled her, and the King stirred forward in his throne. The Queen placed a restraining hand on her lord's shoulder. He could guess the words Gwilliane spoke into her lord's ear: "Give him a little time to speak, sire. For my son, if for no better cause."

Oriel turned to the men. "So I ask you, suitors.

I ask if you will give over to me your claims. If you will do so, all of you, then I will take the lady's hand and count myself the most fortunate of men. If you would choose another, and all agree, then I will bend my knee to him, and count him the most fortunate. I would do much to win the hand and lands of the lady, I have done much and will do more; but I will not reach out to her, or to her people, a hand stained with the blood of so many good men."

The masks were still over their faces and he couldn't read their minds. "What do you answer me?" he asked. His question was for the five, but Griff's face told him that whatever came of this chance, Oriel had acted rightly. Always he had heart-trusted Griff, and now their eyes met again in understanding.

There was a long silent time, while the wind rustled and the King's party grew impatient, and the horses stamped their great hooves upon the soft ground. Then Lilos stepped forward. He looked Oriel in the eye and went onto one knee before him, offering Oriel his sword. He didn't offer the sword as if in surrender but as if it were a gift. Verilan came to kneel beside him, then Wardel and Garder, leaving only Tintage indecisive.

Lilos turned around, with the privilege of princehood. "Don't be a fool, Tintage."

Wardel looked over his shoulder to add, "You know he'll deal fairly with you. And you know he is the best of us."

Tintage's hands moved nervously. There was a stillness in his eyes. Oriel wondered, if only Tintage refused, would it be enough to fight only Tintage? To kill one was much less than to kill many. But he wished to kill none.

He would not have the title, if he must kill for it. He knew that now. He waited Tintage's decision.

At last, Tintage came forward, and went down on one knee, and held out his sword. On the dais, someone broke off a cry.

Oriel had all their swords in his hands. He lifted the handful of swords up over his head, and turned to show them to the King and Queen, and the lady, and then he gave them back, one by one, to the kneeling men, asking the men, one by one, to stand. Then he turned again to face the King.

The King rose, in his robe and crown. His face looked sternly down at Oriel. This was the last danger. Oriel knelt to present his own sword to the King. "Sire, I ask you to name me," he said, "and I ask you to accept my most solemn fealty. For under the law, I am the final contender." Griff had taught him how to argue the law, and Oriel hoped that the King — whom he now forced to act without his advisors at his ear — would choose, again, the deathless way.

"Then I do name you," the King spoke. "And I give unto you in token the sword of the Earls Sutherland, with the falcon's wings outspread at the hilt. I place on your finger the ring of the Earls Sutherland, that your sealed orders may carry the weight of law across the land. I give into your hand this beryl, carved with the falcon, ancient sign of the wealth of the Earls Sutherland."

Oriel felt as if he stood taller at each gift. He awaited the final one, the best of them.

"And I give into your hand," the King said, reaching out to bring Merlis forward, "the lady Merlis, who carries the ancient blood of the Earls Sutherland."

The lady put her hand into his, and her mouth

opened wordlessly — like a woman who looks upon her fate with Wolfers.

He was the Earl now, Oriel knew. He had been named by the King, and the title belonged to him as surely and as absolutely as if he had been born to it. So he must let her go.

Because to see in her such fear and anger and despair, and at his cause, was more than he could bear for her. He opened his mouth to say so to her, reaching out his other hand to her, to give her life into her own holding.

"Tintage!" she cried, as if there were danger. "Tintage!"

There was a movement behind him, and a thrusting coldness at the back, but when he turned to see what it was the thick cold was sucked out of him and he saw only Tintage's eyes, brown as moleskin, and fearful.

Voices, alarms, shrieks rose into the air and his knees buckled and he saw that Merlis had run to Tintage, and hung at his neck with her arms around him, and she looked back over her shoulder at Oriel and Griff held him erect, on his feet, without his knees. Oriel leaned against Griff, to find his breath.

Tintage was surrounded by men, and soldiers. Even Lilos had a dagger drawn against Tintage, who stood with Merlis hanging from his neck.

Oriel's ears rang. He didn't know how much longer he could stand, even with Griff's help, and for the land there was a voice in him that must speak now — before he could measure the danger of the wound Tintage had delivered to him. It didn't pain him, and he thought that must be good. There was no pain, but his back was hot with blood and he didn't think he could have stood without Griff to lean upon.

"This man," he heard himself say, and was glad to hear that his voice rang out as rich as the soil of the southern lands. "This man, Griff, I name my heir. I ask all — Lilos, Wardel, Garder, Verilan — I ask. Your fealty for Griff. As for me." He saw their faces and his knees collapsed under him, and he thought his head was floating away, and he thought, cradling up against the warmth of the breast, of Beryl.

He had treated her unkindly, he thought. He thought, she had given her heart bravely but he had given his as a coward does, only for the equal return. Until the last, he thought. At the last he would have done bravely.

He was dying. How he knew it, he didn't know. Blood bubbled up from his throat into his mouth, and it was bitter to the taste, and his hands were as cold as if they had been trapped in ice. Oriel wept then. He turned his face into the green shirt that covered Griff's chest, and wept hot tears.

He was afraid to die, and unwilling, and he was going to where Griff couldn't come with him. Into such darkness. He would never know what fortune came to his lands.

In the warmth of Griff's chest, Oriel wept for the heart of the lady who wished him dead, and he wept because he had given his heart away to someone who despised it. He was a fool, he wept. He wept for his child, and he could never tell Beryl now how much he understood, and how much he cherished her — even if he could never give her his heart. There was pain now, burning through him.

He had won everything, and lost it all, and he was ashamed of himself to be weeping.

Griff's face was near his own, and Griff's face was wet, and he was sorry to lose Griff but there was something urgent. "Put her under your care," he said. "I ask you."

"I will," Griff said. "I promise."

"I mean Merlis," Oriel said.

"Oh," Griff said.

Griff's eyes were as brown as the earth of the southern lands. The ringing in Oriel's ears made him almost deaf, but he saw the answer he asked in Griff's eyes, as Griff's mouth moved.

But her name eased him, to speak it, so as the darkness rose up Oriel greeted it with her name.

CHAPTER
27

His sleeve was wet with Oriel's blood. His breast
was damp with Oriel's tears. He looked around, for
help. It was Lord Haldern he saw. "Sir, send for
the girl. The puppeteer. You called her Baer? In
Lord Hildebrand's territory. Near the mountains."

Never mind how he and Beryl had last parted.
Never mind his own resolution to leave her in the
solitude she asked of him. She wouldn't deny Oriel.
Griff saw Lord Hildebrand's son among the men
who stood around him, where he knelt on the ground
with Oriel in his arms. "Wardel, sir, can you send

soldiers for her? Can you help me? She knows healing, she knows — "

The young man needed no further word. He spoke to the King's Captain, beyond Griff's hearing, then ran to his horse, and mounted, and turned its head to the north.

Griff struggled to his feet, Oriel a heavy weight in his arms. He thought his heart had been torn from his chest. Fear gave him the strength he needed to lift and hold his friend.

"Where — ?"

He shut his voice off. It was a howl like a wolf's that he barely kept in his throat.

He saw the Queen come forward, among her women, making murmuring noises. He saw soldiers hold a squirming man down on the ground.

Nothing to do with Griff now. Griff had only Oriel to think of. Oriel breathed, but pink foam dribbled out of his mouth.

And Beryl was not here to medicine him. Griff knew nothing of healing. He heard Lord Haldern speak, and there were tears in the man's voice. "Take . . . my house . . . litter. . . ." Some of the words Griff could hear and some never entered his ears.

Lady Merlis, with her cold grey eyes and her long shining hair, stood beside the man the soldiers now held erect.

Servants came to hold out a litter, upon which he placed Oriel, and when the servants lifted it again he stayed with Oriel, in case his eyes might open.

He couldn't understand what had happened. His understanding was trapped at the time when Oriel stood before the kneeling lords, about to be named Earl Sutherland.

What had happened? Oriel had stood in his slender, high-shouldered pride, drawing all eyes to him. There was that in Oriel — and had ever been, even from the first — that drew the eyes, first, and then the heart. The man of eighteen winters, who had claimed the Earldom without shedding blood, who had boldly risked everything, even the woman of his heart — he was no surprise to Griff. That man was the natural kin of the boy who came to the Damall's island and proved stronger even than all the fear the Damall could summon onto his boys. The boy and the man had both walked on the land as if it belonged by rights in their care. The boy and the man had both stood unvanquished — aye, and untarnished, too — and always, Griff thought, worthy of his life's service.

Grief almost knocked Griff's knees out from under him.

Long-robed priests awaited them at Lord Haldern's house, with their books of medicine and their pots of balms. Griff knew them for men who would do the best they could.

When Oriel lay on his stomach, the bleeding staunched by a folded cloth, Griff sat beside him on a low stool. He listened to the thready breathing — in and out. The priests came and went, to study the wound and try to pour spoonfuls of medicine down Oriel's throat. They spread ointments on Oriel's naked back, and his breathing halted, came fast, then steadied.

"My lord," the priest said, a young man with yellow-green cat eyes, "will you not eat?"

It was by then dark and candles were lit. Griff shook his head, to shake away the company, to deny everything. As long as he sat beside Oriel, the breathing continued. He did not necessarily believe that if he were to leave, or to sleep, then Oriel would die. But he knew he must not move from the room.

He had no hunger and no thirst. He rose from the stool only to urinate into a bedpan, which a servant removed, or a priest, he paid no attention, for he sat hunched beside the bed where Oriel lay breathing thinly, threadily, painfully.

If Beryl would only come. If they found her she would come. She would never refuse Oriel anything. Griff had always understood that, even as he grew to know that he desired her for himself. She was the best of women. She would of course choose Oriel.

And if Beryl knew Oriel needed her skill, and help, nothing would keep her from this room. Griff knew her heart.

"My lord," one of the servants asked. "Will you take food?"

It was growing light. Griff shook his head. He hadn't slept, and he wasn't tired. His will held tight to Oriel's will. It was as if he held Oriel tethered to life, through his will. It was as if his will allowed Oriel to fly up, aloft, above the pain of flesh, so that Oriel wouldn't abandon his body, despite the pain that tried to drive him away.

Sometime during the first day, Griff understood what had happened. He remembered Oriel's refusal to fight to the death, and the response of the other contenders, and Tintage's sword driving into Oriel's back. He understood that Tintage must be the lady's chosen lover. He remembered that he was the named heir.

Griff pulled his stool closer to Oriel's bed, and fixed the end of his will more firmly to Oriel's. Griff was not the man to be Earl. He did not wish it. He wished to serve Oriel, Earl Sutherland.

In the winter, in Beryl's house, when they had

first designed the scheme, Oriel had asked Griff if he would want to be the one to make the attempt. It had been asked in jest, but Griff knew that if he had said yes, Oriel would have stood behind him. Oriel had looked at him in the straight way he'd always had, bright eyes unafraid. "We have come too far and paid too dearly, to miss the chance," Oriel said. "You could be the one to try it."

"That I couldn't do," Griff had answered, and Beryl added, "Aye, and if you will rule, Oriel, then you must let people serve you. If you would govern, you must let them give you authority, even those who are also your friends."

Now Griff looked at Oriel, bloody backed, and he remembered what Oriel had said, and what Beryl had said, and felt his will grip Oriel's will tight, that Oriel might live to rule the land that had taken his heart. It was always so with Oriel. Even the mountains had seemed to him objects of wonder. To Griff they had seemed cold, and difficult underfoot, barren, colorless, death-dealing.

Griff sat, Oriel breathed, and Griff hoped of Beryl. He had no thought for any more than that: Oriel breathing, and hope of Beryl.

On the second day, Oriel died.

Beryl did not come.

Griff was alone.

And he must be Earl Sutherland.

After Griff had slept and bathed and shaved and dressed and eaten, after Oriel was buried beside the other Earls Sutherland, after many days, Wardel rode back to report that the puppeteer's holding was uninhabited by any human creature, although the puppets hung in rows in their cupboards and the horse grazed in a fenced field. The news had no meaning.

After more days, they came to him, the contenders, Verilan and Garder, Lilos and Wardel. They treated him as if he were the Earl. They spoke of promises made to Oriel, and their intention to honor their word, and Oriel, in honoring Griff. Griff was still a guest at Lord Haldern's house and there the old lords also came to him. Tseler told him he must first bend the knee to the King, in fealty, and then he must ride into the south, to bring his lands into order.

Griff had no lands. These were Oriel's lands.

"My lord, you must," Lilos said. The others echoed him, and "You must," repeated Lord Haldern, Lord Karossy, Lord Tseler.

Perhaps he must, Griff thought, but that did not mean he would. He could find no words to speak to any of them.

When a boy knelt in the whipping box, the others ringed close around to watch. But for the boy it was as if they were far away, a distance across which their voices didn't carry. For the boy in the whipping box, there was only the cut of the whip and the sharp stones on his knees and palms. He couldn't hear or see anything else, except as you see things underwater, muffled and muted.

It was the Queen whose voice first spoke through to him. She came one day, and held out her hand to give him the beryl, with the falcon carved into its back. Griff wouldn't reach out to take it. "Oriel said," the Queen spoke, then stopped to weep, then spoke again. "He said that this stone should go to the Earl Sutherland, when he had the title. It is time, now, Griff."

Griff shook his head, but she reached her hand up to hold his chin. He saw the fine lines near her eyes and mouth, and the grey in her hair, and the way a stiffness of the back hurt her; he saw the way the years had made marks on her beauty. He felt her little finger where it touched the scar on his cheek. "Do you refuse him?"

Griff shook his head again and this time she allowed it. "I wouldn't refuse him," Griff said.

The Queen was satisfied.

"My lady?" Griff asked. The Queen would know as much as any man of the court, but she was not a man and so she could speak her knowledge when she chose. "What of the lady Merlis?"

Gwilliane turned away from him, and answered him as she looked out of a window, that he might not see her face and whatever it would reveal. "Merlis has placed herself at the traitor's side. She now claims that they were wed in secret, during the summer. She has placed herself at the traitor's side and must be taken, thus, for a traitor to her Earl. If she is a traitor to the Earl then she has forfeited her rights to the title and lands."

So he need not marry Merlis. Griff could have done almost anything for Oriel, and he would be Earl Sutherland because Oriel asked it of him, but marry Merlis he could not. "Thank you, lady."

She turned then, with a rustling of her dress, and he walked with her to the door, and he opened the door for her and he bent over her hand to place his lips on her fingers. "I wish you well, Earl Sutherland," she said.

Four men waited in the hallway, three of them near Griff's age and the fourth older by many summers. These four Griff welcomed. They had seen in Oriel what he himself had seen, and chosen to serve him. Griff gestured them into the room, asked them to be seated around the table, called out for a servant to bring wine and bread, sat down with them, and said what was in his heart. "I can be named Earl, myself, alone, but to be the Earl takes more understandings and skills than I have in myself, alone."

They looked at one another, not understanding.

"I ask your assistance," Griff said. "I've read the law," he explained, "and the history, but I know nothing of how to set taxes, and assess for them. I have little experience of how to judge a man who speaks truly for the people from one who speaks for his own advantage. I know how to fight with sword and staff, but not with an army at my back. I have only the ideas Oriel and I spoke of to tell me how to shield a people from famine in drought or blight, how to plan against fair as well as foul weather, how to cull herds so that they can breed and feed in comfort. I think I know how to serve the King rightly and how to apply the law or change the law for greater justice, but of the rest — how to dress for occasions, who deserves what honors among the people of the court, how to train a servant, how to balance the powers of priests and lords and Majors, how to hold a Hearing Day, how . . . I know almost nothing."

"I will serve you, as I can," Lilos promised, "and so will all of my father's house."

"As will we all," they said.

"I can lead soldiers for you," Verilan promised, but "No," Wardel argued, "the Earl must be known to lead his own men." Verilan was quick to the quarrel, asking Wardel, "Do you think I would seek to reclaim what I have given over? Do you think I am so little to be trusted?" and Lilos was quick to defend Wardel, "You know that isn't what he meant, so don't pick a fight on that account."

Garder spoke, then, with less heat than any of

the other three. "The important thing may be as much what the Earl is seen to do, as what he actually does. If those who serve a man are true to him, as I think we are, there is no danger if Verilan leads Sutherland's troops, as long as Griff rides at their head."

"What about Verilan's place in his father's house?" Wardel asked. "For I am more easily spared, having more brothers, to go into the Earl's close service."

"Unless," Lilos suggested, "there were two Captains over the soldiers, which would be less potential danger than one Captain, for one might grow greedy, or win the loyalty of soldiers and people, against his will. Two divide the dangers."

"Ordinarily it is the brothers of the house who serve this purpose," Garder said. "But if brothers are lacking, then there must be others, to be Captain, and to be steward, too."

"But such men would have to give up their own inheritances," Wardel pointed out.

Then, as if all had earlier agreed that this must be said, Wardel addressed Griff, "My lord Earl — No, Griff, you have to accept the title. My lord Earl, Tintage awaits your justice."

Verilan spoke quickly. "To name the day and place of the hanging."

"But he is a lord," Garder pointed out unwillingly. "Yaegar might make the death of his son an excuse for armed rebellion."

"But we saw how little Yaegar valued his son," Lilos said.

"He dishonorably seduced the lady, too, if you ask my view," Garder said. "Whether he wed her, as she claims, or whether he did not, he will have bedded her, you can count on that. To seal her heart to him, as bed pleasures can, and seal the Earldom."

Griff covered his eyes with his hand, for Oriel had given the lady his heart.

"No one would deny Griff revenge," Wardel said. "To kill an Earl is high treason, and an Earl's sword can answer it. Surely Yaegar will deny the traitor?"

"He denied the son," Lilos observed.

"But he did that for his own purposes," Garder insisted. "I am uneasy in my mind about how to contain Yaegar. For he cannot resist the chance to bend another to his will, if he thinks he can profit of it. We should know more of what is in Yaegar's mind, before anything is decided about Tintage."

"But something must be done!" Verilan cried. "For Oriel was basely murdered."

"And I think soon, before it has the chance to grow in people's minds," Lilos agreed.

They turned to Griff, who had been listening close. "Shall we hear him, then?" Griff asked. "I agree we can't wait, but to condemn a man un-heard — Even if there are witnesses to his deed, he can still be heard. Not just by the Earl, I think, and not just by Oriel's companions, but by all, I think, for it is all he has offended in taking this life. Just as in taking any life, whether great or small, the murderer offends all who have given their free-doms over into the keeping of the law." Griff tried to gather his thoughts together, for they were scat-tering like a flock of flushed birds. "I would ask the King and Queen, also, to hear Tintage. I would ask Beryl, could I find her."

All but Wardel looked puzzled.

"Here they called her Baer, she was with us that first day, but — she is the puppeteer, the — she — " It was too many griefs at one time. "I would have the Queen and one or two of her ladies, if you know of ladies of good judgment, and good hearts, have you a sister, Lilos?" Griff didn't know how to say what he was thinking of. In part, he cared about none of it and wished only to go away — to be perhaps a mountain man, living among ice and blinding light until he could die.

But he had to live and be Earl Sutherland.

"I would ask — I don't know how many, but enough so that no one man's enmity could condemn Tintage, and so that no one man's friendship could save him. Can you find and bring them here?" he asked. "Your father, Garder, and the Lords Haldern and Karossy, Verilan? The King, Wardel? and the Queen, too, and the best of the ladies, Lilos? Lady Rafella, too, she must be here. We gather at midday," Griff said, and rose abruptly from the table.

The four, he thought, would take his abrupt rising and leaving as showing fixed purpose, as the proper action of an Earl. They wouldn't know that grief had come down upon him unbearably, and he must be alone to put his arms around her, and feel her arms around him, to take enough comfort from grieving so that he could return to finish the business of the day. The business Oriel had given into his hands.

There were almost twenty in the great hall. Griff sat alone at the center of a long wooden table, and the rest were behind him, on benches and in chairs. Tintage faced Griff, and thus faced all. Two guards stood close beside him, and his hands were chained in front of him, and two more guards stood at each door, but Tintage didn't look dangerous. He stood straight, as if unafraid, and calm, but his eyes, like moles wandering above ground, shone fearful, and he considered his words carefully before he spoke.

He bowed his head to the King and the Queen, to the other lords and ladies present. He greeted Rafella not by name but by title; not, however, by her title as Lord Haldern's wife, but by her title in relation to himself. "I am glad to see you, Aunt," Tintage said.

At the last, his mole eyes met Griff's.

Griff had fallen into flames. His heart choked him and he could see only Tintage, and he had a sword near his hand —

"My lord," Lilos asked. "Are you unwell?"

Verilan spoke softly. "Let him do it. Who better?"

Griff shook his head, to clear it. For blood called out for blood, when lands and wealth were at issue. If Griff revenged Oriel now, who might revenge Tintage?

He pushed himself back into his chair and gripped its carved wooden arms. He forced himself to look at Tintage — why was the man smiling now? Oriel would have slit the man's throat, if it had been Oriel now in the Earl's chair and Griff buried underground with his stiff fingers wrapped around the hilt of his sword. When the avalanche rolled down toward Rulgh, there had been joy in Oriel's face, as well as long hatred and stern necessity.

But Griff was not Oriel, and couldn't take a blood revenge. Even if Tintage mocked that in him, when the fit had passed Griff knew it had gone forever. He wished, seeing Tintage smile, that he could summon the fiery fit back, but he couldn't. He wasn't Oriel and he never could be.

"You stand accused of treason," Griff spoke the formal words.

Tintage answered, "What I have done deserves my death. I don't deny it. If I could undo the action,

I would. But I cannot and so I must accept your judgment on me."

He spoke like a true man.

Griff smelled falseness on him, like fear.

"It was a madness of jealousy that made me act," Tintage said. He looked now at the lords and ladies, and the royal couple. "With the others I was nearly equal. With the others, some of them your sons, and some of you present to confirm my words, I was in some ways the stronger or more able, and in other ways the lesser. With any of the others, I might fight well. But Oriel — "

Tintage stopped speaking. Griff thought, watching the mole eyes measure the expressions Griff couldn't see on the faces behind him, that he could see the man peeping out from behind the eyes, pleased with the effect of his words on the company.

"It was madness of jealousy. But Rafella knows the truth of my life, and how cruelly I was treated — she will speak of beatings, of being locked into my father's dungeons and given only water, for days, of the shaming. Can you say that for me, Aunt?"

"I cannot deny it," she said.

"What hope had I of honor, then?" Tintage asked.

Griff didn't trust himself to speak.

"My great fault is, I turned my sword against a man I should have offered it to in service," Tintage said.

"You turned it against a man you had just offered it to, in fealty," Griff reminded Tintage.

It was as if Tintage hadn't thought Griff was any danger to him. It was as if he hadn't seen how Oriel honored Griff, and how the others now gave Griff the title they had hoped for. Now he gave Griff his attention, and the title. "Let me live, my lord Earl, and I can promise that you will come to no harm from me. My enmity, like my envy, was for Oriel. For he had everything."

Griff answered, "Everything but the heart of the lady."

"What is a lady's heart without her lands?" Tintage asked, almost gaily, as if he were not standing trial for his life. "He would have had her heart, too, soon enough, I'll wager, once he'd wed and bedded her, once she'd ceased her weepings."

Griff had thought the same, and hoped for it. But he thought Tintage disrespectful to the lady, a coward's disrespect, to say so.

Death would silence that false voice, but death was not the only silencer. And he would always choose not to kill, if he had the choice. As Oriel had once chosen —

And regretted it, Griff remembered, then he remembered better — with grief like a stone at his belly — remembered that Oriel never regretted the chances he took.

"Have you more to say?" he asked. Tintage shook his head. "Then I say to those present that I think of banishment," Griff said. "Lifetime banishment from the Kingdom, never to be lifted, not for any cause, not on any petition." He looked around then.

Haldern stood red-faced but irresolute, Garder seemed doubtful, but it was Verilan who spoke. "If you hesitate to kill him, I offer you my sword."

"I hesitate to kill," Griff said.

"Is that wisdom?" Wardel inquired, after a silence.

"It is my choice," Griff said. "For the weal of the Earldom is not fed by blood, is it?"

Nobody answered him.

"Thank — " Tintage said.

One look at Griff silenced him.

Griff waited, but no one wished to speak, so he said, "I ask my lord and King to banish Tintage, son of Yaegar, from the Kingdom, and for all of his life."

The King spoke the sentence without hesitation, adding, "In three days' time you must be gone. If after that time you are found anywhere in the Kingdom, your life will be forfeit."

Tintage bowed his head. "Thank you for my life, my lord Sutherland. Sire, I thank you. I will obey. I hope — "

Griff stood, was standing up before he knew that was his intention. Silence held the room, and he knew he held all eyes, but he needed all of his strength to hold his hand and let the law rule. "Take him away," he ordered the soldiers, and they obeyed him.

Before Griff could turn away, before the courtiers could rise, before the King could speak whatever formal words he thought befitting the occasion, almost before the servants had closed the doors behind the guards and their prisoner, Merlis ran into the room. She knelt down before the table, her head lowered down into her skirts. Her long pale hair spread around, and when Griff went to her, and asked her to rise, the face she turned to him was paler than her hair, and ravaged by weeping.

"What do you want of this company?" he asked her.

"I would speak with you, my lord Earl," she said, her voice so low he had to bend down to hear her words.

"Then you will," he said.

"Alone," she whispered.

Griff remembered his promise to Oriel, but she had shown herself to be a woman capable of great betrayal. "Not alone," he said.

She clasped her hands over her breast and tears came out of her eyes and she seemed to gulp in air for the breath to ask him, "Let me go with Tintage. I beg you. Don't make me — marry — "

"Never," he promised her. "Have no fear of — "

" — bed another — " she gulped.

" — being forced to marry me, or — "

" — nothing else matters — "

" — any other man," Griff said.

"Please, give me leave. Please, to take his exile with him."

Her request suited Griff's own purposes, but he tried to warn her, "You are a lady of high birth, and wealth."

"I had nothing to do with my birth, and you have my wealth, you've taken it, he would have — All I ask is to go with Tintage."

"Lady," Lord Karossy spoke. She turned to face him, like an animal at bay. "If birth has given you lands and beauty, you can never be as those who have none."

"I don't care!" she cried. "I care only to be with him!"

"Lady," Griff said. The face she turned to him was hopeful, and she accepted the hand he offered to raise her to her feet. "He wouldn't have forced you. Oriel. He wouldn't have struck another man in the back for you, either."

She snatched her hand away. "You didn't see the way he looked at me, my lord Earl," she said, coldly angry now.

"You didn't know his heart," Griff said.

Neither could speak to the other.

But Griff had made a promise to Oriel, and he would keep his word. All he had left of Oriel was word to keep. "You may accompany Tintage, if that is what you wish," Griff said then. That was the most he could do, for now; and if more was needed later, then later he would do more. "If the King agrees, and no other makes objection."

The King agreed. No other made objection. Griff was suddenly tired to exhaustion.

"And what of my personal effects?" the lady asked now. "My horses? my gowns? linens and servants? my jewels, and the carved chests they are kept in, and the tapestries and furnishings of my own apartments at the castle, my dogs?"

Griff turned his back to her. "Lilos, would you — ?" he asked, and stood looking out the window, stood alone, while Lilos gave the lady Merlis permission to take one horse for riding and one for sumptering, and one hundred gold coins to keep her. He forbade her the jewels, which belonged to the House of Sutherland.

"May I take my gowns and cloaks? boots? bedclothes? May I have one of the stable carts to carry my goods?" Merlis asked.

"Yes, lady, you may. And any servant who wishes to accompany you is free to go with you."

"And — "

Griff made himself turn around, to speak again, for she had lost everything. "Lady, I offer you a home of your own, wherever in the southern lands you choose, with fields to keep you in wealth, and servants to care for you, and a dowry should you wish to marry."

She drew herself up. "I am already wed," she said, and he knew she was lying. He knew also that she didn't wish to be saved.

"The man is a blooded traitor," Griff reminded her.

"Yes, while now you are the Earl Sutherland," she answered scornfully, and Griff's heart broke again within his chest.

CHAPTER
28

It was as Earl Sutherland that Griff rode south from the King's city. In towns and villages he was formally welcomed — by the Majors and the wealthiest men from among the people. Others, men of all ages, women of all ages, children of all ages, stared at him, as if they could read in his face what their futures might be. At least once in every town and village someone would find the courage to call out, "Aye, and we'll all miss him, won't we? You as much as the rest of us, my lord." Griff heard how those gathered around all agreed. "Aye, and he was a lovely man." The praise for Oriel made it easier for

Griff to ride out on the tall horse, with its great hooves pounding onto the ground, to wear the long green cape with a wide-winged falcon stitched in gold across his back, to have on his finger the ring worn only by the Earl Sutherland and his heir.

Thus Griff came to the castle of the Earls Sutherland.

Sorrow, loneliness, and labor made the sum of his days. The storehouses and granaries were low, the linens in disarray, the servants confused and frightened, the rooms and the gardens in neglect. The castle seemed without heart, without life. It was Garder whom Griff put in charge of bringing order to the castle. It was Lilos he sent down into the surrounding city, and to the towns and villages beyond, to carry messages of good will, and to find out how things stood for the winter, how the harvest and herds fared. Verilan was busy with the training and accommodation of a troop of soldiers from the north. For the lady Merlis had taken her soldiers with her into the south.

Griff endeavored to learn his way around the many-roomed castle itself, and all the custom it was built on; and to learn the business of the land. He endeavored to go out into his city, where he could be seen and known, where he could make some of the faces familiar to him. For should not an Earl know his own people? And was not the purpose of the Earldom to make life richer for its people, whatever their rank or occupation?

Griff did not want the title of Earl. There was no other man to carry it, but the burden lay uneasy on his shoulders. Only Oriel would have understood, Griff thought.

Or Beryl, perhaps, but Wardel — whom he had sent once again into the north, to seek her whereabouts — had not returned, so Griff didn't even know how things were with Beryl. He thought of her seldom — for the grief of Beryl was like an open wound. The grief of Oriel, who was dead, had at least finality. He awaited Wardel with fear, and grief, and a desire to see Beryl, to be in her company, to hear her speak, of Oriel, and the world, and the puppet tales, and the child she carried. To hear her speak.

And the child she carried. He had forgotten the child.

It was as if Oriel had placed a hand on Griff's shoulder, to comfort him, and to strengthen. Griff could be Earl when Oriel's child was heir. He could hold the Earldom for Oriel's child.

The thought of the child — It wasn't that grief rose from her place in his heart and rose into the air, leaving him. No, grief was his companion. But he was no longer so separated from Oriel when he thought of the child.

More days passed, and the leaves of the trees in the castle gardens became tipped with gold and red. Wardel, at last, rode in and delivered his news. The holding was still uninhabited. None had seen Beryl, in the villages between his father's city and the holding. The spaewife had flown away on a tree branch, some said, who claimed to have seen her traveling across the sky. Others said she would return if they had great need of her. A few spoke only into his ear to hope she had not been murdered, for she was only a girl, with a talent for healing. But she had taken into her house, just last winter, two danger-ous-looking young men, who had ridden to the fairs with the girl between them. Perhaps those young men might be traced? One or two said if Beryl was in need of help she could always ask help of them.

Griff ignored the rumors and tried to accept the reality.

Wardel, the stains of his journey still upon him, sat before the broad fire in the Earl's apartments. Woven tapestries hung down over stone walls, and a tall window opened onto the night sky.

"Beryl's grandfather," Griff said now, "came from the south, from an Inn at the southern edge of the Kingdom, she said, and I think I will seek her there myself, and thereby see more of the people I rule."

"That would take you into Yaegar's territory," Wardel said. He pulled in his legs and asked a direct question. "If you find this lady — but she isn't a lady born, is she? Will you wed her?"

"If she will have me," Griff answered. "She is with child," he told Wardel, "and the child is Oriel's."

Wardel looked into the fire. Griff could see his calculations. "So if you were to wed her, you would be regent for the child, who will have in his veins the blood of the man who won the Earldom."

"I am the Earl Sutherland," Griff said.

Wardel was angry at Griff's answer, which made complicated what Wardel had hoped to keep simple.

"As I was named by Oriel," Griff reminded him.

"And I begin to see why he chose you," Wardel said. "For you have a heart that is stubborn for truth. What of this child, then?" Wardel demanded. "And the woman, when you wed her?"

"If she will have me, for she has already refused me once."

Wardel turned back to the fire, where flames rose up in disorder. "You must have an heir, you know that. And more than one, if you can, an heir and brothers for him."

"I know," Griff said. He would marry, for heirs.

If he couldn't marry Beryl, and Oriel's child, then he would find another lady. There would be many glad to be an Earl's Lady. "All I ask is to know that Beryl is safe." She would not, he thought, be brought to bed for another few months, but he couldn't be sure of that.

"And this child may be a girl and no danger," Wardel said.

Griff didn't argue. He felt a wash of loneliness, or perhaps only grief, that drove him from his chair by the fire, to look out the window. Before winter closed him into the castle, he would go south, to see his people and meet his lords and find Beryl. If she was to be found. This place in the world which Oriel had given to him — he was unprepared for this place. What was good in him was not the same as all those things that had been good in Oriel —

"Lord Griff, I would be of service to you," Wardel said, from his seat by the fire.

"I thank you." Griff turned around. Wardel looked a boy, but he would never let another take unmerited advantage from him. Oriel had found Wardel, and selected him, but Griff knew why the choice was wise. That was all the advantage he had ever had over Oriel. He had known Nikol's heart, and the desire of the sixth Damall to have a heart as foul as his own inherit the island. Oriel had only recognized Nikol's enmity.

Griff couldn't, as Oriel could, gather men to him at a glance, seal them to him with a word. He had himself been the first gathered, the first sealed.

"I thank you for the offer," Griff answered, and not until he saw alarm in Wardel's eyes did he realize that he had already spoken those words. "I will ride into the south," he said, "to seek the lady myself, and to meet my people. I should assure myself of

Lord Yaegar's fealty, I think, for there are rumors."

"I ask to ride with you," Wardel said.

"With no rest?"

"Across the winter, I promise you. I'll rest and grow fat," Wardel said. "But I would go with you into the south, and a troop of soldiers, too, Griff. For Lord Yaegar . . ."

This was business, and Griff got down to it. He called a servant to summon Lilos and Garder to them, and sent another to fetch Verilan from among the soldiers.

Two days later, they rode out. They rode out into grey rain, Griff, Wardel, Verilan, and behind them a troop of one hundred mounted soldiers, trained — as Lord Haldern required — for fighting on horseback or on the ground. Griff knew no more of what they rode towards than did the others, lord or soldier. He feared what might await them, if the rumors were true. On the chance that the rumors were true, Griff had that morning named Lilos as his heir. "His is the highest blood of all of us," Griff had explained.

"And after Lilos?" Verilan inquired.

"That is up to Lilos," Griff decided. Verilan masked his disappointment and thereby revealed his desire to be named if not first, then second. Griff noted that ambition in his Captain, and thought he would be unwise to overlook it.

As they rode through steady rain, Griff surprised himself by this thinking of successions. Then he surprised himself again, when he understood how natural it now felt to him to ride out as Earl Sutherland. He looked back over his green-caped shoulder, to see the soldiers riding four abreast behind him, along the River Way.

The rumors were enough to dismay all but the

most high-hearted. There were rumors of the disinherited lady and her true man, who welcomed all who cared to fight on their behalf for the lady's lands. There were rumors of a troop of discontented soldiers, and some with genuine grievances that had gone unanswered during the years since the Lady Earl had died, and for years before as well, long grievances. There were rumors of rebellion.

For the first two days of travel, as they crossed by fields and villages lying close to Sutherland's stronghold, all seemed well. The people gathered to cheer them. A solitary farmer's wife might look up towards them from the field where she gathered the last onions. Children called out in excitement to see so many armed and mounted men, riding at such speed. Dogs ran out to bark. For the first two days, they rode through prosperous land.

After those first days, however, the land seemed sparsely inhabited. The villages that they rode through were empty, and if they happened to pass a herdsman out with his flocks, that man would pretend not to see them as he drove his goats or sheep in an opposite direction. Midafternoon of the third day they passed a ruined holding, the house no more than charred posts and black beams, the field black stubble. No animal or person remained, except for a solitary cat who stalked birds and mice, as if the holding still needed protection from such thieves. It worried Griff to see the holding in ruins, here in the Kingdom.

By the time they arrived at the village near which they would camp that evening, they had passed two more scorched holdings, and Griff had moved from worry to anger.

The Major of the village came forward to greet them, and the people gradually came out of their houses, to stare at the soldiers without expression. They were not glad to see soldiers, nor afraid to see soldiers, nor sorry to see soldiers. The Major was a wiry white-haired man, bald-pated, whose eyes doubted all they looked upon, whose hands he kept clasped behind him as if they might lead him into trouble. He greeted Griff and the lords with minimum courtesy, although he offered them refreshment. "We have some ale yet left, and bread. But we cannot feed another army of soldiers."

"Another?" Griff asked. He stood at his horse's head.

"Aye, and you don't think yours is the only army about, do you?"

"Is this the way you speak to the Earl Sutherland?" Wardel warned the man.

The Major was not afraid. "How do I know he's the man?"

"Who else would wear the ring?" Wardel asked.

"Aye, and I heard the tale, of a foreigner who without even fighting for it laid his hands on the title, and then he gave it over to his creature. And so the lady could not have her own inheritance from her own father, and his father before him who was the Great Gladaegal. The lady, as I heard, stood helpless until there came a man willing to put his army at her disposal, for the justice of her cause."

Griff silenced Wardel to ask, "What is the justice of the lady's cause?"

"Why, her inheritance, from her father the Earl, and his father the Earl before him."

"Was she named the heir?" Griff asked. If there were an error in justice, he would give the lady her rights, without delay.

"Only the people name their heirs," the Major told him. "Among the lords, as you should know, it is the oldest son who takes the lands and title. The lady, maugre she was the only child of the old blood, could never be the oldest son."

Griff ignored the discourtesies of word and tone, and now he could ignore the lady's claim. Now he had more pressing concerns. "We passed three burned farmsteads as we rode into your village."

The circle of listening villagers fell silent. Griff looked around at them all. They were only eight in number, three women and five men, plus a few children standing hand in hand, or clutching a woman's skirts. One child seemed alone, and pale — he stood behind a woman's skirts but as if he was attached to no one.

"Why were the holdings burned?" Griff asked. He heard but did not look to see his own men, impatient, with stamping of hooves and jingle of spur and sword.

The Major shrugged his shoulders, a helpless gesture.

"Did all the people of those holdings come safely away?" Griff asked. He sensed something wrong here, of which no one spoke.

"Not my father," the solitary boy cried. He was perhaps seven summers, perhaps eight or nine, and he was angry. But his anger was directed at Griff.

About boys at least Griff felt he knew something.

"Lord Tintage told us it was necessary, for the lady Merlis to have a victory. For when the hordes came down to take our lands from the lady, and from us. There is a great army coming out of Sutherland's city." The Major reported this warily, and bitterly.

Griff forced back his own fury. He looked at the boy, and at the Major. "You see the great army. I am the Earl Sutherland," he said. "I am Earl

419

through being named heir by Oriel." He clamped
his teeth together to keep from saying here and now
what had happened to Oriel. He must claim the
Earldom only by himself, for himself; he must not
take it away from Merlis or Tintage. "I have sworn
the Earl's fealty to the King. I wear the ring and
carry the sword. I have the commission to rule over
you."

The Major studied him. The woman before
whom the boy stood held the boy by his shoulders,
holding him back.

"You aren't a lord," the Major said.

"No," Griff agreed. "Neither am I born a man of
the Kingdom. But I ask you to recognize me as your
Earl."

The Major studied him for a long time before
saying, "Aye, and I will. And if I will, so also will
the people of the village, and the people of the
holdings. When we tell them. For holdings should
not be burned out, and crops should not be burned
over, as if winter will never come. A man who has
no need to die ought not to lose his life to save his
holding. When they rode through this summer, I
saw that man. Oriel. If you are his chosen heir, I
serve you."

"I thank you," Griff said. He summoned the boy
forward.

"I promise you," he said to the boy, "that who
breaks the law will answer to the law. Moreover,
that holding will be yours. I give it to you, if it is
in my power to give. I promise to get it for you, if
it is in another lord's gift. So that however wastefully
your father's life may have been taken from him,
you will not lose what he died to keep for you."

"Can you do that?" the boy asked, not afraid of

Griff in his height and splendor — more afraid, perhaps, to hope.

"What else is the good of being Earl?" Griff asked.

A smile broke over the boy's face. Then he remembered to whom he spoke and his face became serious, and he knelt solemnly to Griff. And Griff remembered briefly the Damall's island and the smell of salty air.

"Have you men enough?" the Major asked now.

Wardel leaned forward. "You have seen their army, can you say how many they are? and how well weaponed? Can you tell where they were going, and if they intended battle?"

"Yaegar's city," a woman spoke from out of the crowd. "My husband went with them — but he hoped for booty, not battle. It was booty they promised, holdings and coins, rich cloths. Lord Tintage said his father would bring his own troops in on the lady's cause. He said, forgive me his words, sir, that the Earl would never dare battle. Sir," she said, "my lord, if they burn their way to Yaegar's city there will be famine this winter, and how shall I feed my children?"

"The doling rooms will be no less full than my own storerooms," Griff promised her. "It may be that we shall all go hungry, but," and he could speak as one who understood hardship, "we can survive hunger, I think."

"If we move fast," Verilan said now, addressing Griff but, Griff thought, with the intention that all the village should hear and carry the tale, "then there will be little time for them to burn and destroy crops, or holdings, or herds."

"Then we must ride on tonight," Griff said, and lifted his foot into the stirrup, to mount his horse.

"May good fortune ride with you, my lord," the Major called behind them.

They rode out, rode on. They followed the broad River Way, the path that Tintage and Merlis had taken. They saw more burned holdings and scorched fields than Griff liked, but fewer than he had feared. They rested seldom and ate on horseback. Each man carried a fortnight's rations of oatcakes in his pack; the river gave water to both horse and man; the lords ate and drank and rode just as the soldiers did.

At night, before they slept, Griff and Wardel and Verilan discussed the upcoming battle, what it might be, and where. By the time they reached the stone walls of Yaegar's city, Griff knew almost as much about mounting a battle as did Verilan, who had studied the subject with his father's Captain, and spent his youth fighting mock battles with stones for soldiers against his brothers. By the time they drew their horses up before Yaegar's walls, on the fifth day after they had left the castle, Griff was willing to accept the necessity of battle. His two Captains had persuaded him. The armed men who stood in the crenellations of the stone walls persuaded him. A sharp wind blew off the river as they looked up at the sealed city. Wardel turned in his saddle to order his troops back, out of the range of arrows.

"Is this the place we'll have our battle, do you think?" Verilan asked. "We need to consider the disposition of the men."

"Although I've witnessed many more attacks, I've only actually drawn my blade once," Griff said then. "Therefore, I appoint you two to ride at the head of the troops. If I knew I could count on my own courage, I'd do it, but since I don't know — I prefer not to put my soldiers in any danger or disadvantage. I'll ride with the soldiers," he said. "I'll fight behind you."

"No," they both said at once, and without hesitation.

Griff thought they didn't understand.

"Sir," Verilan said, before Griff could explain again. "You are the Earl Sutherland. You are the Earl I would myself name if I were naming now, for you talk with the people as if you wished them well, and you honor each one of us, lord as well as people."

"My lord," Wardel said, "the Earl must ride at the head of his army. His Captains ride behind him, and all who see know each man's courage. Your soldiers trust you, my lord, and your people trust you, and so do I. We were Oriel's men, and now we are yours."

Griff was silenced. The wind was at his back and stone walls rose in front of him. He was afraid of battle — not for losing it — he didn't think that with Verilan and Wardel for Captains they would be defeated, not with this number of soldiers — but for the pain of it, and the sounds of fear and rage that he could still hear in memory, and for the dangers of it from which no man could be certain to escape. Griff didn't know what would be required of him. He didn't know if he could act well in the events that awaited him. He had no one to stand beside and show him how to act, with Oriel dead. He had only himself.

"What do we do first?" he asked.

"Sound the trumpet for parley," Verilan answered. "It is too late in the day for any battle to start — unless we have somehow ridden into a trap."

Wardel thought they hadn't. "This open field would be a fool's choice of ambush to trap an army," he said. "I'd guess that Yaegar won't risk so much, not right away."

"Shall I sound the trumpet, my lord?" Verilan asked. He seemed impatient. Griff trusted his sense of things and gave the permission. The trumpeter raised the horn to his lips and the gatekeeper answered the summons. Verilan announced that the Earl Sutherland was present and sought to speak to Lord Yaegar. "For there are rumors of unrest," Verilan called up. "Rumors of an army in the land. Rumors of a rebellion in Yaegar's lands. The Earl has come to hear how Lord Yaegar answers the rumors."

The gatekeeper heard them out, then disappeared from view. Griff waited for the word he would bring. Verilan and Wardel had gone over all the possible ways Yaegar might answer and debated the most likely one, but Griff merely waited.

There would be a response, whatever it might be. There would be a battle, whenever, wherever. He awaited the particulars.

After a while, the iron gate was raised and a man rode out, bearing Yaegar's guidon, sky-blue, emblazoned with a wide-winged falcon. "My master demands — "

Griff cut him off. "I am the Earl Sutherland," he said. Pride was in his mouth like wine.

"Yes, I know, and I'm sorry, my lord, but my master — "

Griff cut him off again. "I am the Earl Sutherland and I would speak with my vassal. On his allegiance, I summon him to me."

It took longer, and the sun was sinking beyond the river when at last four men rode out through the gate, and the heavy man in armor at the lead was likely Yaegar. Oriel had described this lord to Griff, in telling of the taking of Rafella. Yaegar was, to look at, as much unlike Tintage as any man might be. The three who rode behind him were enough like him that Griff took them for Yaegar's sons, of whom Oriel had spoken more gently.

Yaegar and his three sons rode up to where Griff waited alone.

When their eyes met, as the horses moved nervously at being brought so close together, Griff nearly turned to flee. Oriel hadn't prepared Griff for the shock of recognition. Perhaps Oriel hadn't seen what Griff saw.

What Griff saw was the sixth Damall. He sensed the similarity immediately, as of a remembered odor. Yaegar watched for Griff's weaknesses, and got ready to take hold of them. Yaegar waited for Griff to reveal the ill that was in his heart, so that Yaegar could turn that ill to his own advantage. Yaegar saw Griff's instinctive fear and he laughed.

Perhaps that laughter saved Griff. Or perhaps he had grown beyond where the Damall, or any man like him, could frighten him with anything more than pain. For whatever reason, Griff overmastered his own faint heart. He couldn't rid himself of fear but he needn't let fear drive him.

Yaegar made token obeisance. "You're too late," he said, not unhappy at the news he told.

Griff sat on his uneasy mount. "Too late for what?"

"Too late to do anything," Yaegar told him. "My soldiers are armed, and ready. The city is guarded at every gate, and at the walls. We are provisioned for the winter. We are resolute."

"Resolute for what?" Griff inquired. Yaegar would

425

have some price he'd want paid in exchange for submission to the Earl.

"You have caused my son to be banished," Yaegar said.

So Tintage was the price of peace.

"The King has banished a man who traitorously and cowardly slew the Earl to whom he had just sworn obedience," Griff answered.

"Tintage is my son," Yaegar said. "What is mine, I rule."

"Tintage has made warlike raids upon my villages and people," Griff answered. "I am here to hang a traitor and a murderer."

"Now you sentence him to hanging?" Yaegar demanded.

Griff feared him, but Griff had his own troops behind him, and he had seen Oriel answer Rulgh. "As a traitor, yes. As a murderer, yes. Under terms of the King's banishment, thrice yes."

"I'll fight this." Yaegar spoke as if hands were at his throat.

"If you fight you'll lose, and you'll lose all — "

"I'll fight," Yaegar promised.

Griff continued, as if he hadn't heard. "You'll lose all to men who keep their oaths."

"You can't threaten me, as if I were a weakling, as if my son were no man's son. You didn't win the Earldom. It was that other one, the pretty-faced boy. You have no right to rule me. By what right do you attempt to rule me?"

Griff gave him one more chance. "By your rebellious words, you give away the inheritance that should go to your sons," he said. "If you fight, you act the traitor with Tintage."

"Father . . . ?" one of the sons inquired, uneasily.

Yaegar jerked back on the reins of his horse, so

sharply that the animal rose up onto its hind legs and nearly fell over backwards. "Quiet! Do you hear me? All of you, follow!"

Griff raised his hand, and ten of his own soldiers charged forward to encircle Yaegar and his sons, to take their weapons and tie their hands at the wrists, and take control of their mounts. This was Verilan's stratagem, to which Griff had agreed, thinking that with Yaegar in the Earl's hands, the city would prove less resolute. It was easy to overcome a man like the sixth Damall when you could both outscheme and outnumber him.

Griff left the questioning of Yaegar and his sons — who seemed now at last to perceive the trap their father had led them into — with Verilan and Wardel. He thought Tintage was no longer within the city, although Merlis might be. Griff thought that Tintage would have fled into the deep forests, to hide within his father's protection. Griff thought that Yaegar would have let Tintage take armed men into the deep forests, to have the use of them — if he chose to, if fortune gave him the opportunity — for Yaegar's own increase, should the Earl be unable to rule the lands that had been given to him.

Griff looked to the forest, where it crowded up behind the city walls, wondering how he could flush Tintage out and into battle, and thus he was the first to see a line of people emerge from the trees. They were dirty and many were blooded and some could walk only with the help of others. There were men of all ages, and women of all ages, and children, and one woman swollen with child, who was Beryl.

CHAPTER
29

Griff, his eyes so full of Beryl that he couldn't see anything else, dismounted and walked toward her. At the movement, her eyes looked up from where they watched the rough ground. She was unsurprised to see him so caparisoned, by which he knew that word of Oriel's death had reached her. There was a stillness of sorrow to her face, and her dark blue eyes especially, and she shook her head at him. Griff turned his attention to the man who led the group out of the trees.

The man was of full years. The group he led

straggled behind, his clothes were stained, and his face showed the strain of exhaustion, but he held himself straight and then went down on one knee before Griff. Griff urged him to stand even while pride — that Beryl should see him so honored — fluttered in his chest like some new-hatched bird. "My lord Earl," the man said. "You have anticipated my need." His voice carried, without loudness.

Griff guessed. "I think you are the puppeteer."

He had amazed the man. "Aye, and I was, sir. Now I farm a small holding, half a day's journey beyond the Inn, and serve as Major for the village. These are my people and they have no homes. As for the people of the Inn — I have no hope for the people of the Inn, I have no — " His voice failed him.

Griff called for food and water, and his soldiers answered him. The Major had regained his voice, but without its showman's qualities now; he spoke in a voice like any man at the end of his strength and his hope. "We fled in the night and have only rested briefly, and some of us are weak, and my niece is with child. They came out of the night at us."

"It's Tintage, and an army," Griff guessed.

The man gulped down water and took enough refreshment from it to speak with scorn. "It is no army. There are four or five soldiers I saw among them, and those try to keep order but with little success. Thieves, those who would rather take than earn, adventurers, opportunists — that's his army."

"How many?"

"Perhaps thirty? They came out of the forest and it wasn't possible to see how many. Many, but not a horde, and my impression — I had to warn the village, you see, and my niece had just returned from the Inn that evening, there was no time for — we were lucky to escape with our lives."

"Were you coming to Yaegar for protection?" Griff asked.

"No, sir, to you. You are my overlord."

"How can that be?" Griff asked.

"The Inn, the Falcon's Wing, is in the Earl's particular gift. The Innkeepers at the Falcon's Wing — this was long ago, long, long ago — were chosen by the Earl himself, as the story is told. The same family has had the Inn ever since, from father to eldest son. The village, being attached to the Inn, lies also in the Earl's gift, not Yaegar's. The holding where I live was given by the Earl Sutherland in perpetuity to my father — or perhaps it was my mother, and we do not ask why. There is a paper in a leather tube and its seal is the Earl's seal, so the gift was made, as I must think. The village has some sixteen families in it, fishermen — for the Inn lies up against the river — and a blacksmith, herdsmen whose pigs root in the forest and grow fat, a few farmers who have cleared fields . . . a weaver, a butcher . . . it is the last village of the Kingdom, isolated. Unprotected."

"How far off does the Inn lie? For mounted soldiers," Griff asked.

"Perhaps a day? perhaps less, at a good pace," the man said.

Griff had two questions, before he left the man to the business of caring for his people. "Do you think Tintage and his men are at the Inn?"

"I know they are. Once my people were safely away I went back, to find out what I could, to help if I could. The Innkeeper at the Falcon's Wing would not have given over his house without a fight, nor would his sons. Aye, and his women, too." The man smiled at the thought. "The women of the Falcon's Wing have never been mollycoddles." His smile faded and he asked, "Let me ride with you, my lord. I have no hope — for the Inn was filled with the sounds of men celebrating, and the Innyard may have been heaped with bodies that it was too dark for me to see — but should there be any man or woman living, a familiar face would ease — "

"No." Griff forbade it and the man didn't question him. "Was the lady Merlis riding with Tintage?"

"I saw no lady. I heard of none. I think they had found the barrels of wine and ale, so I think they will be sodden with food and drink — unless the soldiers can keep some kind of order, which I think they cannot. I can't think, my lord," the man said.

"Then rest," Griff said. "We will do what can be done. I would have word with your niece, who has most recent knowledge of the disposition of things at the Inn."

"I'll send her," the man said. "What can I tell my people?"

"That we ride against Tintage," Griff said. "Can you ask them to await the outcome here? We have Yaegar and his sons in custody, as you see, and the city will send out stores — "

"We can wait. Ours will be the easy part," the man said.

"No part is easy," Griff answered as he thought. It seemed to him that all the parts were necessary, so it didn't matter if they seemed easy or hard to the puppets who played them.

He called Verilan and Wardel to him, leaving Yaegar and his sons sitting bound on the ground within a guard of soldiers, near to a fire that burned against

431

the approaching night, so that the prisoners could be easily seen from the city walls. The soldiers had been given orders to kill all four, first, at any sign of attack. But there was no sign of attempt to rescue; the city gate had been lowered and its walls were lined with citizens, who awaited the outcome of events before they might decide their loyalties.

Griff told his two captains what he had learned from the Major.

"We must move swiftly," Verilan said. "If we are swift — "

"I'm of the same mind," Wardel agreed.

"Can the horses travel by night?" Griff asked.

"If we have luck in the weather," Wardel answered. "Verilan, what's your mind?"

"My mind's as yours. If Tintage holds this Inn, where can we gather for an attack? Does anyone know the way the land — ?"

"For we need a plan," Griff realized. "If we speed there with all possible haste and come upon them by surprise, it were well to know what we will do then. Beryl knows the Inn," he said, for she approached them, then, wearing a brown cloak, with her hair neither loose like a lady nor wound around her ears like a woman of the people. Her hair was the color of leaves in autumn and was twisted into a long braid that hung down her back. "Beryl is of known loyalty," Griff said, introducing her to the two men.

"Lady," Verilan said, and bowed over her hand. "I give you greeting."

Beryl's smile was mischievous, and temporarily drove the sorrow from her eyes. When Wardel greeted her in the same manner she didn't correct him, either, and Griff did no more than note their courtesy. For there was immediate business before the four. "Can you tell us about the Inn?" Griff asked.

"The Falcon's Wing? You need to know how it's situated, is that it? I can draw it on the ground, that will show you best." Beryl didn't hesitate and didn't draw modestly back.

All four bent over her rough map.

"Attack from the forest," Verilan advised. "They'll least expect that."

"In two prongs?" Wardel asked. His fingers pointed, to the kitchen doorway, leading to the yard, and the main doorway into the Inn, facing the river.

Griff wondered, "Wouldn't a fight in the open be more in our favor, since we have such an advantage of numbers? since we have horses, and skilled soldiers? If we could lure them out — "

"Or drive them out," Verilan said. "If a smaller force attacks from the barn side, and catches them unaware."

"With the larger force waiting in the trees, hidden. So that, if the first attack succeeds and they flee out to the meadow, they can be surrounded." Wardel's eyes lit up with the idea.

"And if the first attack fails, then we can fight our way in from two sides," Verilan agreed.

"You'll try first for an open battle?" Beryl asked, "and that failing, to trap them within the Inn?"

"I think that is our plan," Griff said, and the other two agreed. "Tintage must be taken."

"Do we care if he is taken alive?" Verilan asked.

"We do whatever our best safety lies in," Griff decided without hesitation. "He has broken the terms of banishment so the law permits us whatever necessity requires."

"If we leave now, soon — and travel quickly, while the light holds, and then more slowly through darkness — we might even surprise them before dawn," Verilan said.

"No battles are fought without light," Wardel protested.

"No battles have ever before been broached without light," Verilan argued, "and so I think that this battle might go quickly if we dare to begin by darkness."

"But our honor — "

"Maugre honor, when you deal with a murderer," Griff said.

"And traitors," Verilan said.

"We travel this night," Griff decided.

Wardel wasn't unhappy to be overruled. He and Verilan went off together to get the soldiers ready.

"Is it true," Beryl asked Griff, as he gave her his hand to help her to her feet, overbalanced as she was with the weight of the babe, "that he was struck in the back by this Tintage?"

Her eyes were as dark and deep as the sea. "Aye, it is true. He named me heir."

"Will you wed the lady?" she asked him.

"The lady is a traitor, twice over," Griff said. At the sound of something in his voice, she reached her hand to him. Then she drew it back. "And she is unworthy," Griff said.

"Not everyone must see in Oriel all that you saw," Beryl chided him. "As I did," she added, and then added again, "as did most of the world. Aye, Griff, she is unworthy."

Wardel came up then to ask him to charge the soldiers who guarded Yaegar and his sons. "If you ask it of them yourself, Griff, they will not fail their word."

"Why should that be so?" Griff wondered.

"In part for Oriel, for his honor, as all who saw him knew it. In part for you, for the soldiers have ridden with you these many days, and seen how you endure, and they will trust you. In part because they will want you to know that you can trust *them*."

A longing for Oriel drove through Griff like a sword. He almost could not answer Wardel, and he turned away from Beryl. "I'll do as you advise," he said, because there was no use to saying anything else. He watched Beryl return to her uncle's family, the long braid swinging down the back of her cloak, with a few curls escaping its restraint. But he couldn't dwell on loss, or longing, or waste, or even revenge. There was a battle to be ridden toward, and fought. He approached the guards, to give them instruction.

"We ride to meet Tintage," and Griff repeated their orders for the keeping or killing of the prisoners.

One of the soldiers, a youth of perhaps fifteen summers, stepped forward. "Sir?"

His companions pulled at him, but he shook off their hands.

"Let me ride with you, my lord Earl. I am ready for battle, and who knows how long it will be until the next."

Griff could have laughed.

"And there must be a man in your troop who doesn't wish to chance his life," the youth continued boldly. "Someone who would choose to stay guard here if he could. Wouldn't I make the better soldier for you, that longs to bring a traitor to justice?"

Griff would have denied him, for his youth and his boldness, but he gave the lad the choice he wanted. "Your name?" he asked.

"Reid," the lad answered. "Do you give permission, sir? If I can find someone to change places with me?"

"Against my advice," Griff said.

Reid respected that, but was undeterred. "Thank you, sir. Thank you, I — "

"But hurry," Griff interrupted him.

While the light lasted, they rode hard. This was an old forest, with thick-trunked trees and branches tangled overhead. Close to the city, the forest had been cleared of fallen trees and branches, the wood taken for fuel, so the horses could step safely. As darkness came over them, they spread out single file. Riding through the thick blackness of forest night, Griff followed his own breath, which rose like sea smoke, and thought his own thoughts. The sky was still black when Wardel, who rode vanguard, halted.

"The Inn's ahead. We will need some little light, for the men don't know the terrain. You can't ask men to fight when they can't see, especially men on horseback."

"Yes," Verilan agreed. "But at first light."

"I want to parley first," Griff told them, which was where his thoughts during the nightlong ride had tended.

Their three horses stood quietly, halted. Behind him, mixed in with the creaking and scraping of branches and the whispering of leaves, Griff could hear his soldiers waiting — the shifting legs of horses and the creaking of leather, the muffled jingle of metal and the low sounds of men questioning their neighbors.

"Parley why?" Verilan asked.

The two faces of his Captains were blurred in the darkness.

"To offer the chance of surrender, and the chance of amnesty."

"But he's a traitor and has broken the terms of his banishment," Verilan protested impatiently.

"Not amnesty for Tintage," Griff said. "But for the men who ride with him, if they can be tempted to desert him."

"If some surrendered, it would dispirit the others," Wardel observed.

"Added to our greater numbers, and they trained soldiers," Verilan agreed. "But, Griff, you will be in danger."

Griff didn't argue that point. "I can prove my courage, in a dim light where I don't make an easy target, on an occasion where only one of the enemy has everything to lose. For the rest will consider the offer, to measure their own advantage," he pointed out.

"That's true."

"He wears armor."

"So did Oriel. It's not safe."

"Let me offer the parley, my lord," Wardel volunteered.

"Or let me."

"Do any doubt your courage, either one of you?" Griff inquired. "Are either of you unproved?"

Wardel saw his point. "Nor are you unproved," he declared.

"I know that," Griff said. "Oriel knew it, and you do because I have told you so and you take my word. But," Griff explained, "the world needs to see it, just the once, and never again as I hope."

"If you do that, if you trumpet your presence and

437

call Tintage to parley, that will distract all in the house as we move the first attack into place," Verilan realized.

"Yes," Griff said. "For I think we must be quick and cruel." This also he had been thinking of, through the night. "We are likely to win, be the battle long or short, and shorter will shed less blood. Let no man hold his hand when once the battle starts."

"No prisoners?" Wardel asked.

Griff answered, "It troubles me, but it's our swiftest way. It troubles me, but we don't have the chance to try both ways. We can take only one way, and then let the events work themselves out. So that is my choice, unless you overrule me."

"Not I," Verilan said.

"Nor I," Wardel agreed.

Darkness was all around them. Griff couldn't see the sky, to know where they stood in relation to daylight, or if it would be a clear or cloudy day, if there was rain coming. Whatever the weather was, it couldn't stop them; it could only hinder what they were going to do. Hindrance was the worst of the harm the weather could do them; and the most of the good was not to do harm.

At the first paling of the sky, Wardel took a band of twelve soldiers around the Inn, to cut off escape by water or into the trees. Verilan had fifteen handpicked men to follow him on foot in an attack from the rear of the Inn. With him went the young soldier, Reid, who waved his excited gratitude to Griff.

Griff led the remaining soldiers, still mounted, to the edge of the woods, with orders to wait until the horn called attack. He chose the first ten men his eye fell on and ordered them to be ready to ride out of the trees with him at the first light, and then to stay back behind him as if prepared to attack. Let Tintage underestimate their numbers if he determined to settle it in blood.

The air silvered. Over the washing river, watery birdcalls rose. It was Griff's time.

He rode out onto the meadow, the guidonier beside him and the ten soldiers behind. Only the horses' breathing and the clank of swords announced their arrival. Griff and the guidonier left the soldiers in a line and rode up to the Inn.

Behind its closed shutters and closed door the two-story stone building slept, as grey as the dawn.

At Griff's signal, the guidonier raised the horn to his lips, and blew. The single note cut through the air.

The whole dim world grew still, like ice. The forest was silent, and Griff could almost hear the wary stillness that now filled the Inn. A sign hung over the doorway, the same bird that had been carved on the back of Oriel's beryl, with its wings outspread. Were the wings spread for flight? or attack? or to offer protection? Perhaps all three, Griff thought, and gave the guidonier the signal.

The horn sounded again, three short sharp notes, calling.

The shutter of a ground floor window was pulled back. A face looked out, and then the shutter was pulled closed.

Griff sat his mount stiffly. In his motionlessness, he knew he looked at ease, but his heart was racing and his brain was racing. No outcome was certain, he knew that. No man, not even the best of men, could be sure of his life, he knew that, too.

Griff knew what he planned to say, but was not sure his mouth would utter those words, when the time came. He was remembering how he led the

Wolfers down into the mines and then stood in a stony black recess, listening to the killing, waiting to know his own fortune — slave to Wolfers or slave in the mines.

It was better to fight than wait, Griff thought. The one time when they had stood to fight, which he could barely remember for the speed of the events, he remembered a breathlessness and a kind of wild panicked joy — Tamara's passage down the banks to the boat, and the victory of her voice rising up from the safety of the river.

Only, no victory was promised, ever. Only, there could be victory the victor didn't live to enjoy. A cry rose in his throat, displacing the words that waited there. Griff swallowed to keep it down. It rose again.

The door opened. Tintage, armed, stood on the lintel stone.

Griff no longer had time for memory, or fear.

"I come no farther," Tintage said. "Speak what you would say."

Behind Tintage figures moved through the shadows.

"I sue for surrender," Griff said. "Any man here who lays down his arms will be taken quietly."

"Quietly to the dungeons," Tintage said, laughing. Then, not laughing, "Quietly to his death."

"Only one man here stands under the sentence of death."

Griff knew that Verilan and his men were even now creeping towards the Innyard, crossing it as silently as armed men were able. Griff had need to keep the attention of all on himself, and Tintage, at the front of the Inn.

"To all but that one man I offer amnesty. Yours is a cause that can't succeed," he pointed out.

"That's what you say," Tintage was quick to answer. "Oriel wouldn't say the same, now, would he?" He didn't miss the quick fury on Griff's face, or the hand as it moved to the hilt of the sword. "You'd like nothing better than to slay me, I think. I've forgotten your name. You, Oriel's creature, what is your name?"

What his purpose could be for the goading mockery, Griff didn't know, and had no care for. "Griff, Earl Sutherland," he named himself.

Tintage laughed aloud. His laugh rang untroubled, as merry as a lad at the dance with no thought of livelihood or marriage, with thought only for the circling dance, and the notes of the fiddle that lifted his feet, and all watching him with admiration and envy. "Yet you trust me not to have you slain, here? now?"

"I don't trust you for anything," Griff answered quietly.

In the silence that followed his answer, two men pushed out of the Inn door, crowding by Tintage. They dropped swords and knives on the stone. He was blind to their passage across the meadow to where the line of mounted soldiers waited.

"You don't come well armied, for all the riches of Sutherland, which are now yours," Tintage said.

Three more men pushed by him, and two behind them.

Two scurried along, bent over for protection, around the far corner of the building.

Others moved inside, girding on swords, strapping on breastplates.

"Traitor," Griff called out, "I sue for your surrender." He knew, had known from the first word, that Tintage wished battle.

"I scorn your suit," Tintage called in answer from

the doorway. "As I scorn your claim to the Earldom. And this," he unsheathed his sword and raised it high, "is my answer to you, and to all who would bend me to their wills. Scorn is my answer."

Even as he declared his defiance, cries arose from the Inn. Tintage knew what they were. "You have played me false!" he cried, and then he laughed, "I thought too little of you." Before Griff could answer, Tintage had run back inside, his sword out and ready.

Griff gave the signal, the guidonier blew attack, and his soldiers rode out of the wood. The thunder of hooves mixed now with cries from within, and the shouting of the men who came out of the Inn to wage their battle in the meadow.

Griff was down from his horse and heading for the Inn door, to meet the first wave of those driven out by Verilan's soldiers.

When Tintage was taken, that would be the end of fighting.

The cry in his throat rose up again, and he opened his mouth wide. There was noise all around him, and his own Wolfer cry filled the air in front of him. At the same time, there was a deep silence through which he moved.

"Guard, there," came his own voice in that silence, as he drove his sword into an attacker, "parry — turn — quick, danger!" The noise, and some of it was cursing and screaming, seemed to come to him from far away, although the bodies were close all around him, some fighting, some fallen. The noise was deafening.

He moved through the deafening noise, in his silence.

"Tintage," he reminded himself, as he fended off a sword, with a ringing of metal, and felt something sharp along his upper arm as he swept his own sword back, and his sword grew thick as it cut through flesh, and the smell of blood —

The man screamed into his face, but he didn't see Griff, for death had already blinded him. His scream might well have been soundless, for Griff didn't hear it.

"My lord." It was Wardel standing in the main room of the Inn. Most of the soldiers in the room wore green shirts, and were his own men. Griff took a moment to assess, and then headed off.

"Sir," Wardel was at his side, a bloody bruise on his cheek, "keep safe — "

Griff didn't dare to stop to think, and choose. He pushed on, pushing around his own soldiers, once barely escaping a blow from the fist of one of his own officers — who saw at the last chance who it was he threatened, and flushed red, and then laughed, and then bent his shamed head, until Griff's laughter excused him and both men went on about their tasks.

Griff didn't know how long it had been. His chest heaved. He didn't see Tintage, but he thought there were fewer of the traitor's band who offered combat now. He heard groaning, and moans, now, more than steel on steel. He heard voices calling support to one another. "I'm behind you." "At your right." "Any of the bastards left in that room?" Then he stepped out of the back door to the Inn and into the flagged yard.

"Tintage!" he roared.

Tintage and four or five men were running across the stones. Tintage halted, and turned, to hear his name called. The men with Tintage stopped at the sight of the soldiers, Verilan among them, who blocked their way. They crouched with drawn

443

swords and held daggers in their other hands, awaiting attack.

As soon as he saw flight was useless, Tintage strode back towards Griff.

He frightened Griff.

"So we will duel for the Earldom," Tintage said.

"Don't be a fool," Griff said.

Tintage had fought his way out of the Inn, and his shirt showed that. He had lost, and his eyes showed it; for which reason he was determined to match swords with Griff. Griff could almost hear Tintage's thought: The glory of it, if you cannot be Earl, to be the man who slew two Earls. A man who took two Earls into death with him could not be said to have made the journey ill attended.

"We will, whether you choose it or not," Tintage said, approaching with outstretched sword. "Oriel would have fought with me thus."

"Oriel was the better swordsman," Griff said. His pride was for Oriel, not himself. "If you will have a duel, take Verilan," Griff said, stepping aside to let Verilan — who was at his side now, and eager — come into place.

But Tintage didn't care for the risk of dueling Verilan. He tried to run, and was met by soldiers. He tried to fight his way through them, and he was unweaponed, caught, and bound.

It was finished.

Tintage's men threw down their weapons.

Griff leaned against the stone wall of the Inn. He smelled smoke, and saw green-shirted soldiers in a line, passing buckets of water to put out a fire in the barns. He heard voices again, from within the Inn. Soldiers cursed and reported to officers, and asked if it was over. "Quick," they said, and "Short." "Not a proper battle." "Aye, and that's the best kind." "Aye, and that's what the Earl devised." "It's what we all wanted, isn't it — a victory." "A good victory." "Where is our Earl, he isn't killed, is he?"

Griff stood straight, and walked into the Inn kitchens, and across and through the main room, and out onto the meadow.

It had taken no time at all, as the sun measured time. The first daylight was just staining the eastern sky and gilding the river.

It had taken all the time they had, for the three green-shirted soldiers who lay dead.

The prisoners were set to building two pyres, one for their own dead, one for the dead of the Earl Sutherland's soldiery. The wounded were tended by their friends. While the business of cleaning up was being taken care of, Griff looked around for Reid, to see how the youth had fared.

He found him crouched in a corner of the barn, weeping silently, holding his right hand tight against his chest. When Griff approached he stood up, wiping his face dry, wiping his nose, making his face brave. Griff reached out to look at the wound.

A wide slash across the forearm had been bound, to stop the bleeding, but the cruelty was that the fingers of Reid's hand had seized up, and were curled into a claw. Griff couldn't force them open. The sinews that worked his hand had been severed.

"Aye, and it's a hazard of the game," Reid said as bravely as he could manage.

Griff couldn't deny that. "The lady who came among the villagers, she is a healer. The lady with child. I'll send her to you," Griff said. "When we return, and ask her help. The wound could fester, grow gangrenous — she will know."

"Thank you, my lord."

The boy wished to be left alone. Griff would oblige him, soon.

"Afterwards, will you come back to my castle?"

The boy shrugged.

"There will always be work for soldiers who have fought in battle for the Earl Sutherland," Griff said.

"Aye, and what work can I do like this?" the boy cried.

"What task you can do, that you will be set to," Griff answered, and then he turned abruptly away, that the boy might have his privacy before he came out into the day and had to act the man.

Only Tintage remained to be done with.

"What think you?" Griff asked Wardel, who thought hanging, and "What think you?" he asked Verilan, who thought hanging. "Let us do it now, and then bury him, and then sleep before we return to Yaegar's city," Griff said.

"You dare not!" Tintage cried, when his sentence was told him. "You cannot! You will not!" he maintained.

A soldier made the halter, tied the death knot. Tintage was sat upon his horse. The rope was thrown over the high limb of a tree. The soldiers gathered. They wanted to be ribald, but Griff silenced them. "This is a man's death," he said, and they were quiet.

When the booted feet had ceased their twitching, and Tintage had been cut down — his tears still damp on his face and the smell of death about him, his own death and the deaths he'd given that morning — Griff understood truly that Oriel would never again be more than a memory.

When they had taken the body in a boat across

the river, to bury Tintage in the uncleared forests there, beyond the Kingdom's land, Griff understood that he must always be Earl Sutherland.

When they had risen from a short sleep and set off for Yaegar's city, the prisoners to follow under guard, their own wounded to follow as they could, Griff rode at the head of the column. He led the men back along the forest path, in a night that seemed not as dark as the night before. They emerged from the trees once again in silvery pre-dawn light. The voices from the city walls rose up to greet the victorious army, and the Earl who rode at its head. Griff understood then that with Oriel dead and himself Earl, he could once again approach Beryl and ask for marriage.

CHAPTER
30

As they rode out of the woods, the sun lifted itself up over the trees behind them, and looked across the field to the city walls. Under the sun's glance, the piled stones glowed, and a veil of light lay gently along the ground, gilding the autumn grasses, shining on the people who waited to hear the news from the Falcon's Wing. Beryl stepped forward, washed in the golden glow.

Griff barely heard the cheers and the sound of trumpets that greeted his return. He didn't notice the gate being raised, to let the city rush out, bringing food and drink, bringing welcome.

"I am glad to see you well," Beryl greeted him. "I am glad to see you safe returned." Sunlight shone in her hair, and he couldn't gather his thoughts when she looked at him so gladly.

"There is need of a healer at the Inn; will you go?" Griff asked her. "I would name your uncle Innkeeper — for his fears were correct and none live there. I would ask him to keep the Falcon's Wing for me," he said, then wondered, "Would that please him? Is Merlis within the city?" he asked. "For there is news she must hear. When is the baby due, Beryl?"

She had tried to answer each question but he had given her no time. Now, when he needed to hear her answer so that he could frame his next request, she hesitated. Then she told him, "Midwinter, if all goes well. There is no reason to think all will not go well, so it is not long now. It's Oriel's child," she said, and a smile lifted the corners of her mouth.

Griff felt his own mouth lift in response. "Beryl, I asked you once before and you refused me, but I ask you again: If you will be my wife. I won't have your answer now," he said. "Oriel's child is heir to the Earldom," he told her. "You can't deny me that, you can't deny Oriel that. I am the Earl for my life, but my heir is this child and I will declare it. I must be wed," Griff said.

"Yes, I know."

"There needs to be more than one heir, for the hazards of life, and if you were to wed me I would ask for children. More than that I wouldn't ask of you — and if you won't have me I will wed elsewhere. It is only that you are the one I wish for, as wife. But my wishes need not move yours."

"Yes, I know that," she said. Her hands rested on her belly.

"For it was Oriel to whom you gave your heart."
Again she smiled.

"Just as it is you to whom I have given mine."

"Aye, but Griff," she said, speaking in the same tender tone with which she had refused his first proposal of marriage, "and the child might be a girl."

"Still Oriel's heir," he insisted.

"It's a lord's sons must inherit."

"Under the law, that isn't clear. I've read the law, Beryl, and — it's custom that names the sons, not law. Custom is harder to change than law, but be it girl or be it boy, it is within the law that Oriel's child can be named heir to the Earldom. So this baby must be raised in the ancient castle of the Earls Sutherland, and thus — unless you leave it in my care — "

Her face told him she wouldn't leave it.

" — you also will live in the castle, and I would have you live there as my lady and my wife. No, don't answer me quickly this time." Griff was certain that if she answered quickly she would refuse him, and he judged that she would be wise to accept him.

But he would not require it of her. He wouldn't force her, even if he could.

"I'm of a mind to appoint your uncle the Innkeeper of the Falcon's Wing. Did I tell you that? Then Merlis — for Tintage is hanged. Merlis can go to the holding your uncle lived in, with whatever servants she requires, until such time as she wishes to do elsewise with her life, or in perpetuity."

"Is there anything more you ask of me, other than to be your wife?" Beryl inquired. "And not to answer you aye or nay right now? And to accept that this child I carry must be your heir?"

Nothing, Griff thought to answer, but then he thought that was a false answer. And then he thought of how much he was asking of her, twice out of the three. He could find nothing to say.

An officer approached, and Griff needed to deal with his soldiery and where they might be quartered. Another officer waited behind the first to present Yaegar's compliments and inquire what his fate might be. Griff dealt with the two, detailing Wardel to find quarters for the troops, sending word to Yaegar that he must wait until the Earl pleased to find time for him, and he turned back to Beryl with a clearer mind.

"He said you were the best man he knew," Beryl told him then.

Grief was a stone he had swallowed, and his words struggled past it. "When I first — when I was a boy, and we lived on the island, and there was no hope," Griff told her. "When I first saw him, he was a child, but even then . . ." the nameless boy, barefooted on the beach, afraid of the sixth Damall but determined not to give way to fear, his head held high and his shoulders, under rags, held back and brave. "Oriel's child will have the Earldom," Griff said, and somehow that completed the thought.

Beryl watched his face out of her blue eyes.

"There is healing needful, at the Falcon's Wing," Griff said. "The burying has all been done, and the burnings, but some of my soldiers were too badly wounded to travel. There is a soldier named Reid, waiting for you, to look at his arm, and his hand. But when those things are done, I ask you to come back to the castle, and give me your answer, and await the birth."

"What if I were to run away?" she asked.

He hadn't thought of that. The possibility hadn't ever occurred to him, and yet he knew how large the world was, and how easily a woman and her child might be lost to sight in it. He could understand why Beryl might prefer to try her own fortune, with the child. He thought, however, that she would send him word so that he might know of it and look out for another wife; he thought she would deal fairly with him. So he must deal fairly with her.

But he didn't know what answer to make her.

"What if that were my choice?" she insisted.

"You will make your own choices," Griff said, and didn't speak of how empty life was, when Oriel was gone and Beryl also. "I only ask you to take care of what needs care at the Falcon's Wing, and then to come to the castle."

"He said," she said again, "you were the best man he knew, and I didn't deny it."

After Beryl had gone, in company with the people of the village and their Major, who was now also Innkeeper of the Falcon's Wing, followed by the horse that carried the lady Merlis into the south, Griff turned his mind to Yaegar and his three living sons.

He couldn't think, short of hanging, how to answer Yaegar's perfidy. Yaegar had failed in his fealty — not to Griff, but to the Earl, and through the Earl — whoever might hold that title — to the King.

Yet Yaegar was a lord, and many of his people were loyal to the man, however much they decried his actions in this event. His sons had followed their father in failure of fealty.

Griff called Verilan and Wardel to him, and they discussed the matter over bread and ale and cheese, standing before a table that had been brought out from the city to set before them. They were all three tired, and longing for sleep; but they all agreed that the matter of Yaegar, who waited among his sons under the walls of the city, must be determined.

"Lock him in your dungeons," Wardel suggested.

"The sons would try to rescue him," Verilan pointed out.

"As they should," Griff said. "I wouldn't have any man live out his years in dungeons."

"Then they must all four be hanged," Verilan concluded. "Let's get it over with quickly."

"Were they traitors, then?"

"Not precisely," Wardel said.

"You walk too fine a line," Verilan answered. "They gave Tintage the support of weapons, food, safe passage. They aided a traitor proven. They wished him success, and Tintage's success was the same as Lord Griff's downfall. How can you argue that they aren't traitors, who wished to bring down your lord?"

"Do we hang men for what is in their minds?" Griff asked. "There would be many to hang, I think. More than we have ropes for, think you? And who would remain to be the hangman?"

Verilan's dark eyebrows gathered together in irritation; and then, unwillingly, he smiled, and then he laughed in a short swordstroke of laughter. "Yes, my lord, you have the right of it. I have had such thoughts in my mind, such desires in my heart."

"And you do not deserve hanging," Griff said. One decision was now made, and he spoke it. "You deserve, I think, the work of restoring order to this part of the Earldom. Yaegar's moiety is yours, whatever Yaegar's fortunes may be."

Verilan looked quickly at Wardel.

"Wardel will be my Captain, in a brother's place," Griff said. "I would ask this of you, Wardel."

Wardel, his eyes shining with the honor of it, assented.

"So, now, to Yaegar and his sons," Griff said.

"I can keep all four in my dungeons," Verilan offered.

"Wouldn't it be dangerous to let them remain in what were their own lands?" Griff asked.

"Must they be judged together?" Wardel asked.

"Ah." Griff welcomed a new way to see the problem. "No," Griff said, and asked Verilan, "Do you think?"

Verilan agreed. There would be one judgment on the father and another on the sons. After a long argument, during which at one time or another each of the three became so frustrated that he suggested hanging all four traitors, just to have the quarrel between the three of them settled, a decision was reached. Yaegar, under guard led by Wardel, would be sent to the King, and house arrest in the King's city would be the sentence on him, the expenses of his imprisonment to be borne by the Earl's coffers. The three sons would be sent into the north, one to Lord Hildebrand, one to Earl Northgate, one to Lord Arbor, again in Wardel's company, to serve those lords in a country to which they had no claim by birth and where they had no hope of sympathetic followers.

Wardel and his soldiers would then ride back at speed, to be of service to Verilan should he need it and thence back to the Earl's city. Griff and the remaining soldiers would return now to Sutherland's city, where he must be Earl and rule. Verilan would keep a company of his own men with him, until he could be sure of the loyalty of Yaegar's house and people.

"Yours is the most perilous situation now," Griff

said to Verilan even as he thought that the peril would be welcome to the young fighter. "Remember, the Falcon's Wing I keep in my own disposal, under my own man, if you need a place of safety."

Verilan wished to deny the possibility, but couldn't, although he could think it unlikely. "I hope not to need to accept your hospitality," he said.

"As I hope also, and feel I have good reason to," Griff said. But there was no certainty, as he knew. There was only a good plan, and luck, and the intention to deal justly; that was all he could bring to any occasion.

Griff had much work to do, and much to learn, and these would fill the days until he could know how Beryl would answer him. He rode out of Verilan's city two days later, without allowing himself to turn and see where the river flowed away, into the forest, southward to the Falcon's Wing.

CHAPTER
31

Weeks later, the ground was covered with snow, a light white dusting that had fallen the night before, and flurries of snow swirled down through the darkening air. Griff stood in the castle yard, wrapped in his cloak. These were the shortest days of the year, the longest nights; but a messenger had arrived at midafternoon, with news that the lady Beryl was close to the castle. Her covered carriage should arrive before nightfall.

The rooms were ready, two midwives were in residence and a wet nurse also, and Griff had grown too restless to stay indoors waiting. It was cold in the castle yard, but not as cold as he had known in his life. He was warm within the cloak. White flakes of snow blew into his face.

He heard hoofbeats, the steady pattern made by eight hooves on packed dirt. He heard the creak of wooden wheels. A carriage followed those heralding sounds out of the darkness and entered through the broad castle gates.

Griff came forward to open the door, and saw that Beryl was alone. He handed her out, and hurried her towards the warmth. She was already inside before any of his servants noticed that the carriage had arrived, and the cart behind it, and that all needed unloading. Griff hadn't dared to speak to Beryl, not even to greet her. He hadn't dared to look directly at her. Now that the time to know had come, he thought he would prefer another day's delay, lest she bring word of her refusal.

"We'll be wed, Griff," she said quietly, as if she understood how sharply waiting to know hung over him.

Then he did dare to look into her face.

"If you still wish it."

"Aye, and I do," he said. He didn't know what to do with himself, whether to let his knees fold up under him, or to call out for the best wines in the cellars, that all might drink to the Earl's Lady. He didn't know if he could put his arms around her and hold her against his heart — and he thought, as he looked at her swollen belly, that it might harm the child were he to do that.

Griff held out his hand. Beryl held out her own, and placed it in his. He felt her fingers against his palm. She would be his wife.

Servants and lords swirled around them. Beryl, who stood no taller than his shoulder, smiled up at him to advise, "You might make the announcement. The child should be born to the woman who is your wife, I think. And I don't know how long this child will wait to be born," Beryl told him.

Two days later they were wed by the priests, and the marriage was celebrated by the castle and city. Then all settled back, to await the arrival of the heir.

Beryl was restless. Griff thought she might be anxious and sent to the King's city for the midwife who birthed the Queen's children. Lilos came often into Beryl's rooms, to keep her company, and often brought lords and ladies with him, to enliven her days. "I'm never left alone," Beryl complained to Griff. "Except when I sleep, and even then there is some servant nearby. I don't sleep well," she complained. "It's the child," she explained, to the expression on his face. "It's partly the child, coming to its time, but — and we are never alone, you and I, the way we used to talk together, before you were the Earl," Beryl complained.

The Earl had his apartments and the Earl's Lady had hers, down the hallway. Each had a sleeping room and sitting rooms, and a room where the servants could keep out of the way but still be within call. The nursery apartments were down another hall, distant enough so that the sounds of children might not disturb the ears of the Earl, to interrupt his work or his rest, where the sounds of children might not irritate the Earl's Lady. Finally Beryl burst out, "I don't want to live like this. I want my baby near to me. I don't want my baby fed at another's breast, Oriel's child, I want — " and tears fell from her blue eyes.

Garder set to work, having nursery furniture moved in and servants' furniture moved out, making the lady's apartments her own suite of rooms, for herself and her child. Griff wondered if there would be room for the lady's husband, but didn't dare to ask. Let her finish the business of childbearing before he presented himself as husband, he thought, and then thought more honestly, let her finish the business of Oriel.

"How did you leave the lady Merlis?" he remembered to ask one day. They were by the fire in her smallest sitting room, where he had come to bid her good-night. She wore a green cover and she knitted some tiny garment. She often shifted in her chair and Griff wished he could know how to ease her discomfort.

"I left the lady Merlis in the ground beside her man," Beryl said. Her hands fell still and she looked up at him then. "The lady hanged herself, since the man had been hanged. I don't — Merlis stayed on at the Inn, and wouldn't be comforted. Every day she had herself taken in a boat across the river, to the place where he was buried, and left there, all day, day after day. Other wounds healed, other fevers abated, but hers — "

Beryl looked into the fire, where flames had turned logs into grey ash.

"She wouldn't be comforted. I don't know what to believe of her, except — she hanged herself so that she might always lie beside her lover."

Griff was more afraid to leave the thought unspoken, where it might grow in Beryl's mind, than to ask it. "Do you think you cared for Oriel the less because you choose to live?"

"I never thought of comparing the size or worth of our two hearts," Beryl told him. "It isn't who had the greater or better heart that I think of. I think — the lady Merlis was fierce in her heart, like a falcon, as if the man were her prey. I think — she hanged herself for the sake of a man who had murdered another, which second man had given the lady his heart, unasked and unwanted." Beryl stopped speaking and seemed to be listening. "I think," she spoke slowly, while Griff stood at her fireside, watching the restless light on her sorrowful face, "you had best call the midwives to me."

The women came and they drove Griff out of the room. He went as far as the broad hallway that separated his apartments from Beryl's. Women servants came and went from her rooms, carrying water and linens, bobbing their heads at him, but never speaking. Lilos joined him, and so did Wardel, and they spent the night together in the hall, pacing, starting brief conversations that none paid attention to, trying to hear and understand the sounds from the doors behind which Beryl lay in childbirth.

At early light, with Lilos and Wardel slumped asleep at a table, Griff went determinedly back into her sitting room, where just the last night — and he went up to the closed door to her bedroom. From inside he heard her cry out — sharp and frightened, like a bird's call. He opened the door.

The women flew towards him — "You can't!" — "What — ?!" — "Sir!" Beryl lay on her bed, pale of face, her hair tangled and damp with the sweat that ran down her cheeks.

"I am the Earl," Griff reminded the women, which confused them long enough to give him time to continue on to the bed. He sat by Beryl's head. She looked at him as if she didn't know who he was. She held birthing straps in her hands. Her belly rose, and fell, and sweat ran down into her eyes, and she clenched her teeth, and she looked at Griff as if she were his murderer, or as if he were her murderer, and her mouth opened on a high, wordless cry.

Griff took her hand in both of his. Her nails dug into his palm.

"My lord," a woman's voice spoke at his ear, "you can't stay here."

Griff didn't move. "I am the Earl," he said again, and he didn't know if Beryl was clutching his hands any more than he was clutching at hers. She was panting now, and her knees were drawn up. He could do nothing to help her, but he couldn't bear to leave her. He didn't want to stay and have to hear her pain, and see it, but knowing of her pain, he couldn't abandon her to its company.

This was what men did to women, in taking pleasure of them, he thought as her body arched up again. Let this child live, Griff thought, and he would never ask Beryl to bear another.

He heard women at his back, telling Beryl that they could see the baby's head, but he didn't think Beryl heard them. Her eyes were fixed on Griff's face, sometimes as if she knew him. He heard a woman's voice, calm, tell him, "Now you mustn't move, my lord. Stay just as you are, until we tell you."

Griff nodded his head and gripped Beryl's hand and let the calmness of the voice comfort him.

Beryl opened her mouth, and howled, and her face grew red with the effort.

A matching howling cry rose in Griff's throat, but he was too frightened to find voice for it.

Then it was done, it was easy now, and he heard a baby's cry, and Beryl was breathing heavily. They put a bloody child into her arms, and she opened her eyes. She released Griff's hand. Griff could see

461

only the baby's wet head, and shoulder — Birthing was as bloody a business as battle, he thought. The baby was streaked with watery blood. One of the midwives lay a soft white cloth over it, and picked it up. "You have a — "

"Don't tell me," Griff said, more roughly than he intended. The midwife drew back, as if he offered the baby harm.

Beryl sat straight up in the bed. She cried out —

A cry greater than any she had given in the birthing and tears ran like sweat down her face, and she cried out aloud, "I'll never see him again!"

So Griff held her face in his hands. There was nothing he could do to deny it. Helplessly, he held her face, with its unseeing eyes.

"Never!" she cried, stiff and straight in the bed.

When the midwives brought the babe, wiped clean and wrapped in more white cloths, Beryl turned away from them all and turned her head into the pillow, so Griff took the child into his hands.

The baby was all there was left of Oriel in the world.

"Go," Griff said to one of the servants, "Find Lilos where he waits in the hall; tell him to call the household together."

Beryl wept silently, with her back to them all. Griff held Oriel's child in the two palms of his hands, one palm around the little skull, the other around the little backside.

The first time Oriel had seen the whipping box, which Griff knew to fear, he had slipped his hand into Griff's, whether to give or take comfort Griff didn't know. There was, of course, no comfort, and there was no help — there was only the two of them, standing together for whatever came.

Now there was only Griff.

But he held Oriel's child in his hands, and that was something. That was more than the nothing he had had left of Oriel when the birthing began.

Griff stood, the child against his chest. "I'll return shortly," he said to Beryl's back, in case she heard him. The midwives didn't dare protest.

He carried Oriel's child out of Beryl's room and out through her sitting room, into the broad hall, crowded now with his household, Garder, Lilos, and Wardel among them. He held the baby up before them, one hand under the backside, one under the skull. He held the baby up briefly and then gathered it back against his heart.

"The heir is born," he announced. "Let the bells be rung. Let every man and woman in the city be given a holiday, to mark the day. Let every man and woman in the castle be given a measure of wine, to mark the day. This is the heir of the Earl Sutherland."

The baby wailed then, and everyone laughed.

"Is it a boy, then?" Wardel called. "What do you name him?"

"I don't know yet if this is a boy or a girl," Griff answered. His face kept smiling, although the occasion was solemn enough. "I know only that this is Oriel's child."

A brief silence greeted this news, and then voices spoke out in wordless approval, Ho's and Ha's, over other voices that murmured doubtfully. Lilos came forward. "I will drink to the heir of the Earl Sutherland," he announced. "Let us all toast the heir," he said. "Bring wine to the great hall," Lilos gave the order.

Griff left them then, and returned to Beryl, with Oriel's child in his arms. Her face was wet, with sweat and with tears, but she reached up for the baby — which was now wailing, with hunger Griff thought, but even knowing the baby cried for food didn't make it easy to let Oriel's child out of his hands.

He thought his heart must break at the joy of Oriel's child.

When the baby was arranged at Beryl's breast, and sucking, she asked him, "You named the heir?"

Griff nodded.

"Sit down, Griff. You can sit beside me on the bed. They'll mutter but — aye, and among the people a man might stay in the same room for all of the birth, if only because there would be no other room to go to. Do you mind whether it's a girl heir or a boy heir?" Beryl asked.

Griff shook his head. "But, Beryl," he said, "you must never again have to — "

"Aye, Griff," she said, "it's only pain, and there's the child at the end of it — and we two both live, now, the child and I, and I feel — " her eyes smiled at him " — so strong, so — This was easier than when they branded you, I'll wager. For there's the child at the end of pain."

She was sitting up against pillows and with her free hand she reached her fingers out to touch his cheek, where the white crescent scar marked him.

The baby suckled and Beryl sat in the carved wooden bed of the Earl's Lady as she nursed her child, and it was Griff who sat beside them. Not Oriel. Never Oriel.

"He told me," Beryl said, and her fingers were still on the scar, her hand against his cheek. "He said that a man who gave his heart to my child could win my own heart. Oriel told me that. He knew me better than I knew myself in this," she said.

Griff couldn't speak. He thought — he had never

thought — He reached up to take her hand, and the bells of the city began to peal out the good news.

Weeks passed and the question was decided, the child had Beryl's blue eyes but shoulders — as Griff thought the first time he saw the child lying naked before the warmth of a fire — like Oriel's, broad and flat. As the weeks passed, and winter retreated, Griff made other decisions known. Garder, Lilos, Wardel, and Beryl would be coregents, should Griff die by mischance; he wished everyone to know in whose hands the child's welfare lay. The whole castle — and probably the city, too, for the Earl had little privacy in his life — knew the happiness of the Earl and his lady, how they slept in the same bed and had the child in the next room, with neither servant nor nurse in attendance. But with spring coming up upon the countryside, and the new year's business, labors, and troubles rising with the sap, Griff had to attend to the Earldom this baby would inherit. Consequently, he gathered Lilos and Wardel and Garder together, and he asked Beryl to join with them.

Looking down the long table, at which the five of them sat, Griff announced, "All together we will make the council, to rule."

Beryl pushed her chair back from the table, but he asked her with a gesture to wait until she heard him out.

"As Earl," Griff said, explaining his idea, "I can overrule the general will of the council. This will happen seldom, as I hope, because when we are not in agreement we will do nothing. I alone will be responsible to the King." He waited to hear their reactions.

Garder voiced the objection. "We'll never all

agree on anything, and so we'll be bound in inaction and waste our time in quarrels. You must have one man over all, that he may act. It always has been so."

"Might we not avoid unwise decisions if we act in concert?" Wardel asked.

"But what about the wise decisions, which we might be too fearful to see?" Lilos inquired. "Or, unable to admit, in our quarrels?"

"They'd be made eventually, if only because fear has a weak grip on a true heart," Wardel answered lightly. "And I'll claim true hearts for all of us."

Griff thought that Wardel and Lilos were already willingly convinced.

"Sir," Garder said. "I say this with all due reverence. I am not hopeful about this council, if all on it must agree."

"Oh, but I am," Lilos said. "The more I think of it, the more I like it. In time, if a thing is good to do, we will all agree."

"Are we four in agreement that the lady should sit equal among us?" Griff asked.

The three men were.

"Beryl?" Griff asked. "What say you?"

She didn't speak, but just studied their faces.

"No, you must speak," Wardel said.

"Why must I?" Beryl asked. "I will speak when I have something to say. What is this *must?* What I must have is the right to decide when I have something to say, and when I do not, that is my must. Otherwise, I am no more than a puppet, if you can pull the string and I *must* have words in my mouth."

Beryl smiled to Griff, out of dark blue eyes, and he knew what she remembered. No one spoke, however, for none could answer her. It was Griff they all turned to.

And Griff was what Oriel had shown him how to be, and needed him to be, and saved his life to be. Like Beryl, who was his lady, Griff carried on his breast the medallion that marked the house of the Earls Sutherland. This was the treasure Oriel had won, and given to them. This was the medal Oriel had worn at his heart, when they had laid him down into the dark earth — emblazoned onto a disk of heavy gold, the falcon with its wings outstretched.

ABOUT THE AUTHOR

"It seems to me," states Cynthia Voigt, "that the heroic is just as much a part of life as the ordinary, the everyday. The only difference is that the heroic is rare."

The Wings of a Falcon, Cynthia Voigt's nineteenth novel, is the third book in a trilogy that began with *Jackaroo* and *On Fortune's Wheel*. Mrs. Voigt's other works include *Homecoming*, *Tell Me If the Lovers Are Losers*, and *Dicey's Song*, winner of the 1983 Newbery Medal. Her most recent book for Scholastic Hardcover was *David and Jonathan*.

Cynthia Voigt lives in Maine.